A Girl Called Hope

Kay Seeley

Published by Enterprise Books

ISBN 978-1-9164282-0-1

TO: MY FAMILY

with thanks

'Families make you stronger'.

ALSO BY KAY SEELEY

Novels

The Water Gypsy

The Watercress Girls

The Guardian Angel

Box Set (ebook only)

The Victorian Novels Box Set

Short Stories

The Cappuccino Collection

The Summer Stories

The Christmas Stories

Chapter One

London – 1899

With a last look back Hope walked out of the front door, into the street carrying her small bundle of clothes. Pale sunlight peeked through pearl grey clouds. A light breeze blew fallen leaves along the cobbles and a discarded tin rolled into the gutter. She shivered and pulled her shawl closer around her. People were out, going about their business. Children played in the street, jostling one another, laughing. The newspaper seller on the corner called out the latest news about the war in Africa, a cluster of women gossiped on doorsteps.

Everything looked normal, as though the world had stood still, nothing had changed and yet everything had. Her life, their lives, would never be the same again. Her mind spiralled back to last year. Could it really have been only a year ago? It felt like a lifetime, although the memories were fresh as yesterday's. An ache of grief caught in her throat. Everything had been so different then. She recalled it vividly:

She'd finished polishing the pub's long walnut bar and moved on to do the tables. A fire burned in the grate and gas lights on the wall glowed amber giving the room a welcoming glow. She'd glanced out of the window at the persistent drizzle. Despite it being almost eleven o'clock the sun had yet to appear and darkness still shrouded the street outside.

"It looks like this rain's set in for the day," she'd said to her brother, John, busy polishing the beer pumps ready to open the pub. Although a year younger than Hope, John was responsible for running the pub in their father's absence. "This weather'll bring in nowt but muddy boots, damp coats and the odd straggler come in to dry off by the fire."

John snorted. "Best keep the fire well stocked then. I'll bring in some more wood from the yard."

Glancing around the bar she noticed the floor needed sweeping and there were some dirty glasses left from the night before still waiting to be cleared. "What's happened to old Tom?" she said as she picked them up to take into the kitchen. Don't tell me he didn't come in again last night."

John shrugged. "Too drunk to finish up properly if you ask me," he said. "I don't know why Pa keeps 'im on."

"Cos he's a sick old man who works for nothing," Hope said. She sighed. They didn't pay him much, just a few pence, but their ma always made sure he had a pie and a pint every evening when he came in.

Just as she was about to take the glasses to the kitchen and get the broom she heard the thud of horses' hooves and rumble of wheels on cobbles as a hansom cab drew up outside. Drawn to the window she saw the imposing figure of Silas Quirk alight. Her heart sank.

Every time he called the frequency and duration of Pa's visits to The Grenadier, the gentleman's club and gambling den he owned, increased. It would be a new fighting dog or ratter that was 'worth a bet' and Pa would be sucked into spending all his time and money there. It would be another evening he'd be out until the early hours and come home much the worse for drink.

"I'll go and help Ma in the kitchen," she said, hurrying towards the bar door. "You'll manage 'til Pa come down won't you?"

John's eyebrows rose and, from the expression on his face Hope knew exactly what he was thinking. They both knew that, as soon as their pa came down, he'd spend most of the night huddled in a corner with his drinking buddies playing cards or dice. Betting and gaming were food and drink to their pa, William Daniels.

They both jumped as a loud banging on the front door reverberated around the room. John glanced up at the clock on the wall above the bar. "One minute to go before we open," he said.

She glared at the door. "It's Silas Quirk," she said. "We're always open for him. I'll fetch Pa." Although only in his thirties, Silas Quirk was a man used to getting his own way and not one to be thwarted, but, to Hope's mind that shouldn't mean he had the full run of the place. She couldn't understand why Pa was so in thrall to him.

John heaved a sigh and went to open up while Hope went to find her father.

In the kitchen Ma was busy rolling out pastry. Her famed meat pies were a reliable source of income and sold well in the bar.

"Silas Quirk's arrived," Hope said. "I'd best go wake Pa."

"No need," her father's voice boomed out. "He's knocking loud enough to wake the dead." He winked at Hope. "He'll need serving and nothing pleases him more than the sight of a pretty face. Tell 'im I'll be there in a minute."

"John's out there, he'll have served him by now," she said. "I came out to help Ma with the pies."

William Daniels scowled. "Get out there and make out you're pleased to see 'im." He grabbed Hope and propelled her towards the door.

A shiver ran down her spine. She couldn't disobey her father, not when he was trying to please Silas Quirk. His temper flared at the slightest provocation these days and it wasn't worth upsetting him. She stomped into the bar. John had already poured a pint and a whisky to follow which he pushed across to Silas. He knew enough not to ask for payment.

"Pa'll be out in a minute," Hope said, attempting to arrange her lips into the semblance of a smile.

Silas took a gulp of beer, put his glass on the bar and turned to stare at her. Tall and powerfully built; every inch of him oozed power and prosperity. Dark hair curled onto the collar of his immaculately cut overcoat. He had the sort of smile well known to make women go weak at the knees and do foolish things. His mesmerising gaze ran over Hope like a buyer inspecting a cow in the market.

She coloured under his scrutiny.

"You're looking very fetching this morning, Hope," he said. "Come and join me. I hate to drink alone."

Hope stood rooted to the spot. She glanced down at her faded blue dress and worn white apron. Several strands of blonde hair had escaped from under her cap and she hadn't had time to tidy them. Fetching indeed, she thought. Still, she didn't want to displease him and by doing so bring her father's wrath upon her, but on the other hand...

"Good morning, Silas."

"Ah, William. Just the person I want to see," Silas said.

A slow smile spread across Pa's face. The Hope and Anchor offered games of chance and cards but nothing like the blood sports Silas offered in The Grenadier where dog fighting and ratting competitions were fiercely contested and a good size crowd could always be relied upon for those willing to place a bet on their fancy. Hope rued the day Pa'd ever been introduced to such blood-thirsty sport. Games of chance had been enough for him in the past, if it hadn't been for Silas Quirk. She couldn't think of any anguish in their lives that couldn't be traced back to Silas Quirk, or laid at his door.

The door opened and two men came in, shaking the rain from their coats. They made their way to the bar where John stood ready to serve them. Hope took advantage of the distraction to return to the kitchen to help Ma with the pies.

In the kitchen Hope saw her younger sister Violet putting on her bonnet and shawl. "Out again?" she asked, trying to keep the irritation out of her voice.

"You know she has singing lessons on a Tuesday," Ma said sensing Hope's irritation. "Miss Braithwaite says she's doing really well an' all. Calls her the East

End's Cockney Nightingale, she does. That's right in't it, love?"

Hope's eyebrows shot up. "And I suppose I'm the East End's Cockney Sparrow," she said. "Dull and brown in comparison."

Violet giggled in delight. "If the cap fits," she said as she swept out of the door, slamming it shut behind her.

"And I don't suppose we'll see her again today," Hope said. "Her singing and that theatre's all she thinks about."

"Don't take on so," Ma said. "It's her working in that theatre that's brought this on. Turned her 'ead it 'as and given her ideas."

That was true enough. Since Violet had got a job working afternoons and evening in the theatre box office, being on stage was all she could think about.

"You know what she's like. It'll be somat else she's wanting to do next week and another thing the week after."

"And Pa'll go along with it and give her everything she wants, no matter what the cost," Hope said.

"Aye. Like as not." Ma stopped what she was doing. "He's got a soft spot for our Violet that's for sure, but one day she'll go too far and he'll rein her in like the rest of us. You mark my words. Now, come on, let's get these pies in the oven before the hordes descend. Cold morning like this we should do well."

Hope helped her mother in the kitchen while her pa stayed behind the bar with John. Hope knew it was only the promise of some sport after hours at The Grenadier that kept him there once Silas had left, but at least she was spared and could spend the afternoon working on the embroidery samples she had to finish.

When she wasn't helping out in the pub she made use of her talent for needlework by deftly adding delicate stitching to the exclusive garments the local drapery store supplied to high-class establishments in the West End. She loved the work and working with exquisite materials, adding her own unique, decorative touch. Knowing she had a talent for it made it even more of a pleasure, but she could never earn enough to make it a full-time job. The small amount she earned would go towards some new silks and material to make herself a new blouse.

The next morning Hope rose early as she wanted to deliver her finished embroidery to Miss Ruth Godley of Godley's Drapery. Violet was still sleeping so she dressed quietly and went downstairs. The smell of baking greeted her as she walked into the warmth of the kitchen. Ma was already up and her little brother, Alfie, was finishing his breakfast.

"I don't want to go, Ma. Do I have to?" Alfie pulled a face, his body sagged like a worn out chair. "Why can't I stay here? I can help around the place and Hope can teach me all I need to know. Please Ma, don't make me go."

Rose Daniels gazed at her youngest son. "You have to go or I'll have the school board man round again poking his nose into our business." She turned away. "Now, get going before your pa comes down and gives you a clout."

Hope saw her swallow, her face a picture of regret. They all knew what went on at the school and why Alfie didn't want to go.

"I'll walk with him," Hope said. "I need to get these samples to Miss Godley this morning. They should have been finished yesterday."

"What about your breakfast? Can't go all day with nowt in your belly."

"I'll pick something up on the way." She smiled at Alfie. "Go get your coat. I'll be there in a minute."

Alfie brightened up. He limped off, a smile on his face.

"You spoil 'im," Rose said. "Always mollycoddling 'im."

"You know the teachers hit him and the other boys make fun of him because of his leg."

"He's eight years old. Needs to learn to stand up for 'iself."

"Not easy to stand up to a gang of bullies all bigger than you, especially when you can't run away like they can."

"That's somat he'll have to learn to live with. You can't fight all his battles for 'im."

"I can try," Hope said and marched out of the kitchen to go upstairs for her shawl and bonnet.

"An' wake Violet up while you're up there," Ma called after her. "She didn't get 'ome 'til past midnight an' I need her to run an errand for me."

Chapter Two

Upstairs, Violet was already out of bed, dressed and brushing her tangled red hair. Her face was pale and dark rings shadowed her eyes.

"I'm sorry I left you to do all the helping out," Violet said, preening herself in front of the mirror. "I know you don't think I pull my weight around here, but I'm sixteen now and I have to think about my future." She tossed her head so her curls bounced on her shoulders. She smiled, admiring her reflection. "I don't want to spend the rest of my life serving cretins behind the bar of a dingy pub. I've got plans. I want to make somat of meself. I can't wait to move out of this dump and get on."

Hope's temper flared. "This dingy pub has kept you fed, dressed and alive for sixteen years. It's provided a roof over your head and food on the table and paid for your precious singing lessons. I think you ought to be at least a little grateful."

Violet coloured and swung round to face Hope. "Of course I'm grateful but that doesn't mean I have to stay here for the rest of my life. There's a big wide world out there and I'm having some of it. Bert says I've got the makings of a real star. If I keep up the singing lessons I could hit the big time. He even said he'd find me a spot in one of his shows."

"Bert? You mean Albert Shadwick, the magician?" Violet had met the magician, Albert Shadwick, and, Hope thought, a good few other equally disreputable characters at the theatre where she worked. "You haven't been seeing him again have you? You know what happened last time. He led you a merry dance making promises he had no intention of keeping. I wouldn't trust him further than I could throw him."

Violet glared. "You're just jealous – jealous of everything I do, everyone I see. I was only young then. I know better now and I'll soon have him dancing to my tune, you see if I don't."

"Dancing to your tune like the rest of us I suppose you mean. I think you'll find he's a lot shrewder than you give him credit for."

"Well, we'll see won't we?" Violet said. She slammed the brush down on the table, jumped up and stormed out.

Hope shook her head. Trouble on two legs that one, she thought and who'll be expected to pick up the pieces when her hopes and dreams fall apart? Then she remembered how she'd felt about a boy when she was sixteen and too young to know better, and all her irritation melted away. She'd loved Danny with all the passion of her sixteen-year-old heart and dreamt of a future with him. He'd gone with his brother to join a ship travelling to the East Indies. "When I get back I'll have enough money so we can get married," he'd promised. He never came back. She still remembered the pain of parting and carried the memory of him in heart so she couldn't blame Violet for believing in Bert. Hadn't she believed in Danny? It was a raw reminder of the frailty of the human heart.

She sighed and made her way downstairs. Alfie was waiting for her in the bar with John who was preparing the beer pumps and cleaning the pipes ready to open at lunchtime.

"I wish I was big like you," Alfie said. "Then I'd be able to take care of you instead of the other way round."

Hope laughed. "Your heart is big, that's all that counts. And don't take any notice of the other boys. They're just envious because they don't have your brains and can't do the lessons as quick or a well as you."

That was true. Although Alfie was only just eight he had a quick brain and a good memory. He could add up faster than anyone she'd ever seen and in his head too. A valuable skill when you live in a pub. He was a late addition to their family, she'd been twelve, John ten and their sister Violet nine when he came along, but she loved him more than words could say. Even as a baby he had a magical smile and way about him that melted her heart. If it hadn't been for his crippled leg and his club foot, he'd have been a force to be reckoned with. As it was he was just the dearest, kindest, most thoughtful brother anyone could have, she thought.

Outside the air was sharp with frost and noisy with morning traders. Costermongers called their wares, competing with newspaper boys who stood on the street corner. Hope slowed her pace to match Alfie's. The smell of horse manure hung in the air. It was a short walk to the school and they passed people, wrapped up in scarves and hats, hurrying along the narrow pavement, eager to be on their way to work. Hope nodded to those she recognised and bid them a good day, so the walk was pleasant. If only she didn't have to worry so much about Alfie. She thought about having a word with the Master but that might only make matters worse. Nobody likes a tittle-tattler. Perhaps Ma was right, Alfie did need to learn to manage on his own. Her heart dipped at the thought.

When they reached the school gates Alfie hesitated. "Do I have to?" he asked his eyes pleading.

Hope grimaced. "I'm afraid so," she said.

In the boy's playground in front of the building she saw boys pushing and shoving each other, shouting, laughing and running around; their boisterous activity a marked contrast to Alfie's quiet, woe-begotten demeanour. She watched Alfie limp to a bench and sit with his books on his lap, waiting for the bell that meant it was time to go in. Her heart flipped. She could stand it no longer. She strode across the playground into the school and found the Master's office.

He looked surprised to see her.

"Good morning," he said. "It's Alfie Daniel's sister isn't it? Is Alfie unwell?"

"Actually, he isn't well," she said. "I'm very concerned about him."

The Master's eyebrows rose. "How so?" he enquired.

"He has a nasty bruise on his shoulder and several more on his body. It's not the first time I've noticed gashes and welts across his back. I don't know what's been going on here but it needs to stop. I won't put up with Alfie being bullied or beaten."

Colour rose in the Master's face. "Boys will be boys," he said. I expect it's the result of an over-enthusiastic game of football or a scuffle in the playground. High-spirits, that's all, my dear. Nothing to worry about."

Hope knew Alfie would never be able to play football or join in a playground scuffle, but she said, "I trust you'll see it never happens again. I'd hate to have to go to the school board to sort things out."

The Master's lips spread into the semblance of a smile, his eyes narrowed. "Rest assured, my dear, there's no cause for that. I'll keep an eye on young Alfie."

"I do hope so," Hope replied. She knew she couldn't protect Alfie entirely but she hoped her remarks had gone some way towards preventing the worst of the beatings.

When Hope arrived at Godley's Drapery she pushed open the glass shop door and went in. She nodded to the salesgirl who'd glanced up at the sound of the bell and walked through the shop, past the counters displaying colourful fabrics and large wooden cabinets filled with linen goods, to where Miss Godley had a small office-cum-workroom at the back. Hope found her there, going over the orders.

Ruth greeted her, putting down the large order book she was holding. "The samples. Have you finished them?"

Hope handed her the items she'd been working on.

"These are lovely, Hope," Ruth said. "The stitches are so delicate I declare you're the best needlewoman I've ever come across." The work had been commissioned by a fashionable store in the Strand and there was the promise of more to follow if they were satisfied with the samples. "I wish you could work for me full-time," she said, not for the first time.

Hope laughed. "Perhaps one day," she said, but her dream was to have her own workshop where she could design and make her own merchandise and even take on students and pass on her skills as her grandmother,

Amelia Daniels, had taught her. She'd said Hope had nimble fingers. Gentlewoman's fingers she called them. Hope knew that, in the family's financial position, dependent on the brewery for their living, it was a dream that spiralled so far away it would reach the stars, but then, she thought, perhaps nothing's impossible.

"The customers will be delighted and I'm sure we can rely on a very good order." Ruth put the pieces into a box and looked at Hope. "You look worried. It's not the work is it? I can tell them they'll have to wait for the rest if it's too much."

"No, it's not the work. I love doing it. It's Alfie I'm worried about. I've just left him at school and can't help wondering if speaking to the Master about his bruises has made matters worse instead of better for him."

"Yours isn't the first complaint about old Mr Mackitterick I've heard," Ruth said. "I sometimes think the power of being made Master has gone to his head. He thinks he can get away with anything." She frowned. "I could have a word with my father if you think it would help." Ruth Godley's father was the local pastor and on the school board. "A sharp word from him would soon sort things out."

"No, it's all right. I don't want Alfie to be treated any differently from the other boys. I just want him to be treated fairly, but I may change my mind if things don't improve."

"Whatever you say, although if you're worrying about anyone I should think there's more to worry about with your sister."

"Violet?"

"Yes. I saw her the other day when I was in town delivering some sheets to The Grand Hotel. She was with that swindler Albert Shadwick doing the three-card trick in Oxford Street. They were lucky not to be arrested."

Hope was aghast. "In Oxford Street? With that rogue Bert Shadwick?" Hope could well imagine what happened. Bert would have enticed people to 'Find the Queen' a well-known three-card trick. Then, by of sleight of hand, he'd manipulate the cards to ensure that punters betting on a card would lose. A renowned scam as far as far as Hope was concerned. Obviously Bert was using Violet as the innocent bystander who makes the first bet and wins, thus encouraging others. Bert would make sure the rest lost steadily until a warning from his accomplice standing on the corner, alerted them to the imminent arrival of the coppers.

"I've told her that Bert's no good, but she won't listen. Thinks he's going to make her a star."

Ruth shook her head. "I just thought you ought to know."

Chapter Three

Violet was a problem Hope couldn't solve but she could cheer Alfie up with a twist of fudge from the market as a reward for going to school. With that in mind she made her way to Spitalfields where she could stock up on embroidery silks at the same time.

The early rain had cleared and, by the time she reached the market, the sun was attempting to make an appearance. The market hummed with vibrant life. Lively chatter and the voices of market traders filled the air. In one corner a barrel organ played and people jostled at the stalls to be served. Hope squeezed her way past a small crowd gathered around an ironmongery stall, the stallholder pitching the merit of the latest kitchen grinder to a spellbound audience. "Turns the toughest gristle into the tastiest morsel," he said as she passed. Hope smiled at the thought.

At the haberdashery stall she spent some time discussing the various advantages of each colour with a portly woman dressed in a buff apron that covered her from neck to ankle. She wasn't in a hurry to get back to the pub and choosing the right silks, comparing each shade and how they went together was the thing she enjoyed the most. Eventually she decided on two skeins in blue and a pale lilac for some pillowcases and pale pink for a child's petticoat Miss Godley had asked her to embroider.

After buying her silks she walked around the market perusing the various stalls. She slowed her pace as she approached the fruit and vegetable stall where her friend Ned was calling out the benefit of buying his fresh from the farm produce.

"Morning, my lovely," he greeted Hope, doffing his cap, a broad smile lighting up his suntanned face. "You brighten up the dullest morning. What'll it be today? How about some nice Bramleys for your pies. Bring a sparkle to a glass eye they would or, if you prefer, I've got some lovely fresh oranges. Do you a treat they would. So what'll it be?"

Hope laughed. "Oranges? Far too exotic. I'll take some Bramleys though for Ma's pies. Good to get some so late in the season."

Ned picked out half a dozen of the best apples and put them into a bag for her. "I'll call in the pub tonight if you're on," he said. "Always nice to see a cheery face behind the bar."

Hope took the bag of apples. "Where else would I be?" she said with a smile.

Ned grinned. "It's a date then."

Her step lightened as she walked home. She'd known Ned since she was at school. He was a couple of years older than her and she'd always found him level headed and reliable, the sort you could turn to in a crisis. He was popular with the other market traders too, and a good friend who'd brighten up a dull evening. Looking forward to seeing him she made a special effort to look her best. She wore a white blouse with a high collar, trimmed with lace. She'd embroidered delicate blue periwinkles across the yoke and she tied back her freshly brushed hair with a matching blue ribbon.

Her effort didn't escape Violet.

"Ooh. Doing yourself up are you? Someone special coming in?" she sniggered.

"Not especially," Hope said. "I hope I always try to look my best when I'm working behind the bar. Not that you'd know anything about that."

"Don't want to know either," Violet said as she preened herself in front of the mirror in the room they shared. "I've got bigger fish to fry." Violet patted her red hair into place.

"Like Bert Shadwick? I don't think so."

"You're just jealous, jealous of everything I do, but I'll show you, I'll show you all," she said and swung away from the mirror to swagger out of the door.

Hope sighed. She could see Violet was heading for a fall but nothing she could say would stop her. She remembered again how passionate she'd been about Danny at that age, and how stubborn and her heart softened. Violet was no different, and she'd have to learn the hard way, she thought, same as the rest of us. Still, it didn't stop her worrying about her.

The bar was quiet that night and for once Hope didn't mind working there with John. She buzzed around making sure the tables were cleared and the fire stoked so she could sit with Ned when he arrived. Four men grouped around a table in the corner played a noisy game of cards. Hope guessed from the loud explosions of cursing and swearing that one man was losing heavily. Tom, the potman, was supposed to come in and see to the glasses but, as usual he hadn't shown up.

"I thought Tom was supposed to do that," John said when Hope brought their empty glasses to the bar to be washed. "Where is he tonight?"

Hope shrugged. "Same place he usually is these days," she said. "Down the Celtic Harp with his chums I expect."

"Aye, an' he'll come in late half-ratted as usual too," John said.

A few more stragglers came in and every time the door opened Hope glanced up eagerly, awaiting Ned's arrival. At seven-thirty the door opened and a crowd of workers from the docks burst in, pressing up to the bar. "Just the one," she heard the first man say. "Got to get 'ome to the missus." The other men laughed and Hope and John exchanged glances, knowing that one drink would lead to several.

By eight o'clock Ned hadn't arrived and Hope was getting anxious. Perhaps he'd changed his mind and wasn't coming after all. The bitter taste of disappointment rose in her throat. She should have known he was only joking. She ought to be used to that by now, men letting women down. She'd seen enough of it in the bar, just like the men who'd come in for 'only the one tonight' and would stay drinking until closing. They were regulars and it was the calls of 'one for the road', and 'just a quick one, then', that made the difference between a poor night's takings and a good one. She was glad she wasn't married to any of them and wondered how their wives put up with it.

At two minutes past eight the door swung open and Ned walked in. Suddenly the evening looked brighter, the bar warmer and the company more lively. John greeted him, "Evening, Ned. Thought you usually supped at The Bull in Market Street."

Ned grinned. "Well, it's nearer to the market but it doesn't have the same attraction as The Hope."

John glanced at Hope, a wide grin on his face. Hope felt herself blushing, which seemed to please Ned even more.

"And one for yourself and your charming sister," Ned said as John pulled him a pint of best bitter.

John pulled a pint for himself and poured a sherry for Hope. Ned took it to a table by the fire. Hope joined him.

"Cheers," he said raising his glass.

"Cheers," Hope said, her heart fluttering.

"You're looking quite bonny this evening," Ned said. "I was afraid you'd be too busy to talk to me."

"I'm never too busy to talk to a friend," she said. Ned grinned.

Between serving drinks Hope sat with Ned. He told her tales about his customers and the goings on in the market and she told him about the people who came into the Hope and Anchor.

Tom O'Reilly came in after ten, just when Hope had taken some glasses to the bar. "Sorry, I'm a bit late," he said. "Had some trouble wit' me back."

"Aye, getting it out of the chair," John said and walked away. Hope said nothing, but did make a point of collecting all the other empty glasses and putting them on the bar for him to wash. Overall she thought it quite a good evening, despite the earlier spat with Violet.

The rest of the week the weather didn't improve and every day brought more fog and drizzle. Customers complained of the cold, shaking the rain from their coats and stamping the mud from their boots. Even lighting the lamps and stoking the fire all day didn't dispel the dismal gloom. Some days it was so foggy

Hope's shawl was soaked through on the short walk to the market and back.

She worked on her embroidery whenever she had the time and spent her evenings helping John serve customers in the bar. Pa made a brief appearance each evening before heading off to spend the rest of the night at The Grenadier. The only bright sparks as far as Hope was concerned were the evenings when Ned visited the pub. Sometimes he'd come in alone and sometimes with a couple of friends from the market.

"Evening, lovely," he'd say, then asked about her day. He made her laugh with anecdotes from the market and the other traders. If the bar was quiet she found time to sit with him and play a game of shove-ha'penny, until John called, "Glasses need washing, Hope," or came over himself and pointedly picked up their glasses. "Ma's calling you from the kitchen," he'd say, and, reluctantly, she'd have to scurry off to do his bidding.

The weather became colder as November turned into December and frosty air blew in with each of the customers as they opened the door. Pa spent more time out than in. It didn't help that the weeks before Christmas were the busiest of the year, with everyone working every hour God sent. Every day a messenger would turn up with a pile of fresh orders from the drapery store for Hope to embroider before Christmas. The extra work meant she could afford to spend a little more on Christmas treats for the family.

Violet managed to be out most days working at the theatre, helping with the costume making, going over the acts with the performers and generally making sure she was at home for as little time as she could possibly manage. She often didn't return to her bed until the early hours, and when she did she'd be full of the excitement of the shows they were putting on and the magic Bert performed to full houses and standing ovations.

John was kept busy in the bar and Ma worked long into the night making preparations for their own Christmas celebrations as well as adding goose and chicken to the pies she made to sell. William's continued absence stirred up Ma's resentment too.

"I don't like it," she said, "him being out so often. That Silas Quirk is a bad influence. Makes 'im forget he's got a family to support. He's a wrong 'un and no mistake."

Hope couldn't argue. Her pa never came home before the early hours and when he did he was usually staggering with the drink, crashing about as he made his way upstairs.

"I'm at me wit's end," Rose said, "but what can you do. That man has the devil in him and no mistake."

Hope wasn't sure if she meant her pa or Silas Quirk, but it made no difference, there was nothing to be done about either of them.

Friday morning Ma gave Hope the list for the butcher. "Make sure he don't give us short measure," she said. "The meat for the money seems to get less and less every week. You have to watch 'im." She wiped her hands down her apron. "An' get the best sausages an' all. The last lot were all sawdust if you asks me. Shrivelled up to nowt."

"All right, Ma. I'll watch him and I'll ask him to put by extra for next week as we'll be busy coming up to Christmas."

When she arrived at the butcher's shop, instead of being welcomed in and the list taken from her hand, the butcher called her over to the back of the shop. "Can I have word, Miss Daniels," he said. Given the expression on his face Hope guessed it wasn't to pass the time of day or talk about the weather.

"It's about the outstanding account," the butcher said. "I'll need somat off these bills 'afore I can extend any further credit."

Hope took the bills from his outstretched hand, her stomach churning in trepidation. "I don't understand," she said. "Pa always pays these." She glanced around hoping for some sort of answer but none came. "I'm sorry," she said eventually. "It must have slipped Pa's mind, what with all the preparations for Christmas. I'll have a word. In the meantime I hope you can advance us a little more credit to cover today's order, please."

The butcher took a deep breath, shaking his head. "I'm sorry, Miss Daniels. Nothing personal, but I can't afford to supply folk as don't pay their bills. It's been more 'an a month."

A month! Hope stared at the bills in her hand. Sure enough there were four. One for each week. "I'm sorry," she said. "I'll get Pa to see to them right away."

She hurried out of the shop with her head bowed. What on earth was Pa up to? Why hadn't he paid the bill? How were they to make pies without meat?

Thoughts ran through her head like skittering hares. He was the one who paid the tradesmen, sending a cheque at the end of each week, or at least that was what he usually did. Had it slipped his mind because he was out getting drunk every night? The thought filled her mind but she pushed it away, admonishing herself. He was her father. She should have more respect; still she couldn't help wondering if the butcher was the only one. If news of them not paying their bills got around the neighbourhood all their supplies would be affected. Then what would they do? Heart pumping she walked as fast as she could home to see her mother.

"I knew it," Rose said. "Always down that club drinking and gambling when 'e should be at home seeing to 'is business. Leave it to me. I'll get it sorted." Hope saw thunder in Rose's eyes. "Meanwhile, nip down to Ada in the market. Tell her we've bin let down and can she let us have a couple of chickens and a ham. Tell 'er I'll see 'er all right but don't mention butcher's bills. She's a good sort is Ada and she owes me a favour."

Hope swallowed and went back out. Ada supplied the eggs her ma used in the pies and Ma often sent her some of the leftover pies for her expanding family. Hope had no doubt that the 'favour' consisted of a couple of bottles of gin that Rose said she needed to tenderise the meat. "Six kids and no 'usband," Ma used to say. "Needs all the 'elp she can get." Hope also recalled seeing the said kids running around the market wearing her and Violet's cast-offs.

When she got back with the chickens, ham and a dozen eggs Ada had put in for 'extras', she heard her father moving about upstairs.

She could tell from his demeanour in the mornings after he'd been out all night how the evenings had gone. Pa wore his heart on his sleeve. Whenever he won money he was the most generous man on earth. Everyone was his best friend. He'd promise Ma a new dress, Violet a new hat and John a new coat and boots. He'd be on top of the world, handing out drinks to customers and playing the hearty host, sharing his good fortune, until the money ran out. Just lately she hadn't seen that side of him. In fact she couldn't remember the last time he's come home boasting of a big win. He never mentioned mounting losses but he'd been sullen and withdrawn of late, so she knew the storm clouds were gathering. She decided to plead a headache and retire to her room where she could do her embroidery in peace, and await the coming tempest.

Upstairs she closed the door and settled down to her embroidery. She'd only just begun when she heard angry voices coming from the kitchen. She tried to ignore them and concentrate on her work, but the voices grew louder and louder. Her mother's voice became a shrill cry and her father's a roar in response. She couldn't make out the words but soon the voices were replaced with the sound of something being smashed followed by an almighty crash and the slamming of a door.

Perturbed, she put her embroidery on the bed and tiptoed to open the door. She listened on the landing for a few minutes but downstairs appeared to be silent. She eased her way down the stairs, opened the kitchen door and peered in. Lying on the tiles next to the table, blood seeping from her head to pool on the floor, she saw her ma.

"Ma, Ma!" she cried, rushing to her side. "What happened? Are you all right?"

Her mother rolled over and stared up at Hope, her eyes filled with bewilderment. "Oh," she said. "I must have slipped. Not to worry. I'll be fine in a moment." Hope helped her into a sitting position where she could see the wound on her head.

"But you're bleeding. I'll call the doctor,"

"No, no. Don't make a fuss." Fear replaced the bewilderment. "I just slipped and caught my head. My fault. All my fault. I'll be fine in a moment." She paused as if trying to gather her thoughts. "Perhaps a nip of brandy," she said. "Then I'll be right as rain."

Chapter Four

Resentment hovered in the air for several days after the argument, with everyone tiptoeing around his moods. Hope kept a watchful eye on Ma looking out for further evidence of her father's temper, which was as volatile as his red hair suggested. Every time Pa went out the atmosphere eased until his return. Ma carried on as though nothing had happened, too frightened to raise the subject again.

The situation with the traders didn't improve. More of them demanded cash before they'd supply any goods. Several nights, after Hope retired to bed she heard Pa come home. Then there'd be shouting and sudden silences. The next day Ma would be sporting a new bruise, cut or graze which she said was her own clumsy fault, for tripping over, or walking into a door. Hope knew better. The only thing that helped the situation was the thought of Christmas coming and the trade that would bring in. The money taken over Christmas would at least ease some of the debts.

Ever since Hope could remember, the local Chamber of Commerce had hired the function room at the back of the pub to host their Christmas party. It had become a tradition for the most affluent, well-to-do, local traders, businessmen and merchants to gather for an evening of eating, drinking and celebrating or commiseration, depending what sort of a year they'd had. Their wives vied with each other to appear in the most fashionable and expensive outfit, topped with the most extravagant hat. It was the one night of the year when everyone 'let their hair down' and the takings over the bar would guarantee the next three months' rent.

The week before the event Hope and Violet spent every spare moment making cards, crackers and paper chains. Hope loved the run-up to Christmas when they'd be busy getting ready for the festivities. All the shops would be lit up, the window displays filled with gleaming lamps, ribbons, bows and twinkling silver stars. People in the streets would carry bundles of holly or wreaths of jasmine, pine and ivy for their doors. Even the goods in the shops and on the market stalls took on a festive flavour with colourfully decorated baskets of fruit, nuts and sweets.

On Christmas Eve Alfie spent most of the day sitting weaving greenery into ropes of holly, ivy, jasmine and spruce for John to hang in garlands around the walls. Large red satin bows stitched by Hope and Violet held the swags in place. Extra glasses, candles, plates, cutlery, cloths and candelabras for the table were borrowed from the brewery which also provided barrels of beer, wines and spirits on a sale or return basis so there was no fear of running short.

"What about meat for the party?" Hope asked Ma. "We're going to need a lot more than usual."

"We'll have to get it from the market," Ma said. "I'll make a list and ask Ada. Take the money from the till. If anyone asks, refer them to me."

So Hope took the money from the till, putting in a note of the amount taken. She wrote '*for meat for the Christmas party*' so there could be no argument about her taking it.

The short walk to the market was pleasant and, nodding to friends and neighbours she passed Hope could almost forget about the problems they were facing. She prayed that the evening would be a success and that all their hard work and efforts would be rewarded with sufficient takings to at least cover the rent.

At Ada's stall she glanced over the range of meats laid out. "Ma said to get the meat for the Chamber of Commerce Christmas do," she said to Ada, "but I can't afford much more than the usual order."

Ada nodded. "How about a nice ham then? It'll need a bit of cooking, long and slow, but I reckon sliced thin it'll spread to a plate or two. An' I've got a bit of cheese you can salvage with care. There's some brawn left from last week and tongue. With your ma's pickles they'll make a good spread. Your ma can pay me after, when she's got things a bit straighter."

"Ada, I don't know what to say. We can't thanks you enough."

"It's me as should be grateful to your ma. Done me right favour in the past she 'as. Think no more about it."

Hope bought fruit and nuts from Ned, again noticing how he put a 'few extra' in the bag after he'd weighed it. Next she bought flour, butter and sugar from a chap selling groceries that he promised would 'make pastry light as air and only half the price'. Several times she stopped to listen to the exaggerated claims and banter of the stallholders who were always cheery, no matter their circumstances. She couldn't resist buying some toffee, chocolate and fudge to add to the sweetmeats they'd be putting out.

During the afternoon Hope helped Ma prepare goose-liver, chicken and duck pate, cook eggs, savoury tarts, mince pies and several rich plum puddings while

Alfie made sugared plums, almond paste sweetmeats and candied fruits. Ma would cook game pies and sausage rolls during the evening so they could be served hot. That evening they would serve more food than they'd eat in a month.

Hope and Violet laid out the tables with white cloths, candles, crackers and garlands of flowers.

"I'll be making the mulled wine and punch and serving behind the bar. Violet will help me. John, you do the public bar and Hope and Alfie can help serve the food," Pa said when the preparations were finished. He puffed out his chest. "Silas Quirk's coming and he's bringing several influential guests. We need to make a special effort this year. Let people see the Hope and Anchor at its best."

"I'm sure we all do our best every day," Hope said, finding Pa's constant awe of the owner of the most infamous gentlemen's club and gambling den in the area a trifle irritating.

"Remember, everyone, a special effort."

"Yes, Pa," they chorused.

Upstairs, getting ready Hope noticed Violet putting on a forest green gown, cut so low at the neck to be just on the right side of decent. Pulled tight at the waist she wondered how Violet would breathe. There didn't seem to be much in the way of sleeves either. "Is that new?" she asked. "I don't recall seeing it before."

Violet sank onto the stool in front of the mirror, admiring her reflection as she did so. She picked up a brush and started applying rouge to her cheeks. "Yes," she said. "Bert bought it for me. He's generous to a fault, as are all the patrons at the theatre." She sat back to assess the effect of the rouge. Hope wondered what Violet had had to do to earn such a generous gift.

Violet glanced at Hope. "It wouldn't hurt you to dress up a bit," she said. "You could be quite presentable if you made more of an effort."

Hope glanced down at her own light blue dress. It was an old one, but she'd added ribbons and braid to the bodice and lace around the neckline and sleeves. It was serviceable and practical. It accentuated the freshness of her skin, the blue of her eyes and the lightness of her hair, although, she had to admit, it wasn't exactly the height of fashion, but it would see her through until Easter.

"I'm not sure I want to be 'presentable' as you put it," she said, "if I have to dress like a dollymop and paint my face like a Haymarket harlot." As soon as she said it she regretted it. It was mean and unworthy and the fire in Violet's emerald eyes told her that Violet thought so too.

"I'm sorry," she said. "I didn't mean…"

"Yes you did. You're just a jealous cow and I'm not surprised that a barrow boy is the best you can do. I'm aiming for something better than that." She glared at Hope, rose and swept out.

Hope sank onto the bed. The last thing she'd wanted to do was fall out with Violet, but why did she always have to be so exasperating?

Downstairs everything was ready. Pa opened the doors to the function room and guests began to arrive. Hope watched as they came in. Some arrived by hansom cab but a few had braved the frosty night air to walk the short distance from their premises to the pub. Suddenly the room was alive with chattering voices, colour and activity. She breathed a sigh of relief and relaxed, ready to do her part to make the evening the roaring success her parents were hoping for.

The band, three musicians Violet knew and had persuaded to play for food and drink, struck up and music filled the air. The drink flowed; people dug deep into their pockets to make it a night to remember. Hope and Alfie worked in the kitchen under Ma's direction to keep the plates of food filled.

"All right for some," Ma said, her face flushed from the oven. "They'll be up drinking 'til past midnight and me with a goose to roast and plum pudding to boil in the morning afore we can 'ave our Christmas dinner."

"If there's anything left-over tonight we can have it for our tea tomorrow. No point letting good food go to waste," Hope said, surveying the vast amount of delicacies spread out on the kitchen table.

Ma huffed. "We'll be lucky. Never known 'em to leave as much as a crumb for us poor folk. Still, got to make the most of it."

Hope knew she was counting on the takings for the evening to meet the huge bills run up to pay for the food and drink. She picked up a plate of pies. "I'll take these in," she said.

For Hope the best part of the evening was seeing the ladies in all their finery. She recognised most of them and she'd try to guess which local dressmaker had been persuaded to make each garment at cost. The wives prided themselves on using local labour but also on being able to drive a hard bargain when it came to spending their husbands' money. She'd also note which of the women were sporting new pieces of jewellery and which were wearing old favourites. Hope suspected that the new pieces were bought as peace offerings by errant husbands.

As she walked through the bar towards the function room she saw Silas Quirk arrive. She almost dropped the plate she was carrying. He walked in with the easy grace and air of a man who needed no one's approval. His clothes were expertly cut to flatter, his hair shone dark and glossy as a raven's wing, but his most striking feature was the intensity in his blue, deep as the ocean eyes. As well as being known for his ruthlessness in business, he had a well-deserved reputation as a heartless philanderer. A string of ill-fated dalliances followed him like a dog following a hot scent so she wasn't surprised to see the most striking young lady on his arm.

Dressed in a tightly-fitting crimson silk gown trimmed with fur, she moved with grace, elegance and dignity. Balanced on her fashionably styled ebony hair a dashing plum red hat was set at a rakish angle, its ostrich plumed feather secured by a colourful pin depicting a hand of cards. Below the hat Hope saw a finely featured face with high cheekbones, sparkling blue eyes and a smile that would warm the coldest heart. Around her neck a gold chain held four jewelled pendants, each in the form of an Ace depicting Hearts, Clubs, Diamonds and Spades.

John must have seen Hope staring. "That's Dexi Malone," he said. "She's Silas's sister. She works at The Grenadier."

"His sister?" Hope's voice rose in amazement. "She works at The Grenadier?"

"Yes, she's a dealer and the best card player I've ever seen. She's called Dexi because of her dexterity and expertise with the cards." He let out a sigh. "Her husband was a Mississippi riverboat gambler. Taught her everything she knows about card games and how to win them."

"You mean she cheats?"

John chuckled. "Well, if she does she's so good you'd never know it. Sit at her table you don't mind losing. She even makes that a pleasure." He sighed again.

"I guess you've had plenty of experience losing to Dexi Malone, then?" Hope said.

John smiled. "Just an occasional flutter. Can't afford the high-stakes they usually play for, but she's okay. Never pushes you to lose more than you can afford. And I only stick to cards." The way he said it made Hope realise that he was worried about Pa's reckless gambling too.

Throughout the evening Hope was kept busy taking plates of food into the function room and clearing away the empties and the glasses to take to the kitchen for Alfie to wash up. After drying she took them into Pa and Violet in the bar.

She'd just delivered a tray of clean glasses when Silas Quirk caught her arm. "Good evening, Hope," he said. "You're looking well but I can't understand why you're hidden away in the kitchen when you should be gracing us with your presence here at the bar. I must have a word with your father. Shame on him for hiding away the jewel in the Hope and Anchor's crown and the prettiest lady this side of the river."

Hope pulled her arm away. "I think you'll find most people come for the excellent food, drink and hospitality, sir. Not to ogle the ladies or expect them to be part of the entertainment."

Silas laughed. "I like a girl with spirit," he said. "We'll meet again." Hope wasn't sure whether it was a

34

threat or a promise, but she didn't miss Violet's glare as she hurried over to collect the tray of dirty glasses.

By eleven o'clock she saw Alfie was exhausted. "Why don't you go on up to bed," she said. "I can manage the rest. They'll be winding up soon. No need for you to stay."

Alfie looked at Ma. Ma nodded. "Thanks, Hope," he said and took off his apron before limping away.

It must be hard for him, Hope thought, standing so long with his bad leg. He never complained, but she vowed to do as much as she could for him in the future.

It was after midnight when the party came to an end and the revellers started drifting away. A few had cabs to collect them but other were happy to walk home. Calls of 'goodbye' and 'Merry Christmas' echoed in the frosty night air. Hope couldn't remember when they'd had such a large gathering. Seeing so many people enjoying their hospitality lifted her heart. Perhaps things were looking up after all.

As the last of the guests disappeared Hope looked around at the devastation left behind.

"You can leave that until the morning," Pa said, a smile on his face as he cashed up. "It was a good night. We did well thanks to Silas inviting all his big spending cronies. We have a lot to thank him for."

The thought of being grateful to a man known to be arrogant, ruthless and calculating as Silas Quirk filled Hope with despair. Was that what they'd come to? An establishment that picked up the crumbs from Silas Quirk's table?

"He's certainly a charmer," Violet said. "I wouldn't mind being grateful to him for a lot more than tonight."

"Violet!" Ma shrieked. "You mind your manners. There's folk around here wouldn't thank you for saying that. Gratitude's not what they feel for 'im and with good reason. No, it's Chamber of Commerce we should be thanking. Regulars who've stood by us in good times and in bad, not the Johnny-come-latelys like..." she paused as though saying his name would be more than she could bear, "'im".

A strained silence filled the air until John said, "Well, I'm done in. I'm away to my bed before Pa changes his mind about the clearing up."

Hope nodded. "Me too," she said. "Goodnight. I'll make an early start tomorrow."

Reluctantly Violet followed her up to bed and Ma and Pa followed soon after.

Chapter Five

Much to Alfie's delight Christmas Day brought the first snow of the season. Christmas morning he was the first to wake. His whoops of delight at finding something in his stocking woke Hope. She smiled as she imagined his joy, something she knew he had little of most days. Christmas seemed to bring out the best in people and their family was no exception.

She rose from her bed, wiped frost from the window and gazed out. It was as though a fluffy, white blanket had been draped over the city, covering all its faults. Footsteps and wheels moved silently in the snow as magical as a picture post card. It wouldn't last. Soon the sound of church bells, the chatter of people and clatter of carts and carriages making their way along the road would break the silence.

She shivered as she pulled on her warmest clothes. She'd need to get out soon as the market would be busy with people collecting their Christmas fare.

When she arrived downstairs Ma already had the stove alight and was making breakfast. The smell of frying bacon filled the air. Piles of dirty dishes left from the previous evening cluttered up the worktops and the sink. Alfie was sitting on the floor in front of the stove. She bent over and gave him a kiss. "Merry Christmas," she said. "I hope Father Christmas brought you something nice."

The smile on his face showed that he had. "An orange, a chocolate bar, some nuts and a game of

Tiddledy-Winks," he said, holding the box up to show her. "Can you play it with me later? I'd like that."

"I'd love to," Hope said. "Maybe this afternoon after our walk."

Every Christmas they'd follow the same routine. After a breakfast of bacon, sausage and eggs Pa would light the fire in the small upstairs parlour. The room was hardly used so the fire rarely lit, but he'd bring up enough coal to last until late evening. After a dinner of roast goose with all the trimmings and a pudding with custard and mince pies, they'd exchange Christmas gifts, then Violet, Hope, John and Alfie would go for a walk while Ma napped by the fire and Pa read the previous day's paper. It was a routine that never varied and Hope looked forward to it enjoying its familiarity. It was the one day in the year when all the family would be together.

"Good morning, Ma. Merry Christmas," she said giving her mother a kiss on the cheek. "Violet is still abed." She glanced at the piles of dirty dishes. "Should I start on these or do you want me to go to the market first?"

"The market," Ma said. "The others can do that lot. About time they helped out." She served up Hope and Alfie's breakfasts. "Ada is saving us a goose and some sausage meat. The other stuff has been ordered and paid for. You just need to pick it up."

Hope poured Alfie some milk to have with his breakfast sausage and noticed Ma already had a glass of sherry on the go.

After Hope finished her breakfast Ma handed her a basket with three parcels wrapped in brown paper. "Be sure to give these to Ada and tell her there'll be more at New Year."

Hope took the basket. The parcels looked suspiciously like bottles of gin. Ma gave Hope a list of provisions she needed for the Christmas dinner and Hope set off, pulling her shawl close around her.

Outside the air was cold, frosty and sharp but Hope was glad to get out and leave the clearing up to the others. The street was busy with people on their way to church or visiting friends. Most gave a cheery nod or wave as they passed. The atmosphere in the market was like no other day of the year. Many of the traders supplied a warming tipple to their regular customers, street musicians and buskers livened up the air and it seemed as though everyone had a smile on their face. She wished it could be like that every day.

Her first call was to Ada where she picked up the goose, some sausages, bacon and a large ham. "Ma said to say Merry Christmas and all the best to your family," she said as she gave her Ma's parcels.

"And to you and yours," Ada replied. "I've put a bit extra bacon in." She winked. "Tell your ma I'll see her alright next week an' all."

Hope smiled as she walked to the next stall, a great swell of warmth in her heart for these people who were so kind to them. She picked out some sweets to share, which she paid for with her own money, and then went to find Ned.

When she got to Ned's stall he gave her the vegetables Ma had ordered and then handed her another bag. "Somat a bit special for your tea," he said, with a grin.

"What is it," Hope said opening the bag and peering in.

"You'll see."

She gasped as she brought out a fresh pineapple. "Where on earth…?"

Ned tapped the side of his nose. "I've got a mate works down the docks."

"Well, this'll put a smile on Ma's face," she said. Then she leaned forward and planted a kiss on his cheek. "We're very grateful. Merry Christmas."

"Merry Christmas to you," Ned said, his face colouring the shade of a ripe tomato.

All the way home Hope's heart sang.

Pa's optimism of the previous evening carried over to Christmas Day. It was the quietest Christmas Hope could remember. The snow seemed to have laid a blanket of softness over everything, blocking out the noise and bustle of the city. Indoors the smell of roasting goose mixed with rich plum pudding and mince pies filled the air.

Hope and Violet had sherry before the meal and port after. Alfie had ginger beer and John and Pa whisky or brandy.

Pa was in an exceptionally good mood when they sat down to eat, rubbing his hands and beaming at everyone. "Next year'll be better than the last," he said, a gleam in his eye. "You get to know who your friends are when the chips are down."

"What do you mean? What have you done now?" Ma asked, a quiver in her voice as though experience had told her nothing good ever came of Pa's adventures, but she wasn't going to spoil the day if she didn't have to.

"You'll see, all in good time," Pa said. "All we have to do now is enjoy this succulent meal so expertly cooked by my one true love." He raised his glass.

"Here's to good health and plenty of wealth." He took a gulp.

Hope was too surprised to say anything, and it appeared that everyone else was too. Still a flutter of dread filled her stomach. It was a long time since Pa had been in such a good mood and she wondered how long it would last.

After the meal the girls and John cleared up and washed the dishes while Ma and Pa adjourned upstairs. Pa mentioned a piece in the paper he wanted to read about the latest gold strikes in the Yukon Territories in North America.

"Why? Are you thinking of going there?" a surprised John asked.

"'Course not but there's people making fortunes," Pa said.

"Aye and losing 'em," Ma chipped in.

Pa shot her an icy glare.

Once the clearing up was done they sat in front of the fire and exchanged gifts. Hope had embroidered some handkerchiefs for Ma and Violet and bought marbles for Alfie. He hooted with delight when he saw them.

She'd bought woollen scarves for John and Pa who said they'd wear them next time they went out. Violet gave Hope a pair of soft kid gloves, Ma gave her a book with flower pictures in which she could use as patterns for her embroidery. Alfie had bought her some silks in her favourite colours with his pocket money and John gave her a beautiful silk shawl she was sure Alice, a girl who worked on her mother's clothing stall in the market, must have picked out for her.

When they'd finished John said he'd arranged to visit a friend so he wouldn't be going for a walk with the others. Hope suspected the friend was Alice.

"I'll take Alfie to the park with Violet," Hope said.

"I think I'll go into town," Violet said. "Anyone want to come with me?"

"Into town? You mean the West End? You know that's too far for Alfie to walk."

"It's all right, I'll try," Alfie said. "I don't want to hold anyone back."

So they walked towards the West End, but had only gone halfway when Hope could see Alfie was slowing down.

"It's my leg," he said. "It hurts. I'm sorry."

"It's all right. Violet can go on, I'll walk back with you," Hope said. But she couldn't help being annoyed at Violet's thoughtlessness. She suspected that walking into town meant running into Bert, which Violet would say was a complete surprise.

When Hope got Alfie home she took off his leg brace and rubbed some liniment into his leg.

"Honestly, it was thoughtless of Violet to suggest such a trip," she complained to her mother. "I wouldn't mind betting she had an ulterior motive as well."

The rest of the afternoon she sat with Alfie in the parlour, in front of a roaring fire playing his new game of Tiddledy-Winks, which Alfie usually won.

Firelight flickered, candles glowed on the mantelpiece and windowsills and, for once, everything in the pub seemed to be at peace with itself. If only Violet and John were here, she thought, everything would be complete.

Chapter Six

The time between Christmas and New Year was always quiet. It seemed people had eaten and drunk their fill and had enough of visiting and merrymaking. It was a few days in the year when everyone could have a break from the pressures of their usual routines. The streets were quieter, pavements held only the few stragglers out to stock up with things they'd forgotten, even the traders in the market appeared more subdued. The whole town seemed still, as though waiting for the New Year when it would all start again. It felt to Hope as though the whole world was taking a breath before the next onslaught of activities.

"Hardly worth opening," Pa said so they opened late and closed early.

Hope was glad of the extra time to work on her embroidery and John and Pa managed to find their entertainment elsewhere. Violet too managed to make herself scarce most days, especially when there was work to be done or errands to be run.

Ma took the time to see friends or go shopping in town to shops she rarely had a chance to visit and was decidedly more cheerful when she arrived home than she was before going out.

Hope helped Ma in the kitchen or read to Alfie and helped with his homework.

Every day Pa came and went in a cloud of petulance. His good mood of Christmas Day vanished like morning mist when the sun comes out. Every day his mood darkened. Every night he'd be out and his mood even more morose when he returned. It seemed his luck at The Grenadier wasn't getting any better. Added to that the brewery hadn't delivered the usual order. John was seriously worried.

"We'll need to stock up for New Year," he said to Ma in the kitchen, Pa having arrived home shortly before and gone straight up to bed without a word. "If the brewery won't deliver we'll have to get it somewhere else and that'll mean cash which we haven't got."

"Take the money from the till and have a word with Ben at The Bull. Tell 'im we're waiting for our order and we'll see 'im right. He's a good sort is Ben. Known 'im for years. See what you can do."

New Year's Eve fell on a Saturday and, with the market closing early so the stallholders could go home to see the New Year in with their families, the afternoon was the busiest time. John managed the bar borrowing some bottles of beer from the licensee of the The Bull, with a promise to repay with a few extra 'when their order came in'.

"Everyone I spoke to said they were going to a pub by the river to see the fireworks," John said when he got back from The Bull. "Looks like we might as well close up early an' all." Nevertheless, the stock was becoming a problem and John didn't see why he should be the one to deal with it.

"You'll have to do something, Ma," he said. "Speak to Pa. He needs to sort somat out with the brewery."

"I think we can all guess where the money goes," Ma said in a rare fit of rebellion. "Finds enough money to pay for his drink and gaming."

"That Silas Quirk has some sort of influence over him," Hope said. "I don't know why, but he seems to be in thrall to him."

"It's cos Silas lets 'im 'ave credit," John said. "Even gives 'im cash to bet with in the rat pen. I never go there, the bets climb up so fast you soon lose track and then the fight's over and they start again with the next round. You can lose double, triple or even more in one evening. Too rich for me, but Pa seems to like it."

"What, dogs chasing rats? Urg!" Hope said. "There's something I'd never pay to see."

"Nah, but it's got Pa hooked," John said. "I've seen 'im there, he gets that carried away…"

"Well, if he's not careful we'll all be carried away. Evicted if we can't pay the rent," Ma said.

A few days after New Year's Eve the snow lay even deeper and the frost hardened on the ground. Even with the fires lit the air was cold and windows lined with frost until late in the day. Hope sat with Ma in the kitchen to do her embroidery as it was the warmest place. Violet and Alfie spent most of their time playing games in front of the kitchen hearth. Hope could see Violet was itching to get out though. Staying in and helping in the bar when needed was not in her plans.

"There's a funfair over Regent's Park and skating on the pond," Violet said. "You'd like to see the skating wouldn't you, Alfie? Come on, I'll take you."

Alfie's eyes shone. "Really?"

"Really. I'll even treat you to hot chocolate if you're good. Why don't you come too, Hope? It'll be fun."

Yes, fun, Hope thought and a good way to get out of helping in the pub. "Thanks, but I've to go to the market for silks. I may go later," with Ned, she thought, hoping that if she saw him in the market she could suggest it. Going with Ned would be more fun than going with Violet, that's for sure.

"Your loss," Violet said.

"What about Alfie's walking? He won't be able to walk to Regent's Park."

"We'll take the omnibus. You can manage the omnibus if I help can't you, Alfie?"

Alfie nodded. Violet smirked. "Come on, Alfie, let's go and leave these dullards to their work." Alfie didn't need second telling. He scurried as best he could after Violet as she went to get their coats.

"I'll pick up some meat while I'm in the market," Hope said to Ma, "but I'll need some cash. I daren't go to the butcher. I doubt Pa's paid his bill." Cash was kept in a small safe in Rose and William's bedroom. Only John and Pa had keys.

"It's not good enough," Ma said. "Why hasn't the bill been paid? We've had our busiest few weeks. If we can't make money over Christmas when will be able to?" Ma was about as much use as a paper umbrella when it came to reading, writing and figures. She was an excellent cook and her pies were legendary, but that was the full extent of her talents. "I want you to take a look at the books, Hope. There's somat fishy going on and I want it sorted out."

"I don't know, Ma," Hope said. "Pa'll skin me alive if I touch his books. Anyway, he keeps them

46

locked away. Only Pa or John cash up, record the takings and take the money to the bank. I don't know what's paid in and what's not."

"Well, it's about time you found out," Ma said. Her eyes blazed with anger and her jaw set. "Forget going to the market. I'll get the books and you'll check 'em. I'll not have us thrown out for not paying rent because of 'is gambling and drinking. It's about time 'e faced up to 'is responsibilities."

Hope's heart dropped to her boots. It was clear Ma had got her dandy up and there was no arguing. She'd just have to do what she said and hope she could get to the market later.

While Pa was sleeping off the previous night's excess and John busy in the cellar, Ma went up to the bedroom. Hope stood at the bottom of the stairs, hardly daring to breathe, listening to Pa's snoring. A few anxious minutes later Ma came tiptoeing down the stairs, the books in her hand. "It's all right," she said. "I put the key back in his pocket. He'll not know a thing." She handed the books to Hope. "Here you are. Take a look and tell me what's been going on."

Quick as she could Hope checked the banking against the book where the nightly takings were recorded. There were discrepancies, but not enough to cause the bills not to be paid. Then she checked payments out of the bank. The amounts being paid to suppliers were increasing while the amounts being paid in were lessening. Ma was right, trade leading up to Christmas had been good. The takings should reflect that, but they didn't.

"We're paying more out than we're taking in," Hope said. "There may be a good reason…"

"Good reason my arse," Ma said. "The money's short and there's an end to it."

"I think we should check the stock before we jump to any conclusions," Hope said. "If Pa's been stocking up…"

At least Ma seemed slightly reassured by Hope's suggestion. "Aye, that's reasonable, it's time we did a stocktake then. Ask John to help while I spirit these books back into the safe. He's snoring like a rhino, so between us we should have it sorted before he wakes up."

Down in the cellar Hope told John what had been going on. "She wants the stock checked now. You do down here and I'll do the bar. We need to get it done before he wakes up, so get a shift on."

"Wait a minute, Hope. What do you mean paying out more than we're taking in? How do you know? He keeps the books locked away."

"I've seen them. The banking is short according to the takings book and we're buying a lot more stock than we're selling, unless…" She didn't get any further. John sank down onto a barrel, head in his hands. "I took some," he said.

"Took some? What do you mean you took some?"

"Money from the till. I got involved in a high stakes card game. Had a run of bad luck that's all. It weren't a lot, just a few quid. I was going to put it back when I got paid. Should 'ave got extra an' all, it being Christmas."

Hope's jaw dropped. She sank down onto the barrel next to John. Dread circled her stomach. He was turning out just like Pa, she thought. "That's awful, John. I knew Pa was gambling away the takings, didn't know you were too. What am I going to tell Ma?"

"Don't tell her, Hope. I'll pay it back, honest. It was only a few pounds."

Hope's heart stuttered. It wasn't his fault, he was only following Pa's example.

"I've learned me lesson, Hope. I won't do it again, honest, but just for now, please don't tell Ma."

Hope's anger faded. "Don't worry," she said. "We can do a stocktake and I'll tell her you bought some spirits from the market if it was only a few pounds, although, if none of the bills have been paid and there's not enough for the rent it's likely to be much more than that."

Up in the bar Tom O'Reilly was swabbing the floor with his mop. "You're an early bird," she said. "Didn't expect you to come in. What happened last night? You should have cleaned up then."

"Oh, such a terrible thing," Tom said, in his lilting Irish brogue. "Me back was giving me gip so I went 'ome and thought I'd come in this morning to finish. I 'ope as 'ow that's alright wit you."

Hope smiled, relieved that she wouldn't have to do the cleaning as well as the stocktaking. "Perfectly all right with me," she said and started to count the bottles on the shelf.

She hadn't got far when the door opened and Pa burst in. It was clear that a night's sleep had done nothing to dull his temper. "What's going on here," he roared, his face the colour of a purple beetroot.

Hope blanched. "Just doing a bit of cleaning up," she said grabbing a cloth and whisking it across the bar counter. She daren't tell him what she was really doing.

"What the devil are you doing here, Thomas O'Reilly?" He spun round to Hope. "It's not your place to clean up. That's what we pay 'im for," he said. "Not that he makes any sort of job of it." Then, turning back to Tom he yelled, "You lazy git, getting my staff to do your dirty work." Anger swelled his body and, swinging his leg in temper he kicked Tom's bucket.

A resounding clang rang out. The bucket toppled, spilling dirty water over the floor. Tom rushed to pick up the fallen bucket, but couldn't get there in time to stop a bottle of the best brandy rolling out.

A gasp of shock filled the bar. The bottle of brandy lay on the wooden floor, shining and wet for all to see.

"So that's what's been going on," Pa said eventually, his eyes narrowed. "You thieving toe-rag. I'll 'ave the law on you. Get out. Get out!" He sprang towards Tom, picked him up by the scruff of his neck and threw him out of the door into the street where he skidded across the icy cobbles into the gutter. "And never come back."

The commotion brought John up from the cellar. He stared at Hope, who was staring at her pa. They were both speechless.

"Good riddance to bad rubbish," Pa said, slamming the bar door shut. "I never did like the fellow. Far too shallow and conniving."

He walked up to the bar and poured himself a glass of whisky. "Well, get on with whatever you're supposed to be doing," he said. "I need some breakfast." With that he staggered back into the kitchen.

"More reason now than ever to check the stock," Hope said. "Then we can let Pa work out how much has been taken and decide what he wants to do about it." She wasn't about to let on to Pa that she'd seen the books so knew the stock would be short, even if she didn't know the reason.

"Looks like you'll 'ave to add cleaning to your list of jobs an' all," John said. "Still, it's a bad turn as does no one any good." He sauntered off to finish his work in the cellar and Hope realised that John's losses would be added to Tom O'Reilly's misfortune.

Chapter Seven

Hope waited until after Pa had finished his breakfast before handing him the inventory she and John had completed. He'd be in a better mood once he'd eaten.

"I'll need some cash for the market," she said. "All the traders want cash now."

Pa grunted, but he took the list, gave it a cursory glance, took two half-crowns out of his pocket and handed them to Hope.

She left without saying another word. She was glad to be out of the pub. The air was fresh and clear and the sky a cloudless blue. Frost sparkled on trees as she passed and she was glad of the warmth of her shawl, pulling it closer around her. A sharp breeze nipped her nose and coloured her cheeks but the walk to the market was pleasant, bearing in mind what she'd left behind.

Her first call was to see Ada and pick up the meat Ma had ordered. She stopped and chatted while Ada told her all about their Christmas and how grateful she was for Ma's contribution. "She's a diamond your ma," Alice said. "There's lots round 'ere don't give a damn about other people, but your ma's a good 'un."

"I'll tell her," Hope said and smiled at Ada's generous words.

After buying the meat Hope went to see Ned. She waited until he'd finished serving a customer before approaching him. "Just a few of your best tater-spuds," she said, "to go with the meat in Ma's pies."

He nodded and started to pick out her order. "Cold enough for you?" he asked.

"Cold enough for the pond in the park to freeze over," she replied.

"I heard there was skating on Regent's Park pond," he said. "Thought I might take a look this afternoon. Don't suppose you'd care to come with me?" He put the potatoes into a bag. "You could bring young Alfie. He'd enjoy it."

She laughed. "Alfie's gone this morning with Violet," she said, "but I dare say he could be persuaded to go again."

Ned grinned as he handed her the bag of potatoes. "Call round for you after lunch, about two o'clock?"

"That'll be lovely," Hope said. She couldn't help smiling all the way home.

"It was amazing," Alfie said when he got home with Violet at lunchtime. "So many people. We had hot chocolate and Violet chatted up a soldier."

"I did not," Violet cried, eyes wide. "He was merely passing the time of day. We were talking about the skaters."

Alfie shrugged. Hope guessed there was a reason she'd put on her best coat.

"Well, in that case you won't mind going again," Hope said. "Ned's asked if you'd like to come with us this afternoon."

Alfie's lips spread into a grin. "I'd love to," he said. "Violet wouldn't let me go on the ice, but I bet Ned will."

By two o'clock, when Ned arrived in his horse and cart, Hope and Alfie were well wrapped up in their winter clothes and anxious to go. Hope sat up front with Ned and Ned lifted Alfie into the back. He'd brought blankets for them to wrap up in as well. Hope was overwhelmed with his kindness.

Away from the pub and out in the fresh air she was able to leave all thoughts of the troubles at home behind. Being with Ned she felt more alive than she had in ages. If only life could always be like this, she thought.

The afternoon passed in the whirl of excitement. The park was crowded with people, their breath vaporising in the icy air. Frost hardened ground crunched beneath their feet. There was a carnival atmosphere with skaters and people sliding on the frozen pond. Children, their faces shining with glee at the sticks of candyfloss they held in their hands, watched from the bank. The air was filled with the sound of a barrel organ playing and colourful stalls and sideshows added to the noise. Music from a bright carousel with gleaming golden horses going round and round on the other side of the pond drifted over on the breeze.

The ice was full of skaters bent earnestly to the task, enjoying the afternoon light before darkness descended and beacons would be lit around the edges of the pond so they could skate into the evening.

"Are you game for a skate round?" Ned asked Hope, a twinkle in his hazel eyes.

"Who me?" Hope laughed. "I think I'd prefer to stay on solid ground and watch, but you go ahead."

"And me," Alfie begged. "Take me on, Ned."

"Come on then."

Ned hired some skates for himself and Hope watched in amazement as he pushed a delighted Alfie around on the ice. Hope had never seen him have so much fun. Sliding on the ice supported by Ned was one time Alfie's leg brace didn't handicap him or make him any different from the other boys being pushed around or sliding by themselves. After half-an-hour the cold drove them back to where Hope was standing.

"Did you see me?" Alfie said. "I skated, just like the other boys."

"Yes, I saw. Well done. That deserves a hot drink don't you think?"

While Hope and Alfie enjoyed their hot chocolate Ned skated off, weaving around the ice twisting and turning and Hope realised that he was quite an experienced skater.

Afterwards he bought them all a hot pie and paid for Alfie to have a go on the rifle range. Altogether it was a wonderful afternoon and by the time they got home Hope was wishing the day would never end. She felt so at ease in Ned's company she wished it could go on forever. Being with him brought a sparkle to her eyes and, despite the cold of the day, a new sort of warmth to her heart. She had to sit up until past midnight finishing her stitching for Miss Godley but she didn't mind at all as the memory of a lovely afternoon spent over the park with Ned kept buzzing through her mind.

Over the next few days several more traders insisted on being paid before they would make any deliveries to the pub. The takings going into the bank dwindled and Ma became ever more anxious with the rent due at the end of the week. Pa's temper flared on more than occasion when Hope or John asked for cash to pay the traders.

The following weeks brought more snow together with mounting bills. Every night Hope heard raised voices coming from her parents' bedroom and during the day the atmosphere in the pub was so bad she found excuses to go out, just like Violet.

"Ruth wants me to work in the shop today," she'd say or, "I need to go into town for an errand for Ruth." Anything to get out of the pub.

The January trade was slow anyway. The weather remained damp and dank. The street lights barely cast any light or reflection on the wet pavement. Most days there were only one or two stragglers come in for a warm by the fire or a bite to eat before they went back to work in the afternoon so John could easily cope alone. Even Ma's pies weren't bringing the customers in and by the end of the month, when the rent was due, she was seriously worried.

"I don't know what we're going to do," she said to Hope one morning. "It looks like the end for us." She didn't say 'thanks to Pa's drinking and gambling', but Hope could see in her eyes that that was what she meant.

"Somat's got to be done," she said. "And done quick. I'm at me wit's end."

"I have a little money put by, Ma. From my embroidery," Hope said. "I'll draw it out but it won't keep us for long."

"Nay, lass. I'll not take your money. You're gonna need it afore long, 'specially if we're out on our ear. You hang on it to. I'll get Pa to sort it out. It's 'is responsibility."

Ma's pies brought in a few extra sales but Hope was glad to have more time to do her embroidery. She used the money the drapery store paid to buy food in the market and never mentioned the cost to her mother, not wanting to add to her worries.

"It's all right, Ma," she'd say. "Ada let me have it cheap," or, "She said it was going to waste" or, "She had it over. She was wanting to get rid of it before it went off."

The end of the month came and went with no mention of the rent or the bills being paid.

February came and the weather improved slightly. The days grew warmer and the afternoons drew out. The trees in the park began to show green leaves and catkins hung on branches of the willow bringing a breath of spring. Violet spent more time at the theatre, saying they were going to let her help out with the props and scenery.

Hope rose early and would often walk with Alfie to see him into school, making sure Mr Mackitterick was aware of her presence and that she was keeping an eye on Alfie. She wished she could move him to a different school away from the ruffians and bullies but then she supposed all boys would be the same and Alfie could never walk further anyway.

Every morning she went to the drapery with her samples before she went to the market. The money Miss Godley paid her would be used to buy the meat and potatoes for Ma's pies, which, these days were more potato than meat.

Ma was in the kitchen lighting the fire to put the kettle on for tea. After various conversations with her mother, and aware of their dire financial situation, Hope was walking on eggshells when Pa returned home, having been out all night. It was clear from his appearance that he was the worse for drink. His clothes were dishevelled, his eyes bleary and his chin dark with stubble.

"Oh, Hope," he said, his words slurred. "Good news for you. Come next month you'll be working in The Grenadier for Silas Quirk. He's a generous man and he's made me the most generous offer. You're a very lucky lady." With that he turned, walked out of the door and stumbled up the stairs to bed.

Hope's jaw dropped. She stared, open-mouthed, at Ma. "What did he say?" Her knees trembled. She grabbed the nearest chair and sat. "Did I hear right? He's told Silas Quirk that I'll work for him?" It was beyond understanding. "He's joking. Please say it's a joke, Ma?"

Rose too took some time to recover from the shock, not of her husband returning in the early morning from a night's drinking and gambling, she was used to that, but to send Hope to work for Silas Quirk... "No, he can't mean it," she said, although the look of her face told Hope that she too was troubled by what he'd said. "It's the drink talking. He'll have forgotten about it by the time he wakes up this afternoon."

"I do hope so," Hope said, a quiver in her voice. "There's no way I'll work for that man. He's a ruthless womanizer and not to be trusted. I'd rather walk the street."

Violet, who'd been listening in the hallway, walked in. "Same thing isn't it?" she sniggered. "'cept Quirk's girls stay in the dry."

"Violet!" Rose eyed her youngest daughter. "It wouldn't do you any harm to put in a few hours in the bar helping John instead of spending all your time with that wastrel Bert Shadwick."

"Me work in the bar? No thanks, although if Silas Quirk offered me a job I'd take it in a heartbeat. Some of the wealthiest men in the city go to his place. Wouldn't mind meeting a few of 'em meself."

The colour returned to Hope's face as she realised that Ma was right. Pa was half-ratted. He'd have forgotten all about it by the afternoon. She didn't want to fall out with him, but sending her to work at The Grenadier – what on earth was he thinking?

Chapter Eight

The next few days passed relatively quietly and Hope was convinced Pa had forgotten his drunken ramblings about her working at The Grenadier. In fact, since the night he made the pronouncement that struck fear into her heart, the whole atmosphere at home had changed. The rows had stopped. There was no more shouting, storming out, or doors slamming. Instead, Pa took his turn working behind the bar with John or else he'd be in his office going over the books. He started supervising the deliveries and checking the barrels in the cellar. If he did go out it was to visit the brewery or wine merchants, not The Grenadier.

"Ma and Pa must have made their peace," John said one morning while he was bottling up ready to open. "Perhaps we'll all get some peace and quiet now."

The wine merchants started delivering again. "Pa must have had a win," John said, realising that, for once, the bills had been paid.

"Thank goodness. About time our luck changed," Hope said, although she thought they'd all be a lot luckier if he gave up gambling altogether.

Things improved in the kitchen too. The butcher delivered the best cuts of meat for Ma's pies and she smiled more often.

Hope wasn't sure how long the calm would last, or when the next storm would hit, but she was determined to make the most of it, getting out of the pub, going to the market or the drapery shop whenever she wasn't needed in the bar.

Pa said very little to her. She guessed he was embarrassed about his earlier outburst so she was surprised when, one day, near the end of the month, Pa called her into his office. A shiver of fear tingled through her but she pushed it away. Probably wants to apologise, she thought. Things had been going so well lately it was silly to worry. It was her pa and he wouldn't do anything to hurt her. He may be a bit loud and even aggressive when in drink, but most of the time he was a loving, generous man and she needed to remember that.

"Ah, Hope," he said. "Next time you're in the market buy yourself some nice material for a new dress. It's about time you had something new. And get some of those things Violet uses to put her hair up." He handed her a small purse. "Want to look your best don't you?"

Hope glanced down at her faded blue day dress. It was worn, but there was still a bit of wear in it. Perhaps it was time she got something new but it wasn't like Pa to mention it. Perhaps it was his way of saying sorry. She took the proffered purse and, in a daze, walked out of the room.

On Monday, after a late tea a few days before the month end, Hope and John were setting up for the evening trade when the door opened and Dexi Malone swept into the bar, bringing with her the heady scent of orange, jasmine and tuberose. Her full length emerald green coat, lavishly trimmed with white ermine, the epitome of elegance and style, brushed the floor as she glanced around, obviously unimpressed. An elaborate creation of chartreuse fur and feathers perched jauntily on her head and a fox, complete with amber eyes, draped soulfully around her shoulders. Her presence made the bar of the Hope and Anchor look shabby by comparison.

Hope gasped, unable to believe her eyes. John, mouth agape, rushed to serve her. She avoided him and walked over to where Hope stood, the glass she was drying held still in her hand.

"Can I help you?" Hope said, her mouth dry.

Dexi tilted her head to one side, sizing Hope up. "So, you're Hope Daniels, my brother's latest project. You're even more insignificant than I had supposed."

Hope's eyes widened. She wasn't anyone's project and certainly not Silas Quirk's. "I'm the daughter of William Daniels, the landlord, if that's what you mean and if I'm anyone's latest project I'm unaware of it. I'm happy to serve you a drink if that's what you're wanting, nothing more."

When Dexi smiled her face softened and Hope saw why her brother was so beguiled by her. Her eyes sparkled and Hope immediately felt her warmth.

"I understand you'll be joining us at The Grenadier next week," she said. "Silas has asked me to keep an eye on you. I'm to show you the ropes and help you settle in. I do hope we will be friends."

Hope swallowed. Her worst nightmare was coming true. Her work at The Grenadier? Never in a million years. "I'm afraid you are mistaken," she said. She felt herself beginning to quake. "If you'll excuse me. My brother John will be happy to serve you."

She went to turn away as John recovered his composure, which had taken flight at Dexi's entrance, and rushed to serve her. "It'll be my pleasure," he said.

"I'm not mistaken," Dexi said. She turned to John. "Gin. You know the way I like it."

John's reaction made it clear that he did. "Won't you join me? We have much to discuss." She walked to a table and made herself comfortable, clearly expecting Hope to follow.

Hope's stomach churned. What did Dexi know that she didn't? Her appearance here today wasn't a coincidence. It wasn't a good omen either. "I'll have gin too," she said as she went to join Dexi at the table, her heart thumping.

John brought them the drinks. Dexi dismissed him with a wave of her hand and turned her gaze directly onto Hope. "Hmm. With a decent dress and your hair done up you could look passably pretty, I suppose," she said. "Silas must have seen something in you that completely eludes me. I would have thought your sister, Violet, would have been a more suitable applicant for the post, but Silas knows best. I always follow his advice."

Hope's anger flared. "Well, in this case his advice is misguided. I have no intention of working at The Grenadier, now or ever."

Dexi smiled her beguiling smile. "You were unaware of the arrangement? Did your father not mention it?" She sipped her drink.

Thoughts raced through Hope's head. She picked up her gin and, trying to control the rage pounding through her veins, took a gulp. "I know of no arrangement," she said, her voice barely above a whisper.

Dexi sat for a few moments as though considering her response. She put her hand on Hope's arm. "For some reason I fail to understand, Silas wants you working at The Grenadier and what Silas wants, Silas always gets," she said.

Hope pulled her arm away. "In this case he'll be sadly disappointed."

Dexi finished her drink and put the glass back on the table. "You need to speak to your father," she said. "I'll come back tomorrow. Then we will see." With that she rose and swept out of the door.

"What was all that about?" John said, rushing over to take Dexi's empty seat. "Does she want you to work at The Grenadier? I'd give my eye-teeth to work in a place like that. It's always busy, full of wealthy gents and big tippers. It'd be a right step up. Who's the lucky one?"

For once in her life Hope was left speechless. She glared at John, rose and went to find Ma. Ma would sort it out. She always did.

She found Ma in the kitchen rolling out pastry. "We've just had a visit from Dexi Malone," she said, "who appears to be under the impression that I'll be working with her at The Grenadier from next week. She said something about an arrangement and I should talk to Pa. It's not true is it? Please say it isn't true."

Ma stopped what she was doing and stared at Hope. "You need to do as she says then. Go talk to your father."

"Why? What has he told them? What has he said? You must know. Tell me please. What's it all about and why me? I'm the last person on earth who'd want to work there."

Ma bent her head and continued rolling out her pastry. "Like I said. Talk to your father."

"I can't. He's not back from the brewery." She folded her arms across her chest and stomped over to a chair. "Right, I'll sit here until you tell me what's going on." She glared at her mother who carried on cutting out pastry rounds for the pies she was making.

"You can sit there 'til the cows come 'ome," Ma said. "It's got nowt to do with me. It's Pa's doing. It's 'im you need to speak to."

So Hope sat, fuming for another hour until she heard her father arrive in the bar, calling good evening to John and passing the time of day with the customers. When it went quiet she guessed he'd gone into the room he used as an office.

Her anger had abated, but not her determination. The hour waiting for his return had given her time to think and the more she thought about it the clearer it became. Pa had mentioned a generous offer. Then, suddenly, the rent was paid, bills were met, Pa had even given her money for a dress. If he'd won the money as John had supposed, they'd never have heard the end of it. He'd be bragging about his prowess at cards, or luck on the dogs, buying everyone drinks and celebrating. Instead, he'd quietly been going about his own business, saying nothing.

She rose, walked through the bar and into the office to face him. He glanced up from where he was sitting at the bureau. A lamp on the desk lit the small room. There was no other light.

"Did you tell Silas Quirk that I'd work for him?" she asked before her father could draw breath to speak. "Well, I'm here to tell you that I won't work for that man, I'd rather starve."

Pa put the pen he was holding on the desk. "What's happened?" he asked, his voice controlled, his gaze level.

"Dexi Malone happened. She came here to 'look me over'. Said I'd be working with her next week. Well, I won't."

Pa's face began to turn red and a vein on his neck started to pulse. His breathing slowed and he looked as though he was about to explode. For the first time in her life Hope felt fear in his presence. Memories of her mother lying on the kitchen floor, bleeding, ran through her mind.

His voice was frighteningly calm. "I told you. He's made a most generous offer and one I'll not turn down."

Alarm surged through her; her heart raced, her palms began to sweat.

"He's offering you a chance to work in his club. One you should be grateful for." His fists clenched on the desk. "It's for one year, after that you may do as you please, but you'll not be welcome here if you let me down." She saw the storm gathering in his eyes. "It's bar work. Work you're perfectly capable of doing. It's a wonderful opportunity for you."

"An opportunity I have no wish to pursue," Hope said.

He banged his fist on the desk and Hope jumped. "You'll do as you're told and be grateful," he said, his voice getting louder. "You're wishes are irrelevant."

Another thought occurred to her. "And am I to be paid for this wonderful opportunity?"

Pa turned away, his face like granite. "I will deal with the financial arrangements," he said. "They're no business of yours."

"Supposing I don't want to work at that place?"

He turned back to face her and there was no doubt what was in his mind. "Then it'd be the worse for you.

If you're not prepared to do as I say you can start packing. I have a duty to think of the whole family."

Hope wondered why he hadn't thought of them before he lost all their money gambling, but she didn't say anything. At that moment she hated him more than she'd ever hated anyone in her life.

Pa sighed. He seemed to relax a little. "I've made it clear to Silas that you're only to work in the saloon bar. You won't be required to go into the dog or rat pits and Dexi – his own sister – will look out for you and see that you're treated with respect. I gave my word and that's the end of the matter."

He turned back to his desk and Hope realised that the conversation was over.

Back in the kitchen Ma was putting her latest batch of pies into the larder. "Get it sorted did you?" she asked.

Hope stomped to a chair and sat, arms folded. "Apparently I'm part of an 'arrangement' cooked up by Silas Quirk. His sister said Silas wanted me to work there and Silas always gets whatever he wants."

Ma nodded. "Aye, and not only Silas. Most men have the knack of getting whatever they want." She wiped her hands on her apron. "Told you about writing off the gaming debts and the loan did he?"

"Not exactly, but I guessed money came into it."

"Aye, usually does don't it?" Ma said. She went back to the larder. "Come on, let's get ourselves a couple of gins and drink to our good fortune."

"Good fortune?"

"Aye. We could all be out on the street if it weren't for Silas Quirk taking a fancy to you. Is that what you want for Violet and Alfie?"

A vision of Alfie's trusting face ran through Hope's mind. "No. Of course not!"

"Well then. Your working at The Grenadier for a while's a small price to pay isn't it?"

Hope had to laugh. Ma had a way of putting things in their true perspective and bringing them down to basics.

Chapter Nine

The next evening when Dexi came in Hope was a lot more civil and Dexi was as gracious as Hope knew she would be. "It's quite an investment Silas has made," Dexi said. "I'm just here to see he gets his money's worth."

"I'm not sure what your brother expects," Hope said, "but my understanding is that I'm to work in the bar. Nothing more."

"Unless you feel inclined to grasp whatever opportunity comes your way. Many of our clientele are very generous. You could do well."

"Six until midnight serving drinks, Pa said. I'm sure I can manage that."

"Whatever you wish," Dexi said, "but you will need to look the part. As a gesture of our goodwill I can introduce you to my dressmaker…"

"I can't afford…" Hope had thought to borrow one of Violet's creations, but…

"No need. As I said, Silas can be extremely generous when he sees something he wants."

The thought of being further indebted to Silas Quirk horrified Hope but she was in no position to argue.

"She's a little marvel," Dexi continued. "She'll run up something suitable in no time. Would tomorrow suit?"

Reluctantly Hope agreed. "Although I don't know what you expect," she said. "I'll not dress like a dollymop for anyone."

Dexi frowned. "And you wouldn't be welcome in The Grenadier if you did," she said.

The next day the sky was grey with impending drizzle. Dexi collected Hope in a hansom and they made their way to an elegant Georgian house just off Regent Street.

Inside Hope followed Dexi along the pristine, white-walled hall to a workroom at the rear. The room appeared light and airy despite the dullness of the day and the number of tables set out around it. Several girls, dressed in white overalls, sat on benches, cutting or sewing swathes of colourful fabrics, bending over their work with silent endeavour and application.

A stocky woman in a dark dress moved forward to greet Dexi. "Mrs Malone, such a pleasure to see you again," she said. Her gaze shifted to Hope, eyeing her up like a street cleaner eyeing up a particularly smelly pile of filth.

"And you, Miss Lovell," Dexi said. She indicated Hope. "This is Miss Daniels. She'll be working with me in The Grenadier so she'll need something suitable to wear."

"Ah!" the woman said, her grimace morphing into a smile. "Come this way, dear."

Hope followed her into another room, bare apart from shelves filled with bolts of cloth lining the walls and a large table in the centre of the room.

The next hour was spent with Miss Lovell's workroom assistant, Elsie, taking Hope's measurements and noting them in a small notebook, while Dexi and the dressmaker tried swatches of various coloured materials against Hope's skin and discussed possible designs which Miss Lovell drew with remarkable accuracy and verve as Dexi explained to her exactly what was required. "Elegant and refined," Dexi said, "but alluring with a hint of mystery."

In the end they decided on deep sapphire silk, the bodice embroidered with crescent moons and silver stars. It was to be low cut to show off Hope's assets (Dexi's words), the full skirt trimmed and frilled with strands of silver and the waist cinched. Hope's hair would be dressed in high curls with a midnight blue and silver feather clip and Dexi promised sapphire jewellery to finish the ensemble.

"Can you have it ready for Friday?" Dexi asked. "It's quite urgent. The poor girl has nothing suitable to wear and I want her to make a good first impression."

Miss Lovell smiled. "Of course," she said. Hope felt a pang of sympathy for the workroom girls who'd have to work through the night to get it done.

As she left the dressmaker's her mind whirled. She couldn't imagine what she would look like but had to admit the whole thing had been a surprisingly pleasant experience. How easily things come to those who can afford to pay for them, she thought, not for the first time.

Friday morning Dexi called on her again to go together to Miss Lovell's workshop for the fitting. Elsie, the workroom assistant who'd taken Hope's measurements, was standing ready to help her into the sapphire blue creation.

First of all Elsie swept Hope's hair up to rest in curls on the top of her head, showing off the poise and elegance of her long, graceful neck and shoulders. Stepping into the dress and drawing it up for Elsie to fasten, Hope felt herself grow in confidence. She stretched up to her full height and strode towards the mirror with a new sense of assurance. When she glanced in the mirror she hardly recognised herself. The colour of the material brought out the ocean blue of her eyes and the style emphasised her slim waist and pleasing curves. Her eyes seemed to sparkle and her lips spread into a wide smile. She felt different too. As she drew in a breath a bubble of happiness rose up inside her. She was beautiful. She looked so graceful and elegant she felt as though she could take on the world and give them a good run for their money. She could look the devil in the eye and spit in it, she felt so good. If men wanted to be beguiled by her she'd know how to lead them on and slap them down with equal relish. She saw a new way of life opening up to her, one where she would be in control.

"Excellent," Dexi said, clapping her hands and bringing Hope back to earth. "You've done a superb job as always, Miss Lovell." She moved towards Hope. "Perhaps a little lower here and a little tighter here," she said, indicating the neckline and the waist.

The dressmaker nodded.

"Good. Send me the finished outfit this evening. Miss Daniels will need it for Monday and I want to check it again before then."

"It will be done."

"Thank you."

Then, before she knew it they were back out on the street in the drizzle and rain and Hope's dreams and fantasies were whisked away like feathers in a storm, but it was something she'd remember for the rest of her life.

Saturday morning Hope rose early to go to the market, memories of the previous day's fitting still buzzing through her mind. It was something to tell Violet about when she got back. Violet, of course, was still abed after another late night at the theatre with Bert.

Hope collected the list from Ma and set out at a brisk pace. She hummed as she walked along. The earlier drizzle had disappeared and a weak sun was trying to break through the clouds. She loved these early mornings when the streets were relatively empty. Later they would be teaming with cabs, carts and carriages and so noisy you could hardly hear yourself think. The early morning streets always appeared cleaner, fresher and brighter than later in the day when the dirt and grime of the traffic, horses and people had left their mark.

After buying the things on Ma's list she made her way to the greengrocery stall where she knew Ned would be working. Cheerful as ever he chatted to a customer ahead of her and Hope waited. She hadn't told him about Dexi's visit or about having to work in The Grenadier and, for some odd reason she felt a twist of disloyalty for keeping it from him. She felt guilty about having enjoyed the dress fitting so much too, although there was no reason why she should.

She considered Ned to be a friend, and with the gossip in the market being what it was, he'd be aware of her family's financial problems, nothing stayed secret for long, but she didn't feel able to tell him about the predicament her father had placed her in, at least, not yet.

"Good morning, my lovely," he said as the customer walked away. "You're looking well, and I've got something to make your eyes sparkle even more."

Hope giggled. You couldn't stay worried for long, not with Ned. "And what might that be?" she asked, expecting some spiel about extra tasty tomatoes or fresh as a daisy carrots.

"How would you like to go to the theatre tonight?" he said with a grin.

"The theatre? That's more in Violet's line than mine," she said. "Perhaps you should ask her."

"But it's you I want to take out," he said. "Somewhere special. The proper theatre. To see a play?"

"A play?"

"Yes. One my customers has given me tickets for a play he's performing in and there's no one I'd rather spend the evening with than you."

Hope's heart beat a little faster. Her face flushed. "How can I refuse such a gallant invitation?" she said. "Of course, I'd love to go."

So it was arranged. Ned would call and pick her up at six-thirty that evening. They'd have a drink before the performance and a light supper afterwards. An evening alone with Ned would be the perfect opportunity to tell him about Dexi Malone and working at The Grenadier.

When she got home she went in to see Pa to arrange to have the night off. He could hardly refuse, given that it would be her last evening working in the pub. From Monday she'd be at The Grenadier and he'd have to cover the hours himself, or find someone else to do it.

The meeting didn't go well. Hope noticed a half-empty bottle of whisky on Pa's desk where he sat going through the books. When she told him she'd be out that evening, he just grunted. As she left the room she noticed a couple of empty whisky bottles lying on the floor next to the desk.

"You go out and enjoy yourself," Ma said. "Don't worry about us. Alfie'll help. Might as well make the most of it, it may be the last chance you'll have."

Hope spent the afternoon making sure the bar was cleaned and swept and the shelves stocked, so Pa would have no excuse for complaint.

Violet was in their room adding trimmings to a new hat she planned to wear when she went out with Bert that night. "A play?" she said, when Hope told her about the invitation. "How dreadfully boring. Now if it had been the Music Hall…"

Dressing for the theatre, Hope ummed and ahhed about what to wear. She didn't have a lot of choice but wanted to look her best for supper with Ned. In the end she chose her best cream blouse with a maroon skirt and matching fitted jacket. Warm enough for the chill of the evening but light enough to look good, with her heavy shawl against the night frost. Butterflies fluttered inside her at the thought of the evening ahead.

Ned called for her promptly at six-thirty and together they walked to the theatre. Although it was dark, the street lights giving off an amber glow, it wasn't too cold. Spring was just around the corner and the walk was pleasant, better than being in the pub cleaning and setting up for the evening rush. She was determined to enjoy what she thought of as her last evening of freedom.

At the theatre Ned took her shawl and handed it to the girl in the cloakroom. The look on his face showed approval and she was glad she'd chosen the maroon suit.

Walking into the theatre was like walking into a fairy palace. The floor was thickly carpeted, the walls decorated with elaborate plaster carvings, the predominant colour was pale pink, with columns supporting the ornate ceiling. Several huge chandeliers hung along the passageway. As they walked into the bar they were greeted by a large crowd milling around and the buzz of conversation that filled the air. Warmth and the smell of alcohol enveloped her.

To her great surprise Ned knew most of the people in the bar who all appeared to work in the market. Soon they were drawn into the jolly company of costers.

"We all got free tickets," the second-hand clothes dealer explained. "Old Mick wanted to be sure of a full house for his first performance."

"Nothing worse for a performer than an empty theatre," the man from the china stall said.

"Do you know anything about what we're going to see?" another stallholder asked.

"It's a comedy, according to Mick. That's why I brought the trouble and strife. She likes a chuckle."

"It's by Oscar Wilde," the ironmonger said. Hope didn't have a clue who he was but was impressed with the coster's knowledge.

They had good seats in the auditorium and Hope glowed with pleasure. Suddenly she understood Violet's attraction to the stage. It was magical. The whole atmosphere of the theatre was one of carefree enjoyment and laughter, a million miles away from the daily struggle. She found herself entirely captivated. And Violet was wrong. It wasn't at all boring; in fact Hope found the tale of deception, misconduct and self-sacrifice thrilling. The hours flew by and she clapped wildly as the curtain came down. She couldn't remember ever having such a good time.

"Well, what did you think?" Ned asked as he took her arm to lead her back to the cloakroom for her shawl.

"It was wonderful," she said. "The actors were amazing. It's a long time since I've laughed so much, or enjoyed such an evening." It was a memory she vowed to treasure.

During supper at a nearby chop shop she was able to tell Ned about working at The Grenadier. "I've heard of it of course," he said. "Never been well off enough to go there. They say you have to have an income of over five hundred pounds a year to join, or know someone. I didn't know your pa was a member. I'd have thought the stakes a bit rich for him."

"That's the problem," she said. "I think he got in deeper than he could handle. From what I gather he owes Silas Quirk a fortune and I'm to pay the debt."

Ned wrinkled his nose and shrugged. "Silas Quirk? I've heard of him an' all. A good bloke to avoid by all accounts but it may not be as bad as you think. You can't believe everything you hear. I've never met him but, I mean, I don't believe he really has horns growing out of his head."

Hope laughed. "No, he doesn't," she said. That's the thing about being with Ned, she thought, you can't be sad or angry for long.

There was a frosty chill in the air as they walked home in the moonlight, Hope's arm linked through Ned's. It felt so right. She gazed up at the stars in the clear night sky. Her joyous mood of the evening evaporated. Seeing them brought back the memory of the dress, Dexi and her future, something she'd been able to forget about for a few brief hours. Her heart dipped. This would be the last time she'd be able to spend an evening with Ned. Her evenings now belonged to Silas Quirk.

Her pace slowed as they neared home. She wanted to hang on to these precious moments with Ned as long as she could. She heard the clang of bells through the cold night air and shuddered. Distant at first it rapidly seemed to get closer and louder. The sound of galloping horses and rattling wheels over cobbles reached her ears. The smell of smoke hung in the air. The closer to home they got the louder and more urgent the sounds became. They hastened their pace.

She heard shouting. The nearer they got to home the thicker and more acrid the smoke seemed to be, until they rounded the corner and, to her horror, she saw a crowd gathered outside the pub.

Reams of black smoke billowed from the building. A noisy confusion of people yelling, horses stamping and blowing stood in the road spread out in front of it. She heard the clang of buckets and saw a fire wagon, standing at the kerb.

Chapter Ten

Hope gasped, picked up her skirts and ran, heart galloping, towards the commotion where the fire wagon standing in the road pumped water onto the building. Ned was faster, running ahead of her.

"Let us through, let us through," he shouted, pushing people aside. Hope recognised their customers and neighbours as she squeezed past them behind him.

A police constable with his arms stretched wide stopped them. "Stand back. You can't go any closer," he said.

"It's her home, her family," Ned said. "Let her through."

Hope strained to see over the policeman's shoulder. Her heart was pumping faster than the fire engine. A chain of men leading from the pump handed buckets along, throwing what water they could into the adjacent buildings to stop the fire spreading any further. The pub door hung ajar, the windows blank and empty of glass revealing the smoke-filled rooms beyond. She felt sick. Energy seeped out of her, she thought she was going to faint.

The air was thick with acrid smoke and cinders rising past the roof of the building. A cacophony of noise filled her ears until she thought her head would burst. Through the clanking of the buckets, the shouts and the noise of the fire engine pump she heard someone calling that there were still people inside.

She glanced frantically around, looking for her family. "Ma, Pa, Alfie!" The screams tore out of her throat. Ned grabbed her, pulling her close into his arms. She sobbed on his shoulder.

"They're doing everything they can," he said.

She glanced round and saw John, head in hands, sitting on the pavement at the far end of the crowd. A man standing nearby handed him a cup of water to drink.

If John got out so might the others. She pushed Ned away and rushed up to him. "John, where's Ma, Pa, Alfie? Have you seen them? What happened?" She felt like shaking him. A mountain of fear rose up inside her until a great clump of nausea filled her throat.

He shook his head. He was in no state to tell her anything. His face was blackened with soot. Tears streamed over his cheeks, the deepest horror filled his eyes. "I...I...I don't know..." His voice cracked with pain. Her heart turned over.

Violet appeared, dishevelled from her dash to get there with Bert. "We heard about...oh my lord...what happened? ...Where's? ...Oh no..." She screamed. Her knees buckled and she would have hit the pavement had it not been for Bert catching her and setting her gently on the ground.

A fireman staggered out carrying a body over his shoulder. Hope could hardly breathe for fear of what she might see as he laid her mother on the paving.

"She's inhaled a lot of smoke but she's still alive," he said.

Someone splashed water over her face and waived a bottle of foul smelling substance under her nose. She choked, gasping for breath. An ambulance arrived.

Hope grabbed hold of the fireman. "Pa and Alfie?" she sobbed, great blobs of tears staining her face. "Did they get out? Where are they?" Her voice rose in a crescendo of terror. "Has anyone seen my pa and my little brother Alfie?"

She was desperate now, eyes wildly staring round, pushing through the crowd, turning from person to person, desperate to find out anything, speak to anyone. "Have you seen my pa or my little brother," she cried. It was as though her whole world was falling apart around her and there was no one to stop it. "Help, help us please. Can anyone find my pa and Alfie?" She dissolved in tears, her hands covering her face as uncontrollable sobbing wracked her body.

A crack, like a strike of lightning, sounded as a beam inside the building fell, sending up a shower of sparks and a fresh plume of thick black smoke. She screamed.

The next thing she saw was the bulk of a man, blackened with soot and smoke, coming out of the building carrying a dark bundle that could only have been Alfie.

"Alfie, Alfie." She pushed her way to the man's side as the crowd surged towards them. She watched as he laid the bundle on the ground next to her ma. Alfie's face and what was left of his clothing were charred and black. Small, burnt fragments of material fell away as he was laid down. His hair frizzled and singed. The bitter, acrid smell of scorched flesh and cloth filled Hope's nostrils, but Alfie was all in one piece and safely out.

Relief flooded over her. She glanced up to thank the man who'd saved him and shock stole her breath. She was gazing into the eyes of Silas Quirk. Sweat beaded his forehead and his cheeks smudged with grime. A flicker of emotion flitted across his face, so swift Hope thought she might have imagined it, but she'd never been so happy to see anyone as she was seeing him at that moment.

One of the ambulance crew splashed water over Alfie's face and put his fingers in his mouth to clear away the soot and grime. Alfie gurgled and choked. His chest rose as he tried to draw breath.

"He's alive. He's alive," Hope cried. She wanted to hug him, hold him close and never let him go, but the ambulance man held her back.

"Give him some air," he said, pushing her back along with the gawping crowd.

"Best get these people to hospital soon as you can," the fire chief said. Several men moved forward to pick Ma and Alfie gently up and carry them to the waiting ambulance.

"Pa, Pa, did you see my pa?" she said to Silas.

He shook his head. His voice was hoarse as he struggled to speak. "It's hotter than Hades in there and black as pitch. Sorry." His dejected look reflected his despair.

"You best go too," the fire chief said to Silas, and Hope noticed for the first time that the sleeve of his coat had been burned away and the flesh of his skin was raw and blistered from shoulder to elbow.

Silas's feet dragged and his shoulders slumped as the fireman guided him to the ambulance. Hope glanced around. Swirling smoke stung her eyes and caught in her throat. The smell of burnt timber filled the air. She tasted the grit and ash that floated up enveloping them. The fire had gutted the ground floor of the pub. The place was a mess. All she could see were smouldering embers.

"You can't go in," the fire chief said as she moved nearer to the door. "It's not safe."

She looked up. Soot from the smoke streaked the upper walls but they appeared to be intact. "My pa might still be in there," she said, tears burning her eyes. "I have to find him."

"Not now," the fireman said. "My men'll go in when it's safe. If he's there we'll find him."

Hope was torn between wanting to go in and search for her pa and going with her ma, Alfie, Violet and John in the ambulance. Ned made the decision for her.

"Come on," he said. "You best go to the hospital with your ma and Alfie.Violet and John'll need help too. I'll sort things out here and come on later."

Numbed by grief she couldn't think and could hardly move. Taking one last look at the pub that had been her home for as long as she could remember, she nodded and got into the waiting ambulance.

On the way to the hospital all she could think about was Ma and Alfie and where was Pa? Suppose… No. She couldn't think like that, it was too awful. The ambulance bounced and jolted over the cobbles. Each jolt brought a new worry about Ma and Alfie. Bert was holding Violet's hand, John gripped the now empty cup he'd been handed and Silas stared at the floor. No one spoke. The night's events played through Hope's mind as though on a reel and she was left to wonder how what had been the most magical and best night of her life had turned so suddenly into the worst.

Chapter Eleven

They sat in the hospital, mind-numbed, pale and shaking while John was treated for minor burns and Violet and Hope for shock. Silas was led away as his injuries were far greater. All the time all Hope could think was that this was some sort of horrific nightmare, unreal. She couldn't take it in. What about her mother and Alfie? Where were they? Would they be all right? "Can we see them," she asked again and again.

Each time the answer was, "Best not to. Not yet. They're in good hands."

So the painful waiting went on. Violet sat with Bert, her hand firmly clenched in his. Hope noticed how he made comforting noises and stroked her arms. Her stomach clenched at the improper intimacy.

Just before dawn Dexi arrived to collect Silas. "I heard about the fire. I'm so sorry." She hugged Hope. "They're still looking for William..." She broke off as emotion overcame her. "I'm so sorry," she said.

When Silas came out of the treatment room his arm had been dressed and a graze on his head cleaned and treated with a solution of carbolic. He'd disposed of his coat and wore only a white shirt with one sleeve missing over his trousers and boots.

"You might be in shock," the doctor said. "You need to rest." But Silas insisted on going home that instant with Dexi.

"I have a business to run," he said. Hope saw the pain in his eyes as he left the building and a fresh swell of guilt fell over her.

Their lives were now in tatters. They had nowhere to go and worst of all, Pa was missing. She felt sick but despair pushed the sickness away. How had the fire started? Where was Pa? A lot of questions needed to be answered and why Silas Quirk had been there was one of them.

It felt as though they'd been sitting there for hours in funeral-parlour silence as the minutes ticked away, but, soon after Silas left Ned arrived, which was at least some comfort to Hope.

"Betsy from the market takes in lodgers," he said. "She's got a place near the hospital. You, Violet and John can stay there until things are sorted out. She's a good sort is Betsy. She'll see you're all right."

"I can't thank you enough," Hope said. "I wouldn't have known what to do. It's all so very..." Tears threatened to overwhelm her.

"I want to stay with Bert," Violet said. "It's the only place I'll feel safe." Hope doubted that, but was in no mood to argue. People would talk, even in these tragic circumstances, but Violet's reputation was the least of her worries.

It was morning before she was allowed in to see Ma and Alfie. "You can't stay long," the doctor said. "They're both sleeping."

Ma and Alfie were in a small room and, as the doctor had said, appeared to be sleeping. Hope's heart twisted with helplessness. She wished she could stay and sit with them, but the doctor was adamant. "It's best you go home and come later, when they've had time to rest," he said, so, once she had satisfied herself that they were being properly cared for, Hope left with Ned and John.

Betsy greeted them at the lodgings. A short dumpy woman she smelled of home-baked bread and laundry soap. She shook her head and muttered, "Oh you poor things," as she offered them a hot drink. Hope realised they must look terrible and they smelled of smoke.

"They've been up all night. I think they just want somewhere to lay their heads," Ned said.

"Of course. There's beds ready," Betsy said.

"Try to get some rest," Ned said as he left them at the lodgings. "I'll come back later and we'll find out what happened but there's nothing you can do for now except take care of yourself. Ma and Alfie will need you when they're recovered enough to come home."

"Home?" she said. "Where will that be do you think?"

Ned held her close. "Wherever you are with your family, Hope. That'll be home," he whispered. "As long as you're all safe and together, that's what matters."

Hope nodded. In her heart she knew he was right. If only they knew where her pa was.

Betsy led them up the stairs, still muttering, "Oh you poor things." The room she took them to was clean and large enough for two beds, one double and one single set out against the wall. A chest of drawers held a basin and jug for washing, but both John and Hope were too tired to make use of them. John fell onto the single bed still in his clothes and Hope took the double.

Memories of the fire filtered through her brain and she didn't think she'd be able to sleep but, heart aching and overfilled with grief, exhausted by the events of the night and fears of the future, she fell into a fitful slumber. It was a sad end to what should have been a lovely evening.

It was mid-afternoon before Hope was awakened by a soft tapping on the door. She'd been dreaming that she was in the fire looking for Pa, going round and round searching for him. The smell of smoke burned her nostrils and caught in her throat. She awoke with a start as Betsy entered carrying a jug of water and a basket.

"Sorry to wake you," Betsy said, "but Ned's downstairs and I thought you might like to tidy up before you see him. I've brought you some hot water and Ned brought a change of clothes. He thought you might be glad of 'em."

"Oh, yes, yes, thank you," Hope said gathering her wits. Part of her was still in the fire and smelling of smoke didn't help.

"Is there any news? Have they found Pa?"

"I think Ned has some news. He thought you'd like to go to the hospital too. He said your ma's come round. A bit weak though I understand." She gazed at Hope. "Oh you poor thing," she muttered. "If there's owt I can do…"

Hope jumped out of bed where she'd slept in her clothes which were now wrinkled and damp with sweat as well as being blackened with smoke.

"Leave your mucky things, I'll sort them," Betsy said. "Least I can do." She handed Hope the basket which was filled with clean clothes. "I'll have somat hot for you downstairs, when you're ready," she said.

Hope shook John awake before she washed and changed into the thick woollen dress Ned had thoughtfully provided. There was a heavy shawl in the basket too, woollen stockings and a bonnet she recognised as belonging to Ned's sister Clara. He'd supplied trousers, a shirt, waistcoat and a decent top coat for John.

She put the dirty clothes in the basket to take down to Betsy.

Ned greeted her and John downstairs. "I came as soon as I heard," he said. "I'm sorry if I woke you but thought you'd want to know."

"What is it? What's happened? Did they find Pa? Where is he?"

He took her hands and glanced at John. "You'd better sit down," he said, indicating a chair.

"No, please tell me."

"They found your pa. He didn't make it out of the building," Ned said. "I'm so sorry."

Hope sank onto the chair. "What happened? Do they know?"

Ned shook his head. "Not yet. They found him at the foot of the cellar steps. Silas Quirk identified the body earlier today."

"Silas Quirk?"

"Yes. The police are involved. They didn't want to trouble you and he has some standing in the community. There's to be an investigation. That's all I know."

"An investigation? But surely it was an accident?"

"There's been a death. The police are always involved."

Hope swallowed. A great swell of grief was building up inside her but she had to be strong. "Ma and Alfie?" she said. "Have you seen them? Will they be all right?"

Ned gave a wan smile. "We can go to see them as soon as you've had something to eat."

Betsy bustled in with a plate of hot buttered toast and a large teapot on a tray. "You'll feel better when you get these inside you," she said.

Hope thought she was too upset to eat, but found that, once the toast was in her mouth she was far hungrier than she realised and obediently ate three slices.

Betsy took their dirty clothes to wash. "Don't worry I'll get these good as new in no time," she said. "You'll have 'em back by tonight."

"Thank you," Hope said as the realisation that all they had left in the world were the clothes she and John had been wearing gradually sank in. Everything else would have been lost in the fire.

"The pub?" John said. "Is it all gone?"

"It's been boarded up," Ned said. "No one's allowed in until it's made safe. We'll have to manage for now."

Hope thought of Violet. She'd be more distressed at losing her things than Hope would. "Violet?" she said.

"Is being taken care of by Bert and his theatrical friends." Ned smiled. "Violet will always come out on top. You know Violet." Hope sighed; at least that was true. Violet did always have a knack of getting whatever she wanted. Which brought her back to thinking about Silas Quirk and wondering if he had anything to do with the fire in the pub.

"I want to go and check out the pub," John said. "See if it's beyond repair or if it can cleaned up and reopened. If so I'll go to the brewery and see if they'll transfer the licence into my name."

Hope drew breath. She was about to ask how he could think about the pub when Ma and Alfie were in hospital fighting for their lives, when Ned said, "Good idea. You need to sort out where you're going to live and how you're going to make your living. The police will want to talk to you too. They want to know what happened and you were the only one there."

"I'll come with you," Hope said.

"No," John said. "There's nothing to be gained by us all going. You go and see Ma and Alfie. I'm the head of the family now, so it's up to me." It was obviously something he'd been thinking about while she was sleeping. But he was right. With Pa gone their future lay in John's hands.

"You'll need to speak to the fire officer at the station first," Ned said. "I'll go with Hope to the hospital. I've sent a message to Violet to meet us there."

Helplessness fell over Hope like a dark cloak obscuring everything. Memories of the fire swept through her mind. All she'd loved and hoped for was gone. What on earth would she do now?

Chapter Twelve

Stepping out from Betsy's cosy parlour into the cold March wind Hope shivered. A chill slithered into her bones and a storm of grief engulfed her. It was as much as she could do to hold back the tears, but she lifted her chin and strode out, her arm linked in Ned's for support.

Glancing round at the neat row of terraced houses she'd been too tired to notice when they arrived, she wondered how things could be so normal when her world had been turned upside down. People walked along the cobbled street about their business but to her it seemed eerie and strange. Everything that had happened merged into one incomprehensible blur. She felt as though she was walking through a dream, a terrible, unbelievable dream and one she couldn't wait to wake up from.

A woman on a doorstep along the street called a greeting to Ned. He raised his arm, but didn't stop. Several times Hope clung onto him as she stumbled along, trying to make sense of her loss.

It was a short walk to the hospital, but one during which Hope's fears subsided and her courage surfaced. Seeing Ma and Alfie were all right was the most important thing she could do now and she had to be strong for them and for Violet and John.

Violet was waiting for them when they arrived at the hospital. "Bert's gone to see the doctor," she said. "We were told to wait here. Is Ma going to be all right? Have they said anything to you?"

Hope shook her head. "Only that Pa's gone and the pub is in ruins," she said. She swallowed the swell of grief rising up inside her, biting her lip to hold back the tears she knew would come in an uncontrollable flood, reducing her to a sobbing wreck if she let them. "At least Ma and Alfie are all right," she said trying to reassure Violet with more optimism than she felt. Violet may seem frivolous and vain, she thought, but underneath she'd be just as sensitive, scared and lost as I am.

Bert returned. "We can see your ma, but Alfie's been moved. We can't see him yet. He woke up in a state of distress and they've put him under again. He's been badly burned and they fear for his lungs. We can only pray for him," he said. "We can go in to see your ma now but mustn't stay long."

"Thank you," Hope said, her fears for Alfie threatening to bring on another flood of tears. She was seeing a different Bert than she'd ever recalled. Perhaps he does care for Violet, she thought, and will take care of her. With all her heart she hoped that was true. Violet would need all the help and support she could get. If only she could rely on Bert to look after her at least it would be one less thing to worry about.

Bert led them to a room at the end of a long ward. Their boots thudded on the wooden floor and, as they opened the door and entered, Ma's eyelids flickered but didn't open. The smell of carbolic permeated the air. A small window let in a beam of pale sunlight. A nightstand stood by the bed with a jug of water and a glass. Two chairs, one either side of the bed, were the only other furniture.

Ma lay in bed, her face pale as parchment and just as creased. She looked old and shrivelled against the white of the pillow, her once lustrous dark hair grey with the remains of ash. A large bruise darkened beneath her right eye. Hope gulped back the dread rising in her chest. She glanced at Ned. He nodded and she leaned over her mother. "Ma, Ma," she whispered. "It's us. You're going to be all right."

Ma's eyelids flickered again and her eyes opened. Hope took her hand. "I'm so glad to see you, Ma," she said. "Do you remember what happened?"

Ma glanced around, her gaze flitting over them.

"It's me too, Ma," Violet said taking a position the other side of the bed. "I'm here with Bert. He's looking after me."

Ma seemed to register Violet and Bert's presence. "John and Alfie?" she rasped. "Where's John and Alfie?"

"John's fine," Hope said. "He's gone to see about the pub. See what can be saved. And Alfie's here in the hospital. They're looking after him, Ma. He's going to be all right." She hoped with all her heart that that was true.

Ma's eyes closed. "Thank God," she sighed.

She lay silent for a while, Hope sat watching her face. Had they told her about Pa? She hadn't asked about him. Did she already know?

Her breathing was laboured. Hope picked up the glass of water from the side table and held it to her mother's cracked lips.

"You're a good girl, Hope," Ma breathed, patting Hope's hand. "Look after Alfie for me."

"Of course," Hope said. "But you'll soon be out of here and able to look after him yourself."

Ma rolled her head from side to side on the pillow as though denying it before falling into another doze.

Her breath came in deep rasps. Hope's heart fluttered; if they lost Ma and Alfie as well as Pa…

"The doctor said she needs to rest," Violet said, staring at the prone shape in the bed. "Perhaps we should come back tomorrow. Bert's got a show tonight at the theatre."

"You go," Hope said. "I'll stay. I've nowhere else to go."

So, Violet and Bert left and Hope sat with her ma trying to make sense of what had happened. She watched her mother sleeping until Ned said, "There's nothing you can do here, Hope. Go to Betsy's and get some rest yourself. Things'll look better in the morning."

"No, I want to see for myself how Alfie is and the pub. See what can be saved if anything."

"I'll come with you then, if you're sure."

"I'm sure."

A nurse directed them to Alfie's room where they found the doctor who was looking after him. "Just a few seconds," he said. "He's sleeping and shouldn't be disturbed."

"How is he?" Hope asked. "We've all been so worried."

The doctor checked the chart in his hand. "We soaked off his charred clothing in a warm bath and dressed his burns as best we could," he said. "He was concussed from the fall, his leg is broken and he may have cracked his ribs, but the smoke inhalation is the biggest problem. The jumper he was wearing over his nightshirt saved his arms and chest from suffering major burns. It would have been much worse if he'd been left in the fire longer. We've managed to get some herbal infusion down his throat which should ease it a little, other than that all we can do is pray for him."

Hope gazed at the small boy lying in bed. Bits of singed, sandy hair poked out above the thick dressing around his head, his face below the bandage almost translucent. His arms too were bandaged. She touched his hand. "It's me, Hope," she said. There was no response.

"How long before he wakes?" she asked.

The doctor shrugged. "It could be tomorrow or a few more days. The longer he sleeps the more chance he has of survival."

Hope struggled to hold back the impending rush of tears. "I'll come back tomorrow," she said and left with Ned to go and look at the building that used to be her home.

Out in the cold once more Ned insisted they stop at a coffee stall for a hot drink before they continued to the pub.

"You look like death warmed over," he said. "I wouldn't be much of a friend if I didn't look out for you would I?"

"All right," she said feeling a glow of warmth for him. "I think I could manage a few sips of hot chocolate." Her throat still ached from the smoke; her heart ached more.

Ned bought them both a drink. "I know things are bad right now, Hope. But you must look after yourself. How can you look after the others if you don't look after yourself?"

Holding her hands around the cup of chocolate she moved closer to Ned. She was glad of his company and his solid reliability.

When they arrived at the pub they found John already there with the brewery surveyor and the fire officer. The board across the door had been removed and they were just coming out of the damaged building.

"How bad is it?" Hope asked. "Can it be saved? Will we be able to get any of our things?"

"It's too early to say," the brewery surveyor said. "We need to carry out a full inspection. Most of the damage appears to be on the ground floor, but there's no knowing the full extent until we've had a chance to check everything. I'm sorry you'll have to wait a bit longer before any decision about the future of the Hope and Anchor can be made."

The fire officer agreed. "It'll take a few days for my men to complete their report. After that it's all yours," he said to the surveyor.

"Come and see me in a week or two," the surveyor said to John, handing him a card. "We'll have a better idea then."

"A week or two?" John said, alarmed.

"Sorry, son. Best we can do," the surveyor said.

Disheartened they made their way back to Betsy's. John kicked at a can lying in the gutter as they walked. Hope clung onto Ned's arm, grateful for his support.

"I don't suppose your father had any insurance?" Ned asked a hint of optimism in his voice.

John crumpled further. "No. According to the brewery surveyor they had the building insured, that's all. Everything inside will be gone and that includes all our stuff."

Ned shook his head. "Sorry, mate. If there's anything I can do."

"There's nowt anyone can do," John said, his head sinking deeper into his shoulders. "I asked at the brewery if I could take over the licence, but they won't make a decision until they get the fire officer's report." In the glow of the lamplight Hope noted the dampness of his cheeks. "They won't even offer another post until after the investigation. I don't know what we're to do, or even where we're to live."

"You can stay at Betsy's until your ma and Alfie come home," Ned said. "At least that's a start."

"Yes, thanks to you," Hope said. "I don't know what we'd have done without your help. We're truly grateful, aren't we, John?"

John grunted. Hope squeezed Ned's arm.

"I'll come again in the morning," Ned said, "if you want me to."

"What about your stall? You'll need to be there tomorrow or you'll lose business. Bad enough us losing out, no need for you to as well."

"You're more important than my stall," Ned said.

Hope smiled as her heart swelled at his remark. "Thank you, but John can come to the hospital with me. I'll send a message if there's anything else."

Reluctantly Ned left her. Betsy had made them some tea. After tea Hope found that she was too tired to think any more and was happy to retire to bed after what had been an exhausting day.

The next morning, as they were finishing the hearty breakfast Betsy had prepared for them, there was an abrupt knocking on the front door.

"I'll go," Hope said, thinking it may be Ned who'd come to see her despite having to set up his stall in the market. Her jaw dropped when she opened the door to see Dexi Malone standing on the doorstep. Dressed in a bright crimson suit under a short fur cape and matching hat she was a sight to behold.

"May I come in?" she asked.

"Oh, yes. Yes of course," Hope said, stepping aside.

"Silas sent me," Dexi said. "He's worried about you."

"Worried about me?" Hope's stomach flipped. Today was the day she was supposed to start work at The Grenadier.

Chapter Thirteen

Indoors Betsy gaped, just as Hope had done and John looked as though he'd seen an apparition.

"Good morning. I hope I'm not disturbing your breakfast," Dexi said, removing her claret coloured kid gloves as she spoke.

"Not at all," Betsy managed to say. "I'll make a fresh pot. You will stay for a cup of tea?"

"Thank you that would be most welcome," Dexi said.

Betsy bustled out and Hope pulled out a chair for Dexi which she sank into. "I'm sorry about your father," she said. "It's a tragic loss. I'm sure you will miss him dreadfully."

Tears sprang suddenly to Hope's eyes. Her eyes were too full and her throat too choked to respond.

"Thank goodness you're both safe," Dexi continued. "And your mother and little brother. How are they?"

"They're being well cared for in the hospital," Hope managed to say. "And we have your brother to thank for that. If he hadn't…"

Dexi put her hand on Hope's arm. "It was nothing. Anyone would have done the same."

"I'm not sure that's true," Hope said. "Going into the burning building was a brave and reckless thing to do, but we are extremely grateful."

Betsy waddled in with a fresh tray of tea which she put on the table. Hope poured a cup for Dexi. Handing it to her she said, as casually as she could manage, "It was fortunate that he was there. I can't think what brought him to our place so late, although thank the heavens for it."

"Oh," Dexi said. "He wasn't there. We saw the smoke rising in the air and heard the fire engine careering over the cobbles. It was an impulsive act to follow and when he saw it was your place…" Her eyes widened and she shrugged. "He thought you might be trapped inside. What else was he to do?"

The inference that he'd risked his life to save hers wasn't lost on Hope. The words hit her like scalding water.

John, who'd been struck dumb by Dexi's presence, suddenly stood and got himself a cup of tea. "Whatever prompted him we are exceedingly grateful. Alfie's in a bad way but would certainly have perished in the fire if it hadn't been for Silas. We owe him so much, if there's anything we can do to repay him."

Hope was immediately aware that John was right. They owed Silas more than any amount of money could repay. It was a humbling thought and not one easily entertained. She sipped her tea in silence.

"Well, you could both come and work at The Grenadier, when you're ready of course. It'll take a long time to sort your place out, even if it can be saved, unless you have other plans."

John smiled. "We have no plans, other than to work and try to restore the Hope and Anchor as Pa would have wanted. I know I'll be a poor replacement for him but…"

"I'm sure you'll do very well," Dexi said. "But it's the immediate future you need to worry about. Silas is happy for you both to work for us and he'll pay you the going rate, until you're ready to move on."

"That's a most generous offer in the circumstance," John said. Hope said nothing.

Dexi put her cup and saucer back on the table. "There are other financial matters to be sorted out," she said. "I'm not sure if you're aware of your father's arrangements with my brother, but that's for the future. All in good time. Get yourselves settled first, then we can see about the rest."

Hope's heart missed a beat. Dexi stood to leave. "Give my regards to your mother when you see her. Tell her I'm sorry for her loss and will be praying for her speedy recovery. As will Silas." She started to pull her gloves on and turned to Hope. "Please take as long as you need but I look forward to seeing you at The Grenadier when you're ready. I'll pray for your little brother too. I know he means the world to you."

"Thank you," was all Hope could stutter as she showed Dexi out.

"Well, what do you make of that?" John said. "Dexi Malone here, come to see us. And she's offered us jobs which we'll badly need. Whatever brought that on, I for one am thankful. I'm not sure what we'd have done otherwise."

So, that was to be her future. Hope had never felt so wretched in her life, and yet so thankful.

John's optimistic mood didn't last long. Hope was helping Betsy clear the table when a policeman came knocking on the door looking for John. "I need you to accompany me to the station," he said. "They want to talk to you about the fire."

John blanched. "I don't know anything about it," he said. "I was in the bar closing up. First I knew was the smell of burning and seeing smoke. I went to investigate but as soon as I opened the door I saw the hallway was thick with black smoke. I couldn't see owt. I yelled for Ma and Pa. I couldn't breathe; the whole place was on fire. I thought – hoped – maybe they'd got out the back. The heat was getting to me then so I shut the door and dashed out to get help. I ran down the road to call the fire service. I wasn't even there when…"

"They still want to talk to you," the policeman said grabbing John's arm.

He pulled his arm away. "I'll get my coat," he said.

Hope helped him on with his coat. "Should I come with you?" she asked.

"No, no need. I can't tell them anything so it shouldn't take long."

His eyes were full of misery and his face a picture of the greatest sadness.

"No but find out as much as you can. I'd like to know what happened. What started the fire and why Pa was at the bottom of the cellar steps?" Having seen Pa earlier in the day she couldn't help wondering if he'd been so drunk he'd fallen down the stairs carrying the kerosene lamp and thus, inadvertently, started the fire that took his life. She could think of no other explanation.

John nodded. "I'll be back as soon as I can."

Once he was gone Hope helped Betsy with the washing she took in to supplement her income. Out the back of the building a shed, filled with steam and the smell of damp laundry, held a large round boiler, lit from underneath. Into this Betsy tipped the clothes, sheets, bedding and table linen to be boiled, possed, dolly-blued and starched to the nearest thing to clean she could manage. After that they were put through the mangle and, smelling of soap and much cleaner than when they went into the tub, set on two long airers suspended from the ceiling to dry. Betsy's daughter Lydia took the clean dry clothes to her house to be ironed and returned to the owners.

"A proper little industry you have here," Hope said as she followed Betsy out to the washroom. "Perhaps I can help. You've been so kind letting us stay. We have no money to pay rent but I can see to the washing if you like."

Betsy smiled. "No need, my dear. Ned's paid the rent, at least for now, but it's good to have a bit of company while I'm doing it."

Hope sighed. So, she had Ned to thank again for paying their rent. Another man she's become indebted to. She wasn't sure she liked it, but it was Ned, what harm could that do?

"We're very grateful," she said, "but we'll need to find a bigger place when Ma and Alfie come home."

"You'll miss your pa and working at the pub," Betsy said. "It won't be easy for any of you. But that lady that visited, sounds like you'll be all right working for her and, if I heard right, her brother."

"Silas. Yes. He's her brother. I was supposed to start working for him at the gentleman's club he owns today. An arrangement Pa made. It seems we are indebted to him and under an obligation." Her voice sharpened and her heart hardened as she spoke.

"Ah," Betsy said. "There's nowt in life as irritating as an obligation." She sniffed. "A gentlemen's club? Still, you've got your wits about you and you knows right from wrong. You'll do all right."

Hope wished she was as confident of that as Betsy.

It was lunchtime by the time the washing was finished and hanging on the airers to dry. Betsy was setting out some bread and cheese when a boy arrived at the door with a message from Miss Ruth Godley. Hope gave him a ha'penny and opened the note. She read:

'*I was so sorry to hear of your loss,*' it said. '*If there's anything I can do please don't hesitate to ask. Best wishes, Ruth Godley.*'

Visions of Hope's workbasket filled with silks and the samples she'd been working on filled her mind. They'd all now be lost. So blackened and smelling of smoke they'd be useless. Hope shook her head in despair. "My embroidery things," she said. "The silks, the needles, the samples, it's all gone. I won't be able to do any work for Miss Godley without it."

"When one door closes another door opens," Betsy said, but Hope wasn't sure it was a door she wanted to walk through.

Chapter Fourteen

On her way to the hospital that afternoon Hope called at the drapery store to see Ruth Godley. A pale sun had come out and light clouds scudded across an azure sky. The walk was pleasant. Walking past the park she saw primroses in bloom and daffodils dancing in the breeze. It would soon be Easter. Would Ma and Alfie be home by then?

Arriving at the shop she drew a breath. Miss Godley had been so kind to her and the thought of the samples she'd lost played on her mind. She'd offer to work for nothing until they were paid for, but that could take a while and she had nothing to work with.

A bell tinkled as she opened the door. She nodded to the sales girl behind the counter and made her way to the back workroom where she found Miss Godley.

Ruth Godley rose to greet her. "I'm so sorry for your loss," she said. "It must have been a terrible shock. I can't imagine how you must be feeling. If there's anything…"

"Thank you," Hope said. Every expression of sympathy brought thoughts of Ma and Pa rushing to her mind and the memory of her loss brought on the threat of tears. She could hardly speak as her throat tightened. "It's not going to be easy for us with Pa gone, but at least Ma's alive and making a slow recovery. We are praying for Alfie."

"I'll say a pray for you all," Ruth said, "as will my father."

"Thank you," Hope said. "I've come to say I'm sorry but I fear the fire has taken all your samples and my silks. I won't be able to replace them for a while, but if you'll forgive me I'll try to make it up to you when I can."

"Don't worry about the samples," Ruth said. "You're safe, that's all that matters. Material things can be replaced. People can't."

"You're very kind," Hope said. "I feel I've let you down."

"Nonsense. The fire wasn't your fault and I'm sure I'll soon recover the loss, which is more than I can say for you. I dare say it'll be a while before you'll want to take on any more work from me?"

"Ma and Alfie will need to be looked after when they eventually come out of hospital. I will be needed to make a home for them. I don't even know where we're going to live so it might be quite a while."

"Just let me know when you're ready and we'll work something out."

"Thank you," Hope said, but in her heart she knew her dream of becoming a full-time needlewoman and running her own workshop was now as distant as the moon and stars.

"Let me know when you decide about the funeral. I'm sure my father will be happy to waive the usual church fees in the circumstances."

The funeral! She hadn't even considered it. She sank onto a chair as her legs turned to jelly. "I expect John will want to make the arrangements. He's head of the family now," or so he tells me, she thought.

"Well, just let us know. Both my father and I will do everything we can to make things easier for you and your family."

When Hope arrived at the hospital Violet was already there, and, judging by the look on her face her mood was thunderous.

"I've seen John," she said. "I know about the delay in the brewery's decision about the pub. He wants to take over Pa's licence, but if he thinks I'm going to work there for him he's got another thought coming. I'll not skivvy for him for nothing, I've got plans of me own."

"I don't think any of us are in a position to make plans, Violet. We have to wait and see how Ma is and if Alfie will survive. The future of the pub and who works there is the last thing I want to hear about."

Violet's face softened. "I'm sorry, but someone has to think about the future. Bert reckons I've a good chance of getting a place in his new show. It'd only be in the chorus line, but it's a start."

Hope began to wonder if Violet had any heart at all. "How can you think about singing and dancing when Pa's dead and Ma and Alfie are critically ill? Honestly, Violet, I don't think you've quite realised the seriousness of our situation." Anger rose up inside her and years of suppressed rage began to surface. "We're all homeless and virtually destitute and all you can think about is that no-good con man Bert and your relationship. Well, you can forget any chance of dancing on stage or anywhere else until Pa's been decently buried and Ma and Alfie are home, if we ever find a home, that is."

She stomped off into the room where Ma lay, white as marble, sleeping but Violet, so caught up in her own dreams, wouldn't let the matter rest.

"They're going on tour, all over the country," she said, moderating her voice to a whisper in view of her mother's condition. "And I'm going with them."

"Going with them?" Hope whispered fiercely. "You can forget that. You're only sixteen. Far too young to go off with that rogue Bert. John won't allow it, neither will I."

"John? What's it got to do with John, or you for that matter?"

Hope squirmed around to stare at her. "John's the head of the family and you're still a minor."

Violet huffed. "Well, he can say what he likes. I'm going with or without his blessing."

Their whispered quarrel brought Ma round from her doze. Her eyes flickered open.

"Ma, it's us, Hope and Violet," Hope said, her insides still churning with anger. "How are you feeling?"

Ma gazed at them in silence.

"Hello, Ma," Violet said. "I've just been telling Hope that I may have a job in the chorus line of a travelling theatre company. Isn't that grand? Aren't you proud of me?"

Ma's lips turned up into a weak smile. "Heart strong and head weak," she said, her voice hoarse with effort and barely above a whisper. "That's what you are, Violet. Always been a dreamer too ready to follow your heart instead of your head, like Pa." She lay back as though the effort to speak had exhausted her. "Still, sometimes the world needs dreamers," she croaked and dozed off again.

"See," Violet said. "Ma says it's all right. So, if they ask me, I'm going."

Hope was lost for words. Inside she was seething. How dare she? How dare she even think it? It was alright for her, going off with her no-good boyfriend and getting up to God-knows what. And John. John was just as bad. All he cared about was getting the pub back so he could step into his father's shoes while she picked up the pieces of their lives, working for Silas Quirk to pay the rent and looking after Ma and Alfie. The abyss of a future she was about to fall into opened up in front of her. Despair, like a dark shroud, fell over her.

They sat in stony silence, the air between them heavy with repressed anger as they watched Ma sleeping until Violet announced that she had to go to her job at the theatre box office.

"Surely they don't expect you back at work until after the funeral?" Hope said.

"No, but some of us have got to pay rent," Violet said and flounced out.

"Let her be," Ma said, coming round from her doze. "She always was wilful and sometimes, it's like with a frisky horse, you have to let 'em have their head. She'll be back when she's good and ready."

"Oh Ma, I didn't mean to worry you, but Violet has an uncanny knack of rubbing me up the wrong way. I know she doesn't mean it, but still…"

"I know," Ma said. "She's just like Pa, takes after him she does." Her voice faded to a whisper, almost as though she was talking to herself. "I'm sorry about Pa. Not sorry about what I did though."

"What you did, Ma?"

Ma turned her head to look at Hope. "He wasn't always a bad man," she said. "When I met him he was the kindest, most loving man I'd ever met, but life has a way of changing people. The drink, the gambling. He got into bad company, wanted to be like them, the big shots, the men with money. In awe of them he was. They were foot-loose and fancy free, not a care for anyone in the world but themselves. So stupid." She lapsed into silence.

Hope watched her breathing, her chest rising and falling with each rattle of breath. Then a smile lit up her face as though she'd suddenly recalled a fond memory.

"When you came into our lives we named you Hope because that's what you were to us. A new start, a fresh beginning and a chance to make a good life for us all." Her voice drifted off into a mumbled ramble. "We'd just got the tenancy of the pub. Everything looked so rosy. I knew we'd done the right thing. Pa wasn't so sure, but I've never regretted it. Never regretted it for a moment."

"Regretted what, Ma?"

But Ma had fallen into a deep slumber and Hope's question was left unanswered. A nurse put her head around the door. "Miss Daniels?"

"Yes."

"Doctor sent me. You're little brother's coming round. He thought you'd like to see him."

"Oh, yes. Yes please," Hope said and rushed to follow her.

The room Alfie was in was smaller than Ma's room, the smell of carbolic mixed with floor polish fainter. The walls were painted cream, a softer colour than the stark white of the rest of the hospital. A bright shaft of sunlight slotted in through the blinds at the window. It was a pleasant room, Hope thought. Not at all like the rest of the hospital. Someone had made an effort to brighten it up with pictures on the wall and a jug of flowers on a side table.

Lying in the huge bed Alfie looked small, vulnerable and achingly young. Hope's heart crumbled. His little face was as pale as the sheet pulled up to his chin but he opened his eyes as she nearer the bed.

"Hello Champ," she said as cheerfully as she could so as not to worry him more than need be. "It's me, Hope." The bandage round his head looked smaller and less messy, as though it had been newly applied. She felt his cheek. It was warm. His face flushed slightly at her touch. "I'm so pleased to see you," she said. "You've been out of it for quite a while."

"Where am I?" he rasped, his voice unrecognisable.

"In the hospital. Do you remember anything about what happened?"

He shook his head.

"Just as well," she said. "All we need to worry about is getting you better so you can come home." She felt a pang of guilt that they had no home but pushed it aside.

"What happened? What did I do?" Alfie asked his eyes wide with uncertainty.

"You didn't do anything," Hope said. "You were in an accident. You got burned, but you're going to get better. Then we're going to take you home."

"Where's Ma and Pa? Are they coming to get me?"

Hope smiled. "Ma's in the hospital too," she said. "She was in the accident as well. You'll need to stay here for a while until you're entirely better, but I'll come and visit every day. Do you want me to bring anything? Games? Toys? Whatever you want."

He touched his neck with his hand. "Can I have a drink?"

"Of course." Hope jumped up and poured him a glass of water. "Anything else?"

"Books. Can you bring me some books to read and paper and pencil to write with?"

"Certainly. I'll get them on the way home, but the doctor said you must rest and I'm not to stay too long."

Alfie's face fell and the small spark she'd seen in his eyes dimmed. His little chin quivered.

"Don't worry. I'll come back tomorrow and bring some books. I'll even read to you."

He brightened. It was obvious that speaking was painful for him, but the smile on his face was all the thanks Hope needed.

Chapter Fifteen

On the way home she couldn't understand why she was being so hateful to Violet when, after all, she'd suffered the same loss as her and John. Violet could be as irritating as a piece of grit in your eyes, sharp and painful until it's gone, but that was no excuse and didn't explain the raw fury she felt churning inside her.

When Hope arrived at Betsy's an ashen-faced John was waiting for her. Dazed and distraught he looked as though he'd been put through the mangle like Betsy's washing.

"What did they say? Did they say how the fire started? Can we go home now?"

John shook his head. Tears glistened in his eyes but didn't spill over. "They don't think it was an accident," he said. "They think the fire was started deliberately."

"Deliberately? But why? I mean, who would do such a thing?"

"Someone might," John said. "If they wanted to cover up a murder."

"A murder? Who?" Hope's mind whirled. "You mean Pa? They think he was murdered?" Her voice rose several octaves. "That's ridiculous. Who…"

"They think it was one of us."

Aghast Hope couldn't take in what he was saying. She recalled Ned saying Pa was found at the bottom of the cellar steps. Surely that was an accident. "One of us? Who? Why?"

John put his head in his hand. "I don't know, Hope. I don't know but they're asking a lot of questions. Did I owe anyone money? Did I have an argument with Pa? They think one of us pushed him down the stairs and set the fire to cover it up. They wanted to know who was there in the pub. You and Violet were out so that only leaves me, Ma and Alfie so it must have been one of us."

"No, John, none of us would do anything to hurt Pa. He must have fallen." Part of her recalled his treatment of Ma and sometime John, how he couldn't hold his temper when he'd had a few drinks too many. She recalled he'd been on the whisky that night too, before she went out. A torrent of fear rose up in her.

John raised his head. "I told them. All I remember was the smoke, going to look for Ma and Pa and being driven back by the fire. I don't even remember seeing Alfie..." His voice faded as sobs wracked his body.

"Oh John, of course you don't. It's not your fault. You did what you could."

"I should have saved Alfie. I knew he was upstairs, alone and helpless. I should have thought..." The grief on his face was clear, his eyes hollowed with pain and exhaustion.

"You acted on impulse in the spur of the moment. No one would have done any different. Anyway, thanks to Silas, Alfie's going to be all right. We'll find out more when he and Ma are better. Then the police will have to close the case and let us back into our home."

"You think so? I wish that was true, but I fear they're not going to let this go and it'll be the worse for all of us." He picked up his coat. "I asked about funeral arrangements. They won't release his body until the investigation's over. The only reason they haven't charged anyone is because they can't decide which of us did it. It's only a matter of time."

"A matter of time? What do you mean?"

"I mean, they're going to hang one of us whether we did it or not." He stared at Hope, his face hard as carved marble then walked out into the gathering dusk.

Hope's jaw clenched. They think one of the family killed Pa? But that's not possible, she thought. We all loved him. None of us would hurt him.

Her mind flew back over the recent past when his drinking and subsequently his temper had got worse. But things had been better lately, since he seemed to have come into money. Then she recalled how drunk he was that night, before she went out. She recalled the shouting from Ma and Pa's room on more than one occasion, followed by silence. Ma's bruises the next day evidence of his violent temper. She still couldn't believe any one of them would do such a cruel, senseless thing, not unless they were severely provoked. Her mind was in a frenzy. It was true that only John, Ma and Alfie were in the pub that night after closing when it must have happened. Alfie would have been in bed. She couldn't believe John would hurt Pa, but then, if he was drunk and violent… John could have been protecting himself…

Then she remembered Ma in the hospital saying she didn't regret what she'd done and an abyss of dread opened up and swallowed her. Her knees buckled. She sank onto a chair. Had they argued and Ma lashed out? She felt sick at the thought. If so it would have been an accident, not murder.

There must be more to this than John's saying, she thought. She'd go to the police station first thing in the morning and find out for herself. Pa murdered by one of the family? How insanely ridiculous. Who would do such a thing?

The next morning John was still sleeping when Hope awoke. He hadn't returned until the early hours so she decided to leave him and gathered her clothes to dress in the warmth of the kitchen where Betsy was preparing the breakfast.

She dressed in the suit she was wearing to go the theatre with Ned, which now seemed like a lifetime ago. Betsy had done a good job getting out the smell of smoke and the grit that came with it. Hope pinned her hair up, admiring her reflection in the small grimy mirror Betsy kept hanging on the wall next to the larder. She put on the matching hat. If she was going to the police station she didn't want to be ignored or written off and so she wanted to look her best.

Outside the air was crisp and sharp with a late frost. She breathed it in deeply, trying to calm her racing heart as she strode purposefully along. The police station was at the other end of town and walking along the familiar streets felt unreal. Early morning sunlight bathed the pavement, but there was no warmth in it. People went about their business; the usual morning rush of bustle and noise filled the air. The newspaper boy called the news on the corner, milk bottles clinked as they were placed on doorsteps, women stopped and chatted. It all looked so normal. How could that be? It was as though the world had stood still, their lives, everything they knew and loved was gone and yet to everyone else nothing had changed, life went on as usual.

She had to walk past the remains of the pub that had been her home. When she got there she stopped and stared at the now boarded up building, its walls blackened with soot and smoke. It was hard to image that, only a few days ago, it was where they made their living. A great swell of grief washed over her as though ghosts of the recent past had returned to haunt the abandoned pub.

Her heart faltered. A deluge of memories threatened to overwhelm her, the grief making them sharper in her mind. She could hardly breathe. Memories of a lifetime spent in the place buzzed through her mind. She saw Ma making pies in the kitchen, Violet getting dressed for her first day at school and Alfie bawling loud enough to wake the devil on the day he was born. It had been a difficult birth and she recalled Pa's joy at the safe delivery. Cigars and drinks all round that night.

In her mind she saw the pub lit up, full of laughter and happy smiling faces. Visions of Auntie Wyn at the piano and the Saturday night sing-a-longs filled her head. Happy days before gaming tables replaced the piano and their customers drifted away, replaced by out-of-work dockers hoping to supplement their income by betting and gaming. Could it have been so long ago? How things had changed.

What had happened to her pa, that full, florid faced man she recalled from her childhood? The man who loved to entertain and make them laugh? The man they could rely on to put a smile on their faces? The man who'd loved his family above all things?

Then she recalled him in recent years, when they'd had to tiptoe around his temper like timid fawns. What had brought about the change? Was it comparing himself to others and finding himself lacking, as Ma had said? Or was it something else? What had brought them to this – a fire and accusations of murder? What had happened to him in the pub that night? She could understand it if he'd argued with someone and lashed out. Fighting was his nature, but to be murdered? No. She couldn't understand that. She sighed and walked on.

When she finally arrived at the police station she saw a dour-faced sergeant sat behind the counter on a high stool entering something in a large ledger. She asked to see the man dealing with the investigation into the murder of William Daniels. She was asked to wait. So she waited, sitting on a hard wooden chair in what she supposed was the reception area. Policemen came and went and she sat staring at the panelled walls. Eventually a man came out to see her. Tall and slim with brown hair flopping over the forehead of his fine-boned, intelligent face, he looked more like a businessman in a smart suit than a policeman. His lips spread into a smile which lit up the hazel in his eyes. Hope had been ready to do battle with whichever stuck up, patronising, overbearing officer she encountered, but seeing him she was entirely disarmed.

"Miss Daniels? I'm Inspector Penhalligan. How can I help you?" He spoke with a soft country burr which gave Hope a feeling of reassurance.

"I want to see the officer in charge of the investigation into my father's death," she said.

"That's me," he said. "Please come this way." He led her into a small room, obviously used for interviews. A glass panel at eye level, obscured by netting, ran the length of the wall next to the door. The other three walls were blank. She took a seat at the table set out in the centre of the room. She felt like a villain undergoing an inquisition.

"My brother tells me that you think my father was a victim of foul play," she said, not sure how to start the conversation, other than tell him what John had said. "Surely it was an accident? He was drunk. He fell down stairs. Why would you think otherwise?"

"I'm afraid I can't discuss the case with you," he said. "I understand you weren't on the premises at the time. Unless you can tell me to the contrary and saw what happened."

"I wasn't there," she said. "But I saw Pa before I went out. He was in his office drinking heavily. I wouldn't be surprised if he tripped and fell down the cellar steps. It can be very dark there. He would have been carrying a lamp. That's the most likely explanation. It was an accident."

"That's for the police to decide," Inspector Penhalligan said. The shadow of a smile crossed his face but quickly disappeared.

"No one in the family would do Pa any harm. We just wouldn't."

The Inspector smiled a smile that didn't reach his eyes. "Thank you for telling us about his drinking, although it merely confirms what our pathologist has told us. However, whether he fell or was pushed is something for our investigators to establish."

"Pushed? You think he was pushed down stairs?" Her voice rose several octaves. "Pa was a big man and not easily overcome. I can't believe any one of us would even attempt such a thing."

Inspector Penhalligan shrugged. "I'm very busy. Is there anything else? Do you have any concrete information for us? If not I think your time would be better spent at the hospital looking after your mother and little brother."

Hope fumed. "I want to see him. His body. Pa's body."

He shook his head. "No you don't. It's badly burnt. Scarred too. It's already been formally identified so there's no need for you to trouble yourself further. Best to remember him as he was when he was alive, don't you think?" He rose to show her out.

By the time she got outside she was even more cross. She felt as though she'd been brushed off like an annoying piece of fluff on a good suit and vowed she'd get to the bottom of it if it was the last thing she did.

Chapter Sixteen

Her ill-humour evaporated when she saw Ned in the market. His cheery face always had that effect on her. "Good morning, beautiful," he said, moving towards her to brush her cheek with his lips. "How are you coping at Betsy's and how are your ma and Alfie? Any news?"

"Ma's come round a bit and I spoke to Alfie yesterday. He can't remember anything which is probably a blessing."

Ned reached under the stall and brought out a large bag. "The stallholders heard about your pa and they're all very sorry," he said. "So they had a whip-round. This is for you." He handed her the bag. "And this. He took a money bag out of his pocket and handed that to her as well. "It's not much but it'll help."

Hope's jaw dropped. She stared at Ned before opening the bag to glance in. The bag contained fruit, a chicken and some eggs and a ham from the various stallholders. The money bag jingled with coins. It felt heavy enough to contain sufficient cash to keep them for a while, maybe even until the pub reopened. She didn't know what to say. Thank you seemed too little after people's kindness.

"I don't know what to say," she said. "I can't thank you enough. Everyone's been so kind. Please thank all the traders for me. At least now I won't feel so guilty about eating Betsy out of house and home without the means to repay her."

"If there's anything else you need," Ned said, "you only have to ask."

"Well, with this I can get some books, crayons and paper for Alfie. It'll help keep him occupied and his mind off everything."

A broad smile lit up Ned's face. "Will these do?" He leaned under the stall and brought out a pile of books, including several colouring books, pencils and crayons. "I know what it's like to be confined to bed. You need somat to occupy your mind." He passed the pile to Hope.

"Ned, you're a lifesaver," she said. "I could kiss you."

"Go on then."

So she did.

When she eventually arrived at the hospital she was surprised to see John sitting at Ma's bedside. Ma was sleeping, her breath shallow and uneven.

"How is she?" Hope whispered, not wanting to wake her.

John shook his head. "She hasn't woken yet. The doctor says to let her sleep. I just thought I'd stay in case, you know…"

Hope nodded. She showed him the bags of food and the books and crayons for Alfie. "Everyone's been so kind," she said. "I don't know how we're ever going to thank them."

"It's good to know Ma and Pa were so well respected in the community," he said.

There was a gentle knocking on the door and the doctor walked in. "Ah," he said. "I'm glad you're both here. I need to talk to you about your mother."

Hope and John exchanged glances. Hope's heart was racing. It had to be bad news, what else would he need to tell them other than the worst.

"If you'd care to follow me," the doctor said.

They followed him to his office where they could talk in private. Hope feared the worst.

The doctor's office was clean and clinical. A vaguely medicinal smell permeated every surface, filling the air with its distinctive hospital aroma. John and Hope sank into the chairs placed opposite the desk. The doctor picked up a sheet of paper and glanced briefly at it.

"I'm sorry to worry you," he said, "but she's not making as much progress as she should. We've tried everything but she's not responding to treatment. It's as though she's given up and doesn't want to get better." He was clearly exasperated.

"She's just lost her husband and her home," Hope said. "How would you expect her to feel?" She felt the swirling anger of earlier rising up inside again. Surely the doctor knew better than to blame the patient for her lack of progress.

"I'm aware of that," the doctor said. "But this is more than a feeling of loss. It goes much deeper than that. She's totally resistant to any help we're trying to give her."

"She needs looking after and to be given a reason to go on living," Hope said.

The doctor nodded. "Her lungs are badly scarred from the smoke. There is a place that can help. I'd like to move her to a sanatorium in Kent. It'll cost a bit, but a complete change, fresh air and careful dedicated nursing will give her lungs a chance to recover and her mental state too, being away from London and all her…um… shall we say, difficulties, or whatever it is that's holding her back."

"We can't afford…"

"We'll pay," Hope said. She thought about the money Ned had given her. It might go towards the cost but it wouldn't be enough. "Whatever it costs we'll find the money, won't we, John?"

John shook his head in despair. "We can't, Hope."

"She's our mother. We have to find a way."

The doctor smiled. "You've a day or two to make up your mind. Let me know when you've made a decision."

They went back to Ma's room and a great swell of love fell over Hope as she stared at this woman who'd brought them into the world, cared for them, brought them up and would move heaven and earth if she had to for them. And they couldn't even find the money to send her to a sanatorium to save her life.

"We have to find a way, John," Hope said. "It's the least we can do. We owe her that much."

"Really?" John said. "And how are we to pay? There's Pa's funeral will need paying for and a place for us to live. Where are we to find the money for that?"

"If we both work…"

John glared at her. "We'll have to do that anyway, Hope. We can't live the rest of our lives on other people's charity."

"It's only until we get back home, in the pub."

"If I get the licence."

Hope frowned. "What do you mean, if? Have the brewery said anything?"

John shrugged. "Why don't you go and see Alfie. I'll stay here in case Ma wakes up. We don't want to upset her more than we have to, do we?"

He was right. No use arguing in front of Ma, but she felt sure he wasn't telling her the whole story. She huffed. "I'll give Alfie your best," she said and stomped out of the door.

Chapter Seventeen

When she arrived at Alfie's room the blood drained from her face as she bumped into Silas Quirk. Frown lines creased his face and she thought she'd never seen him look so crumpled. His usually slicked back hair was dull and uncombed. He had burn marks on his face and his arm was in a sling.

"What on earth…"

Alfie was sitting up in bed slowly turning the pages of a colourful story book. The bandage round his head had been removed and replaced with a large plaster above one eye.

"I'm sorry," Silas said. "I didn't mean to intrude. I was passing and thought I'd see how the little chap was." The sincerity in his eyes momentarily shocked her. She felt a stab of guilt for all the terrible things she'd thought and said about him. Suddenly he appeared all too human. She remembered how his arm had been burned, the cloth of his jacket smouldering. "Your arm? How is it now? Have they managed to save the skin and relieve the pain?"

"It was nothing, but thank you for asking. It's almost healed. No permanent damage."

Hope forced a smile while her insides churned. Why did she always feel this way whenever she saw him? "You have every right to come and see Alfie," she said. "If it wasn't for you he wouldn't be here."

"I only did what anyone would have done," he said. She doubted that but was thankful all the same.

"I'm glad that, given time, he'll mend. I was sorry to hear about your father too," he said. "If there's anything I can do."

"You've done enough and we're very grateful," she said.

"How's your mother? I understand from the doctors that her progress is slower than expected. The smoke inhalation worse than…" he glanced back at Alfie.

So, he'd spoken to the doctors about her mother too. "Her progress is slow, she is weak," Hope said. "But we are hopeful for a full recovery." His obvious interest in her and her family was beginning to make her blush. "Thank you for the book," she said attempting to divert his attention. "I assume you brought it."

Colour rose in his face and, for the first time ever, she saw he was embarrassed.

He shrugged. "My sister suggested…"

"It's very kind of you, of her, of you both." Now she was the one cringing with embarrassment.

He nodded. He seemed to want to say something but was having trouble getting the words out. He bowed his head. She'd never seen him so discomforted. "I need to speak to your brother, John, too," he said. "There are matters we need to discuss."

"He's with our mother just now, it would be inappropriate to disturb him. Perhaps there's something I could help you with."

Again the embarrassed look and the discomfiture. "No. I need to speak to him."

He picked up his hat from the side table, placed it on his head and tipped it. "I hope we'll have the pleasure of seeing you at The Grenadier when you're fully recovered from your experiences," he said. "Good day."

Hope was left gasping for breath.

She turned to Alfie. He looked a lot brighter than the previous day. She noticed several more books on the side table, including school books.

"Did Mr Quirk bring all these?" she asked.

"No. Violet came and brought me the school books."

Violet thinking of anyone other than herself was a revelation. "That was thoughtful of her," Hope said and realised that she meant it.

"Can I keep them, the books Mr Quirk brought?" Alfie asked, looking dismayed.

"Of course you can."

"Even when I go home?"

"Even when you go home." Hope perched on the edge of the bed and felt Alfie's forehead. It was cool. She brushed his cheek. "You're looking better. How are you feeling?"

"I feel fine. Can I go home soon? I can't wait to see Ma, Pa, John and Violet."

Hope swallowed. Of course no one would have told him about Pa. "Alfie," she said. "How much do you remember about how you got here?"

He shook his head. "I remember going to bed. I wanted to read but the candle guttered out. Next thing I remember is waking up here with a terrible bad head and sore throat. The doctors and nurses said something about a fire, but I don't remember it."

She nodded. "Well, there was a fire, a very bad one and Pa had an accident. I'm sorry, Alfie. Sorry to be the one to tell you but Pa's gone. He's not coming back."

Alfie blinked a couple of times. Silence filled the room as he took the words in.

"You mean he's dead?" he rasped, eventually.

Hope nodded. She picked up the herbal infusion left for him by the bed and gave it to him to take a drink. He shook his head and a tear, like a giant raindrop, rolled down his cheek.

"It wasn't my fault was it? I didn't do anything. I won't get into trouble will I?" The despair in his voice wrenched her heart.

"No of course not," she said, horrified. "Don't even think about it. You were in bed asleep. Like I said, Pa had an accident."

"And everyone else is alright? Ma, John, Violet?"

"Ma's poorly but they're going to make her better. We just have to live somewhere else until the pub is repaired."

"And I can come and live with you?"

"Yes."

He lay back against the pillows, his little face pale and puckered with pain. He looked so small and fragile. Hope took his hand.

"Can I come home today?" he asked his voice merely a whisper.

"No not today. Not until the doctor says you can."

"When will that be?"

"Soon," Hope said, but doubt lingered in his eyes with a shadow of alarm. "I'll speak to the doctor," she said. "See what he has to say."

Alfie perked up. "Can you bring my leg brace and crutches," he asked. "They're by my bed. I'll need them to go home."

Hope forced a smile at his impossible request. She didn't want to lie to him, but she didn't want to give him false hope either. "I'll see what I can do," she said. "But, as I said, the pub's been badly damaged I may not be able to…"

Alfie sank back into the pillow, turning his head away. "You can go home now. I want to rest."

Hope's heart turned over. "Oh, Alfie," she said. "Please don't cry. I'll get your things and make the doctor send you home."

He turned to face her, his cheek wet with tears. "Thank you," he said.

As she left the room, she felt a lump in her throat. Blood rushed through her veins. All she could think about was Alfie and why he had to suffer so much. She was determined to have him home with them as soon as possible and not leave him here a moment longer than she had to.

She was walking along the corridor, looking for the doctor's office her mind still in turmoil when she saw Inspector Oakley Penhalligan of the Metropolitan Police striding towards her. He raised his black felt trilby. "Good day, Miss Daniels. How fortuitous to run into you. I was hoping to have a word with your brother…er," he checked a piece of paper in his hand. "Alfred. I understand he's a patient here."

Fresh anger rose up inside Hope. "Alfie?" she said. "I've just left him and I'd rather you didn't disturb him. He's a confused little boy who's just been told of his father's death. He's in no fit state to answer any of your questions. He needs to rest."

Inspector Penhalligan removed his hat. A frown creased his brow. "I'm sorry but I will need to speak to him at some point. He was in the building. He may be able to tell us something."

"He can't. He doesn't remember anything between going to bed and waking up here in the hospital."

He twisted his hat in his hands. "Your mother?"

"Also needs to sleep. The doctors are concerned about her progress and she's not to be disturbed. I'm afraid you've had a wasted journey."

He smiled and replaced his hat on his head. "Not a wasted journey if it gave me another opportunity to speak with you. May I walk you home?"

"No. Thank you," she said. "I have to see the doctor but you can help me. Perhaps you can tell me when we'll be able to return to the Hope and Anchor. As you know it was our home and all our belongings are there. We'd like to retrieve as much as possible to make our current living more amenable."

"I'm afraid it will be sometime before that happens," he said. "The building's not safe."

Hope grimaced. She took his arm and led him along the corridor away from Alfie's room. "Alfie needs assistance with walking. His leg brace and crutches have been left behind and I need to fetch them. It is a matter of some urgency."

"And where would they be?"

"By his bed."

"Hmm. Well, you can't go in but I could have a word with the fire officer. Perhaps one of his men may be able to brave the stairs and retrieve them. If it's important."

"Very important," she said.

He lifted his hat. "I'll do my best," he said.

"If you could I'd be most grateful."

He nodded and left with what Hope could only describe as a smirk on his face.

She shuddered and went to look for the doctor. Her search proved fruitless. The nurse said to call back that evening when he'd be on duty, so Hope went home, but seeing Inspector Penhalligan had unsettled her.

Why did he want to speak to Alfie? Did he think he was responsible for the fire? Alfie couldn't remember what had happened. Had he got up and tried to go down stairs with his crutch while carrying a lighted candle? Was he the one who'd had a fall and started the fire? He'd obviously had a fall, but the question remained – why was he going downstairs anyway? To get another candle, because he heard something, or for some other entirely different reason?

Chapter Eighteen

The next few days followed the same routine; John going out looking for odd jobs or working at the wood yard to earn some money and Hope helping Betsy with the washing or doing some darning and mending before going to the hospital to read to Alfie or sit with Ma watching her deteriorate, her life slipping away. She tried to talk to her, willing her to respond, to do something to try to get better. Her soul ached with uselessness.

One evening when she came back from the hospital she walked in to Betsy's front parlour to find John was pacing the floor. He looked worse than she'd ever seen him. His face was pale and his hair ruffled up as though he'd been running his fingers through it. "How's Alfie?" he asked.

"A little better," she said. "Sitting up and taking notice. He wants to come home. I said I'd speak to the doctor. I'm sure he'd get on better if we could nurse him here."

"You can't look after him, Hope. Not here. It's not possible."

"Why not? I can stay with him, talk to him help him get over his trauma."

"What, when we're both working at The Grenadier?"

Working at The Grenadier? She couldn't believe what she was hearing. It was barely a week since the fire and Pa had yet to be buried. What on earth was John talking about?

"Why should I work there? I know Pa said... but things are different now..."

"Not much different. I've been to the bank," John said. "The bank manager made it very clear that there's no money and no chance of borrowing any. We will both have to work if we want to eat."

"Well, I could work at Ruth's..."

"For what, tuppence ha'penny? Anyway we owe Silas."

Hope recalled seeing him carry Alfie out of the fire. "I know, but that's different."

"I mean Pa's loan. The loan he borrowed from Silas. The bank manager knew about it. He told me that it was secured on the lease of the pub. If it's not repaid we'll lose everything."

Hope frowned. "The lease of the pub? Why would Silas Quirk want that?" Visions of Silas taking Ma and Pa's place in their home ran through her mind. She shuddered.

"An investment, the bank manager said."

She recalled Dexi talking about Silas's investment in her and telling her that Silas always got what Silas wanted.

"But he can't... I mean...he can't..."

"I think you'll find he can."

She sank onto a chair, defeated. She couldn't believe the man she'd just seen, the man who'd been so kind to her at the hospital, would be so ruthless as to expect them to pay off their father's debt. But he was Silas Quirk. A businessman, they owed him more than a debt of gratitude. Had she got him all wrong? Was his concern for them only about repayment of the debt? "What are we going to do, John?"

He took her by the shoulders and stared into her eyes. "We're going to go in there and make Ma and Pa proud," he said. "Chin up, walk tall. We won't let anyone put us down, Hope. We may be in a bad spot now, but we owe it to Ma, Pa, Violet and Alfie to get on and do whatever it takes to get the pub back and provide a good living for the family."

Brave words, Hope thought. But the future had never looked blacker or more hopeless.

"What about Alfie? When he comes home, he'll need nursing. I won't let him stay in that place a moment longer than he has to..." She was close to tears now.

"I'm sure Betsy will be pleased to look after him," John said. "She seems like a very capable lady. He'll be safe with her."

That was true and Hope knew Betsy would jump at the chance to fuss over him like a mother hen, but it didn't reassure her. She wanted to look after him, to be there for him each day, to make sure he got better. She stared at John. He was her brother but she hardly recognised him. He'd changed. Pa's loss was eating away at him. Did he feel responsible? He was there in the pub. She saw something she couldn't place in his eyes. Was it guilt, or despair at the weight of responsibility that had been thrust so brutally and unexpectedly on him?

"So, when do we start?"

"Tonight," John said. "The sooner the better. I won't be beholden to anyone any longer than I have to be."

So it was settled. They'd both go to The Grenadier that night and offer their services. John had said it would be a new beginning, a fresh start, but for Hope it felt like the end of something she'd never be able to regain.

John explained their plan to Betsy over tea that evening.

"Well, I suppose you know what you're doing," she said, her eyebrows raised. "I only know the reputation of that place from the gossip you hear in the market. I could be wrong."

"I'm going to speak to Mr Quirk and see what I can salvage from the mess Pa left," John said. "I won't let us be treated with disrespect. I believe Pa made the arrangements in good faith and I'll see Silas Quirk sticks to it."

"Pa only said I should work there for a year," Hope said, recalling the meeting she'd had with Pa. "It won't be forever."

John smiled. "From what I've seen on my rare visits there the girls are treated well. You should be all right. And I have experience of working behind the bar. That's the only service I'll be offering."

"Well, I don't envy you," Betsy said. "But you have to do what you have to do these days. Beggars can't be choosers."

Hope's stomach filled with leaden resignation. "My only concern is Alfie," she said. "When he comes out of the hospital. We were hoping you could look after him. I know it's a lot to ask. You have your laundry…"

"Lord luv us, dearie. I'd be happy to. Long time since I've had a young un to look after. It'll be a pleasure. Don't worry your head about it."

At least that was a relief. If Hope had to work at The Grenadier at least Alfie would be safe.

Betsy made them tea with bread, ham and fresh baked scones. "Can't go out to work with nowt in your belly," she said. "And I'll leave some bread and cheese for supper when you get back," she said. "I expect you'll be late so don't bother to wake me nor get up too early in the morning. You young people need your sleep same as us old uns."

Hope smiled. Yes, Alfie would be well looked after.

After tea Hope dressed in her maroon suit and hat. She wanted to make a good impression and show Silas Quirk that he couldn't intimidate them or cajole them into doing anything other than what Pa had agreed. John put on the suit and overcoat Ned had given him. Together they stepped out into the cool night air.

Excitement stirred inside Hope mixed with nervous anxiety. She didn't know what lay ahead of them, but she wanted to show John that she could stand just as tall as him. She didn't want to let him down. It was something they had to do, as she'd said to Betsy, an obligation. She might as well make the most of it. Recalling how she'd felt when she put on the dress that Dexi provided for her she thought that perhaps it wouldn't be all bad.

John slouched along, his mood morose. It had been barely a week since the fire and they were still coming to terms with their loss. "I'm sorry we have to do this," he said. "I know how you feel about Silas Quirk and I'm sorry to put you in this position."

"It was Pa put me in this position, not you. It's not your fault."

"I'm sorry about Pa 'an all."

"I know."

"Pa had his faults but I honestly believe he was trying to do his best for us."

"By drinking and gambling away all our money?" It sounded more bitter than she'd intended.

John sighed. "You don't know what it's like. Going to that club, seeing how the other half live, wanting to be part of it. He told me he had a plan. If we just waited we'd all be rich – eventually."

"Yes. When monkeys fly over the moon. Ma said he always was a dreamer."

"I've got a dream an' all. It won't always be like this. I'm gonna make somat of meself and of the pub. You'll see. This is only the beginning."

They walked on in sullen silence.

When they arrived at The Grenadier a man met them at the door. Heavily built with a fleshy face; a dark shadow of hair barely covered his skull. His beady eyes narrowed when he saw them. "You can't go in there," he said. "Members only. No females."

John pulled himself up to his full height. "We're here at the request of Mr Silas Quirk," he said.

The doorman looked them over. His nose wrinkled. Then the confusion on his face cleared. "Oh. New bar staff," he said, his gaze running lecherously over Hope. "Staff entrance round the back," he sneered.

Hope and John made their way round to the back of the building. "If that's the sort of welcome…" John said, his face suffused to an angry scarlet.

Hope touched his arm. "It's only temporary," she said. "We'll show them what proper service and good manners look like. We'll show them."

Inside they entered a noisy kitchen area where staff were busy preparing the food to be served in the club's restaurant. Although big and noisy Hope noticed the kitchen was spotlessly clean. A large man in white overalls and a tall chef's hat approached them. "What you want?" he asked in an accent betraying lack of English rather than aggression.

"New bar staff," John said. "Come to see Mr Quirk."

"Through door, first on left," the chef said, pointing the way with a large chopping knife.

"Thank you," Hope smiled at him. Their circumstances were not his fault.

Behind the kitchen several doors led off a small hall. They stopped outside the first on the left and glanced at each other. John gave an encouraging smile. "In for a penny," he said.

Hope took a deep breath, knocked and opened the door. Silas's office was not at all as she'd expected. The only items of note were the large mahogany desk in the centre of the room and a tall glass fronted bookcase filled with gold embossed, leather bound volumes which stretched along the wall behind the desk. Blinds shaded the window and several wall lamps lit the room. Gold framed paintings she recognised as being of the dancers at the Moulin Rouge in Paris graced the other walls. Knowing Silas, Hope guessed they were originals not copies. Two red plush upholstered chairs stood in front of the desk on a colourful rag rug covering bare floorboards.

Silas glanced up. Surprise filled his face as he rose to greet them. Hope didn't miss the 'cat that got the cream' look either.

Chapter Nineteen

He walked around the desk, arm outstretched and shook hands with John. His gaze lingered on Hope far longer than was comfortable. "How is your mother?" he asked, "and the boy?"

"They're both being well cared for, thank you," John said.

"Good, I'm glad to hear they're making progress. It must be difficult, with your father..." his voice tailed off.

"We will need to find work," John said. "Dexi mentioned..."

"Ah, yes of course." He indicated the chairs. They sat.

"I believe we have business to discuss," John said.

"Indeed." Silas picked up a quill and wrote something on a piece of paper. He pressed a button on the desk and within half-a-minute a small, dark-skinned boy, dressed in a blue uniform with shiny gold buttons, appeared. A pill box hat sat atop of his thick, black curls. "Abel, please accompany Miss Daniels to Mrs Malone's parlour and give Mrs Malone this." He handed the boy the folded note and turned to John. "I know Esme has been looking forward to your sister joining her in the recreation rooms. She has little patience herself for hosting."

Anger bubbled inside Hope, not only because he'd completely ignored her presence, other than the overlong original glance, but also that her future and the future of the family would be decided by John, who was a year younger than her and whose only interests were swilling beer and playing cards. Alfie had more business sense.

"I'd like to stay," she said. "The business affects us all."

John glared at her.

Silas shook his head. "My sister will be delighted to see you again," he said. "Let's not disappoint her." He strode to the door, opened it and ushered her and Abel through. She'd been dismissed and the volcano inside her was ready to explode. Well, she'd have a thing or two to say to Mrs Esme Malone, otherwise known as Dexi.

Her anger evaporated into breathlessness as she followed the boy, Abel, along a corridor and up a narrow staircase that opened into the most sumptuous hall she'd ever seen. Thick red carpet, laid over polished wood block flooring, led up a grand, curved staircase between marble balustrades. She followed the boy upstairs where tapestries, far grander that Hope had ever expected to see, graced the walls.

The outside of the building, a blank wall with a discrete black door with a brass door knocker in the shape of a guardsman, above which a sign declared it to be The Grenadier, Gentlemen's Club, gave no indication of the extravagance within.

The size and number of rooms contained within the unprepossessing walls surprised Hope. No wonder her father and John were so taken by it. There was more luxury in one square inch here than she'd seen in her whole life. Walking along behind the boy her anger returned. So this was where her father and John spent their time and money while she and Ma slaved away in the pub trying to make ends meet.

The room Abel led her to was even grander than the hall. High ceilings lit by huge chandeliers and panels around the walls, painted to appear as curtained windows lit by sunlight, together with mirrored panels on the opposite wall, gave the room an airy, daylight feel, belying the cold and darkness outside. The whole place seemed to glitter with light. Card tables around the room stood waiting for their occupants in silence. The only sound was the sound of Dexi, flicking cards out of the pack she held in her hand to lay them face up on the table. Four hands had already been dealt although Dexi was the only occupant of the room.

"Master say bring Lady," Abel said.

Dexi took the note. "Thank you, that will be all," she said and boy ran off. She motioned to Hope to sit. "Miss Daniels, may I call you Hope?" She didn't wait for a response. "Good. Her eyes sparkled like a faceted gem but there was the glint of steel beneath the sparkle as she read the note. "Silas says I am to be kind to you and treat you well." She laughed. "Your opinion must be important to him."

Hope's eyes blazed. "Really? So important he sends me away while he discusses my future with my younger brother?"

Dexi sighed. "That's men for you. Not the most sensitive of creatures but what would we do without them?"

Hope thought she'd do very well without the interference of men, but she stayed silent.

Dexi gathered up the cards on the table, shuffled them and dealt four hands. "Pick a hand," she said, nodding to the cards on the table. "I take it you play."

"Not really. I've come here to serve drinks not to gamble."

Dexi placed the rest of the pack on the table. "You can tell a lot about a man's character by the way he plays his cards," she said. "There are the reckless ones who care only for the risk, the cautious ones always dithering over their decisions, the ones who care only for the game and the desperate ones who care only about winning." She picked up the hand of cards in front of her. "Let's play a hand."

"I'm not sure I'm any match for you," Hope said.

Dexi smiled. "I see my reputation has preceded me," she said. "Pick up a hand and you will see that winning, like life, is not about the cards you're dealt, it's what you do with them."

Hope picked up the cards and played them using the chips on the table to bet. She had a pair of tens and drew three cards. Dexi drew one. Hope pushed two chips into the centre of the table. Dexi pushed in a pile. "Raise," she said. Hope guessed she had the better hand and folded. When Dexi lay her cards on the table she had nothing.

"But…"

"You can't understand why I bet so strongly on a bad hand?"

Hope nodded.

"That's the game. Thirty per cent of the time you will get a good hand. Seventy per cent of the time a not so good one. If you only bet on the good hands you will lose more than you win."

"Just as well I only came here to serve drinks then," Hope said.

Dexi laughed. "I can teach you to play cards and to play men. That is what I do. I think we will have fun together." She checked the small gold watch pinned to her dress. "Come now we will get you ready. Tonight you will shine brighter than the stars in the heavens and men will fall at your feet."

"I hope not," Hope said, but followed Dexi to her boudoir along the corridor and up yet another flight of stairs.

Dexi's boudoir turned out to be even more sumptuous than the card room. A large four-poster bed, draped with red velvet curtains, took up most of the room. A delicate Queen Anne dressing table filled with bottles and lotions sat on one side and a large dressing mirror on the other. Dexi led Hope into a side room filled with rails of shimmering gowns, so colourful it was like walking into a rainbow. Hope felt a tightening in her chest. She could hardly breathe.

"Hortense will help you dress," Dexi said, lifting the blue silk gown made for Hope by Miss Lovell, Dexi's dressmaker, from the rail. She touched Hope's hair which hung loose around her shoulders. "She has magic fingers when it comes to styling hair." She smiled. "You won't recognise yourself when she's finished." She handed the dress to a slight, young dark-skinned girl dressed in a maid's uniform. She didn't look a day over fourteen. "Miss Daniels will be working with me in the Saloon," Dexi said. "Please make sure she looks as spectacular as the gentlemen will expect."

Hortense nodded.

"Come and join me downstairs when you're ready," Dexi said to Hope. "Tonight you will dazzle. It will be such fun."

Hope wasn't sure fun was the right word, but a tingle of excitement stirred in her stomach. She'd never seen anything so beautiful as the dress Hortense was holding and the thought of wearing it to glide among the gentlemen who frequented The Grenadier was not one easily dismissed.

Hope chatted to Hortense as she styled her hair, twisting it into large curls around her head. Sitting at Dexi's dressing table she stared in awe at the array of bottles and lotions, all in crystal jars with silver tops. The perfume sprays were likewise cut glass with silver tops.

"How long have you worked for Mrs Malone?" she asked.

"Long time," Hortense said. "She say we free now."

"Free?"

"Not slave."

Hope knew about the slavery in America, but surely that was all over now, as it was here. "What about your family? Are they free too?"

Hortense nodded. "Mrs Malone, she bring us here."

"Us? Who?"

"Me, Ma, Jo and Abel."

"So, Abel's your brother?"

"Yus. And Jo who works in the restaurant."

"What about your father?"

"He dead."

When she'd finished styling her hair Hortense helped Hope into her dress and laced it up, pulling it tight around Hope's slim waist. Stepping into the sapphire blue creation all Hope's fears about the evening melted away. Even her anger at Silas and John abated. Her heart lifted and she felt a growing confidence blossom inside her.

Hortense fixed the deep blue feathered clip into Hope's soft curls. "There, you finished." She stepped back and Hope gazed at herself in the full-length mirror. Dexi was right. Not even her best friend would recognise her. Perhaps that was just as well, she thought, thinking of Ned and how surprised he'd be to see her like this. She couldn't stop the smile that spread her lips wide.

Downstairs in the Saloon Dexi rose and walked around Hope, nodding her approval. "You look just as beautiful as I'd hoped," she said. "And now for the finishing touch." She picked up a box from the table. When she opened it Hope gasped. Dexi lifted the exquisite sapphire necklace from the box and fastened it around Hope's neck. "There," she said. "Just right. Take a look."

Hope moved to gaze in one of the mirrored panels that adorned the walls. The sapphire gleam of the necklace brought out the startling blue of her eyes. She'd never imagined she could look so striking. "It's beautiful," she said. "But I can't—"

"What? Can't accept it? It's a gift from Silas. He chose it himself. You should be honoured."

"I am," Hope said. "It's very kind of him. I can never repay…" Her voice faded at the thought of all she could never repay. She'd be forever in his debt.

"Your being here is repayment enough," Dexi said. "From now on, whenever you're in the club you will be known as Sapphire. It's the name Silas chose for you. It's for your own protection. It'll give you anonymity and add a little mystery. It's always a good idea to keep our gentlemen guessing about our hostesses. Just be sure to give it to Hortense to put in the safe in my boudoir when you leave. It's very valuable."

Hope didn't doubt it. She smiled. Dressed in silk with her hair styled and now with Silas's jewels around her neck she felt like a different person. Here her life would be different too; different from the ordinary life she was leading at home helping Betsy with the washing.

Chapter Twenty

Dexi took her into the bar and introduced her to Poppy, the Chinese girl she'd be working with. Hope guessed she was called Poppy because of her scarlet silk gown and the oriental poppies woven into her glossy, dark as night hair. A ruby poppy hung from a gold chain around her neck. "She'll show you the ropes and keep an eye on you," Dexi said.

Poppy smiled. Her face was gentle, but with an underlying wariness, like a cat that's been teased and doesn't know who to trust. Hope took an immediate liking to her.

"You watch what people drinking," Poppy said. "Refresh glasses. Get drinks from bar. The barmen keep tabs on how many bottles you take. Men pay you with gaming chips. At the end of evening barman give you account which you pay with chips. Rest is for you. You exchange in casino for cash. I show you."

Hope followed Poppy to a cubbyhole with a barred window behind which sat a thin faced man with greying hair and spectacles. Poppy picked a chip out of the pocket hidden in her skirt and handed it to him through a gap below the bars. He put it into a tube which whistled away, returning a few minutes later with a silver half-crown which he gave to Poppy. "See," she said.

Hope laughed. "They have the same thing in the drapery shop in town," she said. "I'm quite familiar with the system."

Then Poppy showed her the different colour chips which each had its value engraved on it. The values ranged from gold and black chips worth £5 down to green ones which represented half-crowns. Crowns were blue, half-sovereigns purple and sovereigns, which Hope soon realised were the most popular, were red and gold.

"You'll need small float," Poppy said, "although not many men bother with change. They'll wave you away once they put chips on tray." She glanced over Hope. "Men good tippers. You do well."

The evening started quite slowly and Hope quickly got the hang of walking round the tables with a silver tray carrying several bottles. Every time she topped up a gentleman's drink a few chips were put on the tray, just as Poppy had said. It didn't take her long to realise that the men at the tables were far more interested in the cards than the girls who served them. Often they were so intent on the game that the chips casually dropped onto the tray far exceeded the cost of the drink.

The evening passed in a flash. The constant light, reflected by the mirrored panels around the room, belied the lateness of the hour and by the time the players thinned out sufficiently for Dexi to send her home it was well past midnight.

Back upstairs Hortense put the sapphire necklace in the safe as Dexi had instructed and helped Hope out of her gown. She hung it back on the rail in the dressing room. "Tomorrow we try a different style," she said as she brushed out Hope's hair. When she said it Hope realised that this was where she'd be spending all her evenings from now on. Unlike Hortense and her family, she was no longer free.

When she got downstairs John was waiting for her. "Couldn't let you walk home alone," he said. "How did the evening go?"

"It was all right. Busy and my feet ache," she said. "Yours?"

"Good. I was put to work behind the bar in the restaurant. You should see the dishes they bring up from the kitchens. I've never seen so much food in one place. I think we've fallen on our feet here, Hope. Did you get many tips?"

"A few," Hope said.

"Good," John said. "With my wages and your tips we should be able to pay Silas Quirk back every penny Pa borrowed. Then we can set about getting the pub licence back and going home."

Hope didn't say anything. Paying Silas Quirk back and releasing them from that obligation was one thing, but the memory of Ma in the hospital and the doctor's advice to move her to a sanatorium played in her mind. Surely the money would be better spent on saving Ma's life than paying Silas Quirk back?

The next morning Hope rose early, leaving John still sleeping. Betsy was up, fussing round the kitchen putting the kettle on and buttering some bread. "Good morning, you're an early bird," she said. "Didn't expect to see you 'til lunch time given how late you was coming in. Not that I'm complaining, mind. You have to do what you have to do, but it makes it a long day."

Hope smiled. "I'm fine. John's still sleeping and I'd appreciate it if you didn't disturb him. I got up early as I want to get to the hospital."

"You'll have time for a cup of tea and a bite won't you."

Hope wasn't going to stop but the hot tea and buttered bread looked so tempting. "Thank you," she said, edging onto a stool while Betsy poured her tea. "I want to talk to the doctor about moving Ma. I know she's in a bad way. It's the least we can do for her after all she's done for us."

Betsy sighed. "Aye. Well, it's bad enough losing your pa and I don't underestimate the effect of that, but to lose your ma as well…" She shook her head. "It's a wicked world we live in. Folks setting fire to other people's property."

Anger brought Hope up sharp. "Where did you get that idea? It was an accident. An accident with an old kerosene lamp…"

Betsy glanced up, then shrugged. "Whatever you say. But other folk seem to think different."

"Well, other folk can mind their own business," Hope said. She gulped down her tea, picked up the buttered bread and stood to go. "I'm sorry," she said. "I know you mean well, but there's no one in the world would want to hurt Ma or Pa. They just wouldn't."

"I'm sure you're right," Betsy said but Hope couldn't help feeling that what Betsy said was probably true. The police certainly seemed to think so. Rumours about the fire not being an accident had spread faster than the fire itself and it would take more than cold water to put them out.

The March morning air was sharp and a chill wind blew as she hurried along. A sudden gust rustled blinds over the shop's awnings as she passed and she pulled her shawl closer around her. Costers wheeling their barrows nodded to her and she smiled back, although smiling was the last thing she felt like doing. A whirlpool of anxiety churned in her stomach. Ma was poorly and she was determined to do everything she could to help get her better.

When she arrived at the hospital she asked to see the doctor in charge of her mother's care. The nurse on duty shook her head. "It's a bit early for visiting," she said. "Doctor's on his rounds. There's no knowing how long he'll be. Can you come back later?"

"I'd rather stay," Hope said. "Can I go in and see Ma?"

"She's probably sleeping. It really would be best if you came back later."

"Please. I haven't got long and I promise to be quiet and not disturb any of the other patients."

The nurse relented. "Oh all right then, but only for a few minutes. We can't have the routine of the hospital disturbed. It's essential that our patients get enough rest."

"Thank you," Hope said and rushed off before she could change her mind.

In her mother's room it was as the nurse had said, Ma was sleeping. Hope sat at her bedside watching the uneven, rasping breath and her mother's fingers pawing at the sheets. Even asleep she seemed agitated. Hope took her hand.

"It's me, Hope," she whispered. She rubbed her mother's hand, but there was no response, only a harsh wheezing sound as she drew breath. "We're going to get you out of here, Ma," she said, more to herself than the sleeping form in the bed. "Take you away to a place you'll be able to breathe fresh air and get well again."

Ma's eyelids flickered and the corners of her lips lifted into the shadow of a smile. Her hand gripped Hope's. Her grip was weak but even the slight movement cheered Hope. "Did you hear me, Ma? We're going to get you out of here."

Ma's eyes opened, watery but still blue she gazed at Hope. "You're a good girl, Hope, a good girl…" her voice faded and she lapsed back into sleep.

Hope sat at her mother's bedside for another hour, the only sound filling the room the sound of her mother's uneven breathing. When she rose it was to pour water from a jug on the side table into a glass for her, or walk to the window to gaze out at the stonemason's yard below. Outside she saw the dust and dirt rising from the stone cutting, the noise and bustle of daily activity on the street beyond and the grime that hung over the city. It's a wonder any of us survive, she thought and became more determined than ever to have Ma moved to a sanatorium in the country.

Eventually the doctor arrived, accompanied by the nurse she'd seen earlier.

"Good morning," he said. "I didn't know we allowed visitors so early in the day."

"It was a special request," the nurse said. "Miss Daniels was wanting to speak to you. I said she could wait here."

"Oh." He smiled, picked up the chart from the end of the bed and looked at it. "How can I help?"

"You mentioned moving Ma to a sanatorium for her health. I wanted to make the arrangements…" she took a breath, "if it's not too costly."

The doctor sighed, the worried look on his face as he read the chart wasn't promising. He put the chart on the bed and moved to feel Ma's forehead. He listened to her chest for several minutes, moving his stethoscope from side to side. "How are you feeling today, Mrs Daniels?" he asked, rather loudly Hope thought.

Hearing his voice Ma opened her eyes and lifted her hand. He moved closer. "How's the breathing?" he asked. "Any pain?"

Ma nodded and he wrote something on the chart.

"Increase the medication," he said to the nurse. "I'll come back tomorrow and see how you are, Mrs Daniels," he said to Ma, but she'd already drifted off to sleep again.

He motioned to Hope to follow him to his office.

"I'm afraid she's not making any progress. We're having to increase the medication daily. There'd be no advantage in moving her now. It would be too disruptive, and having spoken to her I know she's not keen to move." He paced the room. "I'm sorry if I gave any reason for false hope. I'm afraid there is none. All we can do is make sure your mother is as comfortable as she can be in her last days."

"You mean…" His words seemed to hang in the air and she had difficulty grasping them. She gasped as the sudden realisation of what he was saying hit her like a stone falling into her stomach. A quicksand of dread began pulling her under.

The rest of the conversation went in a blur. Hope could take in nothing the doctor said. She heard the words 'miracle' and 'prayers', and 'a slight chance if…' but his comforting smile and pat on her shoulder did nothing to reassure her. Walking out of the hospital all she could think about was that her mother was dying. Her fragile grip on life was slipping away.

There was nothing they could do. It was only a matter of time.

She hurried on unaware of where she was going. Anger churned inside her: anger at Pa for gambling away all their money and leaving them penniless, anger at John for wanting to take over the licence, anger at Ma for not getting better and even anger at the doctor for not being able to save her and the fiercest anger of all for the fire that had taken everything from them.

She walked so fast that in a short time she was amazed to find herself by the river. The water looked murky, dark and deep, constantly moving as it made its way to the sea. Dark clouds filled the sky. She shivered in a sudden breeze. Overwhelmed and numb with grief she sank onto a bench. The doctor's words replayed in her mind and, for the first time since that terrible night, the floodgates of sorrow opened and she gave in to uncontrollable sobbing that wracked her body, until there were no tears left to cry.

Half-an-hour later her sobbing subsided but not the deep grief that went with it. She'd cried as much as she could cry and there were no tears left. A deep empty void opened up inside her. She dried her face and sat motionless on the bench, watching the boats going up and down the river.

She'd cried her heart out but nothing had changed. She wished she could turn the clock back and make everything all right again: Ma and Pa in the pub, her and Violet, John and Alfie all together as they were before she went out with Ned that night. But she couldn't and no amount of wishing would make it so. If she'd known what was to happen she wouldn't have gone, but it was no use regretting it now.

A chill wind had blown up and clouds scudded across the sky. Pale sunlight shone on her face as she sat there, but she didn't feel the warmth of it. Visions of Ma, lying in that hospital bed where she'd likely end her days, and Alfie with his injuries played through her mind. Alfie'd need looking after. Perhaps Violet was right, going out making a new life for herself, not giving a second's thought to what she may be leaving behind.

"It's the future, not the past you need to worry about, girl," she said aloud, although no one was there to hear it. And looking to the future meant looking after Alfie, making sure he had the best opportunities life had to offer, and looking after herself too, making the best of whatever chances came her way, even if it meant working at The Grenadier, being nice to the gentlemen who spent their evenings and their money there. She'd come to realise how much difference having money could make to your life. To her mind all their problems stemmed from Pa's gambling debts. If he'd kept his money in his pocket they wouldn't be in the situation they were in.

As the water shifted in the breeze another shaft of sunlight peaked out from behind a cloud, briefly playing on the waves in front of her. When she left the bench a new determination was growing inside her, like a flame growing steadily brighter, a determination to take control of her own future.

Chapter Twenty One

Despite her new determination Hope's heart was heavy as she made her way to the market. Walking in the chill spring sunshine she passed costers pushing their carts along the cobbles, washerwomen carrying their huge bundles on their hip, a woman pushing a pram shouting at several ragged children in tow behind her. She didn't know what she'd expected to see but the normality of people going about their everyday lives seemed wrong. With Pa gone and Ma soon to follow her whole world had collapsed and been replaced by an aching void in her heart. It was as though she'd expected the whole world to be changed, but it wasn't. She shuddered, feeling more isolated than ever.

On her way to the market she ran into Violet coming in the opposite direction. "I'm on my way to the hospital," she said, "to see Ma. Ned gave me some grapes. These should buck her up." She showed Hope the bag filled with delicious purple fruits.

Hope nodded. She didn't want to dispel Violet's hopes. Not while there was still a chance, the doctors could be wrong...

Then Violet became suddenly serious. "There's a rumour going round that Pa was murdered and the fire set deliberately. Who would do such a thing?"

"Nobody. It's just idle, ill-informed gossip. No one would do such a thing."

"But if it's true? Someone could have had a grudge, someone he'd wronged, or..."

"No. It was an accident. No one would..."

"There might be someone out there with a grudge against us all. If they killed Pa and set our home on fire we could be next." Violet looked terrified. "If there's a mad-man on the loose we're all at risk."

"Utter nonsense," Hope said, boiling inside. Violet's imagination always did veer towards the dramatic and tended to run riot. But putting silly ideas like that into her head – that was unforgiveable. "Whoever put that idea in your head needs sorting out. It was an accident, pure and simple."

"That's not what the police are saying," Violet said. "And if they are out to kill us all it's another good reason to leave town. At least I know I'll be safe with Bert." She stomped away, leaving Hope staring after her.

Was there any truth to the rumours going round? Had it been a deliberate act and were they in danger? Or was it a fight that had got out of hand? She could imagine that. She decided to go and see what she could find out from Inspector Penhalligan. She couldn't think anyone would want to do them ill, but you never knew with people. If they were at risk it was best to know about it.

In the market she'd be among friends anyway. Seeing Ned's cheery face as he chatted to the customers brought a glow of warmth inside her. His eyes lit up as she approached and his smile broadened. "How's my best girl this morning?" he asked.

Hope's resolve faltered. "I've just come from the hospital," she said.

His face fell. "Not bad news I hope."

Tears stung her eyes as she told him what the doctor had said about her mother.

"If it had been a matter of paying we'd have managed something," he said when she told him about the sanatorium. "But you have to be guided by what the doctor says."

"I know. And talking of paying," she fished into her bag and brought out some of her tip money. "I want to repay you for paying our rent. I'll be paying Betsy out of my tips from now on. You've done more than enough for us and I want to repay you."

"There's no need," Ned said.

"Please. It'll make me feel a little better."

Reluctantly he took the offered cash. "If ever you need anything, anything at all, you know you can rely on me."

"I know, and I'm grateful. You've done more than I can ever repay, but at least this will go a small way to repaying our debt."

Ned shook his head. "There's no debt 'atween us, Hope. Whatever I do for you it's cos I value our friendship. Nowt else."

"As do I," Hope said. "I hope we can always be friends but I can't expect you to take on the rest of the family's problems. We have to deal with them ourselves."

"Whatever you say, love. But don't forget, I'm always here for you."

"Thank you." Hope leaned over and planted a kiss on his cheek. "I won't forget."

Her next port of call was the police station where she asked to speak to Inspector Penhalligan. Again she was asked to wait, while a message was sent to him. The messenger reappeared to take her to his office.

He rose as she entered and indicated the chair in front of his desk. "Please take a seat," he said. Today he was smoking a pipe and wearing a tweed jacket. He looked more like a country gentleman than a policeman.

"What can I do for you today?" he asked, smiling as though he had all the time in the world to speak to her. That was one thing she'd noticed about him the first time she saw him. He had an old fashioned grace about him and no sense that his time was more valuable than the next man's.

"I wondered whether you had any more information about what started the fire. There's a rumour going round that Pa was murdered and the fire set deliberately. Surely it was an accident? I can't think of anyone who'd want to hurt us."

The Inspector shrugged. "Perhaps someone your father owed money to? A lesson about paying one's debts?"

"No. Only…" She couldn't bear to say his name. If it was about an unpaid debt there was only one person it could be. And he'd never be so stupid.

"I'm sorry I can't help you," she said.

His smile vanished quicker than it had appeared. "No. And I'm afraid I can't discuss details of the case with you. But rest assured we are doing all we can to find out what happened and why."

"My sister feels that we should be in fear of our lives. If there's a murderer on the loose none of us are safe. He's killed Pa. Who knows who might be next?"

Inspector Penhalligan bit his lip as though trying to suppress an inappropriate response. "I can assure you you have nothing to fear. If indeed your father was a victim of foul play as we suspect it was he alone who was targeted."

"Why? And how can you be so sure?"

"As I said I can't discuss the case with you but I do have something for you."

He turned to the filing cabinet, opened a drawer and took out a strangely shaped parcel wrapped in brown paper. He unwrapped it and laid it open on the desk. "Is this what you were asking about?" he said. The warmth in his voice surprised her.

Alfie's metal leg brace lay in front of her. "Oh yes, thank you. He'll be so pleased to get it back."

"Hmm." The Inspector sank into his chair shaking his head. "There was no sign of any crutch. We can only suppose it got burnt in the fire. Strange though. It wasn't by the bed with the brace."

"It wouldn't be if Alfie had to get out of bed to get to the stairs where he fell. He would have been using it to get down the stairs."

"And why would he get up from his bed in the middle of the night and go downstairs? Unless of course he heard something that woke him and he went to investigate."

"As I told you, he remembers nothing. We can only guess why he was up but we cannot know for sure." Hope picked up the leg brace, wrapping the paper around it and stood up to leave. "So, unless his memory returns, I'm afraid we can be of no further help to you in your investigation. Good day."

The Inspector sprang up and rushed to open the door for her. "Well, if you think of anything, anything at all…"

"I'll let you know."

"Thank you."

As Hope left the building she had the distinct feeling that Inspector Penhalligan hadn't finished with them yet. Not only that, he was enjoying her discomfort far more than she was comfortable with. The memory of Alfie's entreaties about it not being his fault and him not being to blame played in her mind. Why would he think that? And why had he got out of bed? And was Violet right to be afraid? Was there more to Pa's death than they supposed?

Chapter Twenty Two

"I've got something for you," Hope said to Alfie later that afternoon. "Close your eyes."

He dutifully closed them and she placed his leg brace into his outstretched arms. When he opened his eyes a huge smile spread across his face.

"Thank you," he said. "Now they'll have to let me get out of bed and come home."

Hope chuckled. "Not so sure about that," she said, "but it's a step in the right direction. She frowned. "They couldn't find your crutch. Do you remember why you got out of bed and why you were going downstairs?"

"Was I?"

"Yes, that must be when you fell. Don't you remember?"

He shook his head. "The last thing I remember is being in bed. I wanted to read but the candle went out. So I think I went to sleep. Then I woke up here." His eyes filled with tears and Hope decided not to press him any further.

"It's all right. It doesn't matter. You're here and you're getting better. That's what's important. Now, should I read to you?"

He brightened again. "Yes please." He handed her one of the books Silas had brought. It was about a boy's adventures on the Mississippi River. The boy was called Huckleberry Finn.

When Hope arrived back at Betsy's in time for tea before their evening shifts at The Grenadier she found John in a sullen mood. "You left early?" he said. "I wanted to go to the bank to open an account so we could save up to pay Silas Quirk back what Pa owed." He'd obviously expected Hope to hand over her tips to open this account.

"Surely we should be thinking about paying back what we owe first? I've been to see Ned and paid him back some of the rent money. I'm going to pay Betsy the rent from now on and I'll pay Ned back, every penny. We can't go on living on other people's charity."

"But we agreed, Hope. We'd put our money together to pay off Pa's debts."

"No, John. You agreed. I didn't. Running the pub is your dream, not mine. I'll do everything I can to help you, and yes, I'll give you some of my tips towards it, but I'm going to put Ma and Alfie first, then we'll see."

He glowered, his face reddening. "If you don't trust me…"

"I trust you, like I trusted Pa and look where that got us," she said. The memory of him passing his losses off onto Thomas O'Reilly wasn't far from her mind either. "I'll be taking a leaf out of Violet's book and taking charge of my own future."

"But the pub, Ma and Pa's home, our home…"

John's distraught look melted Hope's heart and, against her better judgement, she fished into her bag and brought out her remaining coins. "Here," she said. "But make sure it goes into the bank, not onto the card tables."

"Cross my heart," John said and Hope wished with all hers that she could believe him.

After they'd had some tea Hope offered to help Betsy with the washing up but she hushed her up. "Go on away with you, you get off. I'll sort this."

So, for the second time John and Hope walked to The Grenadier. This time they went directly round to the staff entrance at the back where a porter let them in. Hope went upstairs to change into her dress for the evening and John went to find Jo the restaurant maître d'.

Hope made her way to the boudoir where she found Dexi getting ready for the evening. Hortense was finishing her hair. To her surprise she saw Dexi smoking a small cheroot.

"I didn't know you smoked," she said.

Dexi smiled. "Not many people do," she said. "Silas doesn't approve so I only smoke up here. He still knows though but says nothing." She glanced meaningfully at Hope. "Silas knows everything," she said. She picked up a perfume bottle and sprayed a halo of sweet smelling orange blossom over her head and shoulders. She smiled at her reflection. "How are your mother and brother? Making a good recovery I hope."

"Alfie is a little better and eager to come home," Hope said. "Ma's recovery will take a little longer." She didn't want to admit, even to herself, that Ma would never recover. Miracles happen, don't they? What they needed was a miracle. "Thank you for the books Silas brought in for Alfie. It was a kind thought."

Dexi waved her thanks away. "It was nothing. I know what it's like to be confined to bed for a long period of time. I hope they will provide a means of escape for him, especially after what he's been through."

Another surprise, Hope thought. She'd never even considered that Dexi and, by association Silas, would have had any problems in the past. They had money. Surely money solved all your problems?

Dexi turned back to the mirror and patted a stray curl of hair back into place. "I'll leave you to get ready," she said as she rose from the chair. "When you're finished I'll be in the Saloon. We can continue our little chat there." She nodded to Hortense as she swept out.

Hope sat while Hortense curled her hair with a hot iron which she kept poking into the embers glowing in the grate. "I do ringlets," Hortense said. "Ringlets suit you. Make very pretty."

Hope wasn't sure, fearing the heat of the irons would singe her hair, but Hortense brandished the tongs with surprising expertise and after about fifteen minutes a cloud of golden ringlets bounced around her shoulders whenever she moved her head. Hortense fastened the ringlets into a cascade down the back of Hope's head and then her fingers pulled the strands into thin fronds around Hope's face and, once again she was transformed.

Hope followed Hortense into the dressing room where she again put on the blue dress and Sapphire necklace Dexi had left out of the safe for her.

Downstairs in the Saloon Dexi sat at her table dealing out the cards. She was alone in the room, it being early evening. "Please," she said to Hope, indicating the seat opposite her. "I want to show you something."

Hope sat.

Dexi dealt ten cards in front of Hope, face up on top of each other. Then she gathered them up. "Now, tell me, what cards did I just deal?"

Hope frowned. She recalled three and a possible fourth, but the rest were a blur. Then Dexi did the same dealing a pile of at least twenty cards on the table. After she gathered them up she handed the pack to Hope and recited the order of all twenty cards. Every one was correct.

"That's why I win," she said. "It's a skill that can be learned, if you have patience and time, but not everyone cares enough to learn. They rely on luck to win games. I rely on skill."

"So you would put my father's bad luck down to lack of commitment to the game?"

Dexi shook her head. "Your pa wasn't a card player. He speculated for much higher stakes than you'd find on one of my tables. If I see anyone losing so badly it would affect their lives I refuse to indulge them. They're thrown out until the debts are paid. Then they can try their luck again, but I'm not in the business of ruining my clients. There's no future in that is there?"

She paused and looked levelly at Hope. "I know you think Silas is to blame for your father's many misfortunes, but I can assure you that's not the case. Men choose their own path to ruin. You cannot blame another for their short-comings."

By the time Hope left to join Poppy at the bar she felt she'd learned a valuable lesson. It was true, she did blame Silas for all their woes, but if Pa hadn't gambled here he'd have gambled somewhere else. It was in his nature. Then she remembered Silas running into the burning building and saving Alfie. She owed him more than she could say for that. But she did wonder what Pa speculated on, if not cards?

Poppy was already in the bar putting bottles and glasses onto her silver tray when Hope arrived to start work there. She looked stunning as usual. A spray of crimson silk lilies matching the colour of her gown pinned into the dark rolls of hair framing her face gave her an exotic look few men could resist. Her willing demeanour also made her popular. Only the staff at the club ever caught a glimpse of the steel behind that pleasing facade. Hope knew she could learn a lot from Poppy.

"I wasn't sure you'd come back," Poppy said as Hope arrived in the bar. "Working here is not everyone's cup of tea, but you did well. I hoped you would return."

"Well, here I am," Hope said, picking up the tray Jake, tonight's barman, handed her.

"I suppose you've seen a few girls come and go," Hope said. "Although, personally I didn't find the work too onerous. Dealing with a bar full of drunken dockers is much worse and at least here I get tips."

Poppy laughed. "Yes. It looks easy, but don't be fooled. Dexi is very particular about protocol. Some girls get seduced by gentlemen with money making promises they have no intention of keeping. If you get a reputation as 'the good time had by everybody' you'll be out on your ear pronto."

Hope bristled. "I certainly don't intend to be anyone's 'good time'," she said. "I'm only here under an obligation to pay off my father's debt, then I'll be out of here."

Poppy raised her eyebrows. "I warn all the girls about the consequences of disreputable behaviour, but you'd be surprised how many still succumb to the members' flattery. If it's money you're after many think there are quicker ways to earn it."

"Not me," Hope said.

"We'll see."

Then a couple of gentlemen came in and Poppy left to charm them into buying champagne to start the evening off.

Throughout the evening Hope glided between the tables, topping up drinks, providing napkins and fresh glasses. Several times she felt a pinch in places the members had no right to pinch. She watched Poppy, admiring her skill in avoiding hands put out to grope her and how she always managed it with a smile and a mild rebuke.

During a lull, at the bar Poppy poured herself a gin and one for Hope. "Here, you look as though you could do with this," she said.

Hope took the offered drink and thankfully sipped it. It felt good. "You said everyone has a reason for wanting money," she said. "What's yours?"

"Me? I'm saving up. One day I'll have a place of my own. My club will be the best in London. Everyone will want to come and I'll be calling the shots."

Hope had no doubt that Poppy would one day achieve her dream.

By the end of the evening, which was past midnight, Hope's bag of chips felt even heavier than the day before. She'd spent the evening watching the tables, making sure she topped up the winners who were in a good mood and avoided wasting her time with men who'd lost their stake and expected credit as some sort of compensation.

When anyone won a big pot they'd call for champagne and Hope made sure she was the nearest to fetch it, so her pile of chips grew steadily larger. Watching the tables and the size of the pots, the amount of money bet on even dodgy hands, she soon came to realise that Dexi was right. The people who studied the game, watched the cards, took only minor risks and knew when to walk away finished up with chips rattling in their pockets. It was the others who lost. She also came to realise that the big money was won on the tables, not by waitresses serving drinks.

The evening had quietened down enough for the barman to manage the customers' refills so Dexi allowed Hope and Poppy to go. Poppy disappeared upstairs first so Hortense could help her change into her outdoor things, then Hope went up.

"Do you sleep here?" Hope asked as Hortense unlaced her dress and helped her step out of it. "No. I go home when Mrs Malone retires. Back at six in the morning to help her bathe and dress."

"That's a long day."

"I strong," Hortense said, hanging Hope's gown back on the rack with the other shimmering creations. She picked up the hairbrush, unpinned Hope's curls and began brushing her hair out into soft curls around her shoulders.

Hope's curiosity was aroused. "You've been with Mrs Malone a long time. Did you ever meet her husband?"

"Masser Jack? He very handsome man. Reckless though. Many bad enemies. He come to bad end did Masser Jack."

Hope wanted to enquire further, but Hortense stepped back. "There, you finished," she said, handing

Hope the clothes she'd arrived in which were now neatly pressed.

"Thank you," Hope said.

Hortense nodded. "I see you tomorrow," she said and went back into the dressing room, closing the door behind her.

On the way downstairs, to where John was waiting to take her home, she glimpsed the back of a man disappearing into the corridor leading to Silas's office. A man who looked exactly like Inspector Oakley Penhalligan. What on earth is he doing here, she thought. Her brow creased into a frown. The thought didn't linger long, but she was intrigued and determined to ask him next time she saw him.

Chapter Twenty Three

Walking home with John, whose face was longer than a wet Sunday afternoon and just as miserable, Hope couldn't help thinking about Hortense, the long hours she worked and how little she had to show for it. Perhaps John was right. They had been given an opportunity to do better for themselves and maybe she should be grateful and make the most of it, instead of resenting every minute she spent at the club. John would get the pub licence back, but that didn't mean she had to work there with him. His heart was there, hers wasn't. Perhaps it was time she took charge of her own life and did the same as Poppy, save her money to follow her own dream, not John's.

As the days melded into weeks, Easter came and went and the weather improved, getting brighter and the days longer. Every day Alfie asked about coming home and Hope thought it about the right time, so she asked Betsy about having him there. With them both working they'd have to rely on her goodwill.

"I hate to think of him being left on his own while he's still so poorly," Hope said. "He can sleep in our room and he'll be no bother."

"How's he going to get up the stairs with a gammy leg and the other one broken? No, he's best staying where he is," John said. "Doctors can look after him."

Hope shot him a glare so icy it would turn the devil to stone. "He'll get on better here with us, John, and you know it. If Betsy doesn't mind?"

"'Course not. I can make up a bed for 'im down here if needs be. I'll be glad of the company of an evening," Betsy said. "No point leaving 'im in that hospital when he'd be better off here."

"That's settled then," Hope said. "As soon as the doctor says he's all right to travel I'll bring him home. Thank you, Betsy, we do appreciate it, don't we, John?"

John grunted.

As soon as she could Hope made her way to the hospital to speak to the doctor looking after Alfie. The nurse on duty directed her to the doctor's office where she sat outside awaiting his return from his rounds.

"Miss Daniels isn't it?" he said when he saw her. "Is it about your mother?"

Hope smiled, glad that he'd remembered her. "No, not this time, it's about my little brother, Alfie Daniels. I was wondering when he'd be allowed home."

"Hmm." The doctor thought for a moment. "He was injured in the same fire that damaged your mother's lungs so badly wasn't he? Although, if I recall correctly he's making good progress and should be able to go home soon."

"Thank you, doctor. He'll be happy to hear that, but how soon is 'soon'?"

"How long is a piece of string?" the doctor chuckled, shrugging his shoulders. "His leg is broken but he should be able to walk with crutches. He has his leg brace too, so that shouldn't be a problem. I see no reason he can't go home, provided he keeps taking the infusion, watching his chest, rubbing it with camphor to clear his airways. You'll need to bring him back in a couple of weeks when his leg has healed, but that can be done in the clinic if you can bring him back when required."

"I can," Hope said, although she wasn't quite sure how she'd manage it if he could only walk short distances. "I mean I'll find a way if he's allowed home. I'm sure his recovery will be much quicker there."

"Then, as soon as you've acquired some crutches he can go. Let me know when that's been arranged and transport for him and I'll see the nurse has a supply of his medication."

"Thank you," Hope said. At least with Alfie at home that'd be one less thing to worry about.

Alfie's radiant smile when she told him the news made up for all the anxiety Hope had felt persuading John and getting Betsy on side. At least with Alfie at home they'd feel more like a family again. Then there was only Ma to worry about.

"I'll need to find some crutches for you and make arrangements but, if you're very good, I'll be back tomorrow and then we can take you home," Hope said.

"I won't have to go back to school yet will I?" Alfie said. "Not with my chest and broken leg."

"No, I'll be able to teach you at home for a while," Hope said, aware that getting him back to school was yet another hurdle they'd have to overcome. But that was in the future. One thing at a time, she thought.

After she left Alfie Hope spoke to the nurse about getting him a pair of crutches. She pointed her in the direction of the clinic where she said they had a few she could look at. She chose a pair that would be about the right size for Alfie, gave the nurse a generous donation and arranged to have them taken to Alfie so he could try them out. Then she went to see her mother who was, as usual, sleeping.

"Ma," she whispered. "It's me, Hope."

Ma's eyelids flickered and opened slowly. There was a far-a-way look in her eyes as though wearied by the effort. "How are you feeling, Ma? Any better?"

Ma closed her eyes and drifted back to sleep. It's the medication, Hope thought. Probably for the best to keep her sedated so her body could take its time to heal. "I'm taking Alfie to live with me and John at Betsy's house," she said in case Ma could hear. "He's getting better, Ma. I just wish you were too."

Ma's erratic breathing continued and Hope leaned over and kissed her forehead, hoping that she might be aware of it and it might bring her a little comfort.

"I'll be back tomorrow, Ma," she said. And, with her heart heavy in her chest she left to go and find a cab she could book to collect her and Alfie from the hospital the next day and take them to Betsy's house.

She found a hackney carriage driver with his cab waiting at the rank at the end of the road. He looked approachable and she arranged for him to be available the next morning.

Then she went to the market to buy Alfie some clothes. He'd been wearing a nightshirt when he went into the hospital and a hospital gown ever since. She managed to find some nearly new trousers in his size and a couple of shirts, a jumper, jacket, socks and pants.

"How's he going to manage though, with his leg and that?" Ned asked when she told him Alfie was coming home.

"I've got him some crutches. I hope he'll manage with them."

"Good. I'll pop round after the market tomorrow and see how's he's settling in," Ned said. "I know

Betsy's lovely but she's still a stranger to him. I can take him a couple of oranges and read to him while he eats them."

"You're very kind," Hope said. "He'll appreciate that."

When she got home she told John about the arrangements she'd made. "It'll take a while for the hospital to get him ready," she said. "But we can collect him after breakfast and bring him home."

"Hmm. I still think he'd be better off in the hospital," John said. "But if Betsy doesn't mind."

"She doesn't. In fact she's looking forward to it."

"Well, not much I can do about it then is there?"

"I thought you'd be pleased," Hope said. "At least it shows he's getting better."

John shrugged. "If you say so."

The next morning John went to get the cab while Hope went to the hospital to get Alfie dressed, so they'd be ready when the cab arrived to take them home. She wasn't surprised to see him sitting anxiously on the side of the bed with his crutches ready.

"Have you been waiting long?" she asked.

"Since I woke up," he said. "I was worried you wouldn't come."

She smiled. "I said I'd come and here I am."

She helped him ease himself off the bed taking his weight on the crutches, one under each arm with the plastered leg held out off the ground.

"See, I can do it," he said as his feet touched the floor. "I've been practising with the crutches."

"Well done," she said as she helped him dress. Then she walked with him to the hospital entrance. Progress was slow and she saw Alfie wince as his broken leg touched the ground, but he was determined to do it on his own.

"I can walk almost as good as before," he said. He couldn't but Hope was delighted at his enthusiasm. She glowed with pride as she watched him.

John was waiting outside with the cab and stepped forward to help Alfie in. Hope climbed in after him. It was a short ride to Betsy's house and when they arrived she was standing in the doorway waiting for them.

Once they got inside Betsy fussed over Alfie, just as Hope knew she would.

"I've made some scones specially," she said, ushering Alfie into the front room where he was to sleep. "An' I've borrowed a bed from next door. Didn't want you sleeping on floor, not with a broken leg."

"I'm sure we're very grateful," Hope said.

"Thank you," Alfie said, a bright smile on his face. "You're very kind."

Betsy insisted on them all sitting and having a cup of tea with the scones and jam. Alfie had milk. "Got to build you up," Betsy said. "They don't feed you right in hospital. I know that for sure."

Watching Betsy with Alfie she knew she'd made the right decision bringing him home.

When she was sure he was settled she went to see Ruth at the drapery store and offer her services if there were any items that needed to be hand embroidered.

Walking into the shop she nodded at the sales girl and made her way to the workroom at the back where she knew she'd find Miss Godley.

"I'm sorry," Ruth said, "but since I had the new sewing machines installed I've been able to manage the requests for embroidered items here in the shop. The customers seem to prefer them too. They get their orders so much more quickly. I seldom need hand embroidery now. Of course, if anything comes in I'll happily send it your way."

Hope thanked her. Even if Ruth didn't want her embroidery she thought about embroidering a few items herself which she could sell in the market. She wouldn't get as much as Ruth got from the shops in town, but that didn't mean there wasn't a market for hand-embroidered tablecloths, tray cloths, dressing table sets or pillow cases.

When she told Ned what she had in mind he encouraged her. "You could ask Betsy's daughter Lydia to sell them for you on her stall. I'm sure she'd be happy to oblige."

"Good idea," Hope said. "I'll ask her when she calls round this evening to collect the ironing from Betsy. I'm sure we can come to some arrangement that will suit us both."

That evening, by the time she and John were ready to go to the club, Betsy had cooked them a chicken stew for their tea. Hope had arranged with Lydia to sell anything she made for a small commission they were both happy about.

That evening at the club Hope worried about Alfie, it being his first night home and in a strange bed, but knowing Betsy was there to look after him put her mind at ease.

By the time she left to walk home with John the stars were bright in the clear night sky and a full moon cast a light over the empty streets. There was dampness in the air but the earlier rain had ceased leaving the pavements wet with the unique freshness that comes after a shower of rain. It was as though the streets had been washed and were a little cleaner, but not much.

At home John went straight up to bed but Hope went to check on Alfie in the bed downstairs Betsy had made up for him. The gaslight had been turned low so if he woke and couldn't remember where he was it wouldn't be dark for him. Hope turned it up a little and saw Alfie had been tossing and turning in his sleep. She heard him mumbling. His little body was shaking and his nightshirt damp with sweat. Her heart went out to him.

She leaned over to gently touch his shoulder to sooth him and he called out, first for Ma and then for Pa. "Shush," she cooed softly, stroking his arm to calm him. "It's all right. You're home now and safe."

At the sound of her voice he relaxed, the tension drained from his body and the pain vanished from his face leaving it pale and grey. His breathing deepened and he slept more soundly. She reached out to touch his face. It was wet with tears. It would be a while before he'd sleep peacefully through the night without the nightmare he'd seen tonight, but she felt sure it would come all the sooner for him being home with people who loved and cared for him and could keep him safe.

Once he'd got used to Betsy and sleeping downstairs Alfie was happy to be home. Hope rubbed his chest with camphor every morning and evening, his constant cough receding each day as she did so. After a few weeks the plaster on his leg was removed as he was able to get about more easily on his crutches. As the weather improved and spring turned to summer he would walk a little way with Hope when she went to the market, each day walking a little further. Gradually, as the strength in his leg returned the crutches were discarded, although Hope still insisted he had a nap in the afternoon.

"I'm not a baby," he said. "I don't need a nap," but she did notice that, on afternoons after even a short walk in the fresh air in the morning to build him up and strengthen his leg, his eyelids flickered and closed while he slept for a while in the chair.

Over the following days Hope fell into the routine of helping Alfie with his lessons from books she managed to find in the market. She set him some sums to do and then listened to him reading while she worked on her embroidery. Seeing the neatness of her stitches Betsy suggested she take in some mending and darning. "There's plenty round here would pay to have their clothes mended rather than fork out for new," she said. "I'll put the word out to my customers."

And she did. Hope soon found her work basket overflowing with things to be stitched or darned before she went to the hospital to visit Ma.

John spent most of his time looking for odd jobs he could do in town to earn a little money, going to the pub to see how the work was progressing, talking to the surveyor or going to the brewery about the licence before they both headed off together to their jobs at The Grenadier. He called in to see Ma once or twice but she was so sleepy she hardly knew he was there.

As Hope's mood lightened with Alfie's recovery, John's became more morose and sullen. "The brewery won't make a decision until the work's almost finished," he said one evening. "I keep telling them it's our home and our possessions upstairs, but they just keep saying, 'We'll see'. I don't know what we'll do if

I don't get it. We don't want to work for Silas Quirk any longer than we have to."

"Well, at least the money's good and we can put a bit by," Hope said. She found the thought of going back to the pub and working for John far less appealing to her than it was to him. In fact she enjoyed working at the club, finding it less onerous and more profitable than she'd ever imagined.

"Jo, the maitre d's been telling me about his life in America," John said. "He says there's opportunities there for people like me. People who don't mind putting in a good days graft to get on. It's a young country, he says, and I could do worse than try my luck there."

"Go to America, you mean? Surely that'd mean starting over with nothing?"

"Nothing's what we've got here if I don't get the licence," he said. "Working at the club's all right for now, but I'm not going to spend the rest of my life waiting tables for somebody else. I want my own place, be my own boss."

"Hmm. Nice to have a choice," Hope said. It seemed that waiting tables for somebody else was deemed to be all right for her, but not for him. Then she realised that his bitterness stemmed more from their loss than anything else and she immediately forgave him.

"Well, let's hope it doesn't come to that," she said, although she did begin to wonder which would be worse; going back to the pub and working for him or losing him to some place across the ocean. The words 'rats' and 'sinking ship' came into her mind, but she didn't say them.

Over the weeks Hope had become as adept as Poppy at avoiding the groping hands of men who were old enough to know better and over time her confidence grew. There were one or two incidents she'd happily forget; once or twice men who were the worse for drink forgot their manners and made inappropriate advances, and one man had managed to pin her against the wall, becoming overfriendly, but as soon as a porter or the barman appeared they faded away.

Listening to the talk at the bar, or around the tables, she soon came to know the members' businesses as well as they did themselves. She knew the ones who came from wealth and position, and the ones who'd got where they were by their own efforts. She recognised the chancers and the social climbers, the hangers on, the ones who'd sponge off their friends and the ones who'd be loyal no matter what.

She learned who was in debt and could ill afford to lose and those who seemed to have unlimited funds, which ones kept a mistress and how well they treated them. She found out what they thought about each other and why.

She came to know which ones had enjoyed a distinguished military career and those from wealthy families whose futures were mapped out for them even before they were born. She even felt sorry for the ones who'd had no choice in their careers but had to follow in their fathers' footsteps, although wasn't that what John wanted to do?

"You certainly get to know people in this job," she said to Poppy.

"You see the best and worst in them," Poppy said. "*In vino veritas*, in wine there is truth."

Hope smiled. There was more to Poppy than met the eye too.

Ned called round as often as he could in the afternoons when he'd packed up his stall. Hope would make him some tea, or, if the afternoon was fine, they'd go for a walk together.

"Honestly, Ned," she said. "I swear more business is done in that bar and restaurant than ever gets done in the companies' offices. It's all wheeling and dealing. A man will be pleading poverty one day to a supplier he owes money to, and the next day will be buying everyone drinks and bragging how well his business is doing. I wouldn't trust one of them as far as I could throw him."

"What about the bare-knuckle boxing and the dog fighting," Ned said. "They get some violent coves there for that, or so I've heard, and not always honest ones either."

"I've left by then," Hope said. "Dexi sends us home as soon as the action looks like it's moving downstairs, that's where the fights take place."

"What about Quirk. Do you see much of him?"

"No, not much. I'm in the card room with Poppy and Dexi. He takes care of the more violent parts of the club."

"Good job too," Ned said. He never questioned or criticised Hope's reasons for working there, but she always felt his unspoken displeasure.

The next morning Hope went to the hospital to see Ma. She was surprised to see Violet there, feeding Ma with spoonfuls of broth. "What are you doing? What's that you're giving her?" she said, irritated that Violet should have taken it upon herself to see to Ma without checking with her or John first.

"It's broth with some herbs in. Bert knows this woman. She's a healer. She makes up these medicines. Bert says he's seen really ill people recover after taking her mixtures. I'm sure it will help Ma get better too."

Hope could say little about it as Ma actually did look a little brighter, although that could have been because of her visitor. She didn't want to upset Violet by telling her what the doctor had said, not in front of Ma anyway. If she had to be told she'd do it outside, but doctors could be wrong, couldn't they? Miracles did happen. "Have you been to see Alfie? You know he's at home now don't you?"

"Yes, the doctor told me. I hope he liked the books I brought in for him and I'm glad he's well enough to be treated at home. But Ma's not, so it's up to all of us to do everything we can to make her better isn't it?"

"Of course. How are you, Ma? You're looking a bit better."

Ma smiled and raised her hand but it was obvious that speaking was too much of an effort.

"How's John?" Violet asked, tipping another spoonful of broth into Ma's mouth.

"He's fine. You could go and see him, although he spends most of his time at the brewery. He's hoping to get the licence transferred when the pub's been cleared and the investigation's finished. He wants to reopen when we all move back there." She didn't mention his plans to go away if he didn't get the licence.

"Move back there?" Violet said. "I have no intention of moving back. If John thinks I'm coming home to skivvy for him, working in the pub or taking Ma's place in the kitchen he can think again. Bert's going on tour soon and I'm going with him, like I told you. Ma agreed too, didn't you, Ma?" Ma closed her eyes and let out a big sigh. A dribble of broth ran down to her chin.

Hope wiped it away as Ma drifted off to sleep again.

Outside the hospital Hope said to Violet, "Do call round to see Alfie and John. I'm sure they'd both be happy to see you and see you're keeping well."

"Hmm. I'll think about it," Violet said, but Hope wasn't holding her breath.

Chapter Twenty Four

Over the summer Alfie grew stronger and by the beginning of June was able to go out every day. He helped Betsy with the wash by turning the mangle for her and did bits of shopping. Hope was happy with his progress in reading, writing and arithmetic too.

John told her the pub had been cleaned out and they could now go back and make plans to redecorate the upstairs and salvage what they could of their possessions.

"If we all work at it and clean and sort things out we could be moving back by the end of the month," he said.

Hope recalled Violet's words about going on tour with Bert and not working as a skivvy for John for no pay and very little thanks. "I'll come and do what I can," she said. "But don't rely on Violet coming home. I think she has other plans."

John shrugged. "So she told me. I fear the worst as far as Bert is concerned. If she's relying on him she's in for a disappointment. I hope I'm wrong, but Violet has made her bed and will have to lie in it," he said.

The next morning, while Alfie was out running an errand for Betsy, there was a knock on the door.

Hope opened it and her heart sank like a stone in deep water. Mr Mackitterick the schoolmaster was standing on the doorstep.

"Good morning, Miss Daniels," he said, raising his hat. "I've called to see your brother Alfie and find out when he'll be returning to school."

It was the moment Hope had been dreading. Alfie was physically well enough to return to school, but psychologically was a different matter.

"I'm teaching him at home," Hope told the schoolmaster, keeping him standing on the doorstep. "You can see his work if you like. You'll see he's making excellent progress."

Mackitterick shook his head. "The Law says he has to attend school, unless you can show he is being taught by a bona fide teacher, which I assume you're not, given your previous employment as a barmaid."

"He's been unwell, as you know. He was seriously injured in the fire that took my father and left my mother hanging onto life by a thread. You can't expect a young boy like Alfie to get over that sort of thing in an instant."

"So that's why I've just seen him down the market is it?" It was clear from the smirk on his face that he was enjoying every minute of the encounter. "As you know there's a law about truanting and evading education, Miss Daniels. We don't want him brought up before the school board do we?"

"He's not ready to return to school. I'll let you know when he is. Good day, Mr Mackitterick," she said and, heart pounding, slammed the door in his face. Poor Alfie, she thought. It was true she'd been avoiding mentioning his returning to school because she knew he hated it so much, but as Mr Mackitterick said, it was the law. She'd even considered moving him to a different school, but any other school would be too far for him to walk.

When Alfie returned from the market she told him about Mr Mackitterick's visit. His face fell and the cheery little boy who'd been so brave about his own injuries and losing his father burst into tears. "Do I have to go back?" he said.

"You will have to go back soon," Hope said. "You're almost better. I can't keep you at home forever, you know that."

Alfie nodded, hung his head, limped across the room and flung himself, sobbing, onto his bed. Hope's heart turned over. Why did life have to be so cruel, she thought. And why was it always Alfie that came off worst of all?

At breakfast the next morning Hope could see Alfie was still upset. "I'm going with John to look at the pub" she said. "Do you want to come with us?"

A look of horror filled Alfie's face.

"We don't know what we'll find when we get there," John said. "I don't think we should take Alfie. Best wait until we've cleaned it up a bit."

"Oh, of course, you're right," Hope said. "Sorry, I didn't think." She reached into her bag and took out sixpence and handed it to Alfie. "Here, buy yourself an ice cream or some candy and there's a Punch and Judy Show over the park. You'll enjoy that."

Alfie took the sixpence but his mood didn't brighten. "Thanks," he said.

After breakfast Hope went with John to inspect the pub premises. He'd been told they could go upstairs and see to their belongings. When they arrived the windows of the pub were still boarded and inside was dark and empty. John removed one of the boards covering the window to give them more light. They stood and gazed around in silence. The whole place smelled of new wood and plaster. The beams had been replaced and the ceiling and walls painted. A new oak bar stood where the old bar had been. The walls were bare. Their footsteps on the floorboards echoed in the empty room as they walked through to the back storeroom Pa used as his office. It too was bare and empty, the damaged furniture and fittings having been removed.

Walking around, every room they came to looked bigger than she remembered. She recalled the pictures they'd had on the walls, the crimson curtains that hung on a brass rail, the plush covered benches and the tables and chairs where she'd served drinks since she was ten years old. It all seemed so strange and empty without Ma and Pa's physical presence which had filled the space for as long as she could remember.

Wordlessly John opened the newly fitted cellar door and they descended the freshly painted steps into the cool darkness below. John lit the lamp left there by the workmen and shone the light around bare, freshly plastered walls. There was no sign of the devastating fire that had taken Pa's life. A shiver ran down Hope's spine.

"This looks a little different," John said. He walked over to where the doors opened above them to give access to the pavement. The long wooden chute down which the barrels rolled into the cellar used to be hinged and dropped down once the doors were opened. Now a much bigger metal chute was hinged to the side of the door frame and John had to unlock it before it could be let down to reveal the two metal doors that opened onto the pavement above. These in turn were secured by two hasps and staples each padlocked into place. "This is all new," he said.

"The old wooden doors would have gone up in flames," Hope said. "The metal ones won't."

"Must have been ferocious, the fire," John said. "Probably hot enough to bend metal an' all."

Hope nodded, a sick feeling in her stomach at the thought of it.

As they made their way back up the cellar steps, Hope pushed away the thought of her father lying there at the bottom and being consumed by the fire. It was too terrible to contemplate.

In the kitchen they were pleasantly surprised. The walls had been cleaned and plastered and a gas boiler installed over the sink. The old cooking range had been replaced with a new oven. "This looks a good deal better than it was," John said. "My fear is that with all the improvements and refurbishing they'll hike the rent up so we can't afford to stay anyway." He took one more glance about the room. "Come on," he said. "Might as well face the rest."

Together they made their way back to the small hall behind the bar. The wooden staircase leading to the upper floor had been replaced. John went ahead, still carrying the lamp in the semi-darkness.

Upstairs everywhere the walls were streaked with soot and grime. The air reeked of smoke and burning cloth. Hope raised her handkerchief to cover her nose and mouth, but the smell had got into her nostrils and she thought it would be there forever. What hadn't been damaged by the fire had been ruined by the water from the firemen's hoses.

"Oh, my Lord, John. It's a mess," she said.

The smoke had permeated every fibre of their clothes, furnishings, bedding, rugs and curtains. Opening every door revealed another pile of discarded burnt or damaged things. Hope rushed to open a window to let in some fresh air. She walked around in a daze, picking up garment after garment, sheet after sheet and blanket after blanket, only to drop them in helpless dismay.

"It's dreadful," she said. "Far worse than I ever supposed. Everything is ruined." Tears sprung to her eyes as her mother's precious things, Violet's beautiful clothes and Pa's most treasured possessions fell from her hands.

John also went through everything, turning it over in his hands in dismay. "Can nothing be saved?" he asked.

Hope took a breath and squared her shoulders. "We'll have to sort through what's worth keeping and what needs throwing. I'll take what I can to Betsy to wash. Once we've thrown out the worst we can try washing down the walls and the furniture and it won't look so bad.

"Yes. We mustn't give up. We have to save as much as we can. If you, me, Violet and even our Alfie work together..." his voice faded as though he realised the futility of hoping.

"Well I wouldn't rely on Violet if I were you," she said. "She's going on tour with Bert, remember? She's gone, John, and she won't be coming back."

John raised his eyebrows and shook his head. "Well good luck to her," he said. "She'll need it."

In their parents' room the heavy bedspread had saved most of the bed and bedding from the worst of the smoke and water. Hope pulled it off and laid it on the floor. "Anything beyond saving can go there," she said. "We can take it to the rag man. He'll give us a few pennies for it."

John nodded and started picking the clothes off the chairs and those hanging outside the wardrobe onto the bedspread. Clothing left out had suffered the worst of the damage. The clothing in the wardrobe had suffered less, although it all still smelled of smoke. The brushes and combs on Ma's dressing table were blackened beyond recognition. Hope swept them into a box to be thrown out. She took down the curtains and added them to the rapidly growing pile for the rag man.

After their parents' bedroom, John went to do his and Hope went into the room she shared with Violet. First she went through her own wardrobe and sorted out a small bundle of things that were not too badly damaged. "What should we do with Violet's things?" she called to John, staring at the beautiful gowns Violet was so proud of, now dirty and smelling.

John came in, gathered them all into his arms and yanked them out of the wardrobe. "If she's not coming back I'll not be spending good money saving her stuff," he said and flung them on the pile for the rag man.

In Alfie's room Hope's despair increased. It was a small room and every wall was blackened. He didn't have many clothes but the clothes he did have were scattered around on a chair, on the bed and on the floor. She picked a shirt up from the bed and immediately dropped it back again. Nothing in Alfie's room was worth saving.

The upstairs parlour, being at the back, was the least damaged. By the time they'd gone through all the rooms picking out what could be salvaged, it was time to go home and get ready for their jobs at The Grenadier.

Hope took the bundles downstairs. She would take the smaller bundles of clothes to Betsy to be washed and John the largest bundle to the rag man. He took the things to throw away and put them in the bins in the yard to be collected with the rubbish. All the while a sickening feeling of loss and foreboding swirled in Hope's stomach. She swallowed back the nausea rising in her throat.

Sunday morning John said he was going to see if he could get any hot water on at the pub. "We'll certainly need it," he said.

Hope took Alfie to the market to get him clothes for school and to buy material and silks for the embroidered items Lydia had agreed to sell for her. After completing her purchases she took Alfie to the park to feed the ducks, making the most of the late June sunshine.

Monday morning she helped him get ready for school. She smoothed his hair and buttoned his coat. "It's only a few weeks until the harvest holiday," she said, trying to pacify him a little. The dead, cold as ice look in his eyes told her it hadn't helped.

"I'll walk with you," she said, following him out of the door.

"It's all right, I can go by myself," Alfie said, but Hope wanted to speak to the Master to make sure Alfie wasn't mistreated.

They made slow progress. There'd been rain overnight and the pavements were still wet, but the air smelled fresh and clean. Light clouds scudded across a pearl grey sky, blown by a summer breeze. Alfie dragged his leg to show his reluctance. Her heart went out to him but there was nothing she could do. He had to go to school, it was the law.

She left him in the playground, sitting on a bench, his face filled with misery, waiting for the bell to ring.

"Alfie's better but still fragile," she told Mr Mackitterick. "I've brought him to school and I'll be holding you personally responsible for his wellbeing. If I see one cut, graze or bruise I'll know where to come."

"As I said before, Miss Daniels, boys will be boys. They like boisterous games and sometime indulge in scuffles and rough play. I can't be held responsible for that."

Hope knew he was right, but it didn't make her feel any better leaving Alfie there, knowing how unhappy it made him.

Every day for the next week Hope walked to school with Alfie. After leaving him she joined John in the pub where they scrubbed the walls, ceilings and woodwork in every room, the fittings and the furniture, trying to remove the smell of smoke and the dirt and grime that went with it. Every day, when Alfie came home she looked for any signs of bruising or ill treatment.

On Friday she was with John again working at the pub when they'd taken a break for some lunch. John bought some pies from the shop while Hope made the tea. She was unwrapping the pies when she mentioned that they'd need to think about refurbishing their home.

"We'll need new curtains and bedding in every room before we move back in," she said. "That won't be cheap."

"We can't afford anything new, Hope. We'll just have to manage with what we've got."

Hope stared at him. "I've been giving you my tips every day and with your wages we should have quite a bit put by. Surely we can spend it on making our home more comfortable and I wouldn't mind a new outfit either."

John's face reddened and he looked away.

"How much have we got, John?"

He shrugged. "There's not as much as you think," he said. "I've had expenses."

"Expenses? What expenses?" She couldn't think of anything he'd paid for. She was paying Betsy for their board and lodging and repaying Ned. Suspicion and anger coiled in her stomach. She recalled Thomas O'Leary being blamed for the stock shortages when John had been gambling with the takings. Suddenly the long absences and hours passing when he was supposed to be talking to the surveyor or the brewery made sense. "You've gambled it away haven't you?" she said.

"I've just had a run of bad luck, that's all. I'll get it back."

The red hot fury she'd been holding back for so long surfaced. She jumped up, threw down the pie she was about to put on a plate, wishing she could throw it at him. She glared at him. "If you think I'm working and paying you to go gambling it all away you're wrong," she said. "I'm not going to live my life like Ma, always making excuses and going without because it's been spent on drink and gaming. I'm not going to…"

She didn't get any further, the words died in her throat as Inspector Penhalligan walked into the kitchen.

"I'm sorry," he said. "I hope I'm not interrupting anything only the door was open." They both stared at him. Hope's face burned with embarrassment.

"I'm glad to have found you here as I have a few things I want to clear up," he said.

Chapter Twenty Five

Hope rushed to get Inspector Penhalligan a chair but he remained standing. "I wanted to ask about the cellar doors," he said. "The ones that open in the street."

John didn't look too happy about this intervention. "Yes?" he said. "We open them for deliveries. Nothing unusual about that."

"Did you have a delivery the day of the fire?"

"I'm not sure," John said. "Unlikely, it being Saturday. Delivery days were Mondays and Fridays."

"So, Friday would have been the last delivery before the fire?"

"Probably," John said.

"And the doors would be locked after the delivery?"

"Of course. Pa would have locked them himself. If he wasn't here I'd have done it. What's this all about? What are you saying?"

"I'm not saying anything but the fire officer found this." He produced a tangled mass of metal that appeared to be a heavy lock. "It's been badly damaged by the fire but, if you look carefully there are signs that it may have been forced."

Hope perked up. "You mean someone broke into the cellar? An intruder? Pa saw them so they killed him?" Relief flowed over her at the knowledge that the investigation had moved away from members of the family.

"It's a possibility," the Inspector said, "but they'd hardly be hoping to steal barrels of beer. There must be more to it than that. I wondered if you had any ideas."

"There were wines and spirits down there too," John said. "Could have been after them."

"It still doesn't make sense."

"It makes perfect sense to me," Hope said. "Pa went down to get some stock for the bar or uncork another barrel, disturbed a burglar and got hit over the head for his trouble."

"But why the fire?"

"To cover his tracks."

"The fire officer said the fire was started deliberately. There are traces of accelerant. They found some under the body so the fire was set before your father was killed."

"I don't see what difference that makes," John said.

"It makes a hell of lot of difference," Inspector Penhalligan said.

Hope fell silent.

"Then I'm afraid we can't help you," John said turning his attention back to the pie Hope had put on a plate for him.

Inspector Penhalligan took out his notebook. "We've been looking into your father's financial affairs," he said. "It appears that he borrowed a large sum of money some weeks before he died. Any idea what for? Or where it went?"

Hope and John exchanged glances. "No," John said. "And my father's financial affairs are none of your business."

"He's been murdered. That makes it our business." The tension prickling in the air between the men became palpable. John's body stiffened. He ran his fingers through his hair. Anger boiled in his eyes. The Inspector sighed.

He moved to sit at the table. "I'm trying to catch the person who killed your father," he said. "I could do with any help you can give me. I want to see the killer brought to justice. I would have thought you both want the same thing."

Hope looked at John. "We do," she said.

"Good. Now, did your father keep any paperwork anywhere other than his office? The papers we recovered from there were burnt beyond retrieval. Did he keep his books, or any papers anywhere else? A safe place perhaps?"

"There's a safe in the bedroom," Hope said. "He kept his important papers in there."

John glared at her.

"May I take a look?"

"Only Pa and John have keys," Hope said.

"John?"

Reluctantly John rose from the chair. "We've only just started cleaning up upstairs," he said. "It's a mess."

"I expect it is," the Inspector said. "But anything you could find may shed a little light on the reason for his murder."

John led Inspector Penhalligan upstairs. When they came down the Inspector carried Pa's books and a bundle of other papers. John looked as miserable as the Inspector looked happy. "Thank you," the Inspector said. "I'm sure these will prove invaluable to help solve the mystery."

Hope was seeing him out when a small boy came running up to the pub door. Panting for breath he said, "'ospital sent me. Said as how you was to come, if'n you be Mister Daniels."

Hope called John and guided the lad into the room.

"I'm John Daniels," John said. "What else did they say?"

"Nowt, 'cept you was to come quick."

"It must be Ma," Hope said. "She's taken a turn for the worse."

John's face turned ashen. He handed the lad a penny and moved towards the door.

"I'll come with you," Inspector Penhalligan said.

Hope grabbed her shawl and, pulses racing, joined them on the pavement pulling the door closed behind her. The Inspector waved to the driver of the hansom standing at the kerb waiting for him. "It'll be quicker if we go together," he said ushering them into the cab.

The ride to the hospital was a blur. The cab rattled over cobbles. Hope's heart was in her mouth. Thoughts dashed through her mind as they thundered through the narrow streets, jostled together. Ma must be sinking fast. Violet should be told but they didn't know where she was. Who else would they need to tell? The brewery? Ned? Did she have any distant relatives who'd need know? And, most of all, what was she going to say to Alfie?

When they arrived at the hospital they were greeted by the nurse Hope recognised as the one looking after their mother.

"I'm sorry," she said. "She went quietly in her sleep. There was nothing we could do."

"You mean...?"

"Yes. She passed away about an hour ago. I'm sorry."

"Can we see her?" John asked.

199

The nurse led them through to the room where Ma lay no longer breathing. "I'll give you a few minutes. If you want to speak to the doctor..."

"Yes please," Hope said, still breathless from the dash to the hospital. She moved to the side of the bed. Ma's face was marble white but her lips were turned into the shadow of a smile. She looked as though she was sleeping only without the rasp of breath and the pained rise and fall of her chest. She at last looked to be at peace and Hope was glad of that. She stroked her mother's face. "Goodbye, Ma," she whispered. "Rest in peace. I hope you're happy now."

John's glance was brusquer. His jaw clenched as he said, "At least I can arrange for them to be buried together. They would have wanted that."

"I'm sorry for your loss," the Inspector, who'd followed them into the room, said. "It appears that I'll be looking for a double murderer."

Hope gasped as a dark cloud fell over her. With Ma and Pa both gone their lives would be very different in the future.

She wanted to stay a little longer with her mother, but John was anxious to get away. "What about Violet?" Hope asked. "We need to let her know."

John shrugged. "I'll go to her last known lodgings but if she's moved on...Well, she only has herself to blame. It's not our fault. None of this is our fault." His voice rose as he became more anxious. He was only nineteen, Hope thought. A year younger than her and now he'd be landed with huge responsibilities. Would he be up to it? Or would he, like Pa, take to drinking and gambling and care only for himself?

"If there's anything I can do to help," Inspector Penhalligan said. "Anything at all, you only have to ask."

"We'll manage, thank you," John said, somewhat ungraciously Hope thought.

"That's very kind of you," Hope said. "If we think of anything we'll let you know."

The Inspector smiled. "I'll be off then. I'm just going to have a word with the doctor. I'll need a copy of the death certificate too, to prove she died as a result of the fire."

"I'll come with you," John said. "You can stay here a little longer if you wish," he said to Hope.

"Just a few minutes," she said, although, by the time John returned after speaking to the doctor it was more than half-an-hour. All the while she sat at Ma's beside with tears in her eyes and memories of her childhood running through her mind.

"I'm going with Penhalligan to the station," John said when he returned. "He says they'll release Pa's body so I can make arrangements for the funeral. It doesn't mean the investigation's over. Just that they've got all they need for now. They still want to find out who killed him."

Hope nodded, her mind still on memories of the past.

"I'll go to Bert's old lodgings and ask them to pass a message to Violet wherever she is." He put his hand on Hope's shoulder. "You'd best tell Alfie. It'll be better coming from you."

"I'll let the school know too," she said. "Alfie'll need some time off."

"What about the club? If you need time off too?"

Hope shook her head. "No. I'd rather be working. Can't afford to lose a day's pay if we don't have to."

That evening Hope told Alfie as kindly as she could. It was the hardest thing she'd ever had to do, even harder than telling him about Pa. He was closer to Ma and the loss would be more deeply felt. The confusion in his eyes wrenched her heart.

"I thought they were going to make her better," he said. "Like me."

Hope brushed a clump of hair from his forehead, and gazed into his sorrowful eyes. "They did their best," she said. "She was just too badly damaged."

"Will she be with Pa now?"

"Yes."

"She'd have wanted that wouldn't she?"

"Yes."

The tears that had brimmed in his eyes started to fall. "What about us? What will happen to us now?"

Hope swallowed. It was a question she had yet to find an answer to. "We'll all be together here," she said. "You, me and John. We'll be staying with Betsy for a while. That won't be too bad will it?"

Alfie's bottom lip quivered, his mouth curled downwards and he fell, sobbing into Hope's arms. She held him close, soothing him until the flood of sobs abated. When he sat back she wiped the tears from his cheeks. "There now," she said. "Betsy's going to take care of you. John and I have to go to work. Is that all right?"

Soundlessly he nodded and Hope's heart crumbled again.

John managed to arrange the funeral for the following Wednesday. He spoke to the Master of the Licensed

Victuallers Association who offered to pay towards the funeral costs. "Your pa was a member for over twenty years," he said. "Least we can do is see he has a good send off."

The brewery also offered to make a contribution and many of the licensees of the pubs in the area also took up collections. "I never knew he had so many good friends," John said to Hope when he heard about their generosity.

"Ma and Pa were well respected," Hope said, "and the Licensed Victuallers look after their own."

Hope went to see Ruth Godley to tell her about the arrangements. "Shame about Violet," Ruth said. "She'll be sorry she missed her last chance to say goodbye to the people she loved."

"John's done all he can to contact her," Hope said. "Nothing more we can do."

"It'll be a sad day," Ruth said. "But my father will do everything in his power to comfort you and make it as easy and as least upsetting as he can."

Over the weekend Hope spent as much time as she could with Alfie while John rushed around making the final arrangement and letting everyone know the time and date.

Chapter Twenty Six

"I'll go with you to school on Monday," Hope told Alfie. "And let them know you'll need the day off."

"I'd rather have the week off," Alfie said. "Can I?"

"You don't want to get even more behind in your school work do you? And anyway, John and I are going to be kept busy with the arrangements, so you'll be left on your own. I'd rather know you were in school."

Reluctantly he agreed to go and Hope walked with him. It was a fine morning. Early sunlight reflected on windows and a light breeze blew dust up from the road, busy with traffic. If she'd been going anywhere else, with any other purpose in mind Hope would have enjoyed the walk.

When they arrived at the school she went in briefly to see Mr Mackitterick. He wasn't there, so she left a message about the funeral on Wednesday and Alfie's absence on that day.

After leaving Alfie at school, she was surprised to see Inspector Penhalligan waiting for her outside the school gate. He'd been smoking a pipe while he waited, but tapped it out when he saw her. "Your landlady told me where you were," he said. "I thought I might catch you. I'd like a word if that's all right."

Hope couldn't stop him walking along with her. "I can't imagine how I can be of any assistance," she said.

"Did your father know a man by the name of Lucien Grey? He may have met him at The Grenadier and done business with him."

"How would I know? He didn't discuss his business affairs with me."

"I just thought you might have heard of him. He's a member of the club where you work, a job I understand your father arranged for you."

"A job I neither wanted nor asked for."

"So I believe. But you do work there?"

"Yes."

"Would you, by any chance, have come across this Lucien Grey?"

"Not that I'm aware of."

The Inspector stopped walking and turned to face Hope. "Another man has been killed in circumstances similar to your father's murder. We think it may be the same killer. The only thing this other victim and your father had in common, as far as we can tell, is that they were both members of the same club and, we believe, had dealings with this Mr Lucien Grey. If there's anything at all you can tell me about him it would help our investigation."

Tired from the emotion of the weekend Hope was in no mood to prolong this conversation, despite Inspector Penhalligan's undeniable charm. "I'm afraid I don't know him so I can't help you."

"A few discreet enquiries is all I'm asking. Who were his friends, associates, colleagues? What sort of business did he conduct?"

"I'm sure Mr Quirk would be able to answer your questions far better than I. Why don't you ask him?"

The Inspector smiled. "I have," he said. "He told me the members have a right to their privacy and he's afraid helping the police with their enquiries would harm the club's reputation. Something he prizes above all things."

"So, you want me to risk my job, my livelihood I might remind you, and earn Silas Quirk's eternal displeasure by spying on him and making enquiries for you?"

"If it helps catch your parents' killer..." The Inspector shook his head. "Men like Lucien Grey get away with the most heinous of crimes because they have money and wealthy connections. They have friends like Silas Quirk who keep quiet and won't become involved. Foul deeds flourish in the dark when no one will speak of them. All I'm asking is that you allow me to throw a little light on the subject. He may be the one responsible for you losing your livelihood and your parents."

Hope paused. Of course he was right. What was her job compared to her parents' lives and the family's livelihood? "I'll try but I can't promise anything. I'm only a waitress. They don't tell me anything."

"No but you must overhear a great deal."

"And believe less than half of it," Hope said. "Men have ways of deluding themselves. I'm just an onlooker."

"Who sees most of the game, I'll wager."

Hope smiled for the first time since the previous Friday. Perhaps he had a point. Men bragged about their cleverness in business. If one of them was responsible for her father's losses she'd like to know. And if they were party to the murder, she'd like to see they got their just desserts.

When she got to the club that evening Hope asked the barman about Lucien Grey. She tried to be as casual as she could, dropping his name into the conversation.

"Grey?" the barman said. "Big fellow, equally big mouth. Always bragging about his business in America. Owns a gold mine so 'e reckons. Never believe what they tell you when they're in drink. It's all a fantasy or wishful thinking."

"But if it's true, I mean a gold mine? Really?"

The barman laughed. "Yes and I've got fairies at the bottom of my garden."

She recalled her father's interest in the gold strikes in the Yukon at Christmas and wondered whether there was any connection. Did he know Lucien Grey and have dealings with him?

She smiled and moved away with her tray of drinks, back to the tables where Poppy was already working, topping up glasses, even if they didn't need it.

"Jake behind the bar's been telling me about Lucien Grey," she said. "Does he really own a gold mine?"

Poppy chuckled. "In his dreams. That's him, over there." She pointed out a well built, man in a navy evening coat and matching waistcoat over a winged-collar blue shirt. He was younger than she'd thought he would be. Blonde curls framed his face and a thin beard ran down to his chin. His eyes appeared watchful. A diamond pin, discreet but significant, held his gold silk cravat in place and a matching diamond Albert hung from his heavy gold watch-chain.

"So, what does he do?"

Poppy shrugged. "Some sort of stockbroker I believe. Most gamblers like to play the market. He's mean as a weasel and so oily he'd float on water. Never leaves a tip. I'd avoid him if I were you."

"I was just wondering if he knew my father. He liked to play the market." Hope wasn't sure that was true but if Pa was offered a rock solid way to make a lot of money quickly he might have been tempted.

"More fool him then, especially if his play involved Lucien Grey. I wouldn't trust him to buy me a handkerchief, let alone invest with him. If he was an undertaker people would stop dying, that's the sort of man he is. Don't be fooled by appearances. He keeps fighting dogs and is not shy of a bit of a skirmish himself."

For the rest of the evening Hope kept her eyes on the man Poppy had pointed out. She saw his meanness, the way he manipulated every exchange to his own advantage, how every move was calculated to impress the people around him and how he hated to lose. He was what Ma would have called a 'snake-oil salesman', she thought. If only her pa had been as perceptive.

The next time she saw Inspector Penhalligan was at the funeral. The day had dawned oppressively hot with hardly a breeze to stir the trees. The smell of grass was clean and sweet. Bees buzzed in the still summer air as a sad straggle of people made their way into the church for the service.

Hope pinned a black ribbon bow to her simple black dress and draped a black cotton shawl around her shoulders. A black hat with a veil completed her outfit. She'd found Alfie a dark suit in the market and sewn a black band around his sleeve. He wore a black cap and a worried expression on his little face. "Ma and Pa would be so proud of you," she told him as she straightened his black tie. "Chin up, be brave."

Alfie pouted, but he nodded, holding back the tears that threatened to fall. He looked smart and yet so heartbreakingly fragile. "Stay with Betsy," Hope said. "She'll look after you."

The two coffins were transported to the church, side by side on a brewer's dray pulled by four shire horses, their manes braided, their feet feathered and their flanks glowing. No effort had been spared by the brewery to show the deep respect held for their long-time employees. John, smartly dressed in a black frock coat and a top hat, walked behind the hearse. Hope and Alfie followed in a carriage with Ned and Betsy.

A few of the pub's regulars had turned out, the Brewery Manager also made an appearance. Hope was determined that everyone should see the love for their parents and enormous sense of loss the family felt.

The Pastor greeted them at the door. Inside the sun streamed through the stained glass window, sending a rainbow of light across to the opposite wall. Organ music played softly, murmured conversations rippled along pews, hardly breaking the sultry silence. Hope's heart was heavy with grief.

Following the two coffins felt unreal, like it was happening to someone else. Hope wished it was happening to someone else. John, hat in his hands, head bowed, went ahead first, walking down the aisle worn thin by a thousand feet before them. Ned walked in with Hope but she'd never felt so alone. She saw Miss Godley in the congregation sitting with Lydia. Silas Quirk nodded to her as she passed.

Betsy held Alfie's hand as he limped between the rows of pews and sat with him, holding him close. Hope laid a bunch of colourful day lilies on each coffin. They were her mother's favourite flowers. Violet hadn't come. Hope regretted that.

All through the service her hands were shaking. Seeing the coffins and imagining their contents brought home to her the enormity of their loss. Ma and Pa were gone. Gone forever. She'd been so busy thinking about their immediate problems she hadn't considered the finality of their deaths.

She'd never see them again, never share a happy moment or hear their pride in her achievements. Never hear their praise or their admonishments for something she'd done or hadn't done. They wouldn't be at her wedding, or see their grandchildren and she was sorry. Sorry for all the times she'd let them down, sorry for all the things that might have upset them, but most of all she was sorry they'd gone the way they had and she could do nothing to prevent it.

A torrent of sadness fell over her. It was as though the sun had gone out and she'd never see its brilliance again. The Pastor said a few words, John, tears glistening in his eyes, his voice choked, read a surprisingly articulate eulogy and they attempted the hymns, but it was a poor rendition.

Standing at the graveside as the coffins were lowered a chill ran through her. The Pastor read from the Bible, John scattered earth onto the grave, a few leaves swirled in the breeze and then it was over. Walking away Hope felt empty inside. What would become of them now?

On the way to the gate, Hope heard Alfie sniffle and saw Betsy stoop to wipe his nose. She stood with John under the lych-gate, shaking hands with the mourners as they left. The Brewery Manager was the first to leave, shaking John's hand and saying how sorry he was. Silas walked up with Inspector Penhalligan to shake their hands.

"A lovely service," he said, a note of sadness in his voice. "Your parents would have been proud."

"Thank you," she whispered.

"Will you be coming back to the house for a bite?" Betsy asked him, walking up behind them. "I'm sure you'll be very welcome."

"Thank you, but I don't want to intrude."

"You'd be very welcome," John said, making Hope wonder about his motives. Inviting Silas Quirk to their parents' wake had never been her intention.

Silas smiled. "Thank you, but I have to get back. I don't suppose I'll see either of you tonight. Let me know when you're ready to return to work."

"We'll be there tonight," Hope said. "Both of us." She glared at John.

"Yes, tonight," he said glancing uncertainly at Hope.

"As you wish," Silas said, raising his hat.

Inspector Penhalligan was next to shake their hands and was duly invited back. An invitation he didn't hesitate to accept.

Back at the house Hope made tea while Betsy laid out slices of ham, cheese, bread and butter, tomatoes, watercress, scones with jam and some fruit Ned had provided. She'd also left some potatoes in the oven to cook. John opened a few bottles of beer for the men. "It all looks wonderful," Hope said, as the visitors helped themselves. "But I really couldn't eat a thing."

She piled up a plate for Alfie, who was finding the day all too much and looked overwhelmed.

"Here now, take this upstairs," she said. "And try to get some rest. I'll come up later and see how you are." So he limped off up to the bed he now shared with Hope.

211

As the mourners drifted away with John seeing the last of them off, Hope was able to tell Inspector Penhalligan what she'd learned at the club.

"Yes, Lucien Grey is a member," she said, "but not very well thought of. He's a stockbroker, or so I understand. Perhaps that's a help?"

"Yes, thank you. It's as we thought. We are investigating his affairs. The other victim had recently returned from abroad, where Mr Grey is supposed to own certain holdings in a gold mine."

"Yes, he's always bragging about it at the club."

"Well, the other victim may have found out something amiss and spoken to your father about it. If that's the case we could tie the two deaths together."

"You mean he killed Pa because he found out something about his dodgy dealings?"

Inspector Penhalligan raised his eyebrows. "I've already told you too much. I really can't discuss the case, but thank you for confirming my suspicions."

A few evenings later she was working in the club as usual when she felt as though she was being watched. Every time she turned around she saw Lucien Grey, eyes narrowed, his gaze intently following her as she served drinks. He was also drinking more than usual and at one time she saw him quite unsteady on his feet. He was staring at her, his eyes the colour of slate and just as hard. It was quite unnerving and she found her hands were shaking.

Relief washed over when she saw him leave the room. Sighing and relaxing at seeing him go she went to the rest room provided for the girls to answer calls of nature or redo their hair or make up. Here she took some deep breaths. If Silas found out she'd been asking questions and spying on members for Inspector Penhalligan she'd lose her job and she couldn't bear that. Once she'd regained control of her nerves she stepped back into the corridor.

Before she had time to draw breath or respond she was grabbed and swung against the wall. Lucien Grey held her, his hand like a vice around her neck, his muscular body pressing into hers. "I hear you've been asking questions about me," he said, his flinty eyes boring into her. His lips twisted into a sneer of ill intent.

The shock brought a tightening in her chest, she could hardly breathe. Her knees trembled. She was as helpless as a leaf tossed by the wind. "I ask about all the members," she said, trying to push him away. "It's my job to get to know them, get to know their likes and dislikes. How else am I to serve them?"

He laughed. "Well, in that case you can get to know me better and serve me in private. I know just the place. You can serve me in a much more appropriate and satisfying manner than you can here."

"Unhand me, sir," she said, desperately trying to push him away as he pressed himself against her. He was much stronger than she had supposed and she soon found herself overpowered. His hands explored her bodice and attempted to lift her skirts.

"I'm here to serve drinks, that's all," she cried, trying again to push him off her, fighting to catch his hands as they wandered over her body.

"So, you're one of those trollops who promise so much and deliver so little," he said, grabbing the silk of her skirt and pulling it up so he could caress her thigh. "I hate that in a woman." Fire burned in his eyes as he spoke. His other hand gripped her bodice at the neck and ripped it away, exposing her chemise.

She screamed.

Silas appeared and grabbed Lucien Grey by his collar, pulling him off of her. Two porters materialised, seemingly from nowhere. Each took one of his arms and lifted him off his feet to carry him out of the building.

"A member getting a little frisky with drink," Silas said. "Are you alright?"

Burning with rage Hope steadied her voice. "I'm fine," she said. She didn't want any further investigation into why Lucien Grey had picked her out rather than one of the other girls.

"You'd better get that stitched," Silas said, nodding to her torn bodice. A wide smile spread across his face lighting up his intense blue eyes.

She glanced down and saw more than her underclothes exposed. She quickly pulled the torn fragment across her bosom, her face hotter than a furnace.

"Leave it with Hortense and take the rest of the night off. I'll explain to Mrs Malone," he said.

Hope's heart was pounding. "Thank you," she managed to whisper aware that if he knew what she'd been doing he wouldn't be best pleased.

"I'm sorry," he said. "It's just the effect of drink. There's nothing wrong with the drink itself, it's the demons it releases in some men. It happens but I'm sorry it had to be you he chose to insult tonight. I'll make sure it doesn't happen again."

She nodded silently, her insides writhing with embarrassment. Why did it have to be him who'd seen her and why hadn't she had the sense to fight back and knee Lucien Grey where it hurt? That's what Poppy had told her to do should she be assaulted by a man too drunk to know what he was doing. That would have sorted him out. Berating herself for being so slow to act she took the dress up to Hortense who assured that 'tomorrow it be good as new'.

Walking home in the lingering warmth of the day, Hope could only thank the stars twinkling in the sky above for her lucky escape. If Silas hadn't been there it could have been so much worse. Her only fear now was that Lucien Grey might remember her face and be waiting for her outside one night when Silas wasn't there to protect her. If he murdered her pa he'd be capable of anything. It was something she vowed to remember.

Over the next week Hope noticed several bruises appearing on Alfie's arms and grazes on his leg. One day he came home with a black eye and a cut lip. "What happened?" she asked.

"Nothing. I'm all right. Don't fuss," Alfie said and stomped as best he could up the stairs to their bedroom.

Hope followed him up. "Tell me what happened," she said. "If it's the other boys…"

"You'll do what? Go and punch 'em back? That's the only thing that'll stop 'em. They pick on me because I can't fight back. There's nothing you can do about it."

He threw himself onto the bed and turned to face the wall. Hope's heart broke seeing him so upset and knowing that he was right. He'd have to go back tomorrow and face the same treatment. Nevertheless she was determined to speak to the Master and try to stop it.

The next day she mentioned it to Ned in the market and at least he was sympathetic. "If you like I'll go with some mates from the market. Talk to the lads that did it in a language they'd understand. Just say the word."

"Good heavens, no. I don't want you to do that," she said. "That'll only make things worse and won't teach them right from wrong. You'll be as bad as they are, picking on people weaker than you because you can. No. That's not the answer."

Ned shrugged. "It's the only language they understand," he said.

That evening at the club she could think of nothing but Alfie and what she could do to save him from the beatings. She found her patience sorely tested. When one of the gentlemen made a cheeky remark she slapped him down more sharply than she intended. She got drinks mixed up, filling an empty glass with gin when the customer was drinking whisky. At one time she missed out a whole table and Poppy had to fill in for her. It wasn't long before Dexi noticed.

She called her over to her table during a break. "You're all at odds with yourself tonight. I know you miss your mother," she said, "but a long face doesn't encourage the customers to hang around drinking and gambling. If you need some time off, please tell me and I'll find someone to take your place."

A huge swell of dread threatened to engulf her. She'd lost her ma and pa and now she could lose the job they depended on to keep them going. Not only that she found it was a job she looked forward to, a place she could be someone else and forget her troubles. Her heart clenched at the thought of losing her place.

"I'm sorry," she said. "It's not missing Ma, although of course I do, it's my little brother Alfie. He's being bullied and beaten up at school. I'm worried about him, but you're right. It's not your problem and it's no excuse. It's just that it breaks my heart."

"You have to get used to having your heart broken in this game," Dexi said. "Happens to me all the time."

Again Hope caught the glint of steel beneath the sparkle. She wondered what horrors of the past had caused such pain as to harden Dexi's heart. Still, Hope knew she was right. She needed to toughen up, especially now Ma and Pa were gone and she'd have to rely on John. For the rest of the evening she danced around laughing, flirting and refilling any glasses even half-empty, despite her heart not being in it. As she waltzed past Dexi's table she breathed a sigh of relief when she nodded her approval.

Chapter Twenty Seven

The next morning Hope let Alfie stay at home and help Betsy with the laundry. She sent a note to school saying he was sick.

John went to the brewery as they'd finished cleaning up the mess left by the fire in the upstairs rooms and he was anxious to move back in, take over the licence and see about finishing the refurbishing. "I reckon we can open by Christmas," he said. "Things'll be just like they were before, only I'll be in charge instead of Pa. You'll be taking Ma's place in the kitchen and it'll be a family business, just like before."

Hope's heart buckled. She'd been willing to help clean the place up but she'd pushed the idea of moving back and working there to the back of her mind. The threat of losing her job at The Grenadier had made her realise how much she'd come to rely on it and how much she enjoyed working there: the opulent surroundings, lively company, the men's light-hearted banter, the challenge of avoiding their grasping hands and feeling appreciated in a way she'd never felt before. The warmth and optimism of the club were a million miles away from the dour, dull spit and sawdust company at the Hope and Anchor. She realised how much she'd miss working there in the evenings and the thought of going back to the Hope and Anchor appalled her. She'd miss Betsy too, as would Alfie who'd come to adore her.

"Let's not be hasty," she said. "The brewery might not give you the licence and, in any case, I'm not sure I want to move back. Too many painful memories and it won't do Alfie any good to be reminded of his injuries."

John looked aghast. "Not move back? But it's our home. It's our livelihood too, Hope. Don't forget that."

"We're making a good living working at The Grenadier, aren't we? My tips and your wage and the rent we pay Betsy is a pittance compared to what the brewery want for the pub."

"Working at The Grenadier was only temporary. I want to be my own boss, not work for someone else for the rest of my life. It's our legacy, our security, our future. It's what Ma and Pa worked twenty years for. I'm not going to give it up now, whatever you say and I'll need you to support me. We're moving back and that's an end to it."

Hope wasn't so sure. John was nearly twenty but he had no experience of running a pub. There was no guarantee the brewery would give him the licence anyway, but then she thought of his threat to leave if he didn't get the licence and her mind was thrown into turmoil again.

Later, in the market she saw Ned. "Good morning, lovely," he greeted her as usual. "Why the frown? Is Alfie all right?"

"Alfie's being beaten up by the other kids again so I've kept him home."

"Well my offer still stands. If you want me and the lads to sort it out…"

Hope shook her head. "No. I'm going to have a word with Ruth Godley's father to see if he can do anything. He's on the school board, but it's John I'm most worried about. He's set on getting the licence for the pub and all of us moving back in. I'm not sure I want to go back."

Ned shrugged. "I suppose that's only natural, given the circumstances. But if it's what he wants, and you can all be together again...surely that's a good thing?"

"He wants me to take Ma's place in the kitchen."

Ned nodded. "I expect he does. That'd be the usual thing. Then, when we...I mean... you...later on..." pink flushed his cheeks, "get married and have a family..."

Dread filled her stomach. Is that how he saw their future? Her in the kitchen with a horde of toddlers while he, like her pa, went out enjoying himself? Was that what he thought of her? Visions of her evenings at the club swirled through her mind, the beautiful silk dress she wore, the way she was treated with the greatest of respect, the fun, the laughter...

She picked up the apples he'd put in a bag for her and walked away.

When John returned from the brewery that afternoon he slammed the door at Betsy's and yelled for Hope.

"What? What is it? What's wrong?"

"The brewery," he said. "They won't let me have the licence on my own. They said the Hope and Anchor's always been a family concern. Always has been and always will be. They're going to give it to another family when the work's completed unless I can persuade them to change their minds."

"I doubt there's much chance of that," Hope said. "It's a business decision."

"I thought that with you and Alfie moving back with me they might change their minds. If you sign up as co-licensee and we run it together they might give us another chance. After all, Ma and Pa ran it for twenty years. They can't forget about that."

So, her going back would be useful to him, what she wanted counted for nothing. The courage she'd thought had deserted her rose up inside Hope. "I'm not going back," she said. "Alfie and me are staying here with Betsy. You can do what you like, but we're not moving."

"Then we've lost it, Hope – lost Ma and Pa's legacy and our home. We've got until the end of next month to clear out our stuff, well, what's left after the fire. We're going to be left with nothing." His voice was cold as a winter wind.

Looking at him she saw the fear in his face, the fear of not being good enough, and the helplessness of clinging to the life they'd had and seeing it slipping away and there was nothing she could say or do to prevent it.

She sank onto a chair as her heart dropped into her boots. Ma and Pa were gone, Violet following a path of her own and now she might lose John as well. She'd never felt so desolate and alone.

John glared at her. "We've lost our home," he said. "And it's your fault."

Every evening after that Hope and John made their way separately to the club. John hardly spoke to her. Venom filled his eyes when he looked at her. Several times she almost gave in, but then, glanced around at the fine architecture, the pictures on the wall, the baize tables, the gentlemen with manners, all very different from the Hope and Anchor and her resolve returned. She wasn't going back.

As she was cashing up a few days later, Abel arrived at her side. "Master wants to see you," he said.

Her heart stuttered and missed a beat. Had John asked him to sack her? Told him she could no longer work there, he needed her at the pub? A hundred different scenarios flashed though her mind in the two minutes it took her to walk to Silas's office, her heart pounding. If John has lost her the best job she'd ever had she'd never forgive him.

When she got to Silas's office she stopped to compose herself. She was ready to tell him how grateful she was for the job and how it made such a difference to their lives. She'd say that John was mistaken. Had misunderstood the brewery's intentions. And in any case, even if she lost her job here she wasn't going back to work in the pub.

She squared her shoulders and stiffened her resolve, took a deep breath and knocked on the door. Silas rose as she walked in and greeted her with a smile, which was slightly re-assuring. He indicated a chair for her and waited until she was seated before he sat behind his large mahogany desk. "How are you getting on?" he asked.

The fear that she'd been summoned to be sacked gradually increased, accompanied by the equally great fear that complaints had been made about her work. "I'm quite happy with my working arrangements, thank you. I hope my work has been satisfactory."

"Esme speaks well of you," he said, "and I like to keep an eye on my staff's welfare. She tells me you have a concern about your little brother, Alfie isn't it?"

"Err, yes, Alfie. I was worried about his schooling, but I hope I haven't allowed it to affect my work." Her pulse quickened at the memory of Dexi's comments a few days ago. She'd been worried sick, but that was no excuse for taking it out on the club clientele.

"It's just that I have a friend who runs a school for the sons of merchants and gentlemen. It's in Charterhouse. Merchant Taylors', you may have heard of it?"

Yes, she'd heard of it. It was a posh public school.

"He says they may have a place for your brother, if it suits."

She was aghast. "We can't afford..."

He held up his hand to stop her flow of reasons why she couldn't accept his offer. "They have a scholarship. If Alfie's as bright as I've been led to believe it won't cost anything."

"He's bright as a button and quicker at counting than anyone I know," she said, rushing to his defence.

"Then he'll be all right. Should I arrange for him to sit the exam?"

Her confidence waivered. "Charterhouse? I'm not sure, it's a bit of a way. He can't walk far...his leg...I don't..."

"I have another friend whose son goes to the school. He has a house in Leman Street. If Alfie can make it there he would be prepared to take him with his boy."

Leman Street was just around the corner and in easy walking distance. Words deserted Hope. The offer was more than generous. The idea of being further beholden to Silas Quirk would normally have prompted an early refusal, but the thought of Alfie getting away from Mr Mackitterick and the boys at school who beat him daily...

"I don't know what to say."

"Yes please and thank you, would be appropriate." Mirth danced in Silas's cornflower blue eyes. He was enjoying Hope's discomfort.

"I'll speak to Alfie," she said. "It will have to be his decision," although she knew he'd jump at the chance to change schools to one where there would be less chance of a daily beating.

And she was right. As soon as she mentioned it to Alfie his eyes lit up. "You mean go to a different school? Away from here? Is that possible?"

"Well, there's an exam to pass and you'd have to travel with another boy, a friend of Mr Quirk. But if you pass the exam…"

"An exam?" He pouted. "That's all right. I can do that. When can I take it? Can I start straight away?"

Hope laughed. "No. I'll have to arrange for you to sit the entrance exam and then, if you pass and I have no doubt you'll be able to do that, you can start next term."

"I'll have to study my school books and I'll do my best."

"Good. Then you want me to arrange it?"

"Yes please." Alfie limped off to get his books and start studying. Hope crossed her fingers that she'd done the right thing. It was a chance for Alfie to get away from the daily beatings, what could possibly be better than that?

It was arranged for Alfie to sit the exam the following Saturday. She'd never seen him so eager to sit with his books revising the lessons he'd missed while he was in hospital. It was up to him now, but she hoped with all her heart that he'd pass the exam. To fail now would be a bitter disappointment and one he'd never recover from.

The rest of the week she worried whether she'd done the right thing. She could have refused Silas's offer and Alfie would be none the wiser, but she knew she'd regret it if she did. Alfie deserved this chance and she was determined he'd make the most of it.

Chapter Twenty Eight

On Saturday the air was warm with summer heat. Hope helped Alfie dress in his best suit, the one he'd worn for the funeral. She wanted him to make a good impression, but he looked so small and vulnerable she again wondered if she'd done the right thing. She smoothed down his hair and straightened his tie. "Ma and Pa would be so proud of you," she said.

"I don't want to let anybody down," he said.

"You won't." She smiled at him. "You never have done yet."

She'd hired a hansom to take them to the school. She was acutely aware that it was only Silas's friendship with the headmaster that had allowed them the privilege of the school opening on a weekend so that Alfie could sit the exam. Alfie sat in the cab, so quiet and sombre her heart went out to him.

"You'll be fine," she told him. "Just do your best."

He'd nodded and smiled but she could see how nervous he was. "You won't be cross if I mess it up will you?" he asked, wringing his hands.

"No, of course not. Just think of it as an experience many boys would give their eye teeth for. You'll have done something none of the other boys have and I'll be proud of you for that."

When they arrived she felt Alfie shiver as he got out of the cab. She squeezed his shoulder. "You'll be fine," she whispered.

They both stood and gazed in awe at the magnificent building that had once housed a

Carthusian monastery. The historic architecture and its surroundings were a world away from the dusty, narrow, cobbled streets she was used to. The large square gave the impression of space and light, something else the area where they lived seriously lacked. A reverential silence hung over the square like a cloak, shattered only by the soft breeze rustling through the trees and the sudden chiming of a church bell in the distance. The smell of fresh cut grass and late summer roses filled the air around them. She squeezed Alfie's shoulder again. She didn't want him to be so overawed he'd be unable to do his best.

"It's pretty big and impressive, isn't it?" she said. "But it's what you deserve. Don't forget that."

The ghost of a smile flitted across his lips. "I'll try," he said, his eyes still wide with wonder.

They were greeted by a black robed master who introduced himself as Giles Larkin, the Second Master.

"And this must be Alfred Daniels," he said, checking Alfie's name on a sheet. "Delighted to meet you. I've heard quite a bit about you." He held his hand out to Hope. "And you must be his sister, Miss Hope Daniels. I've heard about you too."

Hope swallowed. What on earth had he heard about her?

"Come this way," he said to Alfie.

With a worried glance at Hope Alfie followed him. Hope sat in the wood panelled corridor, tense with apprehension. What if he failed the exam? What if he wasn't good enough? What if she'd filled his head with false hopes that would be dashed and lead to a disappointment he'd never recover from? The wait seemed interminable. She crossed her fingers and, heart racing, she prayed.

Three hours later the Second Master returned with a smiling Alfie. "You have a very bright young man here," Giles Larkin said. "I'm sure you have no need to worry, but we'll let you know in a few days."

"Thank you," she stuttered. Butterflies fluttered inside her as she walked away, fingers still crossed.

When Hope arrived at the club that evening she was surprised to see Silas in the bar. He didn't usually appear until much later, and then only briefly to see everything was all right. The most acknowledgement she'd had in the past was a brief nod or a smile, although she did often feel as though she was being watched particularly. Not that this bothered her. She supposed he was the boss which gave him the right to eye up any of the girls anytime.

"Good evening, Hope," he said. "I understand Alfie went to the school today to take the exam. How did he get on?"

"Quite well, I think, although it's difficult to say," she said. It was good of him to take an interest.

"Good," he said. "If there's anything else I can do to make things easier for you please don't hesitate to let me know."

"Thank you," she said, taken aback by his kindness. The other girls said he treated his staff well, but his interest in her family was more than she'd expected. Perhaps he wasn't the ogre everyone said he was.

The following Monday being the first in August was the Summer Bank Holiday, given so bank employees had a chance to watch the cricket. However, most gentlemen and wealthier families preferred to enjoy the warm weather by spending the day at the races. The casino was busy with a large party invited by one of the members to celebrate a big win that afternoon at Goodwood. They'd arrived in a state that showed they'd already enjoyed a good day out and were determined to make a night of it. Starting at the card tables, the raucous crowd would inevitably end up in the dog pits when the sport would be lively, loud and last long into the early hours of the morning.

"I'll be glad when they've had enough," Hope said to Poppy as they were picking up fresh bottles from the bar.

"That sort's never had enough," Poppy said. "They'll be here 'til dawn, but at least they'll go downstairs for the livelier sport. Good riddance too."

Hope agreed, and continued topping up glasses and collecting tips as usual. The member's guests were noisy and some of them stepped beyond what was proper in their remarks around her, but at least the drink had oiled their pockets and she found her tips mounting quite generously.

She was about to walk away from one table of regular card players when the man she'd just served jumped up and yelled, "Stop, thief", causing the table to tilt and the other players to call out. He pointed at Hope. "She's stolen my chips," he roared. He came towards her threatening her with this fist. "You thieving…"

Hope was so shocked she almost dropped her tray. Silence had fallen over the other tables at the sudden outburst as the players stopped to see what was happening.

Another man jumped up from the table and grabbed his arm before he got any further. "Hold on,

Jasper, I think you may be mistaken. The girl never touched your chips."

Several of the other men at the table gathered around protesting Hope's innocence but Jasper's eyes blazed madder than the dogs trained to fight downstairs. "She did. She swiped them off the table by my elbow and onto her tray – look, look, on her tray."

Sure enough there were a pile of chips on Hope's tray, her earnings from that evening. Fear, sharp as a knife struck her. Hot blood raced through her veins. Everything was going so fast, she could make no sense of it. Heat flooded her face and exploded crimson on her cheeks. "I never touched your chips," she said. "These are my tips and change from the drinks." She glanced wildly around looking for some support from the onlookers. There was none. He was a club member and bound to be believed whereas she was a mere waitress, who'd believe her? Nausea swirled in her stomach, rising up to her throat. Fear froze her to the spot.

"You wouldn't have seen. She did it so quickly, she's obviously done it before, thieving baggage," Jasper snarled through gritted teeth, his eyes narrowed with anger. "I insist you search her. There was a pile of chips, all my winnings from the evening."

"That's not true," Hope said, despair raising her voice loud enough to attract even more attention. "He's lying."

The man who'd held Jasper's arm looked dubious. "I don't recall you having any winnings, Jasper," he said. "You've been losing steadily all night."

Two large uniformed porters appeared either side of Jasper. "Calm down, sir," the one Hope recognised from the door said. "Perhaps some of these gentlemen saw something?"

The all shook their heads, denying having seen anything. "I was watching the pot, one said. "I saw her top up the drinks, that's all," another said.

"I think we'd better go to the office and sort this out," the porter said. He nodded at Hope. "You too, Miss."

"I want to see the manager," Jasper shouted, his expression determinedly innocent. "He runs a crooked gambling joint and I'll have him arrested." A ripple of concern went through the watching crowd.

Silas was summoned. Hope shook her head in despair, tears filling her eyes. This was the last thing she needed. What would he think of her, after all his kindness to her family? It was too much to bear.

Jasper quietened as Silas arrived, the scowl on his face saying more than words. She saw a flash of temper in Silas's eyes but it was quickly smothered. Silas was mad at her. There was no doubt about it. She'd been employed to serve drinks and keep the members happy and here she was standing in the Saloon having a stand up row and shouting match with one of the esteemed gentlemen members, although she didn't think him such a gentleman. She'd be sacked for sure.

Silas was going to blame her and she'd be thrown out, after all his kindness. She struggled to quell the panic rising in her veins. "I never stole anything in my life," she told him. "Ask the others at the table." The other players had drifted away. The players at the other tables had resumed their games, the excitement being all but over.

"Come with me, all of you," Silas said, his face flushed with the anger that burned in his eyes. As they passed the cashier's office he knocked on the iron door. A barred hatch opened and a man peered out. "Give me the ledger for Mr Jasper Cunningham," Silas said. The bars opened and the ledger was duly passed out.

Following Silas to his office deep dread swirled inside. Hope If this Jasper Cunningham was believed she could be arrested and thrown in jail. What would happen to Alfie and the family then?

Chapter Twenty Nine

In the office, the two porters who'd followed them along the corridor waited by the door. Jasper repeated his allegation. "I had a pile of chips worth at least fifteen pounds," he said. "She came to the table and the next minute my pile of chips had gone. She'd slipped them into her pocket. I insist you search her, although she may have passed them to an accomplice by now."

"It's a lie," Hope said. "I never touched your chips and I've never seen more than a couple of sovereign chips and a pile of half-crowns in front of you."

Silas opened the ledger. A strained silence filled the room, the only sound the turning of the pages in the ledger. Hope trembled with fear and fury. Losing her job and her reputation meant the end of any hope she had of Alfie going to his new school, even if he passed the exam. They'd never be able to afford it and, anyway, the place they'd offered would be snatched away if she was convicted of thieving. Jasper Cunningham, on the other hand, would walk away, reputation and money intact. Tears stung her eyes but, gritting her teeth, she resolutely held them back.

After a few moments Silas looked up his eyes filled with contempt. Speaking quietly, he said to Jasper, "I see you have a number of outstanding IOUs. It appears to me that someone who loses as regularly as you do may seek to mitigate his losses by accusing my staff of theft. I have heard no support for your allegation. On the contrary I'm given to understand that your fellow players refuse to confirm your story."

"They didn't see her. She's crafty as a fourflusher. Who are you going to believe, an upstanding gentleman of breeding and a valued member of this club, or a dollymop out for all she can get?"

Fury rose up inside Hope, banishing her fear. "I'm no dollymop," she said, surprised at the sudden shrillness of her voice. "And you're no better than you ought to be, lying and cheating. I've seen you looking at other players' cards while pretending to take a drink, holding your glass at an angle to see their hand reflected there. Well, it didn't do you any good did it? You lost the game anyway."

Silas suppressed a smile, but couldn't hide the spark of admiration in his eyes. He lifted the pile of Jasper Cunningham's IOUs and waived them in front of his nose. "I take it you don't have the wherewithal to pay off your debts. You dare to accuse my staff of thieving in order to get yourself out of trouble. I've a good mind to call the constable and have you arrested for making false accusations."

The blood drained from Jasper's face.

Silas, his face grim, tore the IOUs into pieces and dropped them into the bin. "Take your cheating, lying body out of my club and never come back," he said. "I run an honest club with a good reputation and I won't have it soiled by people like you. Now, get out."

The two men by the door moved forward, picked Jasper up under the arms and carried him out, protesting loudly. "I'll have the law on you," he yelled. "You can't treat me like this. I'll see you don't get away with it." His protestations fell on deaf ears.

Hope turned to Silas. "I never took his chips."

Silas smiled. "I know you didn't. It's not the first time a bad loser has tried to reclaim his losses by accusing other people of cheating or stealing. We've been watching him for some time. Please don't worry any more about it." He wrote a note on a slip of paper. "Here, give this to the barman."

Back in the bar, still shaking from the experience, she gave the note to Jake, the barman. He read it, poured her a large brandy and handed it over with a wink. "Drinks on the house for the rest of night," he said.

A few days later a letter came by messenger. The thick cream envelope had the crest of The Merchant Taylors' School embossed on the front. "Alfie, Alfie, it's come," she called, giving the boy a ha'penny tip. Her hand trembled. She could hardly breathe.

She stood staring at the envelope. The letter inside could change Alfie's life. A bubble of excitement ballooned inside her quickly followed by a swell of anxiety. It'll be good news, she thought. Please God let it be good news.

She ran in to find Alfie who was helping Betsy in the laundry and hadn't heard her. She waved the letter in her hand. "It's arrived, Alfie. The letter from the school. It's here."

Alfie limped over to take it, holding it reverently in his hands. It was addressed to Hope, so he handed it back. "Open it, please," he said.

Anxiety paled his little face, but excitement shone in his eyes.

Lifting the letter carefully from the envelope she unfolded it and gasped. "You got it, Alfie. You got the scholarship. You can start next term at the school."

She handed him the letter and hugged him with joy, lifting him off his feet and swinging him round.

"I'm so proud of you," she said. "Wait 'til I tell John. He'll be proud of you too." She also found she couldn't wait to tell Silas. He was the one who'd made it possible, and she'd enjoy showing him she'd been right about Alfie. He was a clever child and deserved better than the schooling he was getting.

Betsy made a pot of tea, which was as near as she got to celebrating anything, and together they went over the letter taking in every word and committing it to memory.

Firstly it set out the school's ethos: '*to fashion a gentleman in virtuous and gentle discipline*' and its aim of '*emphasizing individual development within the context of outstanding academic and sporting achievement*'.

It then gave Alfie's date to start, reporting instructions and the name of his tutor, Mr Giles Larkin. It ended by saying how pleased they were to be able to offer Alfred Daniels a place at their school and hoped it would be a mutually enriching experience. The second page set out what he was required to wear, and listed high-class tailor's shops in the city where the appropriate clothing could be purchased. Dinner arrangements stated the boys would eat together in the dining hall. A midday meal would be provided at a cost of two shillings per week, to be paid by the term in advance.

Hope swallowed when she read it, not sure where the money would come from, but determined to ensure that Alfie had everything the other boys had, whatever she had to do to provide it.

The biggest thrill for Hope was seeing the joy mixed with apprehension on Alfie's face.

She couldn't wait to tell John the good news. She was so proud of Alfie and expected John to be the same. As soon as he came in she showed him the letter from the school.

His brow creased as he read it, anger flared in his eyes and clenched his fist. "Whose idea was this? Yours? Well, you can forget it." He crumpled the letter in his hands and threw it to the floor. "Alfie's not going to some posh school I know nothing about."

Fury swirled in Hope's stomach. She stooped to pick the letter up, smoothing it out as she did so. "If you must know it was Silas who suggested it. He thought enough of Alfie to put his name forward for the scholarship."

John gaped at her. "You've been discussing family business with Silas Quirk? Our family business? How could you, Hope? I thought you detested him."

She drew in a deep breath. Defending her feelings for Silas Quirk was not something she thought she'd ever have to do. "I was thinking of Alfie and his future."

"Well, think again. He's not going. For one thing we can't afford it and for another he'll be out of place there. His place is here with us not getting ideas above his station at some school for toffs."

"So you prefer him being beaten every day?"

John looked shamefaced. "No, but a public school, Hope? It's full of uppity snobs with more money than brains. It's a terrible idea. Best forget it."

"Forget it? When Alfie's worked so hard and has a chance of bettering himself? He deserves the best we can get for him and I won't turn my back on any opportunity to get him away from the ruffians at the local school."

"Do you think he'll do any better at a school for toffs? A school where he'll be the poor orphan boy whose family can't afford proper clothes for him and the only one with hand-me-down shoes? It's out of the question." John threw down his bag.

Hope's dreams for Alfie crumbled. She saw them falling into the mud like wounded sparrows. "We can buy him new clothes and shoes if that's all it takes to make him acceptable there. He'll need a proper uniform anyway. It's the least we can do for him."

"Like I said, forget it. Public school's not for the like of us, Hope. I'd have thought you knew that."

"Not for us? What do you mean not for us? We're honest, trustworthy, hard-working and as good as anybody. I won't have Alfie's future blighted because you don't think he's good enough."

John looked as though he was about to explode. "I'm the head of the family and what I say goes. I say he's not going. I'm not spending money to have him dressed up like a nob and turning him into a spoiled brat who thinks he's too good for us. There's an end to it." He glared at Hope and stomped out, slamming the door behind him.

As the door slammed Alfie appeared, his face pinched. "I heard you arguing," he said. "I won't go to the school if it's going to cause trouble. I'll stay where I am."

"No you won't," Hope said, fire and fury blazing inside her. "You passed the exam. You're as good as they are, better than most. You deserve your place at that school and I'm going to make sure you get it."

"But if we can't afford it?"

Hope smiled, her face softened. "I have a little put by. I'll make sure you have new clothes and shoes. I won't have anyone looking down on us."

"B-b-b-but John said..."

"I'll talk him round. He's just upset because he's lost the pub. It was all he ever wanted and I expect seeing you do so well makes him feel even more of a failure." She sighed. "But we'll get over it, one way or another."

Alfie grimaced but slunk back to resume turning the mangle for Betsy.

Hope sank onto a chair. Losing the pub was making John desperately unhappy and he blamed her for it. He couldn't even bear to speak to her. It was as though a wall had sprung up between them and there was no way of breaching it. All she knew was that some deep currents of emotion flowed between them full of unresolved issues.

Chapter Thirty

The next morning, still bursting with pride at Alfie's achievements, Hope went to the market. The sun was shining and her step lightened in the warmth of the summer air. She couldn't wait to tell Ned the good news. Despite John's opposition she was determined that Alfie would go to the school Silas had found for him. She'd find a way to pay for him to have new clothes and new shoes, not second-hand. She knew they'd be expensive, but she worked hard and if she saved her tips… If she didn't have enough she'd even borrow money although she hated to get into debt, knowing what a mess her pa had got into through debt.

Ned greeted her with a grin, as he always did. "Morning, my lovely," he said. "Haven't seen you around for a while."

A stab of guilt pricked her. "I'm sorry," she said. "What with Alfie coming home, helping Betsy and working at the club I've hardly any time to myself."

"I know. I've called round a couple of times but Betsy said you were out. How are things going at the pub? I expect you'll be moving back soon won't you? Then we'll be able to see a lot more of each other."

She forced a smile. She hadn't told Ned about her decision not to move back into the pub but to continue working at the club, nor about John losing the licence. She felt bad enough about letting John down, now, with Ned she felt even worse.

"I expect you're right," she said, "although it's early days yet. We're not quite sure what's happening with the pub. But I've got good news about Alfie."

"Good news?"

"Yes. He passed the scholarship to Merchant Taylors' school. They say he can start in the September term, after the harvest holiday. Isn't that good news?"

Ned's brow creased. "Merchant Taylors'? Isn't that a posh public school? I've heard of it but never knew anyone who went there? Are you sure it's right for Alfie? Won't go giving him ideas above his station?" He turned towards a woman who was inspecting his carrots. "Fresh in today, luv. Won't do better anywhere."

The customer nodded and moved off. He sighed and turned back to Hope.

She huffed. What was it with these men? Did they have no ambition or thoughts about bettering themselves to get a better living than their parents? "No, all it'll do is give him a better education and less bruises than he's getting at present. Now if you could spare me some tater-spuds and apples, I'll be on my way. I've a lot to do today."

Ned pouted. "Sorry. Didn't mean to upset you. But won't it cost a heap of bread to kit him out for a new school?" He started to put potatoes into a bag, twisted the top and handed it to her. "Can't see what benefit he'll get from it neither. He'll need to earn a living when he's fourteen just like the rest of us."

She took the offered bag and handed over a ha'penny. "I'm sure we'll manage thank you. And when he does start work it'll be in a sight better job than on the market." As soon as the words were out of her mouth she regretted it. "I'm sorry," she said. "I didn't mean…"

Ned's face hardened. "Market's been good enough for me and my family for generations. An' your ma and pa didn't do so badly out of the traders drinking in the pub neither." He put several apples into a bag. "I suppose now you're working for that 'oity-toity Silas Quirk you think yourself a step up. Well, you're wrong. Step down more like, serving drinks to 'em as never did a day's work in their lives." He thrust the bag of apples at Hope. "'ave these on the 'ouse," he said and walked away to serve another customer.

Hope felt dreadful. She never meant to hurt Ned but she thought he'd be pleased that Alfie had done so well. Was she the only person in the world who was proud of him and his achievement? Why did everyone else see it as a bad thing? Surely a good education would be better than what was happening to him at school now. She hated arguing with Ned, especially when he'd been so kind to them in the past, but she was beginning to wonder if he was the man she thought he was. Nevertheless, all the way home she tried to think of something she could do to make him see how sorry she was about the argument. Falling out with him was the last thing she wanted. Why did life, and men in particular, have to be so difficult?

Things calmed down over the next week, and John's mood appeared to brighten. He wasn't so moody over breakfast and even smiled as he went out to his job in the wood yard where he'd found he could work during the day when it suited him. It didn't bring in much, but, as he told Hope, at least people could see he was working to support his family which was the most important thing.

One evening he was telling her about the wood that had come into the yard. "Red mahogany," he said. "We don't see much of that. Make someone a grand table that will."

Seeing him in a good mood for a change Hope thought she might broach the subject of Alfie's schooling again. She waited until he was finishing his tea before getting changed to go to the club and said, "It's a good school where he won't get beaten by the other lads. A lot of boys there are from quite humble homes, sons of shopkeepers and the like. They're not all toffs like the men at the club."

"There's nothing wrong with the local school, Hope. It was good enough for you, me and Violet. It's good enough for Alfie."

"Alfie's not like you, me or Violet," Hope said, reluctant to mention his disability, but aware that this was the reason the other boys ganged up on him. "He's not like the other boys at that school either. Most of them are rogues and ruffians who think it's a joke to pick on Alfie because he can't fight or run away. At Merchant Taylors' he'll learn to stick up for himself."

"We had to learn that the hard way. Why should he be any different?"

"He's clever, that's why. He has potential. He won the scholarship. Not many boys at the local school could do that. It'd be a sin to deprive him of this opportunity to use his brain and make the most of himself, don't you think?"

John turned his head away, looking decidedly uncomfortable. "Even if what you're saying is true we can't afford it. We can't afford new books for him, nor clothes and shoes. There's no money."

"No money? But why? We're both working two jobs and make good money from the club." A horrible suspicion entered her head. She recalled their last argument about money and his gambling habit, when she'd decided to only give him half her tips because she didn't trust him. A sick feeling rose up inside her. "Don't tell me you've been gambling again and lost our savings."

John's face turned to stone. "Not gambling, no. I've invested it."

"Invested it? How? Why?"

"To make more of course, not that it's any of your business. I'm head of the family. I decide how we spend our money and what we spend it on and I'm not going to throw it away on fancy schooling for a boy too weak to stand up for 'iself."

Hope took a deep breath. Inside she was boiling with rage. How dare he talk about Alfie like that? What sort of brother was he anyway?

"You may be head of the family but it's my money too. My tips. Plus I'm working for nothing to repay a debt owed by, as you put it, the family. If you've gambled it away I swear I'll not be responsible…"

"I've invested it with a man at the club. He's a toff. Always talking about how much money he's made. Told me I could make more in a week than I'll earn in ten years working behind the bar." John's eyes sparkled as he talked. His face lit up as though a beam of sunlight had suddenly shone on it. "He's a stockbroker. If you must know I've bought a share in a gold mine in Yukon Territory in Canada."

Stunned and bereft of words Hope sank down onto the sofa.

"When the gold comes in we'll be richer than you ever dreamed, Hope. We'll be able to buy Alfie all the uniforms and shoes he wants, just not yet. Not at the moment. The money's all tied up." Enthusiasm shone in his eyes, but Hope's heart sank like a rock in a whirlpool.

"You don't mean you've given our savings to Lucien Grey."

"You know him?"

"Yes. He's being investigated for fraud."

"No. I don't believe it! Who told you that?"

"Inspector Penhalligan."

John sank onto the sofa next to Hope, deflated and confused. "I don't understand. Why would he tell you something like that?"

"He believes Lucien Grey had something to do with Pa's death."

"No," John shook his head. "Why would he say that? Mr Grey's wealthy, a gentleman and a successful businessman. He's a member of the club."

"That doesn't mean he's not a crook," she said, bitterness in her voice.

"I don't believe you."

"Inspector Penhalligan believes he's been selling shares in a Yukon gold mine that doesn't exist and when Pa and another man found out about the swindle he had them killed."

John jumped up. "That's ridiculous. Why would he get involved in anything as monstrous as murder?" Anger boiled in his eyes. "I'll prove you've got it all wrong. I'm going to the club to confront him. I'll sort this out one way or another. If it's true I'll get our money back."

Hope grabbed his arm. "You can't. Inspector Penhalligan told me in confidence. If Grey knows he's being investigated he'll disappear and we'll never see our money again."

He shook off her hand. "I'm going, Hope, and you can't stop me."

Oh hell, she thought as he stormed out. What have I done?

Hope was in a quandary. She paced the floor, dread swirling inside her. What should she do? If John approached Lucien Grey, as he intended, he could end up getting himself killed like Pa and it'd be all her fault. She was the one who told him about the swindle and got him so angry. She was mad with John, but even madder with herself. She could have told him earlier. If he'd known that perhaps she could have prevented him from giving Lucien Grey all their savings.

She thought the best thing to do would be to see Inspector Penhalligan first and tell him what she'd done. She gathered up her things and rushed out after John. If she could get to the Inspector before John found Lucien Grey, perhaps he could stop him.

Terror ballooned in her stomach on the way to the police station. She knew she shouldn't have told John something she'd been told in confidence, but, after all he was her brother and if he'd invested in the same scam as Pa – they'll have lost everything and could end up in the workhouse.

At the police station she only had to wait a few minutes before Inspector Penhalligan came out to see her.

"Good evening," he said. "What a pleasant surprise. What can I do for you? Have you remembered something I should know?"

"Not remembered, but I've done something stupid and I'm afraid I've spoiled your chances of catching that murdering rogue Lucien Grey."

"Good heavens. What on earth could you have done to be so upset about it? I'm sure we can sort it out, whatever it is."

The look in his eyes told Hope that his interest in her was far more than anything she could tell him about the club or its members. His gentle features spread into a smile.

"I'm afraid it's too late. I told John of your suspicions about Mr Grey. He's on his way to the club to confront him. Grey will know you're on to him and..." Tears sprang to her eyes threatening to spill over.

Oakley Penhalligan passed her his freshly washed, neatly pressed handkerchief. His brow furrowed. "Why would he do that? Tell him, I mean. For what purpose?"

"He's given him all our savings that's why. Now we'll lose it the same way Pa did. And he's lost the pub licence too, so we'll have nothing left. I just wanted to warn you." The tears spilled over and trickled down her cheeks. She covered her face with the Inspector's handkerchief.

He touched her shoulder in reassurance. "Thank you," he said. "I'll round up some men and get over there as soon as I can. Please don't worry. It's not your fault. I should have acted earlier."

She knew he was only trying to comfort her. It was her fault, all her fault and she'd never forgive herself if that twisting murderer got away. She'd never forgive John either, but then she realised it wasn't his fault. He'd been just as gullible as their pa. She couldn't blame him for that.

Chapter Thirty One

Hope walked as fast as she could to the club. If she hurried she might be able to catch John before he made a fool of himself. By the time she got there her breath came in quick gasps. She hoped she wasn't too late to stop John confronting Lucien Grey who, as a club member, would have greater standing than a mere waiter. All John would achieve would be to lose his job, get a reputation as a troublemaker and possibly a broken nose. Why had she had to open her mouth? But of course she knew the answer to that. Lucien Grey had stolen her pa's money and now he'd taken theirs in some scam about a Yukon gold mine.

Rushing through the kitchen she saw the porter who'd thrown Jasper Cunningham out, standing by the door on a break. "Have you seen my brother? Has he arrived yet?" she asked.

"John? Yeah. He arrived sometime ago. In a bit of tear an' all 'e was. Never seen a chick with such ruffled feathers. Won't get 'im anywhere though. Never does."

"Thanks." Hope's heart raced. She couldn't go into the restaurant or the bar until she'd changed into her Sapphire outfit. How long would that take? Even if she hurried she'd been at least half-an-hour with Hortense. She picked up her skirt and hurried on up to Dexi's boudoir.

"Goodness," Hortense said, when she arrived. "You all in a sweat. You have to calm down or you spoil your dress." She made her sit in front of the mirror sipping water until the flush faded from her cheeks and her breathing slowed.

"What got you in such a state?" she asked. "Is not good for you, all this rushing about. Ladies is meant to sit and look pretty."

Staring at her reflection Hope saw shadows under her eyes, her face red from exertion and her hair awry. Hortense was right. What could she do that would make any difference? "I'm sorry," she said. "I was trying to catch my brother before he did something stupid. I fear I'm too late anyway."

Hortense grinned. "Men born to be stupid," she said. "Can't change nature."

Hope smiled. Why was it that whenever she spent time with Hortense she felt better? The girl had a calming influence and when she thought of all she'd been through in her young life, she realised how lucky she was and how small and insignificant her problems were.

"You're right, Hortense. I'm sorry. Now, make me beautiful. Tonight I want to shine."

As she dressed in the sapphire silk, her hair piled high on her head and the sapphire necklace that gave her her sobriquet encircling her throat she felt herself growing in stature as she always did. It was like putting on a veil that hid her real feelings. Anonymity gave her confidence she'd never experienced before. She felt as though she were floating as she swished downstairs and was surprised to see Inspector Penhalligan already in the bar.

"Good evening," he said.

She nodded to the barman to fill her tray ready for the casino. Her voice trembled as she said, "Have you caught him yet? What about John, is he in trouble?"

Inspector Penhalligan smiled. "He hasn't appeared yet. I have men waiting outside. Mr Quirk asked me not to arrest him inside the club, it would be bad for his reputation which, as you know, he prizes above all things. We'll pick him up when he arrives."

Relief washed over Hope. "So John hasn't seen him yet?"

"No. As far as I know your brother is in the restaurant working behind the bar."

"Thank you." A warm swell of gratitude filled Hope. Gratitude for this dignified man whose job it was to keep the law and protect them from people like Lucien Grey. "I'll be glad when Lucien Grey is locked up. Will you be able to charge him with the murders?"

The Inspector frowned. "I'm not sure we have enough evidence for that. It's unlikely he did the deed himself. He probably paid someone else to do it, but we will be after him if we can prove it."

The porter came in with a note for the Inspector. He read it, nodded and said, "I have to go."

"Is it him?"

"I'll see you later," he said as he dashed out.

That evening, as she went round filling people's glasses and chatting, she felt happier than she had in a long while. It was as though a great weight had been lifted from her shoulders now that the fear of John getting into a fight with Lucien and being arrested for assault had been removed.

They may not have much money, or any money at all if John gave it all to Lucien Grey, but they both had jobs. She was paying Betsy the rent and had paid Ned back all she owed him. As long as she continued to work at the club Pa's debt to Silas would be paid. They may have lost the pub but they had comfortable lodgings at Betsy's which was enough for her and with Alfie having the chance to start a new school she thought she'd never felt so settled in her life.

She had yet to find a way to pay for Alfie's new uniform, but she was determined he'd have one. She'd sort out how to pay for it later. For the first time since that terrible night when her pa had died she felt optimistic about the future.

She even found herself laughing at the men's witty comments and smiling at their compliments throughout the evening. Several of them said she'd looked like she'd lost a sixpence and found a shilling and winked when they wondered what had caused her to glow so enchantingly.

By the end of the evening, when she cashed up she found her tips had more than doubled the usual amount which brought a wide grin to her face. When she had changed back into her own clothes she found John waiting for her downstairs, more morose than ever.

"Did you hear?" he said. "Lucien Grey has been arrested. Now we'll never get our money back."

She bit her lip to stop from blurting out how glad she was and how happy it made her that he was in custody and no longer a danger to them. "Really?" she said. "Well, I'm sure he deserved it. If he murdered Pa and set the fire I hope he hangs."

John stared at her. "You think he did that?"

"Yes I do and good riddance. That's what I say. Now are you going to walk me home or what?"

John quickly fell into step beside her. He didn't say another word all the way home.

The next morning, after breakfast they decided to go to the police station and see what the position was regarding John's investment. He had the paperwork Lucien Grey had given him so Hope thought he had a good chance of at least getting some of their money back.

Hope strode along with John lagging behind. "I don't know what you think we can achieve talking to the police," he said. "It'll be a fool's errand. It's bad enough that we've been duped without making an exhibition of ourselves at the police station."

Hope had more faith. "At least we can provide the Inspector with the evidence of your having bought shares through Lucien Grey. If nothing else it may help convict him."

"I don't see how. We've only got Inspector Penhalligan's suspicions that the gold mine is non-existent. It's hearsay at best. Without proof..." He grimaced.

Hope noticed his use of the word we when he meant himself. "Well, if we don't ask we'll never know and I for one want to find out all I can about this Lucien Grey. Even if it's a dead-end at least we'll have tried."

John shrugged and they walked on in silence.

When they arrived they had to wait. Hope sat silently praying that the Inspector wouldn't mention her part in identifying him at the club while John sat fidgeting, as though stewing inside and not sure how to deal with his anger.

When Inspector Penhalligan did appear he summoned them into his office. Hope saw his unlit pipe resting on a pipe-rest on the desk, but the smell of tobacco smoke clung to him like cobwebs, impossible to brush away.

"What have you found out?" she asked as John sat sulkily in his chair, glaring at the Inspector, his mouth clamped tightly closed.

Inspector Penhalligan shuffled some papers on his desk then looked up. "He's denying all knowledge of any fraudulent transactions," he said. "We've searched his home and his office and we're going through his paperwork right now, but I must warn you, he has an excellent solicitor. Fraud is notoriously difficult to prove."

John took some sheets of paper from his pocket, leaned forward and put them on the desk in front of the Inspector. "This is what he gave me in exchange for my investment. Confirmation of payment and a certificate showing I own one share in the Klondike Gold Mine. He can't dispute he sold me that."

"He's not denying the sale. He's saying that all his investors fully understood the risk. It's only fraud if the Klondike Gold Mine doesn't exist. If it really is a gold mine and he's authorised to sell shares in it, then you have no comeback. The fact that no gold appears is a risk you, the other investors and the prospectors take."

John's fists curled, his face reddened. Hope saw beads of sweat on his brow. "You're telling me I've been cheated and there's nothing I can do about it?"

"We don't know anything for sure. Until I hear back from the Canadian Police about the existence or otherwise of the mine, there's nothing I, or you, can do."

Hope put her hand on John's leg to try to calm him. "These shares are bought and sold every day," she said. "What would be the position if John decided to sell his share?"

John glanced at her but said nothing.

"Well, if you know, or suspect that it's been fraudulently sold to you, you could be implicated in the fraud if you try to sell it on. On the other hand, if you could persuade Lucien Grey to buy it back at the same price, his willingness to do so would strengthen his case that it's a bone fide transaction, or at least indicate his unawareness of the fact that it's a complete scam."

"And could we do that?" she asked.

"Well, I suppose it's worth a try. Should he be unwilling to buy it back it will of course strengthen our position that he's fully aware of the fraud. I think in that case he might be willing to buy it back."

"So, can I speak to him?" John asked.

The Inspector shook his head. "He's in custody, but I could ask him on your behalf. He has his solicitor with him at the moment. I'm sure, when given the opportunity to prove his innocence, his solicitor's advice will be to offer to purchase the share if you're unhappy with continuing to bear the risk."

"What about Pa's shares?" Hope asked. "Didn't he buy shares from Lucien Grey? At least that's what I understood."

Inspector Penhalligan shuffled the papers on his desk again and picked out one sheet. "This was amongst the papers you gave me from his safe. It's certainly a share certificate for one share in the Klondike Gold Mine." He went through the remaining papers on his desk. "I can't see any receipt for payment. We'll need one to tie the purchase to Lucien Grey, otherwise he may suggest your pa bought it from someone else, for which of course he'd have no responsibility."

"I can have another look in the safe," John said. "But if it was with his other accounts it would have gone up in smoke with the rest of the papers on his desk in the office."

"Do that and please let me know if you find it."

John agreed to leave the matter with Inspector Penhalligan to see what he could do while he looked for more evidence of Pa's involvement with Lucien Grey.

As they left the station Hope felt a little happier, but John slouched along, just as disgruntled as when he arrived.

Chapter Thirty Two

After they left the station John went to his job at the wood yard and Hope called in to the drapery store to see if Miss Godley had any work for her.

"I'm sorry there's not much," Ruth Godley said. "The big orders are done by machine now, but I do have a couple of specialist items I've been asked for." She handed Hope a white linen christening gown and a baby's dress. "They need to be smocked and pink flowers added across the skirts."

Hope smiled. "Fine. I'll have them back tomorrow," she said. She'd only make a few pennies but they would go towards buying Alfie new clothes for school.

She didn't mention to Miss Godley about the scholarship or Alfie's chance of changing schools as, with John still dead-set against it she knew she'd have a battle on her hands to make it happen. She did tell Ruth about Alfie being beaten up again, but as the school was on harvest holiday there was nothing more she could do for now.

She didn't arrive back at Betsy's until mid-afternoon and was surprised to see Betsy open the door as she approached.

"There's a surprise waiting for you in 'ere," she said. "Not sure it's a good 'un though."

Intrigued Hope hastened her step and, peering round the door, she saw Violet sitting on the sofa, listening to Alfie reading his book to her. Well, it looked like Violet, same tangle of red hair but the black eye and swollen lip told a different story.

"Violet! What on earth...?" Hope was lost for words. The rush of exhilaration she felt seeing Violet was overwhelmed by the horror of seeing the cuts and bruises on her face. "What happened?"

"Come on, Alfie," Betsy said. "Come and help me put dinner on. I expect we could do with a cuppa 'an all."

Alfie closed his book and went to get up. "You won't go away again will you, Violet?" he said. "You'll stay with us now, won't you?"

"I'll stay as long as I'm allowed," Violet said, eyes pleading as she looked at Hope. "Do as Betsy says. I'll see you later."

Hope sat next to Violet, thankful for Betsy's discretion in taking Alfie out so they could talk. "What happened? Although I can see for myself the results of whatever it was."

"Bert happened," Violet said, her eyes filling with tears.

"Showing his true colours at last is he? Not what you expected was it?" She hadn't meant it to sound so 'I told you so' and the sliver of satisfaction she felt for being right about him, gave her no joy. She put her arm around Violet's shoulders to comfort her. "Whatever you did you didn't deserve this."

"I got pregnant. That's what I did to deserve this."

Hope glanced down and saw Violet's expanded waistline. "Oh no! Oh Violet!"

Violet burst into tears, holding her hands in front of her face. "He's thrown me out. Says I can't work with him on stage in this condition. He said it's all my fault, but it's not is it, Hope? I never asked for it, honest." She blushed with scorching shame.

"Well, you didn't do it by yourself. Is he taking no responsibility?"

Violet shook her head. A tress of hair fell over her face. "I don't know what to do," she said.

Hope took a handkerchief out of her bag and handed it her sister. "Tell me exactly what happened. How far gone are you?"

Violet sniffed and dried her eyes. "About five months. It happened after the fire. He was comforting me. I wouldn't have done it if I hadn't been so upset about Ma and Pa and that."

"Hmm, comforting himself more like. Well, it's done now and of course you must stay with us. I'm sure Betsy will arrange something."

As she said it Betsy came in carrying a tray with a large pot of tea and three cups and saucers. There was a plate of fresh baked scones too. "I've sent Alfie out the back with an errand," she said. "Thought it best to keep 'im out the way 'til we get things sorted." She put the tray on the table and poured them each a cup of tea. "Now as I see it you'll be wanting a bed for a while at least. I'll make a bed up for Alfie down here, like I did afore and you can share with Hope if that's all right."

"Oh yes, thank you," Violet said, taking the offered tea. "I'm ever so grateful. I don't know what I'd do else. End up in the workhouse most like." Her voice was leaden with gloom.

"No fear of that happening if I've anything to say about it," Hope said, taking her tea from Betsy. "Dreadful place. Wouldn't wish it on my worst enemy."

Betsy nodded. "You can see why folks think they're better off on the streets than in one of them places can't you? Me? I'd rather throw meself in the river."

Her words brought on a fresh onslaught of sobbing from Violet and it took Hope all her patience to stop it. "I don't know what John will say," Hope said. "He likes to think he's the head of the family. He might have something to say about this."

Just as she said it John came in, dropped his bag on the floor and stood staring at Violet as though he'd seen a ghost. Betsy picked up the tea tray and carried it back out to kitchen in the few minutes if took John to recover. Hope was again grateful for her discretion.

"Violet. What on earth…?" he said.

"That's what I said," Hope told him. "That Bert's got a lot to answer for."

"Bert did this?" John said staring at her bruises. "Who does he think he is?"

"That's not the worst of it," Hope said. "She's pregnant. Five months."

John swallowed. "That true, Violet?"

She nodded, biting her swollen lip, her face heavy with sadness. "I'm sorry," she said. "If I refuse he forces himself on me. What else was I to do?" A torrent of tears ran down Violet's face. "It weren't my fault."

"Never is," John said but soon softened. "He'll not get away with it. Tell me where he is and I'll get a few of the lads to sort 'im out. He'll have to marry you. We'll make sure of that."

Fear filled her eyes. "No. I don't want to marry him. He's a beast. Who'd want to marry a man who beats her and forces himself on her? I'd rather die."

"Now, now," Hope said, her arm around Violet's shoulders. "You have to think of the child. Think of its future. No one wants to bring a bastard into the world."

"Bert didn't. He wanted me to get rid of it, but I couldn't, Hope. I just couldn't. An' he can't marry me anyway. He's already got a wife."

Hope looked at John, his face almost puce. "Where is he, the swine? Me and the lads'll sort 'im out."

Violet sat upright and sniffed, her head held high. "You can't. He's gone up North working in the clubs. You'll never find him and I don't want to see him again, ever."

"Where's his wife live? She must know where he is. I'll make her tell me." Anger blazed in John's eyes.

"She won't know where he is or what he gets up to. She doesn't know about the girls he sees, spends the night with them sometimes. I'm not the only one."

"He must have an agent or somat. Someone who does the bookings for him. They'd know where he is."

"If he did I don't know them. He kept that side of the business to himself. Kept the money an' all." A fresh onslaught of tears assailed her. Not for the first time Hope wished Ma was here. She'd know what to do.

"Betsy's said she can stay here for a while," Hope said. "I'll pay her a bit extra for the rent as there's another mouth to feed. We'll manage somehow, till the baby's born."

Her heart crunched as she said the last four words. A baby brought a whole new set of problems and difficulties and she wasn't sure Violet, although she'd be seventeen by then, was anywhere near prepared for that.

"I can't thank you enough," Violet said. "I know I've been a fool but I've learned me lesson. I won't get caught again."

"Hmmph. An expensive lesson an' all, an' too late to do owt about it," John grunted. "This isn't the end of it. Someone's got to pay and if I can't find Bert I'll find 'is missus and see what she has to say."

He turned and clattered up the stairs to get changed for his evening job at the club. Hope too had to get ready to go out. "Don't worry," she said. "Betsy will take care of you. Try to rest. I won't be home until late, but we can sort things out better tomorrow."

"Thanks, Hope. I don't deserve a sister like you," Violet said. "I know I've been a cow to you in the past, but I'm glad to see you today."

"And I'm glad to see you," Hope said and was surprised to find that she really meant it.

John walked with Hope to the club, something he hadn't done for a while, being so out with her. Dusk was gathering and a pale moon shone in the sky. The stars had yet to appear. The warmth of the day lingered in the evening air.

"What we gonna do about Violet?" he said. "She can't stay at Betsy's for long. Not once the baby's born. There's no room and Betsy, kind as she is, won't want a howling brat of a baby keeping her up all night."

"We'll have to find somewhere else," Hope said, but her heart wasn't in making any new arrangements. She had no desire to move, not when they'd got so settled.

"Shame we're not still at the pub isn't it?" John said. "Plenty of room there and we'd be our own bosses. We could have Violet at home if we were back in the pub."

Hope's heart sank. Of course he was right. The Hope and Anchor had plenty of room. She knew what was coming next.

"Do you think the brewery might change their minds now that Violet's back. I mean, they want a family to run the pub and with Violet and a baby on the way..."

Hope took a deep breath to push the thought away. She knew he was hoping she'd change her mind about moving back there if it was for Violet and her baby. She hastened her pace. "Come on, we don't want to be late," she said, trying to change the subject.

"Hmm. Somat to think about though, ain't it?" John said, increasing his stride to keep up with her.

During the evening she was too busy to think about Violet or John, so she tried to put it to the back of her mind, but it didn't stay there for long. The stab of guilt she felt at John losing the pub and his dream grew to an almost fatal wound.

Chapter Thirty Three

The next morning Violet was more like her old self. Betsy had put arnica on her bruises and a cold compress on her face to reduce the swelling. "I looked for you at the pub," she said to Hope as they were dressing, John having gone downstairs already. "I went there first. It was all boarded up so I went to the market and saw Ned. He told me you were staying here and working at The Grenadier." Her voice held a note of reproach.

"It's an obligation," Hope said. "I'm working to pay back the money Pa borrowed. That was the agreement he made with Silas Quirk. I'm to work there for a year without drawing any pay. It wasn't my idea."

"Ned said you've changed since you've been working there. Called it 'that place'. Sounded as though you'd had a falling out. You haven't have you?"

"No," she said, trying to keep the anger at the idea that Ned had been discussing their relationship with Violet out of her voice. "It's just that I don't get much time, what with helping Betsy, taking in stitching and darning and every evening spent at The Grenadier. A romance with Ned is the last thing on my mind."

She hadn't meant to let her irritation show, but wasn't sorry she had. Who was Violet to judge her after all she'd put them through? "Now, don't dilly-dally all day. Betsy has work to get on with as well." She picked up her bag and went downstairs, a dull ache of foreboding in her stomach.

Violet joined them a few minutes later and over breakfast John wanted to know all about her life with Bert and how she'd ended up the way she had. She told them about helping him in the theatre.

"At first I'd do a bit of singing, but that didn't last long. If my songs went well Bert didn't like being overshadowed." She sipped the tea Betsy had poured for her. "If his act went down better than mine, he'd be fine, buying drinks, being nice to me but if it went badly..." Fear shadowed her eyes. "He'd turn into a monster, drink too much and take it out on me." She picked up a piece of toast and bit into it, quite viciously.

"I'm sorry," Hope said. "What about the other performers? Did they know what he was like? Why did none of them help you?"

Violet shrugged. "I think we were all in the same boat. It wasn't as glamorous as he made out. Most of the places we stayed were alive with bed bugs and 'roaches. It were awful."

"Why didn't you come home, or at least write? You know Ma..." Hope said. She was going to say Ma and Pa would be there for her, but of course...

Violet's face fell, her eyes full of regret. "Sorry about Ma an' all. Sorry I missed the funeral. I didn't even know she'd gone. I'll always regret that." Her voice told the truth of it.

"What about performing on stage? I thought you loved that."

Violet's face turned into a grimace. "I would have, if I'd been allowed to sing. All they wanted me to do was stand at the back and take me clothes off."

"You didn't?" Hope was aghast. John choked on the toast he'd just bitten into.

Violet smiled. "No, but wearing them skimpy outfits felt like it."

By the time she'd finished Hope felt quite sorry for her, after all she was young and naive. She was right. She'd had no choice, just like Hope. She'd lost her dream, just like John. At the thought Hope felt guilty all over again.

"You'd like to go back to the pub wouldn't you, Violet?" John said at last, staring Hope in the eye, unblinking, his gaze steady.

"'course I would, that's why I came home. Thought it might be ready to move back in."

Hope recalled her saying she wasn't going to spend the rest of life living in a dingy pub. So, she wasn't the only one who'd changed. She was about to remind Violet, but in the circumstance thought better of it.

"You too, Alfie. You'd like to go 'ome to the pub wouldn't you?"

Hope gritted her teeth.

Alfie looked at them all before he spoke. Then turned back to his plate of bread and butter. "I don't mind where I live as long as I'm with you and Hope and Violet."

Hope's heart melted. At least she had one supporter.

"Well, we'll have to find somewhere else to live before long," John said. "Won't be able to stay here after the baby's born."

That was true. Hope had spoken to Betsy about it and she'd said they were welcome to stay until then, but she was too old to cope with a baby in the house with the crying all night, extra washing and anyway, she had no room for another one. They were squashed up enough as it was with Alfie sleeping downstairs. Hope couldn't blame her, but it didn't help their situation.

"I'm going to have another go at the brewery," John said. "You'd come back and work in the pub wouldn't you, Violet?"

"In a heartbeat if it keeps me and the baby out of the workhouse. I've no other means of support." She lowered her gaze to stare at her now empty plate. Hope's lungs filled at Violet's bare-faced cheek.

"The pub was our living and now the family's all together again…" John glared at Hope, daring her to contradict him. "They owes us somat for Ma and Pa's lives. I'm going to remind them."

"I have an errand to run," Hope said jumping up from the table to get her shawl before John could have another go at her. "I'll see you all later."

She stepped outside and started to breathe again.

Outside in the fresh air she decided to take a walk to the river a place she often went to sort things out in her head. She found a place to sit where she could watch the boats go by, a colourful parade heading towards the docks. It seemed as though everyone was going about their business without a care in the world. If only that could be the case.

A gap in the clouds opened and a shaft of sunlight fell on her face. She felt the warmth of it. The gentle lapping of the water against the boats moored alongside the bank had a calming effect and she began to relax. She was happy to sit here in the August sunshine, but John's words played in her mind. Was he right? It was true they'd had a good life in the pub. If it hadn't been for her pa's drinking and gambling….

She chided herself for thinking like that. She felt her life was all at sixes and sevens. Nothing settled. She watched the birds fly down to the water then, when they'd drank their fill, soared away again, envying them their freedom to go where they pleased with no encumbrances.

She knew where her duty lay. It was to her family. To the memory of her ma and pa. A stone of sadness settled in her stomach at the thought of their absence from the rest of her life. She owed them so much. They'd instilled values in her that couldn't be ignored. Family came first, that's what Ma always used to say, and that hard work and goodness had its own reward.

Was she being unreasonable, denying John the opportunity to take over from his father, follow his dream and carry on his legacy? Could the pub give them a reasonable living? There would have to be changes of course, but wasn't that what life was all about, facing the challenges, facing them and getting on?

She wondered what Ma would say now, but in her heart she already knew. 'Family first,' Ma would say… 'That's the most important thing. We all need family.'

With a heavy heart she walked back into town. She'd sort things out with Ned and with John, but not yet. Just for now she was going to follow her heart and go to the National Gallery to look at the paintings. That always lifted her spirits.

Chapter Thirty Four

By the time Hope arrived home in the afternoon John, Violet, Alfie and Betsy were all waiting for her.

"I'll get tea," Betsy said and shuffled out to the kitchen.

"Have I missed something?" Hope asked as they all sat staring at her.

"You've missed the good news," John said, his face lit up with the broadest smile. "I'm getting the pub back. We can all go home."

Hope's insides fluttered. She didn't want to spoil their joy, but she'd told him she wasn't going back and she wasn't going to change her mind.

"What have you told them – the brewery? What did you say?"

"That now Violet's home with a young 'un on the way we can move back as a family and run the pub just the way they wanted. We can make it a family pub."

"A family without me?"

John's face hardened. "A family like when Ma and Pa were alive," he said. "All of us going back."

"Do say you'll come with us," Violet pleaded. "I'll need help when the baby comes and there's nothing I'd like more than you coming an' all."

"I'm not going if Hope's not," Alfie said. He glared at John. "You promised."

"I'm not asking you to work at the pub, Hope. You can still work at the club, like Pa agreed. Violet can manage the kitchen, although I dare say she'd appreciate any help you can give her." A flicker of doubt crossed his face. "We're all depending on you, Hope. If you don't come…"

Hope glanced at each of her siblings in turn and saw the longing in their eyes. She couldn't let them down, not when they'd all been through so much, but on the other hand…

"The brewery agreed to you holding the licence?" she said, aware that his age and lack of managerial experience would go against him.

He looked sheepish. "Yes. As long as I get someone to sponsor me."

"Sponsor you?"

"Yes. Guarantee the rent, that's all. They wouldn't need to work in the pub or oversee the business, just cover the cost if I can't make it pay."

"And who's going to be fool enough to do that?"

John's lips turned up at the corners. A sly glint shone in his eye. "I was going to ask Silas Quirk."

"Silas Quirk? Are you mad? Why would he be daft enough to put himself in the position of paying your rent if your business fails?"

"Cos it'll be our rent and he's sweet on you."

Hope gasped. "He is not! What on earth put that idea in your head?"

John chuckled. "He is too. Everyone knows it bar you. Why else has he been taking such an interest in our family? Giving us both jobs, finding a school for Alfie?"

She wanted to say it was his kind and generous nature, but they'd laugh. He wasn't known for his generosity only for his ruthlessness. "Because it's good for his business," is all Hope could think to say. "And I doubt paying your rent falls into that category."

"Well, we'll see shall we," John said.

"No, don't," Hope said. "We're indebted enough to him. We can't ask for anything more."

John grinned, picked up his coat and cap and went out, whistling as he did so.

Hope sank onto the settee next to Violet who put her hand over Hope's as Betsy brought in the tea. "It'll be all right," she said. "We'll be together again in the pub, just like before. Ma would have wanted that."

Hope's heart squeezed at the mention of her mother. Violet was right. Ma would have wanted them to stay together and look out for each other, but relying on Silas Quirk? She didn't think Ma would approve of that at all.

All evening, working in the club thoughts of what John had said were never far from her mind. Was she being fair to him? His heart was there, in the place they'd grown up. He wanted to continue Ma and Pa's legacy. Hers wasn't and she didn't. Was there something wrong with her? She questioned why she shouldn't feel the same as John and now Violet. And he was right, it would provide a home for Violet and her baby. Could she deny them that? Then she looked around the opulent surroundings she'd become familiar with at The Grenadier and knew the answer. The fact that that was where Silas Quirk was to be found had nothing to do with it.

Later that evening, after Hope had finished her shift at the club John was waiting to walk her home. The smile on his face told her all she needed to know.

"What did he say?" she asked as soon as they got outside.

"You are looking at the new licensee of the Hope and Anchor Public House," he said, almost doing a jig on the spot. "It's all settled. I told him you'd still be working at The Grenadier and I wouldn't be making any unreasonable demands on your time so he agreed." He chuckled. "Told you he was sweet on you."

Hope dug him in the ribs, but such was his joy at his achievement she didn't have the heart to tell him again that she wasn't going with them. He must have sensed her mood.

"You are coming back with us aren't you?" he said. "For Violet's sake and Alfie's. Although, even if you don't it won't make any difference, now Silas Quirk has agreed to speak to the brewery for me."

"He did that?" Her heart dropped into her boots. It was another thing she had to thank him for. It felt like another obligation increasing Silas Quirk's hold over her family. John was right about his interest in them, but she wasn't sure about John's guess at his motivation. She wasn't even sure he wasn't involved in the fire in some way. What did Silas Quirk want with them and when would he be calling in the favours?

"Yes. Happy to, he said. Although I may have intimated that you'd be moving in too. You will won't you?"

Hope sighed. She stopped and looked him square in the face. "On one condition," she said.

"That is?"

"Alfie goes to the new school and you pay for his uniform and his books."

John paused to think for a moment then his lips spread into a grin. "If I'm running a business I'll be a businessman and people need to appreciate our new status," he said with a twinkle in his eye. "My little brother going to a posh school won't do my standing in the community any harm, in fact it might do it some good. Make people treat us with a bit of respect."

Hope could have thrown her arms around him. All right, she'd agreed to go back to live in the pub, but at least she'd made sure Alfie would be spared a daily beating and that was enough for now.

Breakfast the next morning was a jolly affair with everyone talking at once about their plans for the pub. "There's a bit of clearing up still to do," John said, "but it won't take long if we all muck in."

"Can I have my old room back?" Alfie asked. "With all my stuff."

"What's left of it after the fire," John said. "I propose that Violet has Ma and Pa's room. With the baby coming she'll need extra space and a bit of privacy."

Hope agreed, glad not to be having to share, especially with the baby coming. Working until midnight every night she needed her sleep.

Betsy had her hands full when there was a knock on the door so Hope got up to answer it. Her heart fluttered when she saw Inspector Penhalligan on the doorstep.

"Can I come in?" he said as Hope stood on the doorstep, mouth agape.

"Of course." She stepped back and he joined them at the table. Betsy went and got an extra cup and poured him some tea.

"Have you charged Lucien Grey yet?" John said. "Is that why you've come?"

The Inspector put his cup back on its saucer. "There's some good news and some bad news," he said. "Lucien Grey is still protesting his innocence. I think he realises he has a lot to lose if he's found guilty of the fraud. It would prove motivation for the murders."

"And the good news?" Hope said.

The Inspector smiled and reached into his inside pocket drawing out a small parcel. "He agreed to buy back your shares and your father's."

John reached out to take the package, but Hope was quicker. She grabbed it and tore off the wrapping to reveal a bundle of white five pound notes.

"It's all there," Inspector Penhalligan said. "He wanted to give you a cheque but, knowing how he operates I asked for cash. He didn't have it on him so I had the cheque made out to cash and took it to the bank before he could stop it."

"That's marvellous," Hope said as John leaned forward to take the cash from her. "This'll pay for Alfie's new uniform and his books with a bit left over I wouldn't wonder." She tucked it into her blouse. "We'll go shopping this very day. You'll come with me won't you, Alfie?"

Alfie grinned. His face beamed with happiness.

John sat back and shrugged. "We'll need money for the pub," he said. "I want to make it into a proper family pub. A place where the market traders and local businessmen can bring their wives for a bite to eat. No more gaming tables. I'll be aiming for a better class of clientele and the brewery are upgrading the whole place, so we need to raise our game too."

"I can see you have plans," the Inspector said. "I'll leave you to get on. Thank you for the tea, Mrs Brady."

"You'll let us know about the charges against Lucien Grey won't you, Inspector?" Hope asked. "He's not going to get away with it is he?"

"Not as long as I got breath in my body," Inspector Penhalligan said. "You can rest assured we'll be doing everything we can to bring him to justice."

"Thank you," Hope said as she saw him out. At least getting their money back was a step in the right direction.

Chapter Thirty Five

With John's money tucked into her purse Hope and Alfie went into town to buy him some new clothes. Accompanying the letter of acceptance were details of what pupils should wear and where these could be obtained. They took a cab to city where the gentlemen's outfitter mentioned was located. The cab dropped them on the corner of the street.

The road was wider than the narrow streets they'd left behind with the smell of horse sweat, dung and rotting vegetable, but still bustled with carriages, cabs, buggies and carts. An omnibus made slow progress and the pavements were more crowded than she'd ever seen. They dodged the pedlars offering sandwiches, fresh fish or fruit, pushing their way through the crowds. It would have been unbearably hot in the late August sun were it not for the awnings from the row of shops shading the pavement and the tall buildings casting the street into shadow. Walking along Hope could only stare at the windows with their eye-catching displays.

They were jostled as they walked, Hope slowing her pace to accommodate Alfie. She feared for Alfie in the crush of people bustling along, jostling them but she needn't have worried. He was limping along beside her, mouth agape at the sights and sounds around him. Many of the shop windows were lit with electric lighting. They stared at them in wide-eyed amazement. "Look at that, Alfie," she kept saying as they walked along. Alfie nodded and grinned.

She found Taylor's Emporium, a smart double-fronted shop with large glass windows in front of a display of gentlemen's outfits, the sort one would wear for hunting, shooting or fishing in the country. Could this be right? Could this be the place for boys' school uniforms? Only one way to find out.

She pushed the door open and a bell jangled. She ushered Alfie in and together they made their way past glass-fronted counters standing in front of shelves piled high with various colours of fabrics, suiting, tweed and tartan, in a breathtaking array.

A tall young man in a suit approached them. His nose wrinkled and he sniffed as though suddenly assaulted by a bad smell. "May I be of assistance?" he asked, his eyes belying his intention to help. Hope saw his mouth turned to a sneer as his gaze travelled over her and Alfie, especially Alfie.

She held her head high. He didn't intimidate her. She'd seen gentlemen of greater standing than this twerp and laughed and joked with them in the club. She felt herself equal to the challenge he presented. "My brother needs a uniform for Merchant Taylors' School," she said. I understand you can provide one."

"Erm, yes." His look of sheer amazement was one to relay to John and Violet when she got home. She'd have fun telling them about this visit.

"If you'd care to follow me I'm sure Mr Taylor will be able to…urm…sort you out." He looked unsure, as though uncertain whether Hope was being serious. Perhaps he thought they were going to bludgeon him to death out the back and steal some silk ties, she thought. That made her smile.

"Good," she said. "I'd hate to think we've been wasting our valuable time coming here if he can't."

She marvelled at her own courage. Before she'd worked at The Grenadier she'd never have had the nerve to speak to him the way she did. Perhaps working there wasn't such a bad thing after all.

They followed the young man through to the workroom at the back of the shop where they were asked to wait. "I'll fetch Mr Taylor directly," the young man said, rather grudgingly.

Mr Taylor appeared, hand held out in front of him. "Welcome to my shop," he said. "You've come for a Merchant Taylors' uniform, I understand. Well, you've come to the right place."

Hope took an immediate liking to this bluff, portly man with his ruddy face and thinning hair. "Thank you, yes," she said. "My brother, Alfie, is to start next term and needs to be properly attired."

"Quite right," Mr Taylor said. His face assembled itself into a frown when he glanced at Alfie. "Hmm," he said. "Would I be right in thinking that you are Alfred Daniels? Friend of Silas Quirk?"

Hope gasped. "Yes. How did you know?"

Mr Taylor smiled. "Not many boys going to Merchant Taylors' come dressed as your brother, Miss Daniels, and they usually come with a tutor or valet, not a family member." He paused to glance again at Alfie, nodding as he did so. "You must be the boy I'm to take to school with my son, George," he said. He put out his hand. "I'm very pleased to meet you."

Alfie glanced at Hope before taking Mr Taylor's hand. "Please to meet you, sir," he said.

"Miss Daniels," he said, again offering his hand.

Suddenly it all made sense. This was the friend Silas had mentioned. Why hadn't she realised it before? She smiled at the warmth of his greeting. "I can't thank you enough for taking Alfie to school. It's a weight of my mind to know he'll be in good hands," she said taking his hand.

"Think nothing of it, my dear. I'm only pleased that George will have a companion on the journey and I hope the boys will soon be friends."

"Thank you, sir," Alfie said, his eyes wide. "I hope so too."

Mr Taylor called his assistant and they soon had Alfie measured and his uniform requirements chosen. Hope paled at the cost, but assured Mr Taylor it was fine when he offered to accept payment by instalment. "You'd be surprised how many of my regular customers can't quite find the ready cash for their purchases," he said.

"That's very kind of you," she said, "but we can manage. If there's anything else you think Alfie might need, please add it to the order and the bill." She wasn't going to have Alfie having anything less than the other boys. He'd won his place at the school and she'd do everything in her power to support him and not let him down or have him stand out as being any different from the other boys.

August turned to September, the days became cooler and the nights began drawing in. Hope and John were both working as often as they could and putting their money by for when they returned to the pub. Even Violet helped out doing some sewing and darning and helping Betsy with the washing and shopping in the market. Every time she went out she'd return in a huff.

"It's too hot and sticky. I'll be glad when this baby's born," she said. "The sneering faces of the neighbours don't help. I can see by their faces what they're thinking. Up the duff and no man in sight, that's what they're thinking."

"I told the brewery you were married and your husband was working up North," John said when she'd been complaining more bitterly than usual. "You'd better have this." He put his hand in his pocket and produced their mother's wedding ring.

"Where did you get that?" Hope asked, eyes wide.

"From the hospital," John said. "They gave it to me with her other belongings. I thought Violet could have it…in the circumstances."

"Oh no. I couldn't," Violet said. "It's Ma's."

"No use to her now is it?" John said. "More use to you."

"Yes, you should take it," Hope said. "Ma would want you to have it, especially…" She was going to say in your condition, but bit the words back in time. Violet was still sensitive about 'her condition'.

Violet slipped the ring onto her finger. "I can't thank you enough," she said. "I'll think of Ma an' all, every time I see it. It's very special. Thank you, John, Thank you, Hope." She glanced around. "And thank you, Alfie," she called although Alfie, out the back with Betsy, wouldn't have a clue what he was being thanked for. She hugged both John and Hope. "It's belonging to a family like this that makes it all worthwhile," she said.

The next time they visited the pub they decided that the upstairs rooms needed a lick of paint to get rid of the all-pervading acrid smell of smoke. They also needed new bedding, rugs and curtains.

After fitting Alfie out in his new uniform, with spares of everything, there was still a little left from the money recovered for them to start on the refurbishment.

The morning Alfie was to start his new school he dressed in his new clothes and smarmed down his unruly hair. His face shone with scrubbing and a new sense of pride and confidence shone in his eyes. Hope offered to go with him.

"No need," he said. "I'm a big boy now. I can go on my own."

Seeing him in his smart new uniform, looking every inch a young gentleman, she couldn't help a tear forming in her eye. "I'm so proud of you," she said. "Ma and Pa would be proud too."

"I hope I don't let you all down," he said, suddenly afraid.

"Of course you won't," Hope reassured him. "You passed the scholarship. You have every right to be there. You're as good as the other boys. In fact, even better. They're only there because their parents can afford to pay the fees. You're there on merit. You deserve it."

After breakfast she walked with him to Mr Taylor's house. She'd had a note from him saying how welcome Alfie was and reminding them to be at his home by 7.30 am and he'd drop them off on his way into work.

It was a cool crisp morning when they stepped out and Hope breathed in the fresh air relishing the sense of freedom the early morning always gave her. They passed the coffee stalls, street vendors and newspaper boys on their walk, exchanging a brief 'good morning' as they went along. The people she recognised all stopped to say how smart Alfie looked which brought a warm glow to his face.

The address she'd been given was in a pleasant road lined with trees. The house itself set back from the road behind a small front garden, with a lawn edged by late blossoming summer flowers. As Hope opened the iron gate the front door opened and Mr Taylor, wearing a light coat over a dark suit, stepped out.

"Good morning," he said. "Right on time. I do like punctuality. It shows respect. I'm pleased to see you both so keen to start as you mean to go on."

"Good morning," Hope said. "Thank you once again for taking Alfie. I'm sure he'll be no trouble."

"My pleasure," Mr Taylor said. "Now you must come in and meet George. George," he called loudly as he walked back into house. "Come along, son, you don't want to be late on your first day back."

Inside Hope noticed the wood panelled walls, the thickly carpeted floor. She'd expected the narrow hallway to be dark, but it wasn't. A large stained glass window halfway up the stairs let in the light and threw a rainbow reflection on the opposite wall.

As they stood waiting she heard a carriage pull up outside and the call of the coachman bringing the horses to a halt. A door opened at the end of the hall and a small boy, dressed in a uniform similar to the one Alfie had donned that morning, came out. Bent forward over crutches, one under each of his arms, he made his way unsteadily forward. He looked smaller and more frail than Alfie, and younger, although Hope knew he was the same age from her conversation with Silas. She couldn't stop the gasp that escaped her mouth when she saw him.

Mr Taylor leaned towards her. "Since birth," he said quietly. "We're used to it now and George never complains."

She could see now why Alfie was so welcome. Another boy with a disability who'd been victimised because of it. As she watched him carefully placing each foot on the floor walking towards them supported by his crutches she wondered how many times Mr Taylor's son had been beaten up before they moved him to the new school.

George was followed by his mother, anxiously walking behind him. A nervous looking woman she was slim and well-dressed but Hope didn't miss the substantial bump in her waistline or the worry in her eyes.

"Well done, George," Mr Taylor said when they reached the front door. "This is your new school mate Alfie and his sister Miss Daniels." They shook hands.

"Please don't stand on ceremony," the woman who'd followed George along the hall said, offering her hand. "I'm Margaret and my husband is Harold."

Hope shook her hand. "Hope," she said.

"It'll be nice for George to have a friend," Mr Taylor said.

Alfie grinned. "I'm sure we'll get on famously," he said. It was clear he had warmed immediately to George, and George appeared to warm to him.

Once he was sure the boys had everything they'd need for their day at school, Mr Taylor took them all out to the waiting carriage. Alfie climbed in first, followed by George. Then Mr Taylor kissed his wife goodbye at the gate and climbed into the carriage with them.

As the carriage pulled away Hope felt a bit of her heart go with it.

Admiration for this man and his handling of his son's disability washed over her.

"Now, if you've time you must come in and have a cup of tea with me," Margaret said, leading her back inside.

Chapter Thirty Six

Inside the cosy kitchen Mrs Taylor put the kettle on the stove to boil. "It's cook's day off," she said, "so we can sit in here without bothering her. I do prefer it to the front parlour. I hope you'll be comfortable in here too."

Hope took a chair at the table. "It's lovely," she said, glancing out of the window into the garden, where autumn sunshine dappled grass darkened with fallen leaves. Mrs Taylor noticed her glance.

"Yes, I love to look out over the garden at this time of year," she said. "The changing colours and the knowledge that, when they're gone, they'll come again next spring bringing new life and hope."

"Talking of new life when's it due?" Hope asked nodding towards Margaret's expanded waistline.

Margaret smiled. "Next month, all being well. George came early, so I'm prepared for anything." She spooned tea into the teapot ready for when the kettle boiled. "Harold wasn't sure about having another after, you know, George." She set out two cups on saucers, turning away to avoid Hope's gaze, as though talking it over to herself. "We found out early on that he'd be unable to walk unaided, but he showed such spirit, even as a baby," she said. "We had to do everything we could for him. He brought so much joy into our lives, but the doctors tell us that there's no reason there should be any problem with this one."

She picked the boiling kettle up and made the tea. "Even if it did turn out like George we'd love it just the same. George has brought us so much happiness." She glanced at Hope. "I'm sure you understand, what with Alfie and all."

"Yes," Hope said. "He's my brother not my son, but I'm just as proud of him as I would be were he mine."

Margaret poured the tea and handed Hope a cup. "Every small step George takes, every obstacle he overcomes, fills my heart with love," she said, her eyes shone with pride as she talked about her son.

"I can see you're immensely proud of him. I'm glad Alfie's got such a friend," Hope said. "He's been through a lot too. They'll have something in common."

"Yes, Silas told us about the fire and losing your parents. It must have been awful. I don't know how I'd have coped in such a situation."

Memories of that terrible day flashed through Hope's mind, the sight and ferocity of the flames, the heat, the confusion, the smell of the smoke and most of all the utter desolation and helplessness she felt afterwards. She closed her eyes and bent her head over her tea.

"Alfie was pretty bad," she said quietly, "but the hospital were excellent."

"Harold's hoping they'll help each other through difficult times."

"I'm sure they will," Hope said.

"I hear young Alfie's quite bright. He got the scholarship?"

"Yes, that's right." A warm glow spread from Hope's stomach right up to her face.

"Unfortunately George lags behind in his learning. We were hoping that going around with Alfie would give him the confidence to try harder. It's a worry." Sadness filled her previously vibrant eyes.

"Alfie has a heart of gold," Hope said. "You have no worries there. He'll help George all he can."

"And you work for Silas I understand? He speaks well of you, that's why we had no compunction in offering Alfie a lift to the school. Silas has been very good to us."

Hope smiled, but a shiver of fear ran through her. She knew Silas's reputation and the reputation of the club. How could she explain her work to this nice woman who must think her occupation very risqué indeed? "Yes. I work as a waitress in the bar. My parents ran a pub so I'm using to serving drinks and handling the result of some people's over-indulgence."

"And do many people 'over-indulge'?" Margaret said, sipping her tea. Her eyes alert with interest. "It sounds quite fascinating. I must say I envy you, mixing in such lively company. The most excitement I get is when the butcher's boy calls with the meat. He's always got a tale to tell, not always quite proper, but very entertaining."

Hope laughed. "It's not as exciting as it sounds, in fact most evenings it's quite boring, but we do have our moments." She went on to describe a few and Margaret told her about some of the events run by the Guild that they'd attended. The minutes flew by and before she knew it Hope realised John would be waiting for her at the pub to get on with the cleaning.

"I can't thank your husband enough for taking Alfie to school," she said as she prepared to leave. "It's a weight off my mind knowing he has a friend."

"I'm sure we will become good friends too," Margaret said.

Hope's heart lifted. She was sure Margaret was right.

Hope walked with Alfie to the Taylors' for his ride to school, for the next few weeks despite his protests. "I can go on my own," he'd say, but Hope feared they may run into some of the rogues and ruffians from the local school, who wouldn't hesitate to beat him up, jeer at him and possibly throw stones, mud or something worse from the road at him, especially if they saw him in his new uniform.

Each morning she sat and had tea with Margaret who was glad of the company. She soon learned of Margaret's loneliness and the difficulties she experienced getting George accepted anywhere because of his disability.

Hope told her about the boys at Alfie's school, the beating he'd endured because he couldn't run away and how happy she was that he was no longer there.

Margaret talked about the other wives of the men in the Tailors' Guild. "The adults aren't much better," she said and told Hope about their haughty ways and how competitive they were. Hope regaled her with snippets about the gentlemen at the club and how many of them weren't gentlemen at all.

"I can't get out much nowadays," Margaret said, indicating her swelling bump. "Not in my condition."

Hope thought about Violet and realised that she'd be going through the same thing soon.

"That reminds me," Margaret said. "Talking about my condition. I hope you won't be offended but I have a few things I think might be of use to you." She opened a large bag that had been sitting on a chair next to her and brought out several items of clothing. There was a beautifully tailored suit in a deep marine blue and a couple of good day dresses in lilac and pink.

"I'll never get into them again and it seems such a waste for them not to be worn. You're slim enough to carry them off and I'd be delighted if you could make use of them."

She handed the clothes to Hope who didn't know what to say. The quality was obvious in every stitch. She ran her hands over the material. It was exquisite. "They're beautiful," Hope said. "I couldn't, really."

"Nonsense," Margaret said. "They're no use to me and Harold will make me a brand new wardrobe after the baby's born. Please take them."

"Well," Hope again ran her hands over the rich fabric. They were far better than she'd ever be able to afford.

"There will be several occasions at the school when your presence will be required and, I hope you don't mind me saying, they will require you to wear something a little more, shall we say, fashionable... than you're currently wearing. I can promise you some of those parents are not above expressing their opinions about one another's turnouts, no matter how rude it may be."

Hope smiled. "They are exquisite, far better than I could ever afford. Thank you," she said. "If there's anything I can do in return..."

"Being my friend is thanks enough," Margaret said, "although, I have been admiring your blouse. Is it your own work?"

Hope had put on the blouse she was wearing to go to the theatre with Ned. "Yes. I made it myself and embroidered it. I also do some embroidery for the drapery in town, but the work is falling off these days, what with the new machines coming in."

"I know. Harold is always complaining about the quality of embroidery done by machine on the monogrammed shirts he sells. His customers prefer hand-stitched. I wonder. Is there any possibility that you could show him a sample of your work? He may wish to make use of your services."

"I'd be happy to," Hope said. "The work from the drapery is lovely, but hardly enough to pay the rent. Another outlet would suit me admirably."

Meanwhile work at the Hope and Anchor continued. All the rooms were repainted, new flooring laid and, when they could afford it, new bits and pieces of furniture added. The new baby would need a cot and Violet wanted a nursery chair. Hope and John continued to plough all their money into the pub ready for the grand opening planned for November.

"I've had a word with Elsie, one of the cooks from the club," John said one evening as they were going over plans for the opening. "She's agreed to come along and work for us, at least until Violet's able to take over." He grinned. "Violet's in no condition to do it and anyway, I've tasted her cooking." He pulled a face which earned him a cushion thrown by Violet in his direction.

"What about working behind the bar?" Hope asked. "You won't be able to manage on your own."

"No, I know. I'll have to get someone in for that too, but if things work out as I hope we'll be making enough to cover the extra cost."

"Why don't you ask that girl Alice, from the market?" Hope said. "She's good with money, trustworthy and pleasant. Always has a chat with the customers at her mum's stall. She'd be an asset."

John coloured. Hope knew he was keen on her because of his frequent visits to the market and her mum's stall especially. "Good idea," he said. "I'll do that." He had a satisfied grin on his face as he said it.

Chapter Thirty Seven

Autumn brought a chill to the streets and as the weeks passed the leaves on the trees turned russet and gold. The walk to the Taylors' with Alfie each morning brought Hope joy. She loved the early morning with its clean, fresh air and light, before the rest of the world woke and spoiled it. She'd walk proudly with Alfie in his school uniform and nod to the people she passed, wondering if they knew how special he was and how clever. If she saw any of the boys from the local school they'd be on their own and therefore no danger and they'd walk by on the other side.

Once she was happy that Alfie had settled down in the school and was making friends she buckled down to the task of sorting out their living quarters in the pub with John and Violet.

Downstairs the brewery had refurbished the lounge and public bar to a level of comfort far higher than she ever recalled seeing, with plush red benches and chairs and mahogany tables. They put in new lighting in place of the old lamps. Long mirrored shelving behind the solid oak bar reflected the light making the whole place look brighter.

The kitchen had been refitted too with the installation of a new gas-fired oven, removing the necessity for the bags of coal that left dirt and dust all over the place. Brass and copper fittings still had to be polished and the floor scrubbed, stained and varnished, but the whole place had a more up-market feel about it.

Even the function hall at the back, which hadn't been touched by fire, had been repainted, the floor scrubbed and polished and new red velvet curtains hung over the windows. The cellar had been whitewashed and the bricked floors painted red.

"They're aiming for a better class of clientele," John said. "One who won't mind spending a bit to treat their wives to a night out now and then."

The rent had been increased to cover the extra cost of the refurbishment but John was confident that, with a corresponding increase in prices, he would still be able to make a good living and support them.

Hope, Violet and John worked to get the pub ready to open in time to catch the lucrative Christmas trade.

"We'll have a grand opening," John said. "Everyone invited. All the local shopkeepers and businessmen. Anyone who's anyone will be invited to come."

"I'll get some leaflets printed," Violet said. "I know the printer who used to do the programmes for the theatre. He'll do 'em cheap for me," she winked.

"Hmm. Best wear a big coat then," Hope said, referring to Violet's expanding waistline.

By the middle of October they had most of the work done. John and Hope had done the heavy work while Violet had organised the replacement of the curtains and bedding.

"There's just Ma's dressing table to go through," Violet said, standing in the bedroom she was to take over. She stretched her back, her hands at the base of her spine and sighed. "Can you do that, Hope? I really have to sit down."

Her pregnancy was well advanced and there had been speculation that she wouldn't last out until Christmas, but Violet assured them it wasn't due yet.

"Well, you look to me like you're about to pop," John said and chuckled as he went down stairs to finish the cleaning.

Hope pulled up the dressing table stool and started going through the drawers. She'd already cleared everything from the top as it had been blackened by smoke but the drawers still held the acrid smell.

"They'll need a good scrub, Violet said, "before I put my baby's things in there. Don't want the little mite stinking of smoke."

"I'll scrub them out with carbolic," Hope said. "That'll get rid of it."

So Hope began taking everything out. The long drawer held some of her mother's under-clothes, which she dropped into the box put aside for the things to be discarded. The small side drawers held lots of bits of paper that Ma had kept. She found old cards, bills and letters, some so old they almost fell apart when Hope touched them.

At the back of the drawer she found all the cards and notes she, Violet, John and Alfie had sent during their childhood, from when they started school.

"Ooo. Anything interesting?" Violet asked, perking up.

"No," Hope laughed. "Just Ma's old mementoes and bits and bobs. I'll put them in a box to put aside so we can go through them later when we have more time."

"Great," Violet said. "I'll go and put the kettle on. It must be time we stopped for tea and you and John will need to get changed for work."

Hope hadn't realised how late the time was getting. "I'll just finish this, then I'll come down," she said.

After Violet had gone she emptied the rest of the drawers. She found a bundle of letters addressed to Rose Mercer, their mother's maiden name, tied with pink ribbon. She pulled the ribbon apart and opened the first letter. It was from Pa when they were courting. Reading it brought tears to her eyes. She had difficulty relating the tenderness expressed on paper to the man her pa had become. She wiped the tear way and put the letter back in its envelope. She retied the bundle and put them into the box of things to read later. She thought the letters could be kept and perhaps she'd show them to Violet when she had her baby, to prove there was love between Ma and Pa, at the beginning.

There were cards of congratulation written in a hand she recognised as Grandmother Daniels. The dates coincided with the birth of John, Violet and Alfie. She put them in the 'to keep' box.

At the very back of the drawer, so far back she had to get on her hands and knees to reach them, she pulled out another bundle of letters. These were tied with string and addressed to Mrs R Daniels, but Hope didn't recognise the handwriting.

Intrigued, she pulled the string, took out the first letter and opened it. What she read made her jaw drop and her hands tremble.

Dear Rose,

Thank you is not enough to express how I feel having received your last letter telling me of my baby's progress. I see you have called her Hope, an appropriate name I think. I pray for her every day and

*miss her more than words can say, but will be eternally
grateful that she has been spared the life she would
have had if you and William hadn't been so kind and
generous as to take her in and treat her as your own. I
sleep better at night knowing that she's safe and in
your care. I can't thank you and William enough for
your kindness giving her a home and a better chance at
life than I could have done. Perhaps one day you will
be able to tell her of me and that I loved her beyond
reason and gave her into your care with a heavy heart
knowing it was for the best.*

*I await your next letter, with love and gratitude,
Marie*

Shock, like the kick of a wild, prancing stallion,
knocked the breath out of her. An avalanche of fear
and confusion fell over her as she read. It was beyond
understanding. She tore open another letter and
another. They all carried the same message – thanks for
news about a child given into Ma's care – a child
called Hope.

Hope scrabbled through the other papers she'd
tipped out onto the floor, although she wasn't sure
what she was looking for. Who was Marie? What was
she to Ma? There was nothing else among the papers
scattered all around, only old letters, cards, notes,
nothing of any importance. Birth certificates? If she
could find them… They weren't here, nothing like that
among Ma's papers. Where would they be? Important
documents were kept in the safe, which she couldn't
open.

Her hand shook as she folded the letters, put them
back in their envelopes and tucked them inside her
blouse. She wasn't sure what they meant, but she

intended to find out before she showed them to anyone, especially John, Violet or Alfie; her brothers and sister. Or were they?

When Violet called that tea was ready she gathered up the papers and put them into the box to keep and read later. The bundle of Marie's letters burned against her body, but she wanted more time to study them before she made any decision about them.

All evening at the club she was distracted, thinking about the letters. Dexi raised her eyebrows once or twice when Hope got an order wrong, but didn't say anything. She daren't even look at them again when she got home, undressed and climbed into the bed she shared with Violet. She'd have to keep them safe until she could read them through properly and try to make sense of them.

The next morning when Hope arrived at the Taylors' with Alfie, Mr Taylor was in a terrible state. "The midwife's here," he said. "The baby's coming. The boys will have to go on their own. I can't leave Margaret."

"I'll go with them," Hope said. "And come back with the carriage if you like."

Harold looked her over. She glanced down at his gaze. She was wearing her best suit and shawl, but clearly they weren't good enough. "I'd rather you stayed with Margaret," he said. "The coachman can take the boys. They can manage I'm sure, but Margaret's... Please, go and be with her."

Hope hurried up the stairs and sure enough Margaret was lying in bed, sweat beading her brow, while Mrs Cooper, the midwife, urged her to keep pushing. "It's almost here," she said.

Hope rushed to Margaret's side and took turns with Mrs Cooper in encouraging her when it was time to push, wiping her face and holding a glass of water to her lips between contractions. Margaret squeezed her hand and clenched her jaw and Hope felt her pain. She thought the baby was never going to come, but an hour-and-a-half later, after much swearing and gritting her teeth, Margaret delivered a baby girl.

"Is she all right?" Margaret asked, her eyes darkened with fear as the child let out a lusty cry.

"She's perfect," Mrs Cooper said. "Absolutely perfect."

She handed the baby to Hope while she cleaned Margaret up, mopped her face and brushed her hair back. "There, there, now. The hard work's done," she said.

"She's beautiful" Hope said, cradling her in her arms. Holding the tiny scrap of humanity Hope recalled when Alfie was born. Ma sent her to fetch old Mrs Reilly who'd had eleven children of her own. Pa told her to take John and Violet to a neighbour down the road who looked after them until after the baby was born. When they returned they had a baby brother – tiny, pink and so wrinkled it looked as though his skin was too big for him.

Hope smiled as she handed the tiny scrap to Margaret. Margaret held her for a few moments, stroking her soft cheek and downy hair. "Take her downstairs and show Harold," she said, handing her back to Hope while Mrs Cooper finished cleaning her up ready for him to visit.

Downstairs Harold poured another whisky, which he'd been drinking since early morning. "Is it all right?" he asked as Hope carried the child in to show him. His eyes shone with trepidation.

"It's a perfect little girl," Hope said. "Absolutely perfect."

When Hope left Margaret and Harold with their new baby all she could think about was the tiny form she'd held so briefly in her arms. Was she like that when she was born and her mother gave her into Ma's care? Why did she? When did she? She didn't go straight home, even though today was the day they were supposed to be moving back into the pub and John had told her to come straight back to help with the packing up and moving.

She walked down to the river and sat on a bench. A light breeze blew up bringing a breath of salt mixed with the smell of fish and oil from the barges. Boats on the river chugged by as they'd always done. The skyline across the water, bathed in late autumn sun, looked familiar and yet everything seemed changed. She didn't even know who she was or where she belonged, if anywhere.

She took the letters out of her bag and read them. They'd been written over several months. The last one was received when Hope was nine months old. It became clear that Marie was unmarried and had no means of support. There was mention of where she was going being worse than the workhouse. Had Hope been given away to avoid that terrible fate, whatever it was? Even as she read, teardrops fell from her eyes, wet spots spreading on the paper. She had to put the letters away when she could no longer see through the blur of her tears.

In her mind she formed a picture of what her mother had gone through and how desperate she must have been. The memory of the tiny baby she'd just helped deliver stayed with her. How lucky she was, that tiny one, to be so loved and wanted at birth. Of course she knew of children born to parents who hadn't wanted them. Sometimes the birth of a new baby brought such poverty, another mouth to feed and no time to care for it. She'd always felt blessed. True she sometimes fell out with Violet and John, and Ma and Pa weren't perfect, but she'd always felt lucky belonging in a close caring family.

Now, she wondered who she was. That sense of belonging felt fragile. She didn't really belong, did she? She didn't know why Ma and Pa had taken her in, only that she was glad they had. Memories of her childhood growing up in happy, safe surroundings filtered through her mind. She owed Ma and Pa everything. Would it be so wrong to try to find out more about her real mother?

She sat until a sudden chill got into her bones and a woman stopped in front of her. "You all right, luv?" she said. "Only you don't look so good. Owt I can do for you?"

"No. No, thank you," Hope said coming out of her reverie. "I was just thinking. Lost in a dream. I'm fine. In fact I'll be on my way now. Thank you for stopping." A dream, she thought as she walked away. A nightmare more like.

Chapter Thirty Eight

By the time she arrived at the Hope and Anchor Violet and John were already there.

"Where have you been?" John scowled. "I expected you hours ago," he said, ready to berate her for being so late, but as soon as he saw her dishevelled appearance his expression turned to one of concern. "What on earth happened? You look dreadful."

"You've been crying," Violet said. "What's the matter?"

They both dropped what they were doing and came to comfort her.

"Margaret had her baby," Hope said. "Mrs Taylor. She had a little girl."

"Oh," Violet said, immediately interested. "How was it? Was it really awful? What happened?"

Tears sprang afresh to Hope's eyes at the memory of the Taylors' joy at the birth of their baby. She wasn't sure Violet's child would be so welcomed. "It was fine. Mrs Cooper, the midwife, was there when I arrived. The boys were sent on to school and I stayed with Margaret, Mrs Taylor."

John hurrumphed. "Well, all right. I suppose you're forgiven, but you can come and give me a hand now."

"Oooo," Violet said. "It must have been so exciting." She was blushing as though she had something similar to look forward to, but Hope knew her delivery would be very different.

"I've got a couple of lads coming to help bring the safe downstairs," John said. "You can help me empty it ready."

"Bring the safe downstairs?" Hope said. "Why?"

"Well, I don't want to be having to disturb Violet and the baby every time I need some cash. I'm moving it to the storeroom behind the bar. I'm going to use that as my office."

Hope and Violet looked at each other. He was taking this being the licensee thing really seriously, Hope thought. Still, just as well, because if they couldn't make it pay they'd be out on the street and none of them wanted that.

Hope followed him upstairs and watched while he opened the safe.

"You should give me and Violet each a key," she said. "In case anything happens to you. Silly to have you being the only one who can open the safe in an emergency."

John handed her a pile of papers. "Hmm, I suppose you're right," he said. "I have Pa's key and I can get another one, although I don't see any reason either of you would want to go in the safe. It'll only be the old papers and the nightly takings."

John piled more papers onto Hope's outstretched arms as Violet came in with the two lads who'd come to help. "Is this the stuff out of the safe?" she asked, eyeing the pile of papers in Hope's arms. "Anything interesting?"

"No. Just old papers," John said. "Ma and Pa's marriage certificate, our birth certificates, the contract for the licence, the rent book, and," he stopped and looked at the paper in his hand "the loan agreement from Silas Quirk. You might find that of interest," he said, placing it on the top of the pile in Hope's arms.

"Can I have my certificate?" Violet asked, shuffling through the pile of papers. She extracted an envelope with *Violet – Birth Certificate* written on it. She flipped it open. "Yes. Here I am. *Violet Amelia born 10th September, 1882.* Ma and Pa's details are there too."

She wrinkled her nose. "I'm going to put that scoundrel Bert Shadwick's name as the father. He is after all and I don't want my little one growing up with *Father Unknown* on his or her birth certificate. If he or she ever asks about their dad I'll tell 'em. Not right keeping secrets is it? The truth will always come out so best be honest from the start."

"If you're quite finished, Violet, you can go and put kettle on. I'm sure the lads would like a brew," John said.

Violet put her envelope back on the pile and scuttled out. John and the two lads who'd come to help lifted the safe between them and carried it out. Hope followed, but she took out and the envelope that had her name on it and slipped it inside her blouse to read later.

They were kept busy for the rest of the day. Once John was satisfied that he had his office set up and the bar was cleaned and they could begin stocking up, he sent Hope to the market to buy something for their tea.

At the market she couldn't help running into Ned. "Hello, stranger," he said. "I hear your Violet's back, with more than she went away with. I suppose that's why you've not had time to come round so often. How is she?"

Hope recalled the last time they'd met when she'd found his attitude to Alfie's new school disconcerting. "Violet's well," she said, "and Alfie's doing very well at his new school."

"Yes, I heard that an' all," he said. "Still don't know what good you think it'll do 'im, unless of course you're thinking you're all moving up in the world, now you're back in the pub."

Hope felt her anger rising. "We're going home, if that's what you mean. The home I've lived in all my life. If you think that's going up in the world as you call it, it's not. We're simply going back where we belong." Even as she said it she wondered if that was where she belonged. Knowing about her past she felt more like an interloper than ever. Where did she belong if not with John and Violet and Alfie?

Ned stopped setting out the apples on his stall and stared at her. "But is that where you belong? Way I heard it you're still working for Silas Quirk. A chap can't help thinking as how you might have taken a shine to the work and the place and don't want to see your old friends no more."

Hope's heart skipped a beat. She didn't want to fall out with him, but there was a sliver of truth in what he said. Since the night of the fire her life had changed so much she wasn't sure she could go back, nor even that she wanted to. She felt immediately contrite. Ned had been a good friend in the past. She didn't want to lose his friendship now.

"I'm sorry," she said. "Our lives have been turned upside down. Losing Ma and Pa and all our things, having to start again, I simply haven't had time…"

Ned raised his eyebrows. Again that stab of contrition. She found time to take Alfie each day and go to collect him after school. She found time to sit with Margaret chatting and to help Betsy with the laundry as well as getting the pub ready to move back in. Why hadn't she found time for Ned, who'd been so kind to her?

"And Silas Quirk?" he said.

"Is my boss. It's an obligation. I told you, Pa promised."

Ned shrugged. "I just thought, with John getting the pub back…"

Hope sighed. "Makes no difference. The loan hasn't been repaid. We can't raise that sort of money."

"So, it's not through choice then?"

"No," Hope said, "not entirely, although the money's good and the work is easy and pleasant. I can find no fault in Mr Quirk's treatment of me, in fact he's been more than generous and kind," her voice fell on the last words. It was something she didn't want to admit, but she had come to enjoy working there and looked forward to seeing him on the rare occasions he frequented the bar. "The pub's nearly ready," she said. "We're planning a grand opening. I do hope you'll come."

"And will you be there?"

She stopped for a moment. "I'll make sure I am," she said.

"And will you dance with me?"

She warmed at the twinkle in his eye. "I'll save the first dance for you," she said.

"Good, it's a date." He leaned over and kissed her cheek.

Her mind was in turmoil as she walked away. Was Ned right? Had working at The Grenadier and making new friends changed her expectations? Had she moved on?

Once the living quarters at the pub had been completed to John's satisfaction, he insisted that the family move back in. "We have to start paying rent, might as well make the most of it. No point paying two places," he said, so the next morning they started gathering up their belongings. Not that they had much to pack. Only the clothes they'd stood up in when they arrived and the few things they'd bought since.

Violet was excited about moving back. "I can't wait to have to my own room. Just think," she said, "no more having to share."

"Until the baby comes," Hope reminded her. "Then you'll have someone else to share with."

Violet pulled a face.

"Are my books still there?" Alfie asked, anxiety reflected his eyes. "And my toy soldiers and marbles."

"I'm afraid the books were too badly damaged," Hope said. "But you have new ones now. Most of your other things had a good wash and they've survived."

"So I can have my old room back?"

"Yes."

His face lit up.

Hope sighed. At least the rest of the family were happy to be moving back even if she wasn't. Memories of the past filtered through her brain. Ma's smiling face, the noise of fun and laughter when they were growing up, Pa's gruff voice calling 'time'. It was as though they were all lost, thrown out with the huge pile of rubbish they'd had to discard as too badly damaged to keep. Were her memories too badly damaged? She wasn't sure.

A swell of sadness fell over her as she packed her only remaining belongings into a small bag. Hard to think this was all she had left in the world. She had so little to remember what had gone before. It was as though the vibrant, active, loud, vivid, busy lives of her parents had gone. Nothing remained. No one celebrated their achievements. There was nothing left to mark their passing.

Hope was with John packing up their belongings. Alfie had gone to school and Violet was downstairs with Betsy, resting.

"I think we'll have to manage without Violet at first," John said. "She's nearly due and after the baby she won't have a lot of time to work in the bar."

"I still have to go to The Grenadier," Hope said, "but I'll do as much as I can."

"I wanted to talk to you about that," John said.

"Why, what's the matter?"

"Nothing's the matter. It's just that you've been there best part of a year now. With us reopening the pub I think I could persuade Silas Quirk that you'll be more use working with me than at the club and should be freed from the contract that Pa made. I could even pay off the debt over time if that's what he requires."

Hope sank down onto the chair. That she could give up working at The Grenadier was the last thing she expected to hear.

"Can we manage without my tips?" she asked. "I didn't realise we'd be doing so well."

"It would be a struggle, but if it's what you want, we could manage, if we all muck in."

Hope suddenly felt bereft. Working at the club had become so much part of her life she could envisage no future without it. She'd come to enjoy the lively, company and, she had to admit, the ease and comfort that comes when dealing with people with great wealth. She'd also miss seeing Silas every evening, albeit fleetingly, watching him work his magic on club members, who he held so effortlessly in the palm of his hand.

She smiled at John. "It's not so bad and the money's good for the little I have to do. It's not a hardship to serve in such pleasant surrounding and I don't want to ask Silas Quirk for any more favours. He's done more than enough for us already."

"All right, but it's your decision. If ever you do want to quit…"

"Thank you for the thought, but I'm happy to stay where I am. I think we've all had enough change to deal with this year."

She stripped the beds and folded the sheet ready for Betsy to wash. She was surprised at how little they had to show for a family's belongings.

John and Violet left first and she had one last tidy up and look round at the home they'd shared through the drama of the last few months. Sadness filled her heart at the memories, but it was time to move on.

"Are you off now?" Betsy said, wiping her hands on her apron as she walked in from the laundry.

"Yes," Hope said coming rapidly back to earth. "I think I have everything." She glanced around. "I'll miss this place. You've been so kind taking us in."

"Weren't nothing," Betsy said. "Glad to help. Can't say as how I won't miss you an' all."

"We'll all miss your beef stew," Hope said, a wry smile on her face.

"Aye. Violet never did get the 'ang of the cooker did she?"

Hope laughed.

"Don't be a stranger," Betsy said, giving Hope one last hug. "You're always welcome here."

"Thank you. And thank you for all you've done for us."

"Aw. Twen't nothing."

With a last hug Hope walked out of the front door, into the street carrying her small bundle of clothes. Glancing round into the autumnal air, the sun pale behind the clouds, she took a breath. She was going home.

Chapter Thirty Nine

The brewery had agreed to provide glasses, plates, cutlery and tablecloths for the party. Elsie and John spent some time discussing what they would serve during the evening. They decided to keep it simple and serve canapés and light snacks which Elsie could make up in the kitchen. Alice's younger sister Grace was hired for the evening to serve the food while Alice and John would take turns to work behind the bar or mingle with the guests.

"We need table decorations," Hope said. "They'll make all the difference."

"We could have fresh flowers and fruit," Violet said. "That's what they have in posh houses."

"And you know this how?" Hope grinned.

Violet pouted. "I've seen it in them magazines. You know the posh ones."

"Fruit and flowers it is then," John said. "They won't cost too much if you get them from the market."

"What about candles," Violet said. "Dancing by candlelight, that'll be so romantic." She had a dreamy look in her eyes.

Hope laughed. "Candles on the tables then, with fruit and flowers. Still not sure how much dancing you'll be doing in your condition."

Violet sighed. "I know. Still, a girl can dream."

The day before the party Hope went to the market and ordered flowers and fruit for the tables. Then she found a quiet spot in the park. The envelope from the safe had been burning in her pocket and she needed to find a quiet place where she wouldn't be disturbed to read it. Her hands trembled as she opened the envelope, a heavy stone of dread formed in her stomach at the thought of what she might find.

Folded up inside she found three slips of paper. The first was a faded birth certificate registering the birth of a female child on the day she'd always believed to be her birthday. Her name '*Hope*' was written in slightly darker ink, as though added later, as were the names of her parents. The second piece of paper, similarly faded, registered the stillbirth of a female child to Rose and William Daniels three days prior to her birth. As she unfolded the last piece of paper, also very faded, she recognised the handwriting as being the same as the letters from Marie. She could just make out the writing. Her eyes filled with tears as she read:

My darling daughter, If you ever see this note you will know how much I loved and cared for you and how my heart is shattered into a million pieces at losing you. As soon as I knew I could not keep you I begged Rose to take you in place of the child she lost knowing that she could give you a better life than the one you were destined for. I hope you can find it in your heart to forgive me but, please believe that I gave you to someone who could love and cherish you as I could not. I would not wish the life ahead of me on anyone, but I will suffer everything more easily knowing you are safe and being well cared for. I will pray for you every day and hope with all my heart that, one day, the truth will come out and I will be free, or dead. All my love and prayers, Marie Deveraux

She sat with the papers in her lap, trying to take it all in. She looked at the certificates again, both births registered in North Yorkshire, where her father's family had lived. She wondered how much her Grandma Amelia and Pops, her grandfather, had known about her birth. Did they know about the stillbirth, or did they believe she was Rose and William's daughter?

It was clear that Marie Deveraux was her biological mother. What had happened to her, and what could be so bad that she'd give up a child she obviously loved?

And Ma and Pa? How did they know Marie and why were they prepared to take in her baby in place of their own? More important still, why did they let Hope believe she was their daughter when it was clear she was not?

The questions buzzed around in her head. She tried to imagine how Ma and Pa must have felt, having this baby offered to them in place of the one they'd lost, but it was beyond imagination. Were they happy? Delighted to take her? It had always seemed to Hope that she was loved and she'd always felt as though she belonged. How could she feel any different now? What would John, Violet and Alfie feel about her if they found out? Or did they know already? She doubted it. No, Ma would never tell them and not let her know.

Ma and Pa had taken her in and treated her as one of their own. She couldn't think what sort of life she'd have had if it hadn't been for them. She owed them more than she could say and a new determination grew inside her to do all she could to honour their memory. She'd start by being extra kind to Violet and John and she'd work her fingers to the bone to make the pub a success.

She recalled Ma telling her in the hospital how they'd called her Hope when they got the pub. How she was part of their legacy. Was she trying to tell her then about her real mother and her birth? She sighed. It was too late now to worry about it or try to do anything about it. She tucked the papers away in her bag. She'd tell no one. She'd do what Ma and Pa had done for nearly twenty years and keep quiet about it. That's what they would have wanted, she thought.

Chapter Forty

Walking to the pub with her bundle of belongings John's words ran through her mind. He'd given her a chance to leave the club and she hadn't taken it. She'd see a different life at the club and had to admit that she felt more at home there than she'd felt anywhere.

Working with the family in the pub with the constant memory of Pa's drinking and gambling and the constant dread that John would go that way too couldn't compare to the light-hearted laughter and gaiety she'd experienced working at The Grenadier. Then there was Silas. She didn't want to admit it, not even to herself, but she'd found thoughts of him entering her head more often than was comfortable. The vision of his face, the warmth of his smile, even the scent of him was enough to make her heart flutter.

That evening at The Grenadier, she went down to the bar early. It was empty save for Silas and Jake, the barman, stocking up. Silas smiled as she approached.

"Good evening, Sapphire," he said using her sobriquet as was the custom in the bar. "You're looking particularly lovely tonight." He paused as though he had something on his mind. "Could I have a word?" He led her to a quiet corner where they wouldn't be overheard. A tingle of anticipation ran down her spine.

"I wanted to say how much I…we…appreciate the work you do here. The members speak very highly of you."

Hope felt the colour rising in her cheeks as a warm glow flowed through her. "I've done nothing other than what I was employed to do," she said modestly.

"As a friend of your father's I know he would be very proud of you. I hope the obligation I put on him hasn't been too onerous. You must let me know immediately if you're unhappy here. If you'd prefer to go back and work with your family."

"Oh no," Hope said, shocked at her own reaction to his kindness. "No thank you, that is. I'm quite happy here."

And in her heart she knew she was. The thought of leaving the club had brought a fresh swirl of anxiety inside her. It was the last thing she wanted. She realised that now.

After a frenzied week of activity the pub was ready to open. The invitations to the Grand Opening Party had been sent out to all the local merchants and dignitaries. Silas Quirk and his sister had been invited. "These are our potential new customers," John said. "We want to make a good impression and if he comes, his friends will follow."

"Can I invite Mr Larkin, my tutor?" Alfie asked. "He's a lovely man and I want to show him where we live and how we've done the place up. Please. I won't know anyone otherwise."

"You know Harold and Margaret, George's parents," Hope said, but John overruled her.

"Yes, invite him by all means. You're part of the family and can invite anyone you like. The more the merrier."

John had ordered the stock. "I'm not sure the brewery will give us credit," he said, a worried frown on his face. "After Pa…" But, thanks to Silas's sponsorship the brewery agreed to supply drinks to be paid for with the first month's rent.

Alice's mum had cleaned from top to bottom. Having her buzzing around, shooing everyone out of her way so she could get on, reminded Hope of Ma and she knew coming back to live in the pub with the others was the right thing to do. Ma would have wanted her to and that was enough for Hope.

Violet, in the advanced stage of her pregnancy wasn't expected to do much, but she was going to sing later.

A week before the opening Hope approached Dexi for the evening off. "You'll have to speak to Silas," she said. "If he agrees I won't argue."

When she finally plucked up courage to ask him his response surprised her.

"I've received the invitation," he said. "I'd hoped you would accompany me. There's nothing I'd like more than having you on my arm for the evening. I trust you'll save the first dance for me too."

Her heart sank, but she couldn't refuse, not when he'd been so generous and kind to them. John would never forgive her, but she was appalled at the thought of spinning around the floor in his arms in front of her friends, especially Ned.

She spent some time with Violet wondering what they were going to wear. "I've got nothing suitable for a party," Violet moaned. "And with this lump nothing I've got will fit. I can't go to the party in this old rag. It's not fair."

Hope had stopped thinking life was fair years ago.

"We can't afford new clothes for you girls," John said. "You'll have to make do."

Tears threatened to fall. Violet had always cared so much about her appearance, Hope thought. It seemed a shame she couldn't do something to help her look her best now. "I could ask Margaret if you could borrow one of her outfits," she said. "She was about your size when she had her baby, I'm sure she wouldn't mind."

"Oh really? Would you?" Violet's eyes shone.

How little it takes to make you happy, Hope thought, not for the first time. Violet's vanity was her most endearing feature.

Violet's tears turned to smiles when Margaret sent her a forest green velvet gown she'd worn to a Guild event. It was voluminous enough to hide her bump and yet classy enough to wear for the evening. "You're a saviour," she said to Hope. "Please thank Margaret for me." It was a long time since Hope had seen her looking so happy.

When Dexi heard Hope was to accompany Silas she insisted on her dressmaker running up a new gown for her. "Can't have my brother's guest appearing in something she's worn before," she said. "The deeper shades do look particularly good on you though. Perhaps this time we'll try a rich amethyst."

The dress Miss Lovell made for Hope was the most breathtaking she'd ever seen. The deep purple silk tubular skirt was the latest fashion and accentuated Hope's tiny waist. Swags of silk draped across the front stretched into the small bustle at the back which was topped with a silver bow, its ribbons falling to the hem in a cascade of purple and silver. Lines of sequins on the bodice drew the eye to the neckline, cut low enough to show off Hope's elegant neck and the colour brought out the blue of her eyes.

"How do you feel?" the dressmaker asked when Hope tried it on.

"I feel amazing," Hope said staring at her reflection in the mirror. She'd been transformed.

Miss Lovell laughed. "Good. Most people mistakenly believe it's how the dress looks that's important, but it's how it makes the wearer feel that's the paramount consideration."

"I feel like Cinderella," Hope said. "I will go to the ball." She laughed.

"And I'm the Fairy Godmother," Miss Lovell said with a smile. "I've been called that on many occasions."

Hope was to dress at the club and travel in the coach with Silas, Dexi and Jo, the restaurant manager, who'd also been invited and who was keen to see the pub which was to be run by the man who'd cleared the glasses and washed up for him at The Grenadier.

Hope was getting ready to leave to go to the club to dress and then return with Silas when John called them all into the bar.

"I've got something to show you," he said.

Violet, John and Alfie followed him into the empty bar. There, in pride of place over the mantelshelf, next to a large vase of fresh red roses, he unveiled a brass plaque inscribed:

In Loving Memory of Rose and William Daniels,
Licensees of the Hope and Anchor
18th May 1880 – 1st March 1899.
Always Remembered.

A bottle of champagne cooled in an ice bucket on a table nearby. Hope gasped. "That's lovely," she said.

"I've told Alice to make sure there's always fresh flowers an' all," John said. He opened the champagne and filled four glasses. Let's raise a glass to 'em, and never forget what they did for us." They took a glass which they raised. "To Ma and Pa. Always remembered," John said. They clinked glasses and drank. It was a magical moment to remember.

Later, at the club, when Hope went to dress, she found Dexi waiting for her. Dexi watched and waited while Hortense styled Hope's hair into high curls about her head and helped her into her purple silk dress. When she'd finished Hope was sure no one in the whole world had ever looked as perfect as she did.

"You look stunning, just as I knew you would," Dexi said. "I'm sure Silas will be delighted."

Hope smiled. She wasn't sure where this conversation was going.

"I'm sure you've noticed," Dexi said, "that my brother is attracted to you like iron filings to a magnet."

"It's been remarked upon," Hope said, blushing.

"I'm his sister so it would be odd if I weren't concerned about his welfare."

"I can assure you I mean him no harm." Hope's voice wavered. What was Dexi implying?

"Silas is a successful man. Successful and wealthy. Such success breeds envy, jealousy and distrust. For his own protection he has built himself a reputation that belies his nature. Contrary to popular opinion he is not the heartless philanderer people suppose. He's a man of warmth and passion. He has an innate sensibility and those he smiles upon are truly blessed. I can see no reason for you to have any complaint about his treatment of you."

Hope's eyes shot open wide. "No indeed. He's shown me nothing but kindness and generosity."

"I trust then that you, in turn, will treat him with kindness. I should hate to see him hurt."

Hope swallowed. A vision of his face filled her mind as it seemed to do with alarming frequency that she had no control over. "Always," she whispered, surprised at her own confident assuredness.

"Then I have nothing to fear and we will remain friends," Dexi said. Hope felt with absolute certainty that Dexi could be a good friend and a scarily bad enemy. She was determined that it should be the former.

Dexi's words echoed in her head as she descended the stairs to meet Silas in the hall below. She saw pride shining in his eyes and something else as well. He swallowed as he offered his arm. She realised she'd left him speechless.

Chapter Forty One

As she walked into the pub Hope couldn't help remembering last Christmas and the Christmas Eve party held there where she'd spent the evening in the kitchen helping Ma or running back and forth with plates of food or fresh glasses. How different it felt now, to be part of the celebration.

She glowed with pride when she saw John and Alfie, both dressed in navy blue evening suits, white shirts and blue bow ties, standing welcoming the guests.

John's face lit up when Silas arrived. "Good evening, Silas," he said. "Good of you to come. I hope you find everything to your liking."

"I'm sure I will," Silas said. "I'm already impressed with the improvements." It was true. The bar looked lighter, brighter and much busier than in the past when Pa ruled the roost and the customers were mostly sullen disheartened drinkers drowning their sorrows. Tonight the pub sparkled and Hope warmed to the idea that they could make it a success and provide a good home for the family, including Violet's new baby when it arrived.

There was a glass of champagne for everyone to start the evening off. Hope took a glass and, with Silas at her side, chatted to their guests. When Margaret and Harold arrived, Harold, who'd been a guest at last year's Christmas Eve party, said, "I can't believe it's the same place. It looks so much bigger and brighter."

Silas greeted them warmly. "How's young George? Getting on well, I hope."

Margaret blossomed. "George is fine, doing well at school thanks to Alfie Daniels helping him. Having Alfie as a friend has made an enormous difference. It was an inspiration introducing them. Alfie is a star."

Hope burned with pride.

Silas nodded, his pleasure apparent in his eyes. "I understand you're to be congratulated on the birth of a little daughter. How is she?"

"Charlotte is a treasure. Absolutely no trouble at all."

"You are blessed then," Silas said with a smile.

"Indeed we are."

Hope took Margaret to meet Violet, while Harold and Silas headed towards the bar.

"Please don't get up," Margaret said as Violet struggled to rise to greet her. "I've been looking forward to meeting you. As new mothers I'm sure we'll have a lot in common."

"Hope's told me about your new daughter and how sweet she is," Violet said. "I hope mine turns out as placid."

"What are you hoping for? A boy or a girl?"

"Either would be just as welcome. Getting rid of this huge lump and being able to wear ordinary clothes again would be wonderful." Violet squirmed in her chair trying to get more comfortable.

Margaret laughed. "I felt exactly the same," she said.

Hope was glad Margaret could be a friend for Violet. Margaret knew what Violet was going through. Hope knew Violet missed Ma more than she could say. Margaret wouldn't replace her, but her experience would be invaluable to helping Violet through the coming ordeal. Hope left them to get better acquainted. "I must circulate," she said and went to greet some of the other guests.

When the music struck up Silas guided her toward the space cleared for dancing.

"I've never danced before," she told him. "I won't be very good."

"Don't worry. You'll soon pick it up." He whisked her onto the floor.

In his arms she felt the closeness of him. He smelled of spice and sandalwood. She felt the muscles in his back through the fabric of his jacket and the warmth of his breath on her cheek. Excitement churned inside her. He was an excellent dancer. As he whirled her around the floor she wondered where he'd learned to dance so well. It was as pleasant as it was unexpected. Soon her resistance faded away to be replaced by the joy of the dance. She was sorry when the music stopped and they came to a halt. Only the sight of Ned glowering from the sidelines spoiled her evening.

She made an effort to speak to him.

"Come on, Ned," she said. "I promised you a dance."

Ned glowered. "I can't compete with your first partner," he said. "And I don't want to desert my friends." Hope felt it as a rebuke.

She exchanged words with Inspector Penhalligan. "I hope this is not an official visit," she said when she saw him with his sergeant.

"No, purely social. Everyone seems to be having a good time," he said. He nodded towards John and Alfie, who were circulating among the guests. Even

Violet, sitting in her chair by the side of the dance floor was in animated conversation with a guest. "I'm glad things have turned out so well. You must be proud of your family and the way they've coped with what must be a traumatic and difficult situation."

Somehow, the way he said it brought the memory of her birth mother's letter spiralling back. "Yes, I am," she said, her voice hardly more than a whisper. She wasn't at all sure they were her family.

She saw Alfie beaming with pride as he talked to his tutor, Giles Larkin. "Good evening, Mr Larkin, so glad you could come. I know Alfie's delighted to have you here."

"It's been a pleasure. This is a fascinating building. I understand there's been a pub on this site for over a hundred years."

"Really?"

"Yes. And the name, the Hope and Anchor, which, contrary to popular belief, has nothing to do with the sea. It gets its name from the Bible's Letters to the Hebrews speaking of faith as 'a steadfast anchor of the soul. A Hope'."

Hope tried to see herself as a 'steadfast anchor of the soul', but failed miserably. "I'm impressed," she said. "And doubly glad that you're Alfie's tutor."

"How kind."

Silas appeared at her side. "I hope you're not deserting me," he said. He caught her arm and led her back onto the dance floor. Again she whirled around in his arms. Again the closeness of him, the welcome comfort of strong arms holding her. Again the warmth of his musky body pressed close to hers, his soft shallow breath on her cheek, again Ned's surly glare from the sidelines. When the music stopped she made an excuse to escape.

"I mustn't ignore my other guests," she said, and made her way to the kitchen to help Elsie, hoping for some respite from the heady thoughts racing through her brain, the disturbing feelings and the powerful surge of emotion she'd never felt before.

Later that evening, as the guests were leaving, begging an early start the next day, Hope collected the empty glasses and plates to take back to the kitchen. Passing through the bar she saw Inspector Penhalligan, lighting up his pipe.

"Inspector," she said. "Can I get you anything?"

"No, thanks. I just came out for a quiet smoke. You've all done well tonight. A lovely evening and can I say I've never seen you looking so...so...elegantly beautiful."

Colour rose up Hope's face like a glass filling with wine.

"I couldn't help noticing you with Silas Quirk. Forgive me if it's inappropriate to ask, but is there anything between you?"

"What do you mean?"

He raised his eyebrows in a questioning glare.

"What business is it of yours if there is?" she said.

"No business at all. Just don't want to tread on anyone's toes, that's all. Especially a man like Silas Quirk."

"He's my boss. That's all."

"Will you be working here in the pub with your family from now on then? Now that the pub has reopened?"

"I'll be helping out when I can, but I'll still be working at The Grenadier."

"Hmm. If I had my way we'd close that place down. It's a bad influence encouraging men to lose more than they can afford."

She prickled. "From what I've seen the men who frequent the club are well able to afford their losses and a great deal more."

"Like yourfather?"

For a fleeting moment she was again reminded of Pa and a new doubt in her mind about whether he really was her pa surfaced. Shocked she went to walk away. "Excuse me," she said. "I must get on."

"I'm sorry," the Inspector said, moving after her. "I didn't mean to upset you."

To her surprise she found his presence disconcerting. "I think you'd be better employed trying to find evidence to convict Lucien Grey of murder than worrying about my personal life. Now, excuse me."

She walked away. He followed.

"I'm a detective," he said. "I have to investigate the lives of people involved in any incidents. That includes the victim's family. You have to learn more about everybody than you may wish to know, secrets that have nothing to do with the crime as well as those that do. Things are not always as they seem."

She stopped. Did he know more about her family's past than he was saying? Even about Ma…?

He stopped in front of her. "If I can ever be of any assistance you know where you can find me." He handed her a card.

Her stomach churned. What was he getting at? How much did he know? Hope was left wondering.

Chapter Forty Two

The days after the party were just as busy as the days preparing for it. Since the pub was reopening John decided they would be closed on Sundays. "We're no longer aiming to attract custom from the market traders, it'll give us all a welcome day off and a chance to catch up with the paperwork, sort out the orders and set up ready for reopening on Mondays," he said.

The pub had taken on a new lease of life and there was still the Christmas trade to prepare for. The Chamber of Commerce had booked the hall as usual, but several small Guilds had also enquired about its availability for their Annual events.

At least the future of the pub looked secure. But Hope had other worries on her mind. She dithered for days before she decided to approach Inspector Penhalligan to find out what he might know about her family's past and her parentage in particular.

She visited him at the station on the pretext of finding out how the case against Lucien Grey was going. He was able to give her some welcome news.

"We've heard back from the Canadian Police. There is a Klondike Gold Mine in the Yukon Territories, but Lucien Grey has no connection to it and is not, nor has he ever been, authorised to sell shares in it." He paused a wide grin on his face. "We have him for fraud for certain."

"And the murder?"

"We picked up a man you may know," he said. "Thomas O'Reilly. Picked him up drunk and disorderly and he offered up some useful information in exchange for not charging him. Apparently Lucien Grey paid him five pounds for information about you and your family. He wanted the layout of the pub, your usual routines, deliveries, and, especially where your father kept his papers."

"Thomas O'Reilly was involved? Shame on him. I knew he was a thief, but…"

"Not directly involved I understand, but Lucien Grey did pay him to jemmy the cellar doors a few days before the fire. Tom thought he was going to burgle the place but it's clear he had other ideas."

"But surely Lucien Grey would deny everything? He's no fool and I can't see the words of a drunk standing much scrutiny in court."

"Well, it gave us enough for a search warrant for Mr Grey's house. We found a bundle of old clothes in the cellar, hidden behind a pile of packing cases. They smelled strongly of kerosene and there was blood on the sleeve. We have motive, means and opportunity. I think we have enough to hang him but my guess is that, given the evidence against him, he'll plead guilty for life imprisonment rather than hanging."

"I don't suppose he intended to kill Pa, only to destroy his papers but Pa must have disturbed him."

"I'm sure you're right but it's still arson and murder and I'm pleased to say we'll be charging him. Your brother may be required to appear in court as a witness to the evidence about your father's papers and his involvement with Lucien Grey. Given his evidence and the other case with its similarity I think we can convict him on both counts. Then we will be able to close the case."

"So our family secrets are safe?"

"Yes, for now. Is there anything else troubling you?"

"I wondered whether you'd found anything in your investigation that would throw a light on these." She handed him her birth certificate and note from her birth mother together with one of the letters to Ma from Marie Deveraux. Her heart thudded so loud while she watched him read them she felt sure he must be able to hear it.

His look when he glanced up from the papers gave nothing away. "Is this something you want me to investigate?" he asked. "As far as I can see no crime has been committed, unless you count forging or defacing an official document for pecuniary gain. Although that's clearly not the motive in this case."

"So you can't tell me anything about my…" She hesitated, hardly able to get the words out. "The circumstances of my birth or my birth mother?"

"It appears pretty clear to me," Inspector Penhalligan said. "I see no indication of your having been formally adopted, but an informal arrangement that suits both parties isn't a crime."

"If I wanted to trace my birth mother?"

The Inspector handed back the papers. "My advice would be to forget it. Live the life you have been given. It looks to me like a gift of kindness has been made and accepted, for whatever reason."

Hope felt a tightening in her chest as though a great weight was crushing her.

"Let sleeping dogs lie," Inspector Penhalligan said. "In my experience people who waken them live to regret it."

"And if I don't? Surely it's only natural to want to know where you come from, to find a place you fit in?"

329

The Inspector shrugged. "And in searching you may be led, in all sincerity into discoveries you may be better off not knowing." He picked up his pipe and, watching her closely began to fill it. "It's your family you should be talking to not me. If you are determined to open the door onto what could be a dark and distressing hallway into your past, get their views first. See what they feel about it." He rose to show her out. "Let me know how you get on. If you really want to do it, and I advise you to think very carefully about the possible consequences – you may not like what you find – then I'll see what I can do."

When Hope left the police station her mind was in a whirl. Inspector Penhalligan was right. She needed to speak to John, Violet and Alfie. When she'd read the letter she'd only been thinking of herself and Ma, and recalling what Ma had said in the hospital. Did she mean she never regretted taking Hope in? Was that what Pa was reluctant to do? In a way she was relieved. She'd thought Ma's regret might be something much worse, but with Lucien Grey being charged with the murder and arson, perhaps they could all now relax and get on with their lives.

It was a weight off her mind, but the note burned in her pocket. She walked to the river and sat for a while, thoughts buzzing through her brain like a thousand angry bees. She took the letter out and reread it. What was 'the life ahead of her' that she dreaded so much? What had happened to her all those years ago? Was she even still alive?

She was itching to know more about the woman who bore her and then gave her away for a better life, but not before she'd spoken to the rest of the family.

After the police station she went to the market to collect Elsie's order from Ned. She'd seen little of him since the party and felt there was a rift opening up between them.

The reception she received was cooler than usual.

"You've come for the order?" he said, picking out several bags from beneath the stall. "I could have dropped it round."

"It's no bother. How did you enjoy the party? You left early, so I was concerned you hadn't enjoyed it."

"I didn't enjoy seeing you make an exhibition of yourself with that Silas Quirk."

She recalled how she'd felt dancing with him. Making an exhibition of herself? When she was the envy of every woman in the room? They might look down their noses at him because of the way he made his living, but there was not one of them that wouldn't change places with her in a heartbeat if they could.

"He's my boss. He was gracious enough to give me the evening off to accompany him. I could hardly refuse a dance or two."

"Looked like more 'an that to me. An' you was dressed up like a toffer."

Hope grabbed the bag of vegetables from him. "If that's what you think of me…" her eyes blazed.

"Aww, no. Hope. It's just that you've changed since working at 'that place'. It's as though you thinks yourself too good for us. What with Alfie going to that toff's school an' all and John getting the licence of the pub. Proper uppity he is an' all. Just wondered if you've forgotten where you come from."

Where she came from was a bone of contention she had yet to chew on. "Where I come from is neither here nor there. It's where I'm going I'm more

331

concerned with." With that she turned and strode away, but she couldn't help wondering if she hadn't outgrown Ned, like a too-tight pair of shoes.

A few days later Hope was at Betsy's when Lydia called to collect some ironing and asked to have a word with her. "It's about Ned," she said. "You know, Ned Naismith from the market."

Hope was puzzled. She'd felt for some time that her and Ned were drifting apart, but the thought that he may be so put out that he'd spoken to Lydia about her... that was more than she could bear.

"It's just that...well...I've been seeing a bit of him lately and I didn't want you to think...I mean...I sort of hoped...you wouldn't mind."

The cloud of doubt and guilt she'd been carrying about how she'd treated Ned lifted from Hope's shoulders. "Ned's been the best of friends. I can't think of a kinder, more generous person but as for anything else..." She shrugged.

"He said you were just good friends, but I know you were keen on him and I didn't want you to think I was trying to take him away."

Hope laughed. "We are good friends but nothing more. True, at one time..." she recalled how she'd depended on him and regretted the loss of that closeness. "We have very different expectations now and I don't believe I could make him happy. Nor him me..."

"So you don't mind if I..."

"Make him happy? I'd be delighted. He deserves someone as kind, hard-working and loving as you."

"So, we have your blessing?"

"Yes."

"Thank you, I'll tell him." She picked up the basket of ironing and skipped out, her step lighter than when she arrived.

"That's a nice thing you did," Betsy said, coming into the room. "Lydia's been on her own too long. She deserves a good man."

"And Ned deserves the best too. I think they'll make each other happy."

Betsy nodded. "Time for a cup of tea?" she asked.

"Always," Hope said, surprised at how relieved she felt at Lydia's news.

Chapter Forty Three

The Saturday before Christmas Hope was with Violet making cards and decorations to put up at the Christmas Eve party they were hosting for the Chamber of Commerce.

"These are so fiddly," Violet complained. Do you think we have enough?"

Hope looked at the small pile of gilded nuts, colourful fringed tissue, candied fruit and paper beads threaded onto strings as garlands. "We'll need a lot more if the hall is to look as good as last year," she said.

"Hmm last year," Violet said. "It feels like a lifetime ago." Tears welled up in her eyes. "I had prospects then. A chance to make somat of meself. Now I'm good for nowt. Not 'til I've got rid of this lump, at any rate."

She shifted uncomfortably in the chair.

"Are you all right?" Hope asked. "Is it the baby?"

Violet leaned forward rubbing her back. She stretched to one side and let out a sigh. "No. I'm just impatient. Impatient to finish this, impatient to get this baby born. Impatient to get back to normal. It's so uncomfortable."

"If you want to take a rest…"

"No. It's all right. If I'd have known it would lead to this I'd never have let Bert Shadwick have his way with me."

Hope couldn't help thinking about what she'd discovered about the circumstance of her birth. "It's not your fault. You're not the first young girl to be led astray by fine words and empty promises. At least you've learned a lesson."

"Hmm. What about you, Hope? Any plans to get hitched? I haven't seen Ned around lately, or have you got your eye on a bigger prize?"

"I don't know what you mean."

"Of course you do. I saw you at the party with Silas Quirk. Now, there's a catch. Not that I envy you. He has a fierce reputation which I understand is well earned."

"Oh. So this is the girl who last year said she'd work for him in a heartbeat if I remember correctly."

"I was young and naive then. I'm less trusting now. I dare say he's no different from all the other love-'em-and-leave-'em men around here."

Warmth flushed her face as memories of being in his arms at the party and of their last conversation filled Hope's head. "He's not like that," she said. "I mean...I'm sure he's not like that." Her face grew even redder. "He's been very good to us. You shouldn't listen to gossip, Violet."

"You can't deny the fact that he's taken a great interest in us since the fire. And don't forget Lucien Grey, who's been accused of setting it, is a member of Silas's club. One does have to wonder if he knew anything about the man and his swindles. His interest could be sign of a guilty conscience."

Hope's anger rose like lava in a volcano about to explode. "One doesn't have to wonder, Violet. One knows full well that Silas knew nothing about it. All his time is taken up with running the club. He doesn't have time to enquire into everyone else's business, unlike you."

335

"Ooooh. Pardon me for living. I see I've hit a nerve. Never realised you were quite so keen on him."

"I'm not keen on him."

"Well, people think you are."

"People are just…" she was going to say jealous, but that would fuel Violet's argument. "Just wrong," she said.

"Well, you should know, being so close and all."

"Violet. I swear it's not like that."

Violet's eyes widened. "So who are you keen on? That Inspector Oakley Penhalligan's been a regular visitor. Now he'd be a good catch. Regular job, good future prospects and single."

"Single? How do you know that?"

"I asked his sergeant at the party. Yes, Oakley Penhalligan's single, eligible and quite keen on you I understand."

Hope almost exploded. "Violet Daniels, you do talk a lot of rubbish," she said. "This pregnancy's addled your brain," but she couldn't help smiling at the thought.

That evening at the club Hope was distracted. Hortense was helping her dress when Dexi noticed. "Is anything wrong?" she asked. "Has someone upset you?"

"No. No, not at all," Hope said. It's just…" A great bubble of grief she'd been holding back rose up inside her. Finding out about her birth mother had been a shock. She didn't know where she belonged or who to. It was all too much. She had to confide in someone, someone closer than Inspector Penhalligan. Someone who may understand. So, sitting in Dexi's boudoir with Dexi sitting on the bed, it all came bursting out in an unstoppable torrent, as though a dam had burst and she could no longer hold it back. "I don't know what to do," she said. "Part of me wants to keep it secret, like my parents did, but there's another part of me that wants to find out all I can about her, what happened to her, who she was."

Dexi pouted. "You should speak to Silas. He may know more about it than you realise."

"Silas? You mean Silas knows?" Her brow furrowed in dismay.

"I told you, Silas knows everything. Drink is a great liberator of secrets. A man in his cups will spill confidences like water slipping over cobbles. If they're not bragging they're confessing. It goes with the territory."

Of course, she was right. She'd seen it herself, men confiding in the barman when they'd had a drop too much. But her pa? Telling a man like Silas Quirk? What was he thinking? Or obviously not thinking at all. She rushed downstairs to find out.

She found Silas in his office.

"Good evening, Hope. What a lovely surprise, what can I do for you?"

"You can tell me all you know about these," she said thrusting the bundle of paper under his nose.

He glanced at them, his face emotionless. When he looked up there was a well of tenderness in his eyes. "Your father told me about it. He'd had a heavy drinking session and wanted to get it off his chest, as many men do when they're in that state. He never told you?"

"No."

"I must admit I found it intriguing. Once I knew I could see how different you were from the rest of the

337

Daniels family. You seemed to have an inborn elegance and charm I found – find alluring."

"Did he tell you anything about my birth mother?"

"No. Only that she was a friend Rose met in the hospital who'd had a baby at the same time as they lost a child."

"So you don't know what happened to her?"

"Sadly no. Only that her family had disowned her for some indiscreet alliance and she was destined for a bleak future."

"In the workhouse?"

"The workhouse or worse. From what I can gather William and Rose Daniels did your mother a favour, taking you in. At least that's how he saw it."

That explained a lot about Pa's attitude towards her and his favouring Violet and John.

"I'm sorry, Hope, this must have come as a dreadful shock to you, and coming on top of your loss…"

"That Pa told you before his family? Shock is too small a word," she said. She gathered up the papers and stormed out.

She carried the papers around for several days, gathering her thoughts. She needed to tell John, Violet and Alfie, everything she knew about her birth and her birth mother. Silas and Dexi knew, Inspector Penhalligan knew. How long would it be before the town gossips got hold of it and it became common knowledge?

It would be as much a surprise to them as it had been to her so she needed to choose her time. She decided it would be best to broach the subject while at breakfast, when they were all there, before she took

Alfie to the Taylors to go on to school. Neither Elsie nor the cleaner would be in until later.

Gathering all the courage she possessed she waited until they were all sat at the kitchen table and then said, "I have something to tell you. Well, not exactly tell you, more show you."

She took out the envelope containing her birth certificate and the note from her birth mother.

"Your birth certificate. What of it?" Violet, who had woken up in a bad mood anyway, said.

"It's this letter I found with it." She handed it to John. Violet leaned across to read over his shoulder. He read it aloud.

"But what does it mean?" Alfie asked, his eyes shadowed with fear.

"As far as I can make out," John said, 'it means Hope was handed over to Ma when she was a baby. Ma's not her mother at all."

"I have these too," Hope said, passing round the letters from Marie addressed to Ma.

They sat in silence reading, until, a good ten minutes later, John threw the letter he was holding onto the table. "I can't say I'm not shocked because I am. It'll take while for this to sink in. Strange though. I know Ma always doted on you, Hope, and I was so jealous of that. Pa doted on you, Violet. I always felt if anyone in the family was left out it was me." He turned to look at Alfie. "Of course we all loved Alfie, right from the when he was born, but I must say, this has come as a bolt out of the blue."

"Well I can't take it in either," Violet said. "But I'm in no position to say owt." She looked down at her expanding stomach. "If it hadn't been for you, Hope and John, I'd have been in the workhouse and this little one," she stroked her bump, "would be taken away from me anyway. If I was in that position and found someone who'd take care of my baby and give it a better life who knows what I'd have done. I can't condemn anyone for doing the best they could for their child. It's only natural they would."

John took a deep breath. He wasn't the most articulate of people but the look on his face showed how serious he was about what he had to say. "It seems to me that Ma and Pa did us all a good deed taking you in. You've contributed more to this family than any of us. You're part of it and I'll fight anyone who says different."

"I agree," Violet said at last. "We may have had out differences in the past, but I wouldn't have anyone in your place. And with the baby coming…" Sadness filled her face. "I can't imagine how awful it must have been for her to give her baby away."

"We don't know the circumstances," Hope said, "but from her letters she must have been in dire need."

"Well, if she was going to give her baby to anyone I'm glad she chose us," Alfie said, still not sure what it was all about.

"As far as I'm concerned," John said, "and I'm sure I speak for all of us, this doesn't make one jot of difference. You've always been our sister. I don't see any reason to change that."

"I don't want any other sister," Alfie said. "I only want you. You won't go away will you, Hope? I couldn't bear it if you went away."

"No. I'm not going away," Hope said. "I just thought you should all know about this as I was as shocked as you to find out about it. But, having done so, I want it out in the open. There shouldn't be any secrets between us. Not if we're to remain a proper family."

"So that's settled," John said. "Things will carry on as normal. I need to get the bar stocked, and Alfie, you need to get ready for school."

Hope sighed. That was one hurdle crossed. She felt settled now, but didn't rule out the possibility that, sometime in the future, she may wish to trace her birth mother. That the family knew about her and would support her lifted a great weight from her mind.

Now that the family knew about her parentage and it was no longer a secret, the imperative to find out about her birth mother faded. It was something she'd always know about, but it wasn't a worry anymore. She was who she was and loved by her adoptive family even if they hadn't known she wasn't related. That was enough for her, for the time being anyway.

Chapter Forty Four

Christmas Eve the pub heaved with people come for the festivities. Women wore their best outfits and most expensive jewellery. John at least was happy.

"The last three months have been busy and with tonight's takings we should have made enough to cover our rent and stock for the next three months," he said.

The brewery manager and surveyor, Harold and Margaret Taylor and Alfie's tutor, Giles Larkin, were all invited to the party along with Silas and Dexi and Inspector Penhalligan and his sergeant. Much to Silas's discomfiture and Dexi's delight, the Inspector bagged the first dance with Hope.

"I thought you were saving that for me," Silas said.

Hope laughed. "Oakley Pengalligan has been very good to us," she said and glided around the floor taking great pleasure in watching Silas watching them from the sidelines.

He didn't stay on the sidelines for long. The next time the music struck up he whisked her onto the floor. He held her close. Again she felt the nearness of him, felt the roughness of his jacket and smelled the fresh lime scent of his aftershave. As the music died down he held her hand, reluctant to let her go.

As well as the dancing the guests were to be entertained by a magic show put on by another of Violet's friends from the theatre, a recitation by a local actor and Violet was going to sing some of her old Music Hall favourites accompanied on the piano by a young Italian lad called Dino. Dino had a habit of following Violet around with puppy-dog eyes and sat enthralled as she recounted her adventures touring with Bert and her appearances on stage before she got 'knocked-up' as she put it.

Hope watched as Harold and Margaret danced together and Inspector Oakley Penhalligan bagged a dance with Alice. The gentlemen from the Chamber of Commerce and their wives were enthusiastic dancers and soon the floor was full of colourful couples in each other's arms twirling round in time with the music. Hope thought it a wonderful sight to behold.

At quarter-to-ten John called a halt to the proceedings. He banged a fork on the side of his glass to get everyone's attention. Hope glanced around, looking for Violet. The entertainment was about to start and she wouldn't want to miss it.

"Ladies and Gentlemen, fellow merchants and traders, friends and guests, before the entertainment begins I have an announcement to make," John said. A buzz went through the crowd. "Many of you who drink regularly in the bar will have been served by our lovely barmaid, Alice."

Alice, who was standing at the side of the small stage, blushed to the roots of her chestnut hair.

"I'm delighted to announce that tonight Alice has agreed to become my wife." He beckoned Alice over onto the platform that served as stage and put his arm around her waist. "So I hope you'll all join me in a glass of champagne on the house."

A huge cheer went up mixed with calls of congratulations from the audience.

The brewery manager stepped up next to John. "That's not the only thing we're celebrating tonight," he said. "Tonight I'm pleased to announce that John

Daniels has been granted the full tenancy of the Hope and Anchor and we hope him and his wife will be your landlords for many years to come." He raised his glass. "To John and Alice," he said.

Everyone in the room raised their glass and echoed, "To John and Alice."

"Let the entertainment begin," John called and, to huge applause, Marvo the Magician stepped onto the stage.

Hope, standing talking to Margaret, glanced around looking for Violet who should be getting ready for her spot. Despite her size and constant complaints about her discomfort and how she looked, Violet loved performing. She came alive on stage and put her heart into every appearance, lapping up the applause of the audience, revelling in their appreciation and reaction to her songs. She always said it was what she was born to do so Hope was surprised not to see her waiting for her turn on go on.

A worried John appeared beside her. "Where's Violet? She's on soon. Shouldn't she be getting ready?"

"I'll go and look for her," Hope said.

In the kitchen Elsie said she'd seen Violet going upstairs. "She looked worn out, poor love. I think she may have gone for a lie-down."

Hope flew up the stairs. Violet wouldn't miss her cue unless something was terribly wrong.

Violet was lying on the bed in obvious distress. She stared at Hope. "I think it's coming," she said. "The baby. It's coming."

Hope ran to the top of the stairs and called down to Elsie who was standing at the bottom. "Send someone for Mrs Cooper," she called. "Tell them Violet's baby's on the way."

Back in the bedroom she helped Violet out of the gown she'd put on ready to perform. "Take some deep breaths," she said, remembering what the midwife had said to Margaret when her baby was coming.

Margaret came into the room. "I heard the baby was coming," she said. "Can I help?"

"Ask Elsie to put on some hot water and get some towels. Mrs Cooper will be here soon."

Hope sat with Violet who was in increasing pain.

"There's plenty of time," Margaret said, soothing Violet every time she became anxious. "You're doing fine."

Holding Violet's hand and wiping her brow Hope was glad to have Margaret beside her talking Violet through her ordeal. The minutes turned to hours with Violet swearing and cursing more loudly at every bout of pain. Hope and Margaret took it in turns at Violet's side, holding her hand while she squeezed theirs at every bout of pain and wiping her forehead, or holding a glass of water to her lips at every respite.

It was after midnight when Mrs Cooper arrived.

"Busy night," she said. "I've just delivered a baby boy at the Old Coach-House. Poor Mrs Bailey didn't even know she was expecting. Now, what we got here then?"

She quickly examined Violet, running her expert hands over her extended belly. "Twins is it?" she said. "You never said that."

"No," Violet cried.

"Well I can feel two babies in here ready to come out. Two for the price of one. Lucky girl."

From the look on her face Hope guessed Violet wasn't feeling very lucky.

"Big push," she said as Violet writhed at the next contraction and Violet's first baby slipped effortlessly into her hands.

Hope stared in wonder at the new arrival.

"You have a daughter," Mrs Cooper said, lifting the baby up and wrapping her in a towel. The small bundle of skin and bone in her hands gave a cry and Hope breathed again.

"There's another," she said and sure enough, a few minutes later, with another supreme effort and big push, another tiny body fell into Mrs Cooper's hands. "And a son," she said lifting up another scrap of skin and bone and wrapping him in a towel to hand to Margaret.

John, waiting downstairs with the others, must have heard the babies crying. He rushed upstairs and burst into the room. His words came in great gasps. "What is it? Is it all right? Is Violet okay?"

"Violet's fine. You're an uncle twice over," Hope said. "You have a darling little niece and nephew."

John stared wide-eyed at the scene of Violet, now cleaned up, sitting in bed while Hope held one of her babies and Margaret held the other. "Twins?" he said.

"Yes," Mrs Cooper said. "She's been twice blessed."

"Wow! Two babies? Trust our Violet not to do things by half." But the smile on his face showed how delighted he was.

Alfie, who'd taken longer to get upstairs but was just as anxious, limped into the room.

"Alfie. Come and see your new niece and nephew," Hope said, handing the first born to Violet to hold. She made room for him at the side of the bed where he could see the baby.

Margaret placed the second child in Violet's arms. "Congratulations," she said. "Any idea what you're going to call them?"

Violet looked down at the babies in her arms, now sleeping. The deep love in her eyes shone for all to see. "I'm going to call her Rose," she said. "After Ma and Hope after her aunt and him William, after Pa and John after his uncle. She'll be known as Rose Hope Daniels and he'll be William John Daniels.

The week after Christmas John closed the pub so he could take Alice out and they could spend time together other than working. "Pa always said it wasn't worth opening," he said.

Hope and Alfie had enough to do too, helping Violet with Rose and William and clearing up the hall and bar after the Christmas party. It was a time they could rest and catch their breath.

The memories of the previous Christmas were never far from Hope's mind. She found that grief came at her from all sides when she least expected it: the sight of a beautifully browned pie in the baker's window, the beery smell of stale ale that followed in Pa's wake, little things that brought on a frenzy of memories. Sitting with Violet one afternoon, doing some stitching while Violet rocked the cradle holding Rose and William she asked, "Do you ever think of them now, Ma and Pa? Do you ever wonder what they'd be thinking of us all now, and you with the little ones?"

Violet gazed at her sleeping babies while she pondered. "I do think of them but you have to remember the good times and be thankful for the time we had with them. Not everyone's so lucky."

"Yes," Hope said. "I remember Ma's kindness and common sense and I try to remember Pa's generosity when he was in a good mood, usually because he'd had a big win. Will you tell Rose and William about them, when they're bigger?"

"Of course. I want them to know where they came from…Oh. Sorry, I didn't mean…" At least she had the grace to look contrite.

"No, of course you didn't," Hope said. Just being your usual insensitive self, she thought, and realised nothing had really changed. Well not that much.

"Do you ever think about your real parents or wonder where they are now?" Violet said, pulling the covers closer over the sleeping forms in the cot.

"Rose and William Daniels were my real parents," Hope said. "They took me in, loved and cared for me for twenty years. They made me the person I've become, I owe them everything."

"Not even a tiny bit curious?" Violet's eye brows rose as did her voice.

"No. Not even a tiny bit." That wasn't entirely true. She did wonder sometimes but as she was never likely to find out more about them she put them to the back of her mind. Even thinking about who they might be felt like the worst kind of betrayal. Ma and Pa were more real to her than a name on a piece of paper. They were the ones who held that special place in memory for people she'd known and loved. How could it be any different?

They reopened on Friday, at lunchtime to catch the weekend market business and did a good trade in

Elsie's pies which John said were 'almost as good as Ma's'.

Silas gave Hope the week off too. "I expect you'll want to be with Violet and the new babies," he said. "Poppy and Dexi can cope. The club will be quiet with most of the members going to their country estates to spend time with their wives and families."

New Year's Eve fell on Sunday and Silas organised a ball for his friends, club members and local dignitaries at Somerset House, overlooking the Thames where there would be a gigantic firework display to welcome in the new century. Many of the local traders were invited. Harold and Margaret were there. John took Alice who had a new gown for the occasion.

Hope restyled one of Margaret's old dresses for Violet and she wore the purple dress Miss Lovell had had made for her. Alice's mum was looking after the twins.

When they arrived a footman took their coats and showed them through to the ballroom where Silas was waiting to greet them. Dexi stood beside him resplendent in scarlet velvet. She wore her signature necklace of Aces and a rose coloured hat with a tall red feather held in place by the brooch depicting a hand of cards.

Silas greeted them warmly and they passed on towards the bar. "This is some place isn't it?" John said, glancing round to take in the room's airy interior. Crystal chandeliers hung from the ceiling, the walls were panelled in the finest oak and glass doors along one wall opened onto a wide terrace overlooking the Thames.

"Breathtaking," Hope said.

"Magnificent," Violet said. "It reminds me of the grandeur of the grandest, upmarket hotel or theatre. Silas looks entirely at home here."

Hope glanced back to watch him greet his other guests. He had a dignity about him, a charm that defied explanation. His mesmerising smile and the warmth in his eyes as he greeted his guests made her heart beat a little faster. Naturally his clothes were expertly tailored to flatter and with his dark hair glossy as a raven's wing he looked remarkably striking. She envied his self-assurance and grace of movement. She'd never seen even a moment of self-doubt in him. She envied that too. Suddenly she felt hot enough to melt ice.

Oakley Penhalligan stood by the bar with a drink in his hand.

"What a pleasant surprise," Hope said. "I didn't expect to see you here."

"Silas invited me," he said. "I think he feels that, running the sort of business he does, it's best to have the law on your side."

"Well, I'm glad to see you," Hope said, "and I know Violet will be thrilled too."

Oakley's smile widened. "It was you I hoped would be thrilled to see me. Don't tell me Silas has worked his charms on you already, before I've even had a chance to blind you with my wit."

Hope laughed. "Silas is a charming man but I've become immune to men's flattery. I intend to remain independent and not rely on anyone to support me in the future." Even as she said it she knew it wasn't true. Silas's kindness and concern for her had seeped through her defences and, by the time she realised her feelings for him, it was too late.

"Hmm, that sounds as though you've had a bad experience at our hands. I'm sorry about that."

"Not me, but when I think about the life Ma led…" She frowned. "But tonight is supposed to be a celebration. We're putting the past behind us and welcoming in the New Year with all its opportunities."

"Bravely said." They clinked glasses and drank to the New Year.

Hope saw Giles Larkin standing with Alfie staring out of the glass doors up at the stars in the night sky. He was pointing out the constellations and naming them.

"Good evening, Mr Larkin," she said. "So good of you to take an interest in Alfie. He's benefitted so much from your tuition."

Giles Larkin smiled. "He's a joy to teach. Picks thing up so quickly. I hope he'll do well in the future."

Alfie beamed. Hope's heart sang. Memories of the beatings and bruises he used to come home with filled her mind. "He's lucky to have a teacher like you," she said and ruffled Alfie's hair.

"When are we going to see the fireworks?" Alfie asked.

"Later."

"I'm afraid he's bored by the thought of dancing the night away," Mr Larkin said.

"I hope you'll find time to dance with me, Alfie," Alice, who arrived at Hope's side, said.

"And there's a buffet later too," Hope told him.

"Aw. All right then," he said brightening.

Once the band struck up and the music began Hope found herself being whisked onto the floor by Oakley Penhalligan, who insisted on having the first dance. Then she danced with John, who cut a surprisingly dashing figure on the dance floor. Violet danced with one of the gentlemen Hope recognised from the club.

It was quite late by the time Silas approached her for a dance. It felt like something she'd been waiting for all evening. Was it her imagination or was he holding her closer than she'd seen him with other partners? She chided herself for her foolishness.

Don't go getting ideas above your station – she heard Ned's disapproving voice in her head. She dismissed it without hesitation.

A bell ringing announced the opening of the buffet and the dancers left the floor. Silas led her out onto the terrace. A crescent moon hung in a clear night sky drenched with stars.

"Are you warm enough? I could get you a wrap."

"I'm fine," she said, not wanting to feel the void his short absence would bring.

"I see John's brought Alice. They make a lovely couple. I'm glad he's found happiness after what must have been a terrible year."

"Yes."

"And you, Hope. Have you found some sort of contentment?"

"Contentment? I suppose I have."

"I can see that now John's tenancy is secure, his future more certain and Violet now with responsibilities of her own, you may wish to spend more time with your family, or pursue a different path of your own choosing." He hesitated, glancing up at the sky as though finding the words difficult. "It's just that I'd hate to lose you, both as a waitress and as a friend."

Hope smiled. "You can rest assured that I'm happy where I am. I have no plans to follow another path."

Silas took her hand. "There are some things I'd like to say to you, but perhaps now is not the time."

Intrigued she begged him to carry on. "Please feel free to say whatever it is you want. I can assure you I won't be offended."

He bowed his head. His voice softened. "It can't have escaped your notice that I have had a special interest in you and your wellbeing," he said.

"It has been remarked upon." Her whole body was growing hotter but she was determined not to show it.

"The truth is I admire you greatly. I admire your fortitude and the way you've coped with a great loss. I admire everything about you and carry the hope that one day we may become more than just friends."

Hope couldn't have been more surprised if a full orchestra had risen up from the floor in front of her. "I don't know what to say. You've always been so generous and kind. I never thought..."

"Never thought I might have designs upon you. I'm not propositioning you if that's what you think. I can assure that my intentions are entirely honourable. I merely hope that one day you may come to regard me as more than just a friend."

"I already do," she said.

He smiled, slipped his arm around her waist, pulled her into his embrace and kissed her soundly. She responded with all the pent up passion she'd been holding back for what felt like forever. She felt a tug in her heart as he let her go.

"I've wanted to do that for such a very long time," he said.

"Me too," she whispered, her voice breaking with emotion.

He picked up his glass of champagne and raised it to her, a devilish gleam in his eye that sent hot blood rushing through her veins. "You must know by now how I feel about you," he said. "How empty and meaningless my life would be without you. You're the only one who can fill the empty space in my heart. "

"You mean…?

He dropped to one knee "I love you, Hope. Marry me and put me out of my misery."

She laughed. Her heart was so full she thought it might burst. "I will," she said.

He took her in his arms and kissed her again. In his arm all her doubts evaporated. She knew he was a man she could love absolutely and without reservation.

Gazing out across the river, the lights dancing on the water and the vast, starlit sky above, Hope knew she must follow the path that destiny had laid out for her, no matter how surprising it may be.

As midnight approached they were joined by the rest of the party coming out to see the fireworks. Hope stood with Silas, his arm holding her close. John, Alice, Violet and Alfie stood alongside them. John raised his glass. "To the New Year and a New Century," he said.

"Yes," Violet said. "If anyone had told me a year ago I'd be standing here, having had twins, seeing in the new century I'd never have believed them."

"Just goes to show," Hope said, smiling at Silas. "Anything's possible."

He grinned back, warmth and passion shining in his eyes as he looked at her.

Big Ben struck twelve and the sky came alight with exploding fireworks scattering sparks among the stars. A cacophony of bells, boat whistles, excited cheering, music and explosions filled the air.

The crowd from the ballroom came out onto the terrace. They all raised their glasses and in unison said, "Here's to 1900 and a Happy New Year."

"And a new era," Hope said.

Epilogue

On a bright sunny day in June, 1900 Hope and Silas were married in the church where her parents had been laid to rest. She felt their presence as she walked down the aisle on John's arm and imagined them, puffed up with pride, watching her.

When she saw Silas standing there, waiting for her, her heart swelled with love. It had taken time but she now saw his strength, his steadfastness and his compassion. He turned and smiled and her heart almost burst with joy. She trembled when he took her hand, she felt so blessed.

After the service the wedding bells rang out and her spirits soared with the resonating sounds. It was the happiest day of her life and one she'd never forget.

The reception was held at the Hope and Anchor. "You'll be next," Hope said to Alice who was handing round the champagne Silas had provided. Even Violet seemed to be enjoying herself as her twins, dressed in their Sunday best, were the centre of attention for the wives of the local traders and merchants who'd been invited. They oo'd and ah'd over their cots and remembered when their children were young.

Dexi, who'd arranged everything from Hope's oyster satin gown to the couple's honeymoon in Paris, kissed Hope on both cheeks. "I know you'll make Silas happy," she said "Or you'll have me to answer to."

Hope laughed. "I aim to make him the happiest man alive," she said and realised she meant it. All she wanted in life was his happiness, everything else faded into insignificance.

She glanced over to where he was talking to Oakley Penhalligan. Silas caught her gaze, His eyes sparkled with the deepest affection. He lifted his glass to toast her and the world stood still. Nothing else mattered, just the two of them together. She knew then that nothing would ever tear them apart. She was his forever, and, better still, he would always be hers.

About the Author

Kay Seeley lives in London She has two children, both married and three grandchildren, all adorable. She is a novelist, short story writer and poet. *A Girl Called Hope* is her fourth historical novel. All her previous novels have been listed as finalists for The Wishing Shelf Book Award. She also writes short stories for women's magazines She has published many of these in her short story collections. Kay's stories have been short-listed in several major competitions. Kay is a member of The Alliance of Independent Authors and The Society of Women Writers and Journalists.

If you have enjoyed Kay's book let her know by leaving a review.

or

Contact: www.kayseeleyauthor.com

Acknowledgements

Firstly my thanks go to my family for their unending patience and support especially to my lovely daughters for reading the manuscript.

Thanks to the members of my writing groups, you know who you are, for their helpful suggestions and to the brilliant Helen Baggott whose eagle eyes and sound advice helped in the production of this book.

A huge 'thank you' to my writing friends, ALLi members and supporters for their continued encouragement and, once again, to Jane Dixon-Smith for another wonderful cover.

Lastly I want to thank the readers whose enjoyment of my previous novels prompted me to keep writing and made it such a pleasure.

If you have read and enjoyed this novel I would love to hear from you via my website:

www.kayseeleyauthor.com

I would also appreciate a review on the appropriate Amazon page

Many thanks.

If you enjoyed this book you may also enjoy Kay's other books:

The Guardian Angel

When Nell Draper leaves the workhouse to care for the five-year-old son of Lord Eversham, she has no idea of the heartache that lies ahead of her.

Robert can't speak. He can't tell her what makes him happy or sad. Nell has to work that out for herself.

Not everyone is happy about Robert's existence.

Can Nell save him from a desolate future, secure his inheritance and ensure he takes his rightful place in society?

A love story.

Betrayal, kidnap, murder, loyalty and love all play their part in this wonderful novel that shows how the Victorians lived – rich and poor. Inspired by her autistic and non-verbal grandson, Kay Seeley writes with passion and inspiration in her third novel set in the Victorian era.

The Water Gypsy

When Tilly Thompson, a girl from the canal, is caught stealing a pie from the terrace of The Imperial Hotel, Athelstone, the intervention of Captain Charles Thackery saves her from prison.

The Captain's favour stirs up jealously and hatred among the hotel staff, especially Freddie, the stable boy who harbours desires of his own.

Freddie's pursuit leads Tilly into far greater danger than she could ever have imagined. Can she escape the prejudice, persecution and hypocrisy of Victorian Society, leave her past behind and find true happiness?

This is a story of love and loss, lust and passion, injustice and ultimate redemption.

The Watercress Girls

Spirited and beautiful Annie Flanagan's reckless ambition takes her from the Hackney watercress beds to dancing at the Folies-Bergère in Paris. She returns to work in an establishment catering to the needs of wealthy and influential gentlemen.

When she disappears, leaving her illegitimate son behind, her friend Hettie Bundy sets out to find her. Hettie's search leads her from the East End of London, where opium dens and street gangs rule, to uncover the corruption and depravity in Victorian society.

Secrets are revealed that put both girls' lives in danger. Can Hettie find Annie in time? What does the future hold for the watercress girls?

A Victorian Mystery

You may also enjoy Kay's short story collections:

The Cappuccino Collection 20 stories to warm the heart.

The Summer Stories 12 Romantic tales to make you smile

The Christmas Stories 6 Magical Christmas stories.

Please feel free to contact Kay through her website www.kayseeleyauthor.com She'd love to hear from you.

Or follow Kay on her Facebook Page https://www.facebook.com/kayseeley.writer/

Manufactured by Amazon.ca
Bolton, ON